The Golden Age of Lesbian Erotica

Edited by
Victoria A. Brownworth
& Judith M. Redding

First Magic Carpet Books, Inc. edition January 2007

Manufactured in the United States of America
Published by Magic Carpet Books, Inc.

Magic Carpet Books, Inc.
PO Box 473
New Milford, CT 06776

Library of Congress Cataloging in Publication Date

The Golden Age of Lesbian Erotica
Edited By Victoria A. Brownworth & Judith M. Redding
$17.95 /Canada $24.95

ISBN 0-9774311-4-2

Book Design: P. Ruggieri

Dedication

for Tee A. Corinne
1943-2006
this book is a tribute to our long and abiding
friendship, our love for you, and a thank you for
always breaking new ground in lesbian eroticism
and
for Madelaine Gold
with much, much love

Table of Contents

Introduction

Victoria A. Brownworth
THE GOLDEN AGE OF LESBIAN EROTICA: THE SACRED AND THE PROFANE

Paris, with its romantic beauty, has long been deemed the city of lovers–lovers of all sexual orientations and persuasions. Thus, it was natural that the literal and metaphorical flowering of lesbian erotica found its fullest blossom there with the *fin de siècle* and *nouvelle siècle*.

Prior to the Stonewall Rebellion in Greenwich Village in 1969, which gave birth to the modern queer movement, Paris was *the* place to go if you were a homosexual or "invert." The sexual openness of Parisian society made sexual difference–the *outré–accepted*, if not outright embraced. It was to this world of inclusion and enticement that many an expatriate American and British lesbians fled.

The more well-known lesbian writers and artists of the period–Renee Vivien, Natalie Barney, Gertrude Stein, Alice B. Toklas, Romaine Brooks, Radclyffe Hall, Djuna Barnes, Janet Flanner–each notorious in her own way, lived at one time in Paris in the Montparnasse district, which saw the birth of a multiplicity of artistic and creative genius throughout the period now termed "The Golden Age" (*l'Age d'Or*). Parisians with whom these lesbians became acquainted–Pierre Louys, Colette, Andre Gide, Josephine Baker–cultivated the eroticism of the expatriate lesbian milieu, even at times interpolating that eroticist personae into her or his own art. The exploration and exposition of sensuality between women became a keystone of this demi-monde that had as its icon a lusty and wholly lesbian (if highly unhistorical) version of Sappho.

Introduction

It was, ironically, a heterosexual man who penned the most exquisite and sensual poems of the love between women that became the core myth of Sappho and her various lovers that would later be embraced by lesbian writers. The series of poems, *Songs of Bilitis*, by Pierre Louys (selections of which are published here) are intensely, provocatively sensual in their subtle but demonstratively lesbian sexuality. The *sensibility* is also distinctly lesbian. The lesbian reader would naturally presume they were written by a woman. (In 1955, one of the first lesbian organizations in the United States called itself "Daughters of Bilitis," in homage to those poems and lesbian sensibility.) From a revisionist lesbian-feminist perspective, it's difficult to imagine the poems were in fact crafted by a man; but Louys, despite being heterosexual, had his own gay sensibilities. He was the close friend and confidante of two of the best-known gay male writers of his time, Andre Gide and Oscar Wilde. Louys was well-known for his fealty to the queer community of Paris.

Louys' exquisite poems provide a nexus for later works by lesbian writers in Paris, most particularly those by Vivien and her lover, Natalie Barney.

Vivien's poems are not nearly as well-crafted as those by Louys, which are breath-taking in their quality as well as sensuality, but Vivien's poems are intensely authentic and provocative as they detail the various love affairs she engages in with a range of women, including Barney. Vivien's work includes paeans to Sappho and Mytilene, but excessive artifice occludes much of her work. Yet in the poems reprinted here, which were first translated from the French in the 1970s by Naiad Press, there is a declarative lesbian voice that avows what we have come to know of The Golden Age: authentically lesbian sexual/romantic yearning. Vivien is bitter, angry, persuasive, aching for love, immersed in desire. Hers is a voice of true lesbian desire, not a replicated historicity purloined from Sappho. In Vivien's poems about her lovers, although her imagery repeats again and again, it is the imagery of authenticity–a wholly new voice of lesbian evocation and eroticism. These are not just poems about a long-lost icon–Sappho–and her coterie, these are poems about a modern woman in love with and lusting for other women: now, today, immediately and in the present. No historical parallelisms required.

The visceral nature of Vivien's love poems is what defines them as erotic. This isn't Keats, Shelley, Byron, or any other male Romantic poet evoking "la belle dame sans merci": this is a female poet writing provocatively and sensually about her female lovers. Lips to lips, breast to breast, thigh to thigh.

When Vivien writes of "the sweet hour of hand in hand," we envision the fingers of lovers intertwined in bed–and in each other.

Conversely, Gertrude Stein's work has a far more elliptical, if equally resonant, lesbianism. In her long poem *Lifting Belly*, which was considered too provocative to publish until after Stein's death, the very term has a fleshy, sensual, almost pornographic tone to it. In the literal sense, lifting the belly reveals the genitalia–the pubis, the vulva, the clitoris.

Thus, when Stein writes:

"Lifting belly is so satisfying...Lifting belly is strong and willing...Lifting belly is my queen...Lifting belly oh lifting belly in time...Lifting belly is a language...lifting belly is here" [1]

she is very much chanting the song not just of love, but of lust, of sensuality and, most definitively, of desire. These lines and phrases aren't just indiscriminate words flung down on the page. They are words of aching sensuality, evocative of the whispered sex talk between lovers in bed during sex.

No wonder the piece wasn't published until after her death.

Meanwhile, other members of the Montparnasse set were also creating works of Sapphic sensuality. Natalie Barney's work has remained largely untranslated (Vivien was British and Barney American, but both wrote only in French); however, her work also reflected a visceral eroticism that was given voice by the tenor of the Parisian demi-monde of lesbian passion and sexual intrigue. Barney wrote about love between women in all its variance.

Barney was a figurehead in that Montparnasse circle; she had been lovers with nearly everyone, much to the chagrin of those like Vivien who hoped to reel her in for a monogamous relationship. Lovers changed hands steadily and readily in this group: Vivien, Barney, Radclyffe Hall, the American artist Romaine Brooks, Djuna Barnes, Colette, Janet Flanner. Stein and Toklas knew these women, but did not play with non-monogamy. Flanner was close with Barnes, but was the best friend of Toklas. Flanner chronicled the period in her letters from Paris for *The New Yorker*; but although her lesbianism was well-known, she kept a low profile when it came to flaunting it on the streets of Paris.

In this cast of Montparnassian lesbians, Stein and Toklas were not of their set.

And the set was decidedly and emphatically sexual. Barnes, who had written so provocatively of her lesbian relationship with Thelma Wood in her

Introduction

roman à clef–an explicitness edited out by her closeted gay editor, T.S. Eliot–wrote a catty expose of the revolving bedroom doors in *Ladies Almanack*. Barnes had much to say about the goings-on among the dyads and triads of the Montparnasse lesbians. Radclyffe Hall, in her classic novel *The Well of Loneliness*, also exposed the lusty world of these lesbian expatriates.

Until her later years, when she met Evguenia Souline, Hall lived in a "marriage" with Lady Una Troubridge (although she was rumored to have had many affairs, including one with the African-American actress Ethel Waters). After Hall became infatuated with Souline, the three lived in a discomfiting ménage until Hall's death. Hall wrote passionate love letters to both women over her lifetime, but in her final years her obsession was clearly Souline, to whom she wrote in October 1934: "My beloved, I send you all my heart–all my thoughts and all my desire. I kiss your beloved hands & your feet–I kneel down and worship you my most blessed woman–you who for my sake became a woman." The letter is signed: "Your John." [2]

In the phrase "you who for my sake became a woman," Hall elicits what lies at the heart of much of the erotic writing–in fact all lesbian writing–of the period. A lesbian, mannish/butch in character turns a girl into a woman–a sexual woman–in a kind of ritualistic defloscheoing (this occurs quite literally in the Violet Black story, "Shop Girls Wanted") that takes away the girl's virginity and also her heterosexuality.

In another letter from October 1934, Hall writes even more provocatively to Souline, who clearly has never before been involved sexually with another woman: "Just say to yourself 'I'm a normal woman, and when my John loves me my response is normal–my body loves John and John gives it joy–and will give it that joy many, many times.'…There are one or two lesser things that I will tell you when you and I are together again–things that concern us and our way of loving–they are unimportant except in as much as they give more or less pleasure as the case may be–But I'd rather tell you about this when we're together. For the rest you now know all the essential facts, and the right and proper person to tell you was John, your deeply adoring lover."[3]

Clearly these were not platonic relationships, but passionately sensual ones in which sexual desire was pre-eminent–to such a degree that Hall could not keep herself from writing about her own desire for Souline (or Una, in other letters).

The Golden Age of Lesbian Erotica

It was Hall's fiction, however–not nearly as provocative as her personal love letters–that eventually drew the eye of the censors. The *fin de siècle* world of Paris on the eve of The Golden Age had been sensual and even profligate, but in the Montparnasse there was a wink and a nod over the rondeau of lesbian *affaires du coeur*. The women were mostly young, in their twenties, rich–and not French. No one appeared to care too very much about what they did, as long as they paid for it at the end of an evening. But when Vivien began an affair with a married woman, the Baroness Hélène de Zuylen, one of the Parisian Rothschilds, and Colette, who was married, began a public affair with another woman, Mathilde de Morny, the Marquise de Belbeuf, the mores seemed to shift, and rather suddenly. Society was shocked by these affairs. What had passed for American and British extravagance (what we would today call "celebrity"), now had a different cast. *Families* had become involved. Husbands were being cuckolded by these women in velvet trousers with pastiches of penises between their legs. There were children involved in some of these broken marriages and the scandal was simply inexcusable. The social flirtation with lesbianism appeared at an end.

By the time Lady Una Troubridge, the wife of a British admiral with a young daughter, left him to become the "wife" of Hall, the tone had definitely shifted. Where before no one had cared if Natalie Barney rode half-naked on horseback down the *Champs de l'Elysses* at dawn like some lesbian Lady Godiva, when the security of family was provoked, the wink and nod changed to a cold and unforgiving stare of disapproval, if not outrage.

Whither lesbian eroticism under these circumstances?

Radclyffe Hall was no longer a young woman when her obscenity trial was convened in 1928 for *The Well of Loneliness*. At forty-five, she was very much middle-aged–no mere schoolgirl who could plead innocent and naive. Nor, mannishly attired, with her hair cropped short and combed straight back like that of men of the day (and with that appellation by which all who knew her well called her: John), Hall was no *Penthouse* or *Follies Bergères* nymph. She was, to many, a woman masquerading as a man. And not just that, but one who wrote about the sexual and romantic affairs of women like herself as if they were normal.

Ban the book and ban the idea, seemed to be the impetus behind *The Well of Loneliness* obscenity trial.

This mannishness and insistence on a lesbian "lifestyle" of pseudo-marriage was, to most, simply unacceptable. Renee Vivien, in her Little Lord Fauntleroy suits and ruffled shirts and long, ringleted hair, seemed mostly an errant tomboy with a school-girl's crush–even at thirty-three, when she died. Barney was voluptuous and deeply, obviously feminine. Her sensual exploits had been legendary in Paris–and the subject of titillation to men as well as women. But Hall was another story; she was the obverse of the Sapphic myth. She was the man mothers warned their daughters about–except she was herself a woman.

How much did Hall's persona influence the obscenity trial against her? That's difficult to ascertain with anything other than historical revisionism. What *is* certain is that concomitant with Hall's obscenity trial came a tectonic shift in perception about lesbianism, if not about homosexuality in general. (Hall would fairly soon after be vindicated by explosive sales of her book. She would also win several literary awards for her work.) Years before, Oscar Wilde had been the victim of a trial over his homosexuality. For many, the obscenity trial of Radclyffe "John" Hall seemed more a trial of lesbianism, than anything else. There's nothing that could be termed obscene in *The Well of Loneliness* by today's standards–or even by the standards of that era. It's barely erotic in "the good parts," and certainly nothing like Henry Miller's *Tropic of Cancer* or even James Joyce's *Ulysses*–both banned for sexual references. Hall's novel was more like D.H. Lawrence's scandalous *Lady Chatterley's Lover*; it's not that there was so much overt sexuality in the books as that the sexuality referenced was itself considered obscene–crossing class and morality lines that were taboo.

What *The Well of Loneliness* was, since it was definitely not obscene, was a book that made a case for a genetic predisposition to lesbianism and also presented lesbian lovers as "normal" women–much as Hall describes lesbian sexuality in her letters to the neophyte Souline. In *The Well of Loneliness*, the book's protagonist, Stephen Gordon, is raised as a boy by her parents, who yearned for a son, and having been raised as one, feels herself to be a man in all the important ways.

In the twenty-first century, we might consider Stephen Gordon more of a transsexual than a lesbian, passing for male as she does. But the heart of the tale as written is Gordon's love for other women–while herself being a woman. *The Well of Loneliness* is, in essence, the first lesbian novel.

Hall's story pivots on the psychological theories that were prominent at that time–that "inversion" was perhaps a psychological defect caused by nature or nurture, difficult to discern which, or perhaps a confluence of both. Henry Havelock Ellis is said to have coined the term "homosexual," and his book *Sexual Inversion* became a prototype for discussion of gay and lesbian sexuality, later adapted by Sigmund Freud. Havelock Ellis's theory of inversion is at the core of Hall's novel. Stephen Gordon refers to herself as an invert and seems to make a distinction between women inverts born to the breed, as it were, and other women, like Stephen's paramour, Mary Llewellyn.

In a review of the novel when it debuted, *The Times Literary Supplement* declared the following on August 2, 1928:

Miss Radclyffe Hall's latest work *The Well of Loneliness* is a novel, and we propose to treat it as such. We therefore rather regret that it should have been thought necessary to insert at the beginning a "commentary" by Mr. Havelock Ellis to the effect that, apart from its qualities as a novel, it "possesses a notable psychological and sociological significance" as a presentation, in a completely faithful and uncompromising form, of a particular aspect of sexual life. To the book as a work of art this testimony adds nothing: on the other hand, the documentary significance of a work of fiction seems to us small. The presence of this commentary, however, points to the criticism which, with all our admiration for much of the detail, we feel compelled to express – namely, that this long novel, sincere, courageous, high-minded, and often beautifully expressed as it is, fails as a work of art through divided purpose. It is meant as a thesis and a challenge as well as an artistic creation.

There is no ambiguity about the nature of the thesis. Stephen Gordon, the central figure, was meant by her parents to be a boy; and a boy she was born in all but the physical characteristics of sex. Her painful story, beginning in infancy and continuing to middle age, is mean to express the bitter cry of the female invert, the man-woman, born through no fault of her own into a world which denies her a place in it and persecutes her kind by isolating them from all the happy and fine contacts of life, without regard for their highest mental qualities or for the invert's consciousness of loving no less nobly than any other human being. Stephen's life is one long tragedy, first in incomprehension, as one contact after another in childhood warns her that she is unlike other girls – and this part of the book, the childhood at Merton, passed under her loving but bewildered father's protection, shows all this writer's quality of evoking beauty and visualising human scenes with an extraordinary clarity of outline – then of horrified repugnance when a man friend woos her, and of a romantic passion for the wife of a neighbor, ignobly betrayed and leading to an irreparable break with her home and her mother: thereafter of a long effort to forget herself in work, and finally of love realized with the girl called Mary Llewellyn, of the hideous exiled life in Paris to which such women are condemned, and of the last agony, when, by a desperate simulation of unfaithfulness, she drives Mary into the arms of the man who wishes to make her his wife – the very man-friend of her own early happiness. There is no relief; the stages of an abnormal person's life succeed one another inevitably, with a profusion of detail which, though adorned with a high and poetic literary talent, is excessive for the work of imagination. More and more, towards the end, one feels the artistic inspiration fade and the desire increase to probe to the bottom the pains of an abnormal growth upon the social body. The tone rises into that of a challenge, now angry, now pitiful, to the world and, as the heroine bows in her last agony, to the Creator. The final chapters, describing the unhappy, segregated, unreal life of Stephen, Mary, and their congeners in Paris are extremely painful, as they are intended to be. As such we must leave them to the interested reader, with all the discords unresolved; yet undoubtedly in this book the recognised talents of Miss Hall in themselves are as conspicuous as before, and against any feelings of repugnance against her uncompromising sincerity must be set respect for her intentions, frequent admiration for her treatment, and only regret that the statement of an insoluble problem so passionately presented itself as a theme.

The attempt to proffer a fair-minded review of the book seems brave on its face, but falls flat as the reviewer makes clear he sees Hall's book as more of an aberration, and the pleas for acceptance as hollow–and unacceptable–requests. A "thesis" on an aberrant sexuality. That the reviewer comments that the foreword by Havelock Ellis redefines the book in terms of this sexual aberration merely underscores the point about unacceptability.

Then a nanosecond later, the obscenity trial was convened, Hall lost, and all copies of the book were destroyed. The book was also banned in the United States as well as Britain.

The references to Havelock Ellis in the *TLS* review foreshadow what was to come in lesbian literature for the entire period of The Golden Age. Psychology had a tremendous influence over homosexual themes in literature, particularly with regard to women, who were simply not perceived as having any nascent sexuality of their own. Psychiatry and psychology, from Havelock Ellis to Freud and his followers, framed all female sexuality in the context of men and *their* sexuality. Any sexual experience that women had without men–be it masturbatory or lesbian–was viewed as infantile and undeveloped. "Mature" sex was solely between a woman and a man. (Interestingly, gay male sexuality is not described this way.) But characters such as Stephen Gordon–and in real life, Radclyffe Hall–were almost like men themselves. So how to define them–if not as Stephen Gordon explains herself, "congenital inverts"–that is, women born queer and thus to love other women, not men. (Although the case can easily be made in the twenty-first century that Stephen Gordon is in fact transsexual, rather than lesbian.)

Havelock Ellis was himself married to a lesbian, although he was heterosexual. But his open discourse on the topic of homosexuality, which he did not denounce, as well as his theories on inversion and how some homosexuals might indeed be born as such, became a fundament for the anti-homosexual backlash that arose in this Golden Age period. If this sexuality was aberrance, then it should be treated as such, or at least hidden. Parading it out in the open was unacceptable. Which is why it appears that the censorship trial for Hall was as much about her own sexuality and lifestyle–she had then living with her formerly married female lover for more than a decade–as it was about the assertions in the book.

Thus, with the psychologizing came the censoring. If "inversion" or homosexuality was aberrant, then shouldn't it be stopped, rather than promoted in literature? While in the early part of the century lesbianism had been exalted in poems and prose, now it was indeed the love that dare not speak its name or an obscenity trial might ensue.

Lesbian sexuality went underground. It became hidden and obscured, its depiction encoded. In the writing of The Golden Age and even later, into the era of lesbian pulp fiction, lesbian sexuality was damped down, muted. When written about it was largely off the page–the bedroom door closed and the sex remained unseen. It would not be until the 1970s that lesbian sexuality would flower as openly and provocatively in literature as it had in the early years of the twentieth century.

Inadvertently, Hall's novel also created a sub-genre in itself: In *The Well of Loneliness* Stephen feels compelled to give up the love of her life, Mary, so that Mary can live a "normal" life with a man–marry, have children. The concept of inversion in Hall's depiction puts the sexual element wholly aside. It's all about love. (Which is why it's difficult to comprehend the obscenity charge.) Stephen loves Mary so much she gives her up. Mary loves Stephen as well, but in Hall's paradigmatic re-tooling of the Sapphic myth, the draw of normalcy trumps love. (It just can't trump congenital inversion.)

This theme of the lesbian woman giving up her lover so that the other can lead a "normal" life runs through nearly all the fiction of the era and bleeds into the 1950s and 1960s pulp novels. Lesbian lovers are simply not allowed to live happily ever after. One of the first such couples to do so are Therese and Carol in *The Price of Salt*, the 1951 novel by Patricia Highsmith, first published under the pseudonym Clare Morgan.

In *The Price of Salt*, Highsmith breaks the rules of lesbian misery–it is the first novel to refute the standard set by Hall in 1928 that there can be no lasting relationships between lesbians–there can only be love lost, and the punishment of life-long misery for being "abnormal."

The misery quotient undergirds most lesbian writing, particularly if it is erotic, throughout this period. Yet lesbianism remains a pervasive and titillating theme, for heterosexual writers as much as queer ones.

In Lillian Hellman's 1934 play *The Children's Hour*, Hellman uses this same structure of unrequited lesbian desire as she tells the tale of Karen and Martha, life-long friends who start a girl's school together. One of their students, Mary, a bad seed of a girl, gets her hands on some psychology books (Havelock Ellis, no doubt) and re-crafts their relationship, telling her grandmother that she's "seen things" and witnessed the two women kissing through the keyhole late at night and that she's heard "strange sounds" as well. Mary hasn't actually seen anything between the women–she's a girl who constantly gets in trouble and plots her revenge with the information she has gleaned from her tattered copy of *Psychopathia Sexualis*.

What ensues after her shocking revelation is yet another trial, this one more like the Oscar Wilde trial, in which Karen and Martha are convicted of having "sinful sexual knowledge of each other." The school is closed and the women become the town pariahs. Karen's fiancé, Joe, leaves her, if reluctantly.

In the play's final act, Karen and Martha have the following exchange:

KAREN: But this isn't a new sin they tell us we've done. Other people aren't destroyed by it.

MARTHA: They are the people who believe in it, who want it, who've chosen it. We aren't like that. We don't love each other. I don't love you. We've been very close to each other, of course. I've loved you like a friend, the way thousands of women feel about other women.

KAREN: Yes.

MARTHA: Certainly that doesn't mean anything. There's nothing wrong with that. It's perfectly natural that I should be fond of you.

KAREN: Why are you saying all this to me?

MARTHA: Because I love you.

KAREN: Yes, of course.

MARTHA: I love you that way–maybe the way they said I loved you. I don't know. Listen to me!

KAREN: What?

MARTHA: *I have loved you the way they said.*

KAREN: You're crazy.

MARTHA: There's always been something wrong. Always–as long as I can remember. But I never knew it until all this happened.

KAREN: Stop it!

MARTHA: You're afraid of hearing it. I'm more afraid than you.

KAREN: I won't listen to you.

MARTHA: You've got to know it. I can't keep it any longer. I've got to tell you how guilty I am.

KAREN: You are guilty of nothing.

MARTHA: I've been telling myself that since the night we heard the child say it. I've been praying I could convince myself of it. I can't, I can't any longer. It's there. I don't know how. I don't know why. But I did love you. I do love you. Maybe I wanted you all along, maybe I couldn't call it by a name, maybe it's been there ever since I first knew you. [4]

Martha goes on to tell Karen that these feelings have always been there, dormant in her, until the night that Mary told her lie–"the lie with the ounce of truth to it," as the screenplay of the 1961 William Wyler film version reads.

After Martha finishes her soliloquy, she exits, and shoots herself.

The Children's Hour was Hellman's first play, written when she was twenty-six. The play opened in New York to stunning success for the young Hellman, but soon was banned from being performed in other cities, including Chicago and Los Angeles. When the play was turned into a film directed by William Wyler in 1936 titled *We Three* (for which Hellman wrote the sanitized screenplay), the pivotal scandal is changed to heterosexual infidelity.

When Wyler re-made the film in 1961, starring Audrey Hepburn as Karen and Shirley MacClaine as Martha, the titillation of lesbianism was restored along with Hellman's original plot. Advertisements for the film read: "What made these women different? Did Nature play an ugly trick and endow them with emotions contrary to those of normal young women?"

Hellman's play may or may not pass judgment on Martha and Karen. Is Hellman saying that homophobia is the culprit or the self-loathing queer–Martha–is to blame for the downfall? What is the true sin of the play–the lie told by Mary and believed by her grandmother, Mrs. Tilford, or the lie told by Martha about her own life?

In 1952, in an interview, the increasingly cantankerous Hellman stated that the play was not about lesbianism, but about lies. The interview, however, was done as Hellman was testifying before the House UnAmerican Activities Committee (HUAC); lying was an issue more important than lesbianism at that moment, and it would appear that Hellman wanted to make a point about the poisonous nature of lies in the McCarthy era, more so than make a statement about homophobia.

Regardless of what Hellman said later about her intent, the play speaks for itself and reflects the censoring voice of the time in which it was written: Homosexuality was not just "queer" and *demi-mondaine*, it was an aberrance that normal people were to be shielded from and children protected from. Anyone might come in contact with one of these people–these queers–as Karen does, and her fiancé does. Thus, when a seemingly normal woman like

Martha reveals herself to be something else, that dark thing, a lesbian, then there was only one answer to be had: suicide.

This suicide theme later becomes common in lesbian erotic pulp fiction, although usually the women get to bed each other before the shots ring out. The paradigm that Hall first devised (and which is reflected in many of Vivien's poems) as a plot twist in her novel suddenly becomes a pattern: The lesbian must "lose" in the end.

In D. H. Lawrence's 1923 novella *The Fox*, March and Banford live together as apparent lovers, until one day a young man, Henry Grenfel, arrives and things go fatally awry:

The two girls were usually known by their surnames, Banford and March. They had taken the farm together, intending to work it all by themselves: that is, they were going to rear chickens, make a living by poultry, and add to this by keeping a cow, and raising one or two young beasts. Unfortunately, things did not turn out well.

Banford was a small, thin, delicate thing with spectacles. She, however, was the principal investor, for March had little or no money. Banford's father, who was a tradesman in Islington, gave his daughter the start, for her health's sake, and because he loved her, and because it did not look as if she would marry. March was more robust. She had learned carpentry and joinery at the evening classes in Islington. She would be the man about the place. They had, moreover, Banford's old grandfather living with them at the start. He had been a farmer. But unfortunately the old man died after he had been at Bailey Farm for a year. Then the two girls were left alone.

They were neither of them young: that is, they were near thirty. But they certainly were not old. [5]

Banford is the classic "female" member of the couple: small, delicate, unable to do anything strenuous. Her father intuits that she will not marry–why? And March has, inexplicably, learned carpentry and joinery. Hardly common female trades in the 1920s. And she is "the man about the place." This is a male-female/butch-femme lesbian couple, to be sure.

Enter the fox and his metaphoric human representation, Henry. March intuits that the fox who is killing the chickens must be shot, yet cannot shoot him, just as she cannot force Henry to leave the farm.

In the end, Banford is killed, in an apparent accident, by Henry who in classic Freudian (Lawrence's wife, Frieda, had previously been lovers with

Introduction

Freud's pupil, Otto Gross; less than six degrees separated Freud and Lawrence) masculine umbrage, takes March away from her "infantile" relationship with Banford–but perhaps not for the better.

Sometimes he thought bitterly that he ought to have left her. He ought never to have killed Banford. He should have left Banford and March to kill one another. But that was only impatience: and he knew it. He was waiting, waiting to go West. He was aching almost in torment to leave England, to go West, to take March away. To leave this shore! He believed that as they crossed the seas, as they left this England which he so hated, because in some way it seemed to have stung him with poison, she would go to sleep. She would close her eyes at last and give in to him.

And then he would have her, and he would have his own life at last. He chafed, feeling he hadn't got his own life. He would never have it till she yielded and slept in him. Then he would have all his own life as a young man and a male, and she would have all her own life as a woman and a female. There would be no more of this awful straining. She would not be a man any more, an independent woman with a man's responsibility. Nay, even the responsibility for her own soul she would have to commit to him. He knew it was so, and obstinately held out against her, waiting for the surrender. [6]

Heterosexuality wins out in *The Fox*, but not happily. March would never have left Banford for Henry; Banford had to be killed to make it possible. And Banford, as "the woman" of the couple, would not have let March go–it's the "male" prototype in these lesbian triangles who must let the woman go to be with another man–a heterosexual man–as opposed to a mannish lesbian. March is more masculine than Henry, and the triad is a confused one, fraught with complexity–not the least of which is Henry's determination to win March away from another woman. Henry even thinks that March must submit to him–it's as if he alludes to raping her–and then she can be a woman, no longer the man. No longer independent.

These themes–the "masculine" and independent woman and the triangulating theme of three people together, each vying to become a dyad with the signal woman, plays out again and again. This latter is a predicate for lesbian erotica of the period, a precursor to the lesbian pulps of the 1950s and 1960s where the lesbian sexuality is far more overt, but as the sexuality is enhanced, so too is the unpleasant ending. And the end is always the same: misery. The choices are limited: suicide or the non-mannish woman of the couple leaves to be with a man, no longer able to sustain herself in the twilight world of the demi-monde.

In Hellman's play, the possibility of lesbianism is raised as something that could happen only in the dark, in the anonymity of cities, among degenerate and decadent people. At the end of *The Children's Hour,* Mrs. Tilford, whose granddaughter's accusations brought about the ruination of the school and Martha's suicide, begs forgiveness, but it comes too late. Karen is left alone with the knowledge of what Martha told her before she killed herself.

With all this apparent misery at the heart of the erotic writing of the period, why call it The Golden Age?

Consider this assessment: gold is that precious, rare and expensive commodity. Consider its source: a hidden ore, mined from far beneath the earth, inveigled in layers and layers of obscuring rock and soil.

Mary Daly writes of dis-covery of women's work and history. We must dis-cover–uncover, remove the layers from the obscured thing, be it history or literature or simply attribution. Finding the stories and excerpts collected here required intense research and a great deal of digging. This Golden Age may be the most hidden period of lesbian erotic literature: In the past few decades lesbian Victorian tales have surfaced as have the lesbian pulps of the 1950s and 1960s. But despite the fame of women like Stein and Barnes or Vivien and Barney, the lesbian erotic writing of this particular era remains hidden, difficult to access.

In addition to being the untapped ore of lesbian erotic literature, The Golden Age also serves as the Golden Mean–the middle between two extremes, in this case between the repression of the Victorian era, which was secretly ribald, and the repression of the McCarthyism of the 1950s, which was terrorized into silence. Both periods made homosexuality a crime. But between those two points, there was an exploration of lesbian sexuality in erotic literature that was both provocative and authentic and which set the precedent for real lesbian sexuality on the page–written by and for lesbians, not by men for the titillation of men: the felicitous Golden Mean equals Golden Age.

Lesbianism has always flown under the radar, as it were–before The Golden Age and after. Queen Victoria disbelieved its existence, yet mostly was concerned that no one "frighten the horses" with her sexual exploits. Lesbianism had long been–as it continues to be, if Internet porn is any indicator–a titillation for men. Actual lesbian sexuality has always been cast as a seeming afterthought to its primary function–a sexual aid to male sexual desire/excitement.

When a woman isn't classically feminine, or takes on the "male" role–what then? Where is the place for the man to enter the bedroom and take charge of the two fumbling nymphs who are all breasts and vulvas–where's the penis, which in Freud's perspective, could be the only true sexual organ? In this particular lesbian henhouse, whither the fox?

The Well of Loneliness leaves no room for a man; the man's place has been filled already by Stephen Gordon–a manly woman with a man's name and a man's job and a man's presence. Yet with a woman's sensitivity to the needs, romantic and sexual, of another woman.

As the erotic writing of this period evolves, it becomes evident that the standard continues to be the Sappho/Atthis paradigm: an older, somewhat masculine if not wholly passing-for-male lesbian, with a younger, somewhat naive, feminine, maybe lesbian, maybe just bi-curious partner. This proto-type for lesbian erotica gets formalized with the poems of Louys, which although they were written at the *fin de siècle,* were not translated into English until the 1920s.

Certainly lesbian erotica existed prior to The Golden Age. The Victorian era was rife with tales by various anonymous writers who penned quite a few stories of errant maid servants misbehaving in the kitchen or dressing rooms, or boarding schools for girls with a curious kind of curriculum. Spanking is the answer for many of these wayward girls–spanking at the hands of a head-mistress or lady of the house, and almost always with a man in the shadows, ready to take on the tasks at hand.

Those Victorian tales were obviously written by and for men. In them the lesbianism is bawdy and at times even humorous, with lots of jiggling breasts, spanking of rosy bottoms and quivering of quims. This writing, while erotic in its own fashion, is devoid of what evolves in lesbian erotica of The Golden Age: a truly lesbian sensibility in which lesbians themselves, like Vivien, Barney, Hall, and Barnes (in her classic novel of lesbian seduction, *Nightwood*), are telling the stories of their own authentic lesbian sexuality. *Lifting Belly* for the demi-monde.

It is, however, a complex period, no less so because of the encroachment of psychology with its definitions and theories of female sexuality. Freud divined his penis envy and deemed lesbianism an infantile form of female sexuality. Havelock Ellis defined homosexuality as aberrant, yet also seemed to embrace it. While these psychologists and their followers tried to gauge what was aberrant and what was not, lesbian sexuality was censored on the page, if not behind closed doors.

What defines much of lesbian erotica of this period–erotica written by lesbians as opposed to men–is the over-arching psychologizing and its impact on actual lesbians. In the work of American writers of the 1930s, for example, who are not expatriates and not writing about Sappho or her daughters, the setting is often a college or a dormitory or some other "closed society" of women in which men have no entrée and thus women are drawn to each other as they would be in prison. This often occurs first as a "schoolgirl crush," but then develops into something far more tantalizingly sexual, far beyond the arm-in-arm walks or quick pecks on the cheek. In the works of Lois Lodge and Gale Wilhelm, for example, the women are sexual with men, find it distasteful or unsatisfying, and then find it is women who excite them.

In Lodge's provocative *Love Like A Shadow*, Alice and Jean are college girls fondled over-much by the grappling boys of a nearby college. Jean is particularly revulsed by the attentions of men and takes note that Alice is as well. Soon Alice is asking for a Christmas present unlike those the other girls are getting that year–1935.

What's compelling about Lodge's work is how naturally these young women lay around in each other's arms among their friends. It seems readily acknowledged that a girl's college is much like a prison–one is gay for the stay. No one looks askance at their flirtation, in part because the true depth of their sexual relationship remains hidden from even their closest friends. They might peck each other on the cheek in public and even lie on the sofa in each other's arms, but the hot and heavy lesbian sex happens when everyone else has gone and the lights–and sexy nightgowns–are off.

Still, the paradigm remains the same: Alice eventually runs off to marry a man, the fear of gossip leavening her every move. She loves Jean, but doesn't feel Jean can give her the life she wants. Jean is left alone to seek another partner.

In Wilhelm's remarkable *We Too Are Drifting*, the entire plot revolves around the lesbian love triangle of Jan, the masculine, mannish artist, and the two women–intensely feminine–who vie for her love and sexual attention.

Introduction

There is the femme fatale Madeline, whose sexual set point is clearly very low. This woman heats up quickly and can get out of an evening gown with similar speed. She knows how to work her feminine wiles and does so repeatedly with Jan. In scene after scene, Jan attempts to extricate herself from her intense sexual desire for the rapacious Madeline, because Madeline is also a dangerous and volatile woman who damages everything and everyone in her wake. But while Jan adores Victoria, the love of her life, the sexual enticement is simply not as strong as it is with Madeline. Madeline is the classic bad girl, while Victoria is the good girl—the one Jan wants to "marry." Alas, it is Madeline she inevitably and repeatedly beds.

The entire novel pivots on lesbian sexuality and desire, which although subtle, is intense and heated. At one point, Madeline arrives, unannounced (the only way she ever seems to get into Jan's place) and tipsy. (Wilhelm never uses quotation marks in her dialogue, adding to the intensity of the scenes.)

She was quite drunk and very beautiful...

Could a lady have a drink?

Come in, Jan said. I'll see what I can do.

She got the brandy and got a brandy glass and polished it. Madeline closed the door and locked it and put the key down the neck of her dress. Jan filled the glass and brought it, saying, here you are, and put it into Madeline's cold fingers... She closed her eyes and bent her head and lifted it and said, Kiss me, darling.

Jan kissed her and said, Now drink it or put it down.[7]

The scene goes on between the two women—Madeline in her evening dress attempting to seduce Jan and Jan attempting to steadfastly refuse Madeline's advances. The scene positively simmers with sexual heat. In 1935.

In *Torchlight to Valhalla*, there is once again a triangle, but this time it is Morgen at the center. On one side is Toni, the woman she is in love with, and on the other Royal, the man who wants to marry her.

This is heady and highly charged sexual territory for 1938, when the book was published. Morgen has sex with Royal, who takes their night together as the sealing of a pact: He expects to marry her. But Morgen sees the same act as a quiet goodbye, a farewell present. It's perfectly adequate sex, that's apparent. But it is by no means the scintillating sensuality she feels with Toni.

Wilhelm structures both novels around the pivot of love and desire—and at times these feelings war with each other. While in *The Well of Loneliness* Stephen pretends to have sex with Valerie so that Mary has reason to leave and go have a "normal" life rather than that of an invert, in Wilhelm's work there are varying levels of sexual desire. If there were no Toni, we are led to believe, perhaps Morgen would indeed marry Royal. She's not revulsed by him, as are the women in Lodge's tale by the men who crush their dresses at the college dances and paw at them and try to go all the way. Wilhelm's lesbians *make* choices–their sexuality is somewhat fluid. But their desire is not. Their desire is fixed. And it is lesbian. Not because they are revulsed by men, but because they are enchanted and enthralled by women. The lesbian sexuality in these novels is wholly authentic. It's difficult to remember that these books were written seventy and more years ago.

Violet Black's stories combine some of the classic contrivances of Victorian erotica with the authentically lesbian cast of the Golden Age. A young woman goes for a job interview and finds that the position is quite different from what she expected. Like Mary in *The Well of Loneliness* or Toni in *Torchlight to Valhalla,* Rose is a seemingly uncomplicated girl with no apparent lesbian proclivities. When she enters the shop where her interview is to take place, she is crestfallen–she knows she simply isn't the right type for the upscale Manhattan business.

But apparently she is. Her freshness and naiveté are exactly what the proprietress is looking for. A complex and highly detailed initiation of the girl ensues at the hands of the classically mannish woman–who is French (which explains her *outré* sensibilities)–and her assistant, who is seductively feminine, but far from naive.

These women do all the things that Hall alludes to in her letters to Souline and Wilhelm hints at in the scenes between Jan and Madeline.

Yet although the Black story, "Shop Girls Wanted" has a heightened and fully revealed eroticism to it–the sex is explicit–it follows all the same "rules" set during the era. Rose is not a lesbian–or at least does not appear to be. She has had flirtatious petting with the boys back home in Indiana and with the local butcher in Brooklyn, who fancies her. Yet when she is initiated into the (literally) hidden world of Frederique and Muriel, her natural desire is released. But is it lesbian desire or just pent-up desire? She forms an attachment to Frederique, not unlike similar heroines in other Golden Age stories. However, like Mary or any one of the other feminine women in these erotic tales, Rose clearly traverses both sides of the sexual fence. She has, until the moment she entered the shop, been a heterosexual girl. Yet she opens herself to lesbian desire–at the hands of a mannish lesbian–quite readily.

As does Dolores in "A Flapper's Beads," a story ostensibly about a number of male/female couples at a party in a small coal-mining town. Until one girl–the one without a boyfriend–gets hold of another while no one is paying attention. Ribaldry ensues, if briefly, and then life returns to normal–literally. But the lesbian interlude did indeed happen. Then it evaporated, as if it never had.

This is another consistent theme in lesbian erotica of this period. There are "true" lesbians, like the ones writing the stories: Hall, Vivien, Barney, Stein, others. And then there are the women who fall in love with them, but who come from relationships with men to those women, those "inverts": Una Troubridge with her admiral husband and young daughter; Souline; the Baroness de Zulyen with her two children; even Colette who seemed unable to settle on her husbands or her women lovers as her definitive desire.

There is no certainty for the "male" lesbians in these stories or even in real life during this period: the "female" partner seems to have a fluid sexuality that can take her to one side or the other of a seemingly bisexual fence. But for the women who identify as/with men–the dominant party in the coupling–they have no recourse but to seek out other women. Yet they seem to be drawn almost inevitably to women about whom they can never be completely sure, women like Hall's Souline to whom the specifics of lesbianism have to be explained, in detail.

The bisexual nature of many of the women now embraced by queer historians as wholly queer (much as lesbians of 1920s Paris embraced Sappho–who had been married to men–as the standard bearer of pure lesbianism) seems to find its way into these tales of lesbian erotica again and again. Gertrude Stein was certainly fully lesbian–and yet all her attention was focused on men. Other women of the Montparnasse set, like Barnes, also walked the fine line of bisexuality, as did that other American expatriate, Josephine Baker.

Stateside women like Ma Rainey and Bessie Smith were icons of the Golden Age–and seemed incapable of deciding whom they wanted more, men or women.

Yet another theme is that of the expatriate, or outsider. In A.N. Graeme's "The Artist's Model," the protagonist is an American expatriate in Paris and her model with whom she is obsessed is a refugee. Again we have a masculine lesbian whose sexual desires are for women whose sexual orientation is obscure at best.

What undergirds the panoply of lesbian erotica of this period is a slow evolution toward fully realized lesbian sexuality. Where Louys opens the door to the possibility of sexuality wholly between women–no men are at the keyhole in *Songs of Bilitis* –Vivien authenticates it with poems that are utterly devoid of anything but her aching desire for other women.

Stein celebrates that in her elliptical prose poem *Lifting Belly*. As does Wilhelm in her novels.

The over-arching desire of women for each other, regardless of the revisionist definitions we have come to append in the twenty-first century–lesbian, bisexual, transsexual–is what unites the very disparate erotic tales from The Golden Age. The other unifying thread is authenticity: the sexuality is very much lesbian, even if all the players do not appear to be so at the time. Wilhelm's Madeline, for example, is a gorgeous woman, intensely and provocatively feminine and deeply, unrelentingly sensual. Yet she is no crossover character. She does not flit between men and women. She is definitively lesbian, as Wilhelm crafts her, and her desire is for Jan–not for her husband or for any of the men in the novel.

The elliptical nature of much of the sexuality in the stories from this period–the "off the page" sex in a majority of the pieces (although more than half of the stories collected here have fully realized, on-the-page sex)–led us to publish three stories from each of the decades of the period. These stories are written in the tone of the eras in which they are set and are emblematic of important moments in those decades–the eras of the flapper, the Hollywood starlet, and women serving in World War II. The women in these stories don't waver in their sexual choices: it's all lesbian. And the sex has the explicitness that was rare in the actual period of the Golden Age, because censorship was rife and psychologizing of lesbians often damped down the sexuality in their writing, or led to the kind of stridency one finds at the end of *The Well of Loneliness*.

Ultimately, the Golden Age opens another curtain on lesbian history. The revelation that lesbian sexuality and its representations could be authentic, rather than crafted by men for men, was huge–and a tectonic shift in perspective. The influence of Havelock Ellis and Freud on those representations was unfortunate, and yet it didn't repress them completely: despite obscenity trials and references to lesbianism as either aberrant or unfinished female sexuality, women were living fully authentic lesbian lives, replete with excesses of sex, as evidenced by the Montparnasse set or Hall's love letters.

What do we get from *The Golden Age of Lesbian Erotica?* Tales of real lesbians having real sex–a first. Whether the sex is muted, but simmering, as in Wilhelm, or explosively overt, as in Black, it is all very, very real and representative of a turning point in the perception of what lesbians actually were and what they could be, whether behind closed doors or with the doors flung wide. In the end, despite the repressions of the period, the Golden Age of Lesbian Erotica is an ore that has indeed been tapped, and from it flows the well-spring of today's explicit and thoroughly joyful lesbian erotic literature.

1. Stein, Gertrude. *Lifting Belly.* Edited by Rebecca Marks. Tallahassee, Florida: Naiad Press, 1989.
2. Glasgow, Joanne, editor. *Your John: The Love Letters of Radclyffe Hall.* New York: New York University Press, 1997.
3. Ibid.
4. Hellman, Lillian. *Six Plays.* New York: Vintage Books, 1979.
5. Lawrence, D.H. *The Fox.* New York: Penguin Books, 1977.
6. Ibid.
7. Wilhelm, Gale. *We Too Are Drifting.* Tallahassee, Florida: Naiad Press, 1984.

Prologue

Pierre Louys
From THE SONGS OF BILITIS
1898
Translated from the French by Alvah C. Bessie
1926

Sappho's lyrics have long been popular with European readers. In 1894, French writer Pierre Louys hit on a beautiful fraud: a translation of the poems of Bilitis, a contemporary of Sappho's, whose tomb and writings had recently been discovered. In his book, Louys wrote briefly about Bilitis' life and even provided a faux bibliography to give credence to his creation. Because of then-current censorship laws and the sexual nature of the songs, about half of which discuss lesbianism, it was impossible to publish the book in English translation in the United States. The only way to circumvent the censorship statutes was to privately publish "subscribers-only" editions in limited numbers. The following translation by Alvah C. Bessie first appeared in 1926 in just such a privately printed edition; one year before, Edwin Marion Cox's now-standard translation of Sappho had been published.

The Songs of Bilitis was so popular that in 1898 Louys' close friend Claude Debussy composed a song cycle for piano and voice based on the poems. In 1955, one of the first American lesbian organizations chose to call itself the Daughters of Bilitis, in homage to Louys' sensitive and sensual character.

–*Judith M. Redding*

THE LIFE OF BILITIS

Bilitis was born at the beginning of the sixth century before our era, in a mountain village situated on the banks of the Melas, towards the east of Pamphylia. This country is solemn and dreary, shadowed by heavy forests, dominated by the vast pile of the Taurus; streams of calciferous water spring from the rocks; great salt lakes remain on the highlands, and the valleys are heavy with silence.

She was the daughter of a Greek father and a Phoenician mother. She does not seem to have known her father, for he takes no part in the memories of her childhood. He may even have died before she was born. Otherwise it would be difficult to explain how she came to bear a Phoenician name, which her mother alone could have given her.

Upon this nearly desert land she lived a tranquil life with her mother and her sisters. Other young girls who were her friends lived not far away. On the wooded slopes of the Taurus, the shepherds pastured their flocks.

In the morning, at cock-crow, she arose, went to the stable, led out the beasts to water and busied herself with milking them. During the day, if it rained, she stayed in the *gynaeceum*, spinning her distaff of wool. Were the weather fair, she ran in the fields and played with her companions the many games of which she makes mention.

In respect to the Nymphs, Bilitis retained an ardent piety. The sacrifices she offered were almost always dedicate to their stream. She often spoke to them, but it seems quite certain that she never saw them, for she reports with so much veneration the memories of an old man who had one day surprised them.

The end of her pastoral life was saddened by a love-affair about which we know little, although she speaks of it at considerable length. When it became unhappy, she ceased singing it. Having become the mother of a child which she abandoned, Bilitis left Pamphylia for mysterious reasons, and never again saw the place where she was born.

We find her next at Mytilene, whence she had come by way of the sea, skirting the lovely shores of Asia. She was scarcely sixteen years old, according to the conjectures of Herr Heim, who has established, with an appearance of truth, certain dates in the life of Bilitis from a verse which alludes to the death of Pittakos.

Lesbos was then the axis of the world. Halfway between lovely Attica and sumptuous Lydia, it had as capital a city more enlightened than Athens and more corrupt than Sardis: Mytilene, built upon a peninsula in sight of the shores of Asia. The blue sea surrounded the city. From the heights of the temples the white coastline of Atarnea, the port of Pergamum, could be seen.

The narrow and perpetually crowded streets shone with parti-colored stuffs, tunics of purple and hyacinth, cyclas of transparent silks and bassaras trailing in the dust stirred up by yellow sandals. Great gold rings threaded with unfinished pearls hung from the women's ears, and their arms were adorned with massive silver bracelets, heavily cut in relief. Even the tresses of the men themselves were glossy and perfumed with precious oils. The ankles of the Greeks were bare amidst the jingling of their periscelis, great serpents of a light metal which tinkled about their heels; those of the Asiatics moved in boots of soft and painted leather. The passers-by stopped in groups before the shops which faced on to the streets, and where finery only was displayed for sale: rugs of sombre colors, saddle-cloths stitched with threads of gold, amber or ivory jewelry, according to the district. The bustle of Mytilene did not cease with the close of day: there was no hour, no matter how late, when one could not hear, through the open doors, the joyous sounds of instruments, the cries of women and the noise of dancing. Pittakos himself, who wanted somewhat to regulate this perpetual debauch, made a law forbidding flute-players who were too young to take part in any nightly revel; but this law, in common with all laws which attempt to change the course of natural customs, found no observance, but rather brought about a secret practice.

In a society in which the husbands were so occupied at night by wine and female dancers, it was inevitable that the wives would be brought together and find among themselves consolation in their solitude. Thus it came about that they were favorably disposed to those delicate love-affairs to which antiquity had already given their name, and which held, no matter what men may think of them, more of actual passion than of dissolute curiosity.

Then Sappho was still beautiful. Bilitis knew her, and speaks of her to us, under the name of Psappha, which she bore in Lesbos. No doubt it was this admirable woman who taught the little Pamphylian the art of singing in rhythmic cadences, and of preserving for posterity the memory of dearly cherished beings. Unhappily Bilitis gives few details about this figure today so poorly known, and there is reason for regretting it, so precious would have been the slightest word about the great Inspiratrix. In return she has left us, in thirty elegies, the story of her friendship for a young girl of her age named Mnasidika, who lived with her. We had already known this young girl's name, through a verse of Sappho's in which her beauty is exalted; but even this name was doubtful, and Bergk was nearly convinced that she called herself simply Mnaïs. The songs which will be read further on prove that this hypothesis should be abandoned. Mnasidika seems to have been a sweet and naïve young girl, one of those charming creatures whose mission it is to allow themselves to be adored; the more dear, the less effort they make to merit what is given them. Unmotivated loves last longest; this one lasted ten years. It will be seen how it was broken up through the fault of Bilitis, whose excessive jealousy could not understand the least eclecticism.

When she felt that there was nothing to keep her in Mytilene any longer except unhappy memories, Bilitis made a second voyage: she proceeded to Cyprus, an island both Greek and Phoenician like Pamphylia itself, and which must often have recalled to her the aspect of her native land.

It was there that Bilitis commenced her life for the third time, and in a fashion for which it will be more difficult for me to obtain sanction without again recalling how sacred a thing was love among the ancient races. The courtesans of Amathus were not fallen creatures, like our own, exiled from all worldly society; they were girls sprung from the best families of the town. Aphrodite had given them the gift of beauty, and they thanked the goddess by consecrating their grateful loveliness to the service of her cult. All cities which possessed, as did those of Cyprus, a temple rich in courtesans, cherished the same respectful solicitude over these women.

The incomparable story of Phryne, such as Athenaeus has handed it down to us, will give some idea of this kind of veneration. It is not true that Hyperides needed to display her nude in order to prevail upon the Areopagus, and nevertheless the crime was great: she had committed murder. The orator removed no more than the upper part of her tunic and only revealed her breasts. And he begged the judges "not to put to death the priestess and the *Inspired of Aphrodite.*" Contrary to the usage of other courtesans, who went about clothed in transparent mantles, through which all the details of their bodies were apparent, Phryne was in the habit of enveloping even her hair in one of those great wrinkled robes, whose grace has been preserved for us in the figurines of Tanagra. No man, if he were not one of her intimates, had ever seen her arms or shoulders; and she had never appeared in the pool of the public baths. But one day an extraordinary thing happened. It was the day of the Eleusinian festivals; twenty thousand people had come from all the countries of Greece and were assembled on the beach when Phryne advanced towards the waves: she took off her robe, she undid her girdle, she even removed her undergarment, "she unrolled all her hair and she stepped into the sea." And in this crowd there was Praxiteles, who designed the *Aphrodite of Cnidos* after this living goddess; and Apelles who caught a glimpse of his *Anadyomene.* Admirable race, to whom Beauty might appear nude without exciting laughter or false shame!

I would that this were the story of Bilitis, for, in translating her Songs, I fell in love with the little friend of Mnasidika. Doubtless her life was quite as marvelous. I only regret that it has not been further spoken of, and that the ancient authors, those at least who have survived, are so poor in information about her. Philodemus, who pilfered from her twice, does not even mention her name. In default of happy anecdotes, I beg that all will be good enough to be content with the details that she herself gives us about her life as a courtesan. That she was a courtesan cannot be denied; and even her last songs prove that, if she had the virtues of her vocation, she also had its worst weaknesses. But I am concerned only with her virtues. She was pious and devout. She remained faithful to the temple as long as Aphrodite consented to prolong the youth of her purest worshipper. The day she ceased being loved she ceased to write, she says. However, it is difficult to suppose that the songs of Pamphylia were written during the time they were being lived. How could a little mountain shepherdess have learned to scan her verses according to the difficult rhythm of the Aeolic tradition? It would be found more plausible that, grown old, Bilitis pleased herself in singing for herself the memories of her far-off childhood. We know nothing about this last period of her life. We do not even know at what age she died.

Her tomb was rediscovered by Herr G. Heim, at Paleo-Limisso, by the side of an ancient road not far from Amathus. These ruins have almost disappeared in the past thirty years, and the stones of the house in which Bilitis may have lived pave the quays of Port-Said today. But the tomb was underground, according to the Phoenician custom, and it had even escaped the depredations of treasure-hunters.

Herr Heim penetrated into it through a narrow well filled with earth, at the bottom of which he found a walled-up door which it was necessary to demolish. The low and spacious cavern, paved with slabs of limestone, had four walls, covered with plaques of black amphibolite, upon which were carved in primitive capitals all the songs which will be read hereafter, with the exception of the three epitaphs which decorated the sarcophagus.

There it was that the friend of Mnasidika rested, in a great terracotta coffin, beneath a lid modeled by a careful sculptor who had carved in the clay the face of the dead: the hair was painted black, the eyes half-closed and lengthened by a pencil, as in life, and the cheek scarcely softened by a slight smile born from the lines of the mouth. No one will ever solve the mystery of these lips: both clear-cut and pouting, both soft and dainty, touching each on each, but still as though drunk to kiss and clasp again. When the tomb was opened she appeared in the state in which a pious hand had laid her out twenty-four centuries before. Vials of perfume hung from earthen pegs, and one of them, after so long a time, was still fragrant. The polished silver mirror in which Bilitis saw herself, the little stylus which spread blue paint upon her eyelids, were found in place. A little nude Astarte, relic forever precious, still watched over the skeleton, decked with all its golden jewels and white as a branch of snow, but so soft and fragile that the moment it was breathed upon it fell to dust.

–*Pierre Louÿs*
Constantinople, August 1894

THE TREE

I undressed to climb a tree; my naked thighs embraced the smooth and humid bark; my sandals climbed upon the branches.

High up, but still beneath the leaves and shaded from the heat, I straddled a wide-spread fork and swung my feet into the void.

It had rained. Drops of water fell and flowed upon my skin. My hands were soiled with moss and my heels were reddened by the crushed blossoms.

I felt the lovely tree living when the wind passed through it; so I locked my legs tighter, and crushed my open lips to the hairy nape of a bough.

THE OLD MAN AND THE NYMPHS

An old blind man lives on the mountain. For having looked at the nymphs his eyes have long been dead. And from that time his happiness has been a far-off memory.

"Yes, I saw them," he told me: "Helopsychria, Limnanthis; they were standing near the bank, in the green pool of Physos. The water shimmered higher than their knees.

"Their necks were bent beneath their heavy hair. Their nails were filmy, like the wings of grasshoppers. Their breasts were deep, like the calyx of the hyacinth.

"They trailed their fingers upon the water, and pulled long-stemmed lilies from the unseen silt. About their separated thighs, slow circles spread…"

THE ACCOMMODATING FRIEND

The storm had lasted all night. Selenis of the lovely hair had come to spin with me. She stayed for fear of the mud, and, pressed tightly each to each, we filled my tiny bed.

When young girls sleep together sleep itself remains outside the door. "Bilitis, tell me, tell me whom you love." She slipped her thigh across my own to warm me sweetly.

And she whispered into my mouth: "I know, Bilitis, whom you love. Close your eyes, I am Lykas." I answered, touching her, "Can't I tell that you are just a girl? Your joke's a clumsy one."

But she went on: "Truly I am Lykas if you close your lids. Here are his arms, here are his hands…" and tenderly, in the silence, she flushed my dreaming with a stranger dream.

PSAPPHA

I rub my eyes… it is already day, I think. Ah! who is by my side?… A woman? …By Paphia, I had forgotten! …Oh, Charites! how hot with shame I am!

To what country have I come, what isle is this, where love is comprehended in this fashion? If I were not so tired, I should think I had been dreaming... Can it be that this is Psappha?

She sleeps... She certainly is beautiful, although her hair is cut in virile fashion. But this strange face, this mannish bosom and these narrow hips...

I had best leave before she wakens. Alas! I am lying by the wall. I must step over her. I am afraid to brush against her hip, afraid that she might try to hold me back.

THE DANCE OF GLOTTIS AND KYSE

Two little girls had led me to their home, and as soon as the door was closed they touched the wick unto the fire and wished to dance for me.

Their unrouged cheeks were tan, just like their little bellies. They grasped each other by the arms and chattered joyously.

Seated upon a raised and padded trestle, Glottis sang in a sharp voice, and struck her noisy little hands together.

Kyse danced in quick staccato fashion, then stopping, winded with laughter, grasped her sister by her breasts, bit her shoulder and turned her roundabout much like a playful goat.

COUNSELS

Then Syllikmas entered, and, seeing that we were so intimate, sat down upon the bench. Taking Glottis on one knee and Kyse on the other, she began:

"Come here, my dear." But I remained away. Then she went on: "Are you afraid of us? Come closer: these children truly love you. They can teach you things you do not know about: the honey-like caresses of a girl.

"Man is violent and lazy. You doubtless know him well. Then hate him. He has a flattened breast, rough skin, short hair and shaggy arms. But women are entirely beautiful.

"And only women know the art of love; stay with us, Bilitis, do stay. And if you have a truly ardent spirit, you'll see your beauty as within a glass upon the bodies of your mistresses."

INCERTITUDE

I do not know if I shall mate myself with Glottis or with Kyse. As they are not much alike, one cannot soothe me for the other's loss, and I greatly fear to make an evil choice.

Each has one of my hands, and one of my breasts too. To which, I wonder, shall I give my mouth? To which my heart, and all one cannot share?

For it is shameful to stay this way, all three within one house. They talk of such things here in Mytilene. Yesterday before the temple of Ares a passing woman did not say "Good-day."

'Tis Glottis I prefer; but I cannot disown Kyse. What would become of her all by herself? Or shall I leave them together as I found them, and take another lover for myself?

DESIRE

She entered, and passionately, with half-closed eyes, she joined her lips with mine, and our tongues knew each other... Never in my life had there been a kiss like that.

She stood against me, amorous and willing. Little by little my knee rose between her warm thighs, which spread as though receptive to a lover.

My wandering hand upon her gown sought her secret body, which alternately swayed in undulation, or arching, stiffened with tremblings of the skin.

With maddened eyes she looked upon the bed; but we had no right to love before the wedding, and we separated hastily at last.

THE WEDDING

The wedding feast was given in the morning, in Acalanthis' house whom she had taken for a mother. Mnasidika wore a milk-white veil, and I the virile tunic.

Then after, in the midst of twenty women she donned her festal robes. Perfumed with bakkaris and spread with gold-dust, her cool and rippling skin attracted furtive hands.

In her leafy chamber she awaited me, as a bridegroom. And I led her out in a little two-wheeled cart, seated between me and the nymphagogue. One of her little breasts burned in my hand.

They sang the nuptial song: the flutes sang madly. And carrying Mnasidika, my arms beneath her knees and round her shoulders, I passed the threshold, strewn with blushing roses.

THE LIVING PAST

I left the bed as she had left it, unmade and rumpled, coverlets awry, so that her body's print might rest still warm beside my own.

Until the next day I did not go to bathe, I wore no clothes and did not dress my hair, for fear I might erase some sweet caress.

That morning I did not eat, nor yet at dusk, and put no rouge nor powder on my lips, so that her kiss might cling a little longer.

I left the shutters closed, and did not open the door, for fear the memory of the night before might vanish with the wind.

MNASIDIKA'S THREE BEAUTIES

That Mnasidika may be protected by the gods, I sacrificed two doves and two male hares to laughter-loving Aphrodite.

To Ares I have given two armed cocks, and sinister Hecate has received two dogs who howled beneath the knife.

Nor have I wrongly prayed these three immortals, for Mnasidika bears upon her face the imprint of their trinal godhead:

Her lips are red as copper, her hair shines blue as steel and her eyes are black as silver.

MNASIDIKA'S BREASTS

Carefully, with one hand, she opened her tunic and tendered me her breasts, warm and sweet, just as one offers the goddess a pair of living turtle-doves.

"Love them well," she said to me, "I love them so! They are little darlings, little children. I busy myself with them when I am alone. I play with them; I pleasure them.

"I flush them with milk. I powder them with flowers. I dry them with my fine-spun hair, soft to their little nipples. I caress them and I shiver. I couch them in soft wool.

"Since I shall never have a child, be their nursling, oh! my love, and since they are so distant from my mouth, kiss them, sweet, for me."

TENDERNESS

Softly clasp your arms, like a girdle, about me. Touch, oh, touch my skin like that again! Neither water nor the noon-time breeze is gentle as your hand.

Today you shall fondle me, little sister; 'tis your turn. Remember the caresses that I taught you last night, and kneel beside me who am tired, and do not say a word.

Your lips sink from my lips. And all your unbound ringlets follow them, as the caress follows fast upon the kiss. They fall upon my left breast; they hide your eyes from me.

Give me your hand, it is so warm! Press mine and do not leave it. Hands join with hands more easily than mouth with mouth, and nothing can compare with their passion.

SHADOWLIGHT

We slipped beneath the transparent coverlet of wool, she and I. Even our heads were hidden, and the lamp lit up the cloth above us.

And thus I saw her dear body in a mysterious glow. We were much closer to each other, freer, more naked and more intimate. "In the selfsame shift," she said to me.

We left our hair done up so that we'd be more bare, and in the close air of the bed two female odors rose, as from two natural censers.

Nothing in the world, not even the lamp, saw us that night. And which of us was loved and which the lover, she and I alone can ever tell. But the men shall never know a thing about it.

THE KISS

I shall kiss from end to end the long black wings spreading from your neck, oh, gentle bird, captive dove whose heart throbs wild beneath my hand!

I shall take your mouth into my mouth as the child takes its mother's breast. Tremble! for the kiss sinks deep and should suffice for love.

I shall trail my light tongue along your arms and round your neck, and I shall drag the long drawn kiss of my nails along your tender sides.

Hear roaring in your ear all the murmur of the sea... Mnasidika! the expression of your eyes makes me ill. I'll clasp within my kiss your lids which burn as warmly as your lips.

JEALOUS CARES

You must not dress your hair for fear the iron might burn your neck or singe your lovely locks. You'll let it rest upon your shoulders, and spread along your arms.

You must not dress yourself, for fear your girdle might redden the fine-drawn lines about your hips. Remain naked like a little girl.

You must not even rise, for fear your tender feet might become sore with walking here and there. You shall remain in bed, oh Eros' prey, and I shall dress your wound!

For I would not see upon your body any other mark, Mnasidika, than the mark of a kiss too long-impressed, the scratch of a sharpened nail, or the purpled bar of my own embrace.

THE HEART

Panting, I took her hand and pressed it tightly beneath the humid skin of my left breast. My head tossed here and there and I moved my lips, but not a word escaped.

My maddened heart, sudden and hard, beat and beat upon my breast, as a captive satyr would beat about, tied in a goat-skin vessel. She said to me: "Your heart is troubling you..."

"Oh, Mnasidika!" I answered her, "a woman's heart is not seated there. This is but a little bird, a dove which stirs its feeble wings. The heart of a woman is more terrible.

"It burns like a myrtle-berry, with a bright red flame and beneath abundant foam. 'Tis there that I feel bitten by voracious Aphrodite."

LOVE

Alas! if I think of her my throat is parched, my head is drooped, my breasts grow hard and make me ill at case, I tremble and I weep the while I walk.

If I see her my heart stops, my hands shake, my feet grow cold and fire mounts in my cheeks, while my temples pulse sadly on and on.

If I touch her I grow mad, my arms stiffen and my knees grow weak. I fall before her and curl up like a woman wont to die.

I am hurt by everything she says to me. Her love is like a torture, and the passers-by can hear my constant plaint... Alas! how can I call her Well-Beloved?

SCENE

Where were you? –At the florist's. I bought some lovely irises. Behold them, I have brought them just for you. –And you took all that time to buy four flowers? –The merchant kept me waiting.

–Your cheeks are pale, and your eyes are shining. –The weariness of walking such a way. –Your hair is wet and tangled. –The heat is great, the wind has tossed my hair.

–Your girdle was untied. I made the knot myself, and not as hard as that. –So loose it opened; a passing slave tied it up for me.

–There is a spot on your dress. –The flowers dripped. –Mnasidika, my little soul, your irises are far more beautiful than can be bought in all of Mytilene. –How well I know it, oh, how well I know!

TO GYRINNO

Do not think that I have loved you. I have eaten you like a ripe fig, and drunk you like a draught of burning water, and worn you about me like a girdle of flesh.

I have amused myself with you, because you have short hair and pointed breasts upon your slender body, and nipples black as little dates.

As one must have fruits and water, a woman also sates a living thirst; but already I no longer know your name, you who have lain within my arms like the shade of another loved one.

Between your flesh and mine a burning dream has claimed me for its own. I pressed you on me as upon a wound, and cried: "Mnasidika! Mnasidika! Mnasidika!"

RENDING MEMORY

I remember... (at what hour of the day is she not before my eyes!). I remember the way she had of lifting her hair with pale and dainty fingers.

I remember a night she passed, cheek against my breast, so sweetly that happiness kept me long awake; and the next day she had the imprint of the nipple on her face.

I see her holding her cup of milk, and looking at me sidewise with a smile. I see her, powdered and with her hair new-dressed, opening her great eyes before her mirror and touching up the rouge upon her lips.

And above all, if my despair is everlasting torture, it is because I know, minute by minute, how she trembles in the other's arms, and what she asks of her and what she gives, herself.

THE MYSTERIES

In the thrice mysterious hall where men have never entered, we have feted you, Astarte of the Night. Mother of the World, Well-Spring of the life of all the Gods!

I shall reveal a portion of the rite, but no more of it than is permissible. About a crowned Phallos, a hundred-twenty women swayed and cried. The initiates were dressed as men, the others in the split tunic.

The fumes of perfumes and the smoke of torches floated fog-like in and out among us all. I wept my scorching tears. All, at the feet of Berbeia, we threw ourselves, extended on our backs.

Then, when the Religious Act was consummated, and when into the Holy Triangle the purpled phallos had been plunged anew, the mysteries began; but I shall say no more.

INTIMACIES

You ask why I am now a Lesbian, oh, Bilitis? But what flute-player is not lesbian a little? I am poor; I have no bed; I sleep with her who wishes me, and thank her with whatever charms I have.

We danced quite naked when we still were small; you know what dances, oh, my dear!: the twelve desires of Aphrodite. We look at one another, compare our nakedness, and find ourselves so pretty.

During the long night we become inflamed for the pleasure of the guests; but our ardor is not feigned, and we feel it so much that sometimes one of us entices her willing friend behind the doors.

How can we then love men, who are rude with us? They seize us like whores, and leave before we can attain our pleasure. You who are a woman, you know what I feel. You pleasure others as you would be pleased.

TO HER BREASTS

Flesh in blossom, oh, my breasts! How rich and heavy you are with desire! My breasts in my hands, how soft you are, and with what mellow warmths and young perfumes.

Formerly you were frozen like the breasts of a statue, and hard as senseless marble. Since you have softened I cherish you more, you who have been loved.

Your smooth and swelling form is the pride of my nut-brown body. Whether I bind you in the golden gauze or free you naked to the open air, you precede me with your splendor.

Be happy, then, tonight. If my fingers give forth soft caresses, you alone will know until the dawn: for tonight, Bilitis has paid Bilitis.

THE LAST LOVER

Child, do not go on without having loved me. I still am fair, beneath the cloak of night; you shall see how much warmer my autumn is than any other's spring...

Do not seek the love of virgins. Love is a difficult art in which young girls are not highly versed. I have spent my life in learning it, to give it to my last lover.

You, I know, will be my last lover. Here is my mouth, for which a nation has grown ashen with desire. Here is my hair that the great Psappha sang in measured verse.

I shall gather together for you all that is left of my lost youth. I'll even burn my memories themselves. I'll give you Lykas' flute... Mnasidika's girdle.

Gertrude Stein
from LIFTING BELLY
1917

When Naiad Press published Gertrude Stein's *Lifting Belly* in 1989, it was with the fanfare of uncovering a new perspective on lesbian sexuality written by one of the most famous lesbians of the early twentieth century. Because of its overtly lesbian content, *Lifting Belly* had not been published in Stein's lifetime and had been out of print since 1958, prior to the Naiad Press revival.

Naiad Press editor Rebecca Mark wrote, "*Lifting Belly* is a radical story about lesbian sexuality, about writing about lesbian love making and about loving writing about lesbian sexuality and about loving while writing on lesbian sexuality and about Alice and about Gertrude and about Gertrude loving Alice while writing *Lifting Belly*, and about Alice loving Gertrude about ways of being a loving one and about you and about me and about our loving and about kissing and about kissing with a fire and about..."

Gertrude Stein, known for her obscure and oblique prose as well as her long-term relationship with Alice B. Toklas, takes on the delicate folds of lesbian sexuality in ways that are encoded but also overt. Yet another example of the many facets of lesbian erotic writing in the golden age, *Lifting Belly* reveals that hidden-ness of lesbian sexuality that so characterizes this period of lesbian erotica. Playful as well as sensual, Stein's prose poem takes us into daily lesbian sexuality as experienced between Toklas, whom Stein called "Pussy," and Stein, whom Toklas called "Lovey." The two met in 1907 and lived together until Stein's death in 1946.

Stein often wrote love notes and poems to Toklas, leaving them on her pillow:

"Baby precious Hubby worked and loved his wifey, sweet sleepy wifey, dear dainty wifey, baby precious sleep."

The intensity of the eroticism of their relationship was also remarked upon in Ernest Hemingway's 1964 Paris memoir, *A Moveable Feast.*

—*Victoria A. Brownworth*

Part II

Lifting belly. Are you. Lifting.
Oh dear I said I was tender, fierce and tender.
Do it. What a splendid example of carelessness.
It gives me a great deal of pleasure to say yes.
Why do I always smile.
I don't know.
It pleases me.
You are easily pleased.
I am very pleased.
Thank you I am scarcely sunny.
I wish the sun would come out.
Yes.
Do you lift it.
High.
Yes sir I helped to do it.
Did you.
Yes.
Do you lift it.

* * *

Kiss my lips. She did.
Kiss my lips again she did.
Kiss my lips over and over and over again she did.
I have feathers.
Gentle fishes.
...Lifting belly is so strange.
I came to speak about it...
    Don't speak about it.
My baby is a dumpling. I want to tell her something.

* * *

Please be the man.
I am the man.

Lifting belly praises.
And she gives
Health.
And fragrance.
And words.
Lifting belly is in bed.
And the bed has been made comfortable.
Lifting belly knows this.

Renee Vivien from THE MUSE OF THE VIOLETS
1923
Translated from the French by Margaret Porter

Renee Vivien was born Pauline Tarn in 1877 in London. A British poet who wrote solely in French, Vivien lived a flagrantly lesbian life in Paris, where in 1900 she became lovers with American heiress and poet Natalie Clifford Barney. (Vivien is reputed to have been the great love of Barney's life.) Vivien and Barney were greatly influenced in their work and personal lives by the tales of Sappho and the Isle of Lesbos. Greek and Sapphic imagery abound in the works of both women, but Vivien has numerous poems devoted solely to the worlds of Lesbos and Mytilene. All of Vivien's work resounds with lesbian imagery and lesbian love. A majority of her poems are lesbian love poems to various lovers, the best of which were written to or about Barney. Vivien lived a complex and often reprobate life, as recorded in Colette's *The Pure and Impure*, a lifestyle which contributed to her early death at only thirty-two. Vivien published only one slim volume of poetry before her death in 1909. Her complete poems were published in Paris in two volumes between 1923 and 1924. They were not translated into English until 1977, the translation which appears here.　　　　　　　　　　　　　　　　*–Victoria A. Brownworth*

VELLEITY

Loosen your feverish arms, oh my mistress, dismiss
Me. Set me free from the yoke of your bitter kiss.
Far from your lascivious, oppressive scent,
Far from the languors of the bed where our hours are spent,

Oh the breath of the wind I shall breathe the sharp salt air,
The acrid tang of the algae; till clean and bare,
I shall go towards the wild profundity of the sea,
Pale from solitude, drunk with chastity.

THE TOUCH

The trees have kept some lingering sun in their branches.
Veiled like a woman, evoking another time,

53

The twilight passes, weeping. My fingers climb,
Trembling, provocative, the line of your haunches.

My ingenious fingers wait when they have found
The petal flesh beneath the robe they part.
How curious, complex, the touch, this subtle art–
As the dream of fragrance, the miracle of sound.

I follow slowly the graceful contours of your hips,
The curves of your shoulders, your neck, your unappeased breasts.
In your white voluptuousness my desire rests,
Swooning, refusing itself the kisses of your lips.

LUCIDITY

You fill your leisure with the delicate art of vice,
You know how to awaken the warmth of desire in ice.
Every movement of your supple body is a subtle caress;
The odor of the bed mingles with the perfumes of your dress.
The too-sweet blandness of honey is like your blond charm,
You love only the artificial, what does harm,
The music of elegant words and murmurings.
Your kisses graze the lips like transient wings.
Your eyes are winters starred with icy isles.
Lamentings follow your steps in dejected files.
Your word is a shadow, your gesture a pale reflection.
Your body has softened from kisses without affection,
Your soul has become withered, your body has been abused.
Languorous, lewd, your cunning touch you have used
Till it does not know the loyal beauty of the embrace.
You say the artful speeches one would hear, to one's face,
Beneath feigned sweetness a watchful reptile lies.
Dark as the sea without reflecting skies,
The tombs are less impure than your bed. But the worst,
Oh Woman! Only your mouth will quench my thirst!

Anna Elisabet Weirauch
from THE SCORPION
1920
revised translation by Victoria A. Brownworth

Qui vivens laedit, morte medetur. "What life wounds, death heals."

These excerpts from Anna Weirauch's stunning novel *The Scorpion* detail the full range of what lesbians of the period – here, 1920s Germany – were faced with. Twenty-year-old Myra must cope with psychiatric intervention, homophobia, being cut off from her family, as well as her own intense emotional and sexual awakening at the hands of the beautiful, slightly older and highly manipulative Olga. Although Weirauch does not explore the sexual side of Myra and Olga's relationship in vivid detail, she does repeatedly refer to and reveal the sexual side of their relationship and, most definitively, Myra's obsessive love for Olga, which is clearly of a romantic/sexual nature. What surprises in Weirauch's fiction is not how well-crafted her prose is or how well-drawn her characters, but how true to the present her writing remains. Myra could as easily be a young woman in Middle America as she was a young woman in Mittle Europe.

–Victoria A. Brownworth

After Myra Rudloff had graduated, she remained at home with her father and Aunt Emily for a few years, bored and boring, filled with yearning. To tweak her interests she took the *de rigeur* piano lessons, practicing the requisite number of hours. But Myra had no innate musical flair, although she did suffer from an elevated sensitivity – she suffered from her own inability to achieve the musical range she ached for, without being able, in effort or talent, to make up for her deficiencies.

During this period of flux and inertia, her moods were as quixotic as weather in April – sunny one moment, stormy the next. She longed for what she could not have: to be dead, or to come of age, to be alive in another century, or some other part of the earth, to be a nun or so beautiful as to ravish the entire world.

Throughout this period of emotional drought, the days stretched on into nothingness – there was nothing to stir Myra, nothing to augur the kind of change that might make her life seem less empty. The emptiness was so pervasive that later Myra could barely recall that time. If others raised questions in conversation about that barren, empty era of her life, be it some journey, or even something as significant as a birth or death among their acquaintances, or even some dramatic event in the news, Myra always had to think long and hard about when such a thing might have happened and how old she would have been.

Conversely, there was another signpost in her memory that resonated, a time when people and events stood like commemorative icons for her because she associated them with Olga: before or after Olga's death, when she was together with Olga or separated from her, when she had kissed Olga and when she had not. It was all Olga, because Olga was a talisman – her talisman. Olga was when Myra's life – her life that had been spent in useless reverie – became fully, sensually, excitingly alive.

It was indeed The Moment – the moment when Myra felt her life really began –and it was accompanied as all such great moments are with an almost violent crescendo: hundreds of loud, implacable voices, rendered with a background music that would never again be quiet, but would resonate, first in a major clef, then in a minor, with accompaniment of fullest orchestra, first from the violins, then the cellos, now from one argumentative oboe. It was all in a million intricacies, a million nuances. Then there was the final, dramatic closing chord. That musical flourish, that presentiment was The Moment: when Olga Radó opened the door at Consul Moebius's house and walked into the room. Forever after Myra's memory would flash on the time before and the time after Olga. Memory and Olga were inextricable.

Myra, nor anyone else, could complain about the Moebiuses as companions. Aunt Emily herself had cultivated their acquaintance particularly for Myra. Fannie and Emmie were both younger than Myra, both strawberry blondes, fussy and neat about their clothes and hair. They were also, to Myra, amazingly insignificant. So much so that after watching them day after day in visit after visit, Myra had ceased to know whether they had anything compelling about them at all – were they attractive or not? And did she care? Neither stirred her. Her boredom was complete.

With time, Myra could also no longer discern what their connection to Olga Radó had been. In the beginning, when everything about Olga seemed fresh and new and intensely exciting, the Moebius girls (as well as Aunt Emily and the others) all raved about Olga. Then, when each girl had a crush on her, she was "our cousin." Afterward, after all the unpleasantness, no one could nor cared to remember a connection that resembled blood or kinship.

As for Olga herself, she never commented much on her relationship with Consul Moebius, before or after, for good or ill. What was clear is that Olga would never have visited the house had she not been begged to do so, repeatedly. They all were in love with her.

Myra, Fannie, Emmie, and Erika Hanneman had their own clique. Once a week they got together to do what bored girls do: they plied needlework or read French plays, each girl taking different roles. This was in that period when Myra was perpetually bored and these get-togethers bored her to distraction: she failed to pay attention when her friends read and always missed her cue.

On a typically tedious Wednesday afternoon in April, Myra and the other girls were sitting, complacent and feigning interest, on their white-lacquered chairs in Fannie and Emmie's elegant room when the door opened, and in came Olga Radó.

As Myra remembers it, Olga must have accidentally left another door open behind her, for when she entered, a breath of air as fresh as a mountain breeze accompanied her. Here again was that moment. The partially opened window blew wide with her entrance, and with that, the white faille curtains breathed in and out of the casement. The pages of the books rustled and fluttered and some flies buzzed up around the light. All around it seemed as if the veil of clouds had been torn outright from the face of the sun: with Olga's entrance a dazzling brightness and a cool breeze filled the room to its darkest, dankest corner.

Then the presentiment of what was to come: the door slammed shut, the window rattled back, the air went out of the curtains' billow, and a veil once again covered the sun.

Myra missed each one of these prescient announcements of what was to come, however, because her gaze – every aspect of her being, actually – was riveted on Olga Radó. Myra could neither take her eyes nor her thoughts from contemplation of Olga. Nor could she for some time to come. Olga's entrance had not just ripped the veil from the sun, it had also torn apart Myra's empty little world.

Olga was beautiful. Very tall and quite slender, her face was perfectly chiseled. She had smooth, thick dark hair which exposed much of her high forehead. Thin black brows drew together at the top of her nose, giving her steely-gray eyes an almost threatening expression. Her speech was crisp, almost to hardness. But her voice itself was soft and deep, mellifluous. The contrast was as compelling as her visage.

Myra admired Olga's style, as well, although she failed to find appropriate definition. Olga's dress could not be described simply as tasteful, elegant, or smart. All Myra could discern about her own response to how Olga looked was "That is how I should like to dress."

So there she was, the beautiful and imposing and very different Olga, now in their midst and having swept each of them up, yet none so much as Myra. Myra felt her throat get dry and her heart pound frantically when it was her turn to read. Myra never remembered having felt such nervousness in school – akin to panic – no matter how unprepared she had been. Every word seemed to snare her. She mispronounced everything, made a fool of herself. Irrevocably, she thought. How did she know so little French? Myra decided then and there that she would go to her father and ask him to let her take French lessons. He would be overjoyed to have her come to him with such a request.

There was nothing but relief when she had finally stammered out her few lines. Then came Erika's turn, and then Fannie again, with all the pathos at her command. Myra had lost the moment for charming Olga – and then they stood to leave.

As they gathered before the mirror, putting on their hats, Myra noticed with an inexplicable joy that she was nearly as tall as Olga Radó and, more importantly, much taller than the three fair, plump misses with whom she must vie for Olga's attention.

The three young women left the Moebiuses together – Myra, Erika and Olga – and walked part of the way together. Erika did most of the talking.

Olga commented here and there, saying, "Really? – No! – Indeed! – Oh! – No?"

Myra was silent.

Finally, Erika bid the two good-bye and left. Olga and Myra walked briskly side by side for a while. Myra should long ago have turned off if she had wanted to take the shortest way home. She was aware – and somewhat shocked – that she kept right on going, following Olga wherever it was she was going, ready to follow Olga anywhere, or so it seemed. Despite having traveled so far out of her way, Myra was far too happy to stop now that Erika had finally left them: the air seemed to have become purer and one could stride along more freely, now that it was just her and Olga. It was a joy to keep up with this lovely, regular pace, and Myra reminded herself that nobody knew where she lived anyhow. She had just as much right to walk where she chose as anyone else. And where she chose to walk was with Olga.

And yet she knew the end was coming. Myra glanced at every house nervously: was it at this one or the next that Olga Radó would stop with a hasty good-bye, and the heavy door close behind her, leaving the street empty and lonely, as her life had been before Olga's entrance into it?

At last they had reached a house in front of which Olga Radó suddenly halted.

"My home," she said, "if you can call a boarding-house home. But after all, what can you call home? Are you familiar with the Pension Flesch?"

"I don't know any boarding-houses," Myra murmured.

"Lucky girl! You live with your parents?"

"With my father."

"Oh, the house is quite nice. I have lived in worse. Drop in once in a while and have a look at my little garret!"

"I'd love to."

Myra's response was no mere manner of speaking. For the next few days and nights Myra pondered how she could accept this vague invitation and visit Olga Radó. Once she actually started out to see her. Then she returned because she thought it better to announce her call by telephone. But then again, it did not seem proper to disturb Olga by a telephone call. She would rather write. But that gave the visit too much importance and formality, making the serendipity of dropping by wither away. And what if Myra received a polite refusal? Then all possibility would be gone of making a further attempt. But if she simply went up and did not find Olga at home, she could leave her card with a few words – and wait for a reply.

Anna Elisabet Weirauch from *The Scorpion*

She went, went as far as the house, but again she did not go in. She walked up and down the street and stood for a long time, lost in thought, in front of a few utterly uninviting shop-windows. All she could think of was Olga. Maybe Olga would leave the house now, while she was pacing the street, or even better, she might be returning home. In any case, she would ask Myra to come in with her, wouldn't she? She'd have to – to do otherwise would be rude.

When she wasn't hoping to come across Olga outside her own home, Myra was ruthlessly cultivating her friendship with the Moebius girls, now with renewed vigor. She invited them to her house as often as Aunt Emily permitted, she went to see them as often as she was asked. And she phoned them repeatedly in order to make arrangements for her visits. She borrowed books that had to be fetched and returned. Myra's efforts to be amiable were so excessive that the Consul's wife was quite charmed with her, and kept telling Aunt Emily how much Myra was changing for the better. Such insinuations did not please Aunt Emily, who was all but offended by the remarks.

This game went on for weeks, but Myra did not lose patience. It was enough for Myra to hear the Mobieus girls let slip a comment here or there about the object of her desire, Olga. "As Olga always says" or "Olga likes that so much." It was enough, almost too much in fact, to catch Fannie saying, "Olga was here briefly last night, I thought she looked terrible!" Or to have Emmie, who had herself become infatuated with Myra, observe with a hint of her own passion, "Myra has such remarkably beautiful hands, almost as beautiful as Olga's…."

For Myra, the vicarious thrill of holding the girls' little black dog on her lap while calling it Sophonisba, the pet name Olga had given it, was almost – but not quite – enough.

All these tiny subterfuges promised hope and created suspense for days on end. Finally, through her desire for Olga, Myra began to find life beautiful again.

But she had yet to know it was Olga who made her feel this way.

* * *

Myra spent her time aimlessly — practicing piano at home, studying French. When she had passed a little time doing these tasks, she would throw herself on the divan and stare at the scrap of blue sky netted with silvery telephone wires which she could see from where she lay. Then she would think all manner of things – how incredible it would be to understand all the languages in the world or to master some instrument perfectly or to have a wonderful voice or to be ravishingly beautiful. But since she could never attain these things, perhaps it would be best to be dead.

That is when she would go out, inevitably to pass the house, Olga's house. Naturally she would slow her pace, gaze up at the windows, peer down the street. Naturally she would sit for a time on a bench in the Square and watch the children playing. Was it every day that Myra found herself in front of a shop window looking with profound attention at gloves, ribbons and laces? Was her attention so focused because there was a mirror in the shop window that reflected the door of the house – Olga's house – behind her? Whenever the door opened, Myra jumped, her heart pounding.

Once when Olga came out of her house, Myra barely recognized her. Olga wore a loose cloak, both hands were thrust in her pockets and she had no hat. She ran, rather than walked, two houses farther down to the mailbox, and posted a letter.

Myra rushed across the street to catch her when she returned. Her heart was pounding so much that she had to gasp for breath. She quickly thought of a million things to say and do when she caught up with Olga, but rejected each as soon as she thought of them. She would say something to Olga. No – she would pass her with a silent greeting. But suppose Olga didn't recognize her! She had to say something to her. But what?

Fate intervened. While Myra was crossing the street, Olga saw her and waved. "Hello, Myra! Were you coming to visit me?"

"Not exactly," Myra said, pale with excitement. What was she thinking? She should have said yes.

"Yes, exactly." Olga took Myra's arm. "Come up for an hour. Or shall you be neglecting something? No? Well, then, fine! Wait, I must buy some cigarettes. Will you come, too?"

Myra was flushed and flustered. She followed Olga mutely. Never had Myra seen such a charming tobacco shop as the one Olga patronized. Never had anyone pleased her so much at first sight as the wizened old man, with the trembling hands, from whom Olga bought her cigarettes. Every little nuance was one more joy for Myra, now that she was with Olga.

Back in Olga's flat, she sat at the broad desk of black stained oak, her legs crossed in a Luther chair, leaning somewhat forward, both elbows resting on the high arms. Myra sat facing her in the easy-chair. She felt like she was being tested, although she didn't know what the test was. She gritted her teeth and said to herself, "I will pass this test, I will pass it."

The visit seemed easy at first, with idle chatter between them and Myra able to disguise the excitement she felt at being with Olga, even as she gazed at her as any lover might. They talked of the Moebius girls and Erika and Olga's aunt, the Consul's wife. Myra talked about her home life, about Aunt Emily and the beautiful days of her childhood.

Suddenly Olga leaned forward and said, "Tell me frankly, how did you come to be friends with my so-called cousins?"

"I don't know," Myra stammered, "Aunt Emily…"

"I don't mean to say anything against them," Olga said quickly, "they are as good as gold. But aren't you bored to death?'

"Yes," Myra replied, "but I'm always bored, anyway."

"Oh, how awful!" Olga replied, shocked. "I'd rather be dead than bored. Don't you really know anybody but these girls and your Aunt Emily?"

Myra hesitated. "No. It's probably my own fault. I've never had a friend. But then I've never wanted one." Until now, she thought.

"It is not so easy, making friends – the right friends, the people we are meant to meet," Olga reflected. "We often miss those who will be our best friends by a century or more. We find them in books and pictures. But that's it. Those born after us – we don't know anything about them. That's why I so envy people who create. They can keep themselves alive in pictures, words or deeds. Yes, in deeds, too. It is like a mantra: Thus I am, thus I was, love me! And if in their own lifetimes they have never found anyone –perhaps in a hundred years, or maybe two hundred, somebody will be born who will love them as they desired to be loved. Who will understand them as they desired to be understood. We poor creatures – once we're dead, we most certainly will never be loved again. Sometimes I would like…" her voice trailed off and her eyes were very dark and almost menacing under her deeply furrowed brows.

She broke off and then began again, this time in another tone.

"Do you know," Olga said with fervor, "there are a great many very congenial people of the Renaissance. We should have lived four or five centuries sooner. I should certainly have been friends with Margherita Sforza. I have just read a wonderful story about how she held her brother's possessions when Julius Caesar was sent against them."

Myra felt her head reeling, felt a wave of vertigo. Renaissance – she knew what that meant. And she had a hazy memory of the name Sforza. But, "Julius Caesar," she muttered to herself, disconcerted and adrift. As Olga talked on of people, writers and places Myra knew nothing about, she began to feel stupid, dull and out of her depth. She was failing the test, and miserably. How could she hope to charm this woman when she couldn't even keep up with her in conversation?

Myra was wounded and lost. "I don't know… no… and yet…"

Olga's eyebrows arched at this comment by Myra. Suddenly she burst into laughter, loud and merry laughter. Olga laughed with more abandon than Myra had ever heard when she was with Olga and the other girls. But even though she knew Olga was laughing at her ignorance, she wasn't hurt by it. Instead she was full of something, some different feeling than hurt.

"You poor dear!" Olga exclaimed, still laughing. "I can't imagine what your mind looks like! So disorganized! I'd like to straighten up the mess there."

Myra felt her heart quicken. "Do," she said, fervently. "Please, please, do!"

Suddenly her laughter ceased and Olga's expression became serious and reflective.

Myra was terrified. Had she lost her connection to Olga? "No, no," she protested. "Excuse my impertinence. After all, I can't have you teach me, like a governess!"

Olga leaned forward suddenly and placed her soft hands on Myra's. "Oh my dear – are you really so sensitive? You have no reason to be."

Olga continued to hold Myra's hand. "Why not come and study here with me? Come up and study, why don't you? Come up here to see me as often as you wish until you are bored."

Bored with Olga? "I will never be!" Myra insisted, as if she were taking a sacred oath.

Olga was musing ahead. "You know, before we can really dig into anything, you will have to make a general survey. First you'll have to work your way through a history of the world. Here are eighteen volumes. One volume after the other. Yes, my dear, Heaven won't help you this time! If you can't do more, at least you can read a hundred pages a day. And when you're finished, every few days you'll come up and exchange your book for another and we'll have tea and chat a little. Do you like the idea? Let's do it!"

That is the way it began, Myra and Olga.

* * *

One day Uncle George suddenly turned up in the city. Myra had always had special feelings for Uncle George. She liked his distinguished appearance, masculine manner and seriousness. He was the only one of her relatives who compelled her respect.

But on this occasion she was nervous about him. Even his greeting to her was odd, full of a studied warmth and an affability that exuded ruse, as if to say: "Pretend that my being here has nothing to do with you. Even though it does."

Suspicion flooded over Myra, her antennae picking up something distinctly awry. That suspicion was confirmed when Uncle George, along with Father and Aunt Emily, disappeared into the study. Then the key clicked in the lock.

Why were they locking themselves in? What could that mean? Was it about the servants or about her?

Myra had never shown any interest in family conferences. Until now. The careful snap of the key in the lock aroused an uneasy curiosity in her. She crept past the door several times. But all she could hear was the low susurration of voices. They were whispering. About her. Myra longed to escape the oppressive and unfriendly atmosphere of the house.

After dinner, during which only Uncle George had spoken, going on about how beautiful their little city was until Myra finally asked a question: "You are all going to take a nap after the meal, aren't you? May I spend an hour with my friend before tea while you sleep?"

Silence. The three looked at each other, co-conspirators. Nobody looked at Myra and nobody answered.

Her father glanced uneasily and beseechingly at Uncle George and Aunt Emily. Uncle George tapped his fingers on the table and waited. Aunt Emily cleared her throat and screwed the corners of her grim little mouth into a rictus meant to pass for a smile. Still nobody spoke. Aunt Emily waited to see if the men would reply, but they had left it to her. So she drew herself up, making a face intended to express empathy and concern. Yet Myra felt Aunt Emily was more gleeful than somber, and just a tad malicious.

"You will have to cancel that plan today, my dear," she said, feigning gentleness, yet her voice was sharp as a knife. "We are expecting a visit this afternoon. A visit concerning you."

"Me?" asked Myra, seeking out her father.

Her father covered his eyes, attempting to control the nervous twitching of his lips. He said nothing.

"Yes, dear, you," said Aunt Emily as if she were announcing something marvelous to Myra.

Suddenly, Myra felt danger threaten her. She felt as if she were caught in a net, which could pull her in with just the slightest twitch of Aunt Emily's bony fingers. Myra felt as if all the doors were locked and guarded, as if nothing could save her now. She felt that without hesitation, without a second thought, she should jump out the window, and run, as long as her breath lasted, to rush in mad flight through the streets to Olga.

And so she did. She turned pale and started to run. It was not even a start, but Uncle George sensed it. "Now, now, Myra!" he said with exaggerated kindness. "Just keep cool, my girl! Nobody's going to do anything to you. You must have confidence in us and just tell yourself that everything that happens is happening for your own good. But you have to help us. We just care about your welfare. Please do not make our task more difficult. We just need to get through all of this together. Later you will be grateful to us for having used a little love and force to put you on the right track. Then you'll look back on all of this as if it were a bad dream."

This pronouncement turned Myra's vague uneasiness to mounting fear. It was all so mysterious and incomprehensible. What had happened? What was about to happen?

"Out the window! Out the window!" was all she could think of. But then the door-bell rang, and she knew that it was too late.

The maid came in stealthily, as she would if someone were ill. She handed Myra's father a card.

His hand trembled as he took it from the little silver tray. He had to support himself against the table in rising. His face was distorted, drawn.

"Have you taken the Professor to my room? I will be there in a moment." He quickly poured himself a glass of water, his hand shaking. He left the room, still shaking.

The remaining three sat in silence. Myra wanted – needed – to leave. She kept thinking of Olga. She could not bear another moment. When she rose, Uncle George moved to detain her. But she did not leave, she wouldn't try to escape. She merely went to the window and gazed through the drawn lace curtains down at the street.

The door opened behind her. Her father's controlled and rather hoarse voice called, "Emily, will you be so kind as to come here a moment?" Then the scraping of a chair and the rustle of skirts. Myra did not turn.

The door closed.

Alone with Uncle George, she could have asked him for an explanation. Of the three he was the one she felt she could trust. But now he, too, was a stranger to her.

"Mother!" she thought as a sob rose in her throat. "Dear, good Mother, why did you leave me alone, all alone in this world?"

Then her father appeared. Nervous, without looking at her, he said, "Please, come with me, Myra." She was ready. She walked briskly, smiling a superior, even disdainful, smile.

When she entered the room, a slight man with sharp features and piercing eyes rose from her father's chair. He had a well-manicured black beard with several premature white hairs.

No one introduced him; he murmured his own name, with a slight bow, and gave the others a look that demanded they leave.

He pulled up a chair. "Please sit."

Myra sat, obediently.

The man in front of her leaned forward. "And now, my child," he said in a soft, almost ingratiating voice, "tell me that you will trust me."

Myra stiffened. "I certainly shall not, Professor!" she said quietly.

The man pulled back, surprised. "What does that mean?"

"It means," Myra said, her heart pounding as if it would burst, "that my Aunt called you in, and that I distrust her. No doubt she wants to shut me up in an insane asylum, and you are to declare me mentally deranged. She held a similar party for me when I was quite a little girl. But if you are a psychiatrist, you know that the feeling that one is being observed can induce something resembling insanity, even in the most normal person. And you will make allowance for that in my case."

The physician smiled – a shrewd smile.

"I have not the slightest reason to question your sanity. On the contrary, nobody questions it. And neither has anyone the slightest intention of shutting you up in an insane asylum. I came here to talk with you a little, because of certain scientific and human interests. May I ask you a few questions?"

"Certainly!" said Myra, "I probably will answer your questions better if you will permit me to smoke a cigarette."

"Gladly!" said the Professor, obligingly.

Myra took the cigarette case from the table and offered him one. He accepted and while he held the match for her, asked in a casual tone, "You are a confirmed smoker, are you not?"

"I got into the habit while studying," she said. "It helps me concentrate. And as I can't rid myself yet of the suspicion that you will construe some stupid answer into feeble-mindedness…"

The Professor laughed. "I would have a hard time doing that. However, you are right, one can chat much more easily over a cigarette. But tell me now, what kind of wicked designs did your estimable aunt have on you when you were a little girl?"

"Oh," said Myra, "she called in a children's psychiatrist because I took the silver from the side-board."

"Why did you do that? Did you like silver?"

"No, I pawned it!"

"Pawned it!" The Professor laughed aloud. "How did such an idea ever get into your child's head?"

"It was not my own," Myra responded. From the hazy past the image of Frieda rose clearly and distinctly. "My governess led me to do it. I was completely under her influence, which was not a very good one."

"Are you easily influenced? You do not look it. Probably there is nothing on earth that could make you do such a thing now!"

"The Devil!" said Myra in sudden terror. "I forgot to redeem that stupid silver!"

The Professor was tremendously amused, but he did not let her see it.

"What," he asked, "the silver you pawned ten years ago? It certainly must be lost by now!"

"No," said Myra frankly. "The silver I just pawned. I clean forgot it!"

"Don't worry about it," said the Professor amiably, "it has already been redeemed."

For a moment Myra did not quite comprehend. "How can that be? Nobody knew about it."

"The ticket was found in your pocket."

"Found!" Myra jumped up. "Found? You mean that shameless person has been going through my things again! Oh, what a pity that I did not catch her at it – I think I would have throttled her with my bare hands!"

"Please sit down," said the Professor. "If by 'that person' you mean your aunt, I should urge her, as a man and a physician, to supervise you more closely than is customary among adult human beings."

"I am an adult human being," said Myra angrily.

"You are a child," said the physician condescendingly. "A child that does not even suspect the danger it is getting into, but who will be very grateful to us all once it has grown up and learned to understand from what we protected it."

"I believe you are mistaken," said Myra, in an icy voice. "I am not in any danger. But if I were, I can protect myself."

"As long as you are not of age, you cannot refuse our helping hand. I question whether you would find in yourself the necessary strength to break with the friend who is at present influencing you."

The blood rushed suddenly to Myra's heart. "What do you know about my friend?" she asked bluntly. She couldn't breathe.

The physician smiled a superior smile. "In any case, more than you."

"I doubt that," Myra interrupted, her tone disdainful. The Professor remained unruffled.

"I know," he said, his tone firm, "that you are under the influence of a woman who can do you a great deal of harm. I understand you quite well. You are a child. I will not deny that the lady possesses intelligence and charm. You are proud of this friendship and would be willing to sacrifice anything for her. You would let this friendship start you on a path of crime…"

"Oh, please!" said Myra.

"Just let your cool intelligence take over for a moment. Think logically. You purloin silver from your parents' side-board. You ask your father for money for lessons and spend it on trips with your friend, on champagne and tickets for the Opera. You pay your friend's dressmaker's bills with money that you have come by in problematic ways. My child, don't you see for yourself what an abyss you are headed for?"

How could they know all that, Myra wondered. Suddenly Myra thought, they had had a detective watch every step she took. Wherever she went, strange eyes had been glued to her, due to Aunt Emily's spying.

Myra sat very still and did not move. She felt exposed – exposed by Aunt Emily. Slowly, slowly, Myra's fingers clenched to a fist. She bowed her head; the corners of her mouth twitched and she swallowed hard.

Again the Professor's voice came softly and soothingly. "Just think back on your childhood. Didn't you love this young woman who influenced you as a child? And aren't you glad and grateful now that you were separated from her? Well, you will be just as grateful to us later on when you are capable of judging. If you stop to think, you know it now in your heart of hearts. It is you who are the true friend. It is you who love, who sacrifice yourself. It is you who are used, are treated as a plaything, or denied on occasion, and sooner or later tossed aside. Do you imagine that this is the first case I have seen? Meanwhile you will be ruined for the rest of your life, made sick in body and soul, robbed of every possibility of happiness. What is left for you? Death or suicide. I have seen terrible tragedies come about in this way…"

Myra strove in vain against the impact the words made on her. She felt cold. It seemed to her like a warning from a dark future. Death – the end! A fearful something strode inexorably toward her, casting its cold shadow in advance. She shivered. She had to make an effort to regain her outward calm. She dug her nails in the arms of her chair and swallowed once or twice.

"All that is quite beside the point," she said. "Tell me why they really called you in and what they have decided. If not an insane asylum, do they intend to shut me up in a cloister, or a reform school, or send me to America?"

The physician smiled. "None of those things. But you will leave in a short time to stay with your Uncle George and his family. There in the fresh air and amidst quiet surroundings, your nerves will grow strong again and you will be in a position to make sane and healthy judgments unassisted."

"When do I leave?" asked Myra curtly.

"Today."

Anna Elisabet Weirauch from *The Scorpion*

"I have to pack my suitcase!"

"It has been packed while we have been talking."

That was what she had feared. Myra felt the walls, the handcuffs. She glanced about her like a hunted animal driven into a trap. No escape anywhere, no possibility of flight.

They were separating her from Olga. That was bad, but not the worst. They were doing it by force. They should have asked her to take this journey, they should have allowed her time, time to say good-bye, time for an explanation, time to pack her own things, her books. Now Aunt Emily was at her bureau, was packing for her, was rummaging around. In an hour she would be sitting in the train, without having been able to tell Olga anything. Uncle George would be sitting across from her like a jailor. What would happen here in the interim – to her desk, her books, to Olga…

She had a desire to tear something to pieces, to dash out her brains against the walls. She did nothing. She rose from her chair, quite pale.

"Is that all?" she asked.

"I am delighted," said the Professor, rising at the same time, "that you agree to this."

"Agree?" said Myra with contempt. "I submit to coercion because I know that all resistance is useless. If my aunt wished, she could drag me off in chains, and my father would look on, and all the courts in the world would uphold her."

The Professor opened the door. "Miss Myra and I find ourselves in perfect agreement," he announced cheerfully. "I have prescribed a little change of air, and she is overjoyed to pass a few weeks under your hospitable roof, Herr von Seyblitz!"

Uncle George rubbed his powerful hands, Franz Rudloff attempted a feeble smile, and Aunt Emily made a surprised, and it seemed to Myra, disappointed face.

She rushed up to the Professor and hissed in a low voice, but loud enough for all to hear, "But you told me, Professor, that you wanted to examine her, to see if there were not some physical abnormalities… and I think…"

The Professor endeavored to silence her with a slight motion. It was too late. Myra had already heard. Had suddenly, instantly, understood. It was too late. She was conscious only of the fierce desire to see this hateful creature die at her hands. She wasn't aware of moving, but the floor moved under her feet. She heard a gurgling that was strange and hideous, and yet seemed to come from her own throat. She felt her fingers close on a thin, withered neck, felt at the same moment her own wrists gripped by hands that were like iron, gripped so tightly that all the blood seemed to stop in her veins and she thought she would die. She felt she could not endure this torture one heartbeat longer.

"Let me go!" she yelled. "Let me go!"

The physician immediately released her right arm, and a moment later Uncle George released her left.

Her wrists ached and she rubbed them mechanically. She felt exhausted, quiet, shattered. She was almost happy at the thought that she must leave this house, these people.

She turned to the physician. "When does the train leave? Isn't it time to get ready?"

"We are going the same way, I think," the Professor remarked casually when the auto had drawn up before the door. "Have you room in the car?"

Myra looked at him in surprise and scorn. "Subterfuge is unnecessary, Professor, if you want to take me to the station. My family will gladly forego the pleasure. It is better for all concerned."

She gave her father her fingertips, which he clasped in both hands. "Good-bye, Papa, take care of yourself."

Aunt Emily drew back against the wall as if she feared a new assault on her life, but Myra passed her with a contemptuous glance.

The trip was longer than she expected. Myra watched intently out the window, striving to remember the name of every station, every village, every crossing. It was possible that she would have to return on foot. Return to Olga.

She had no money – whether she would have the opportunity to pawn or sell valuables was doubtful. She glanced at the mileage-signs – fifty miles from home. She could make four miles an hour with ease. Too bad it wasn't summer. It wouldn't be pleasant passing the night in the open at two below zero.

* * *

Uncle George and Aunt Antonia were pleased by Myra's behavior. They had expected – and been warned of – an unmanageable child they would have to tame, by force, if necessary. Instead Myra was the ideal young lady, well-mannered and sweet. Since she was not as they had expected, they were loathe to restrict and supervise her, and allowed her one liberty after another.

Myra took advantage of these liberties; she began preparing to flee. She had never had any other intention but to run from this place, and her constant preoccupation with her plans kept her in a state of almost wanton excitement.

But there was the problem of money. Myra sold everything she could, but it was not enough. Then she began to dispose of articles from her uncle's household. That was difficult and impractical. First, her thefts might be discovered before she was gone, and then all would be lost. Second, the results weren't worth the trouble, and it hurt her to see valuable things that weren't even hers given away for a song.

One day, Uncle George received a large sum of money by mail, and locked it away in the desk, in Myra's presence. She stared as if hypnotized at the locked desk. Here was all she needed, but how could she get it?

She lay all night without sleeping, or even trying to. Her mind was racing. Should she break into the desk right now, tonight? There was no train to get her to the city before daybreak. Maybe she should take a wax impression of the lock. But the locksmith might be suspicious if she asked him to make a key. Could she steal the key ring? No. They would miss it immediately and search the whole house. Should she remove the key to the desk from the ring? No. They would immediately notice that this most important key was missing.

The next day Myra procured a half dozen keys from the locksmith. She told him a tale about a key to the bookcase which she had lost, and was delighted at the assured and unembarrassed manner with which she told it. She had become an accomplished liar in her desire to get back to Olga.

That night she crept down to the study and tried each of the keys. Nearly all were easy to insert, but none unlocked the desk. She was crushed. A new plan would need to be devised.

In the morning Myra asked for her uncle's keys so she could get a book from the library. While she was kneeling in front of the bookcase, she removed the key to the desk from the ring. In its place, she attached one resembling it. She took a book from the case without seeing what it was.

As she handed the keys back to Uncle George, Myra was sure he could hear the furious pounding of her heart. She thought her face must be as white as chalk and made an effort to set her frozen lips in a smile.

Her uncle took the keys without glancing up from his newspaper, and with a brief "thanks," thrust them into his trousers pocket.

Myra packed her suitcase and sent a telegram. Late in the afternoon, she carried the suitcase to the station.

At half past seven they sat down to supper. The train left at half past eight. During supper Myra complained of a headache. At her request, Uncle George gave her a headache-tablet. He advised her to lie down right away.

Myra left the table, wishing all a good night.

In order to reach the stairs from the dining room, she had to pass through the darkened living-room. While she listened to the voices in the adjoining room, expecting at every moment to hear a chair scrape as someone rose, she unlocked the desk and crammed a handful of bills into her pocket.

Myra had left her coat in the hall. She slipped into it and opened the back door that led to the garden. She did not dare pass the dining-room windows in front.

There was nothing difficult about lifting herself over the low garden fence. She looked back once. That side of the house was completely dark. She listened. Not a door opened nor window rattled. Then she turned and ran as if the Devil were after her, across the fields, to the station, to the train, to Olga.

* * *

During the train ride, she fought against her fear. She saw herself pursued, hand-cuffed. The train seemed to crawl along unbearably slowly, seeming to stop much longer than required at each station. At times she felt it would be better to get out and run, simply to run and run and run until she had no more breath or strength. Better that than to wait, a static, restless captive, until the lazy engine finally delivered her to her destination.

A sudden terror gripped her. What if her telegram did not arrive in time or Olga was not at home to receive it? What in God's name would she do if Olga were not at the station?

She couldn't go home. She could already feel the straight-jacket and hand-cuffs. Should she rush through the night to Olga? Ring a strange doorbell and wake up the people in the pension? What right had she to do that? What right, other than her desire to be with Olga?

There was nothing left but to take a room at a hotel for the night. But where would she be safe? Early next morning they would be searching everywhere for her. She shuddered to think of what lay ahead. She shuddered, too, at the thought of a lonely night in a strange room.

There were moments when she was shocked by her own actions, terrified by her daring. Suddenly feeling the bills crinkling in her waist, she asked herself, amazed, how had she done it?

It was eleven-twenty when the train arrived at the depot. The light and the bustle in the station whose vast vault was lost in darkness, was even more alarming that the silent night of the fields.

But Olga Radó was there, which meant all of it, everything, had been worth it.

In the sea of people hurrying and searching for those they were to meet, Olga stood perfectly still – tall and lovely as ever. Surrounded by what Myra saw as only stupid, stolid and ugly faces, Olga's face was beautiful and glowing. From under her tightly knitted brows, her dark eyes sparkled, peering along the line of coaches.

Myra flung open the door even before the train stopped. She forced her way through the crowd, jabbing her suitcase into people with no care. She stretched out her hand, no, she clutched like a falling man at a support, crying between tears and laughter, "Olga!"

Olga's face, which had turned abruptly to her, did not return her joy. Not the ghost of a smile relaxed the knitted brows or grimly set lips.

"Myra!" she exclaimed. "My dearest girl, what are you up to now?"

Myra was stunned. A little taken aback. She had hoped for a different reception, but no matter – Olga was there. Myra gazed into her face, held her hand, listened to her voice. Now everything would be – already was – all right.

"Are you angry?" asked Myra, her eyes glittering as she clung to Olga's hand. "If you really are angry, you old Philistine, I won't even dare confess all the wicked things I've done just to be here, with you!"

"I'm not angry," Olga replied, earnestly, "I simply refuse to be in any way responsible. If you've run away, that's your affair! I know I have not influenced you in any way. I knew nothing about this escapade of yours. I want to get that straight now and forever." Her voice was passionate, but not in the way that Myra had hoped for.

"Yes," said Myra, "but tell me whether or not you're glad to see me."

"If I must be candid," said Olga with a vague smile and without looking at Myra, "I'm not unhappy that you're here, but I'm a little disturbed. Have you thought at all about what is to become of you now?"

Myra had indeed thought about it. She had thought of herself as coming to Olga in order to be with Olga, to remain with Olga, to love Olga. She had pictured herself in Olga's comfortable room, the one room in which she had known blissfully happy hours. She had meant to hide herself there, never to go into the street, never to go home. Now she was aware of the folly of her plan, such as it was.

"I don't know," she said pitifully. "I only know that I can never go home, never, never, never! I'll look for a job as a nursemaid or a chambermaid – anything rather than go home." Anything rather than leave you, she thought.

"Then you might just as well have stayed where you were. They certainly wouldn't have beaten you or let you go hungry. Or do you expect that you'll have more freedom as a maid?"

"Yes," said Myra defiantly, "at least I'll have my Sundays free and nobody can forbid me to spend them with you." Didn't Olga realize that this was all for her? That her family had sent her away because of Olga, and that she had fled them for the same reason – to be with Olga, unrestrained?

"Do what you like as far as I'm concerned." Olga stood still and closed her eyes for a moment. She looked frightened. "You are positively brutal, Myra. Don't you see how you're going to incriminate me? I can't accept responsibility for this, for you. I can't!"

The two were still standing on the platform, which was by then almost emptied of its swarming crowds. Only a few night-travelers were still rushing toward the exit. Myra felt tired and shattered. Her light suitcase was like a dead weight in her hand. The draft in the vast hall made her shiver.

"Can't we sit down in the waiting room for a few minutes?" she asked dejectedly. "Perhaps if I think about it quietly, something will occur to me that I can do. But if you feel so tired, why don't you go home?" She hoped Olga would not choose to exercise this option. She was already devastated by Olga's distance from her. She had expected so much more.

"Yes," said Olga, "and leave you sitting here all night in the depot! Have you gone stark raving mad?"

They sat in the empty waiting room, warming their cold fingers on glasses of hot tea. Myra related the story of her flight. She took the crinkled bills out of her waist and thrust them into her pocket.

Myra had almost expected Olga to laugh. While she was telling the story, the whole business struck her as an incredibly comical adventure. But Olga's face remained dark and serious.

"And now?" she asked.

"I'm going to a hotel!"

"And I?"

"You are going back to your pension, I suppose."

"I won't leave you alone."

"Come with me, then," said Myra with a flare of hope.

"Yes," said Olga, her tone bitter, "and the first thing tomorrow morning the police will come and arrest us. No thank you. I'll probably be accused of making you commit grand larceny. You haven't thought of me at all, have you?" But Myra had thought only of Olga.

"Then," said Myra after further reflection, "in that case we'll have to behave like real embezzlers. That is, take the next train and keep going. We'll simply get off at some station or other and go to a hotel. From there I'll write my father, and beg him first of all to straighten out the money business. Perhaps he'll be reasonable and I'll be able to come to some agreement with him. In six months, I'll receive the trust fund from my grandmother. If my father won't give me anything, I'll borrow against that: it can be done somehow." Myra looked at the huge schedule. "The next train leaves at midnight."

Olga's face had lost its stern expression. Her eyes now glowed with a deep joy. But she still hesitated.

"You're absolutely crazy!" she said, her voice warmer. "No night-dress, no toothbrush!"

"I have linen enough," said Myra eagerly, "and we can buy a toothbrush!"

"What ideas you do have!" said Olga slowly.

Myra saw that she was already half convinced.

"Grand ideas!" she said radiantly. "Fascinating, entrancing ideas. Don't you think so?"

"Yes, but I never would have thought of it," Olga insisted. "You talked me into it. It's your idea and no one's else!"

"Absolutely! I'm much too proud of it to let anybody else claim the authorship."

* * *

Over the broad arch of the dark entrance a tin star was swaying and a blue lantern, swinging from a beautifully curved arm, illuminated the words: "At the Sign of the Blue Star. Hotel and stable accommodations."

"Look," Olga exclaimed, "a hotel!"

They looked for a night-bell. But they could not even find a door. Beside the entryway was a handle for ringing a large bell at the end of a rusty iron rod. It was difficult to reach, but Myra made an attempt.

"Don't bother," Olga said. "That's not for poor travelers like us. What's more, we'll wake up the whole town. Let's try inside instead."

They ventured into the dark cavern of the entrance, but did not get far. Before the passage could open into a court, a huge rack-wagon barred the way. But beside the wagon they found a flight of steps and a little wooden door in the wall. They felt a metal knob and tugged at it. A shrill ring made them jump as it shattered the silence. Then, steps, voices, a light.

A man appeared in the doorway, looking half-asleep, in slippers and grayish-yellow underwear, over which he had pulled on a jacket that he held closed under his chin with his left hand. In his upraised right hand he carried a candle.

Olga did the talking.

She told the sleepy man a story about the train by which they had just arrived, and of how the "Blue Star" had been recommended to her, and how she regretted having had to disturb his sleep, but the trains arrived at such ungodly hours, and of course, they were young women, they couldn't remain on the streets, and people at the station had directed them here.

The man was now more awake. "One moment, please!" He vanished and left them standing there.

Olga and Myra looked at each other and laughed. They waited. After some time a gas-lamp without a globe was lighted farther up the stairs, and the man reappeared, this time in black trousers.

He was collarless and wore neither a jacket nor stockings, but he was still clearly the proprietor and gracious host.

He led them into a big, dark, and quite cold room. He jumped up on the cushion of a chair and lit the gas-jet. This was clearly the "Blue Star's" most impressive suite. The high, broad bed and the ponderous plush sofa almost disappeared into the vastness of the large room. Between the windows stood a huge, gilt mirror before which, on the console, were artificial flowers under a glass. The walls were elegant with numerous prints, most of them in heavy gold frames.

Their host stooped and lit the gas-heater. A row of little blue flames puffed up, and were reflected in a grooved copper cover that cast a warm, golden glow onto the shabby carpet.

"Splendid!" Olga pronounced, tossing her gloves on the big, round table. "Now it will be nice and warm. Perfect! No, sir, we don't need another thing. We should like to have breakfast here in the morning. Is this the bell? Wonderful! Thank you! Good night!"

The door closed behind him.

"Marvelous!" said Olga, including the entire room with all its accoutrements in a wide embrace.

"Are you serious?" asked Myra timidly. "I was afraid your sensibilities would be offended. Those pictures! And those artificial flowers, and the plush upholstery!"

"No, it's simply marvelous," Olga repeated. "It just couldn't be any different. I'd have been terribly disappointed if those fighting stags were not here, or that wonderful Empire maiden with the apple-tree in bloom. Do you think I want to see Chippendale furniture in "The Blue Star?" God forbid! As it is, I think it's simply heavenly!"

Myra shrugged and began to unpack her suitcase, spreading nightgowns on the bed, setting bottles and boxes on the wash-table. Olga walked about noiselessly, whistling with soft, sweet flute-tones. She stopped before each picture, studying it with childish enthusiasm, while she made up long stories about it.

"Here," said Myra shyly, laying her silk kimono on the chair, "you can put that on."

"And you?"

"I have my wrapper, that's all right for me."

"Now all I need is warm feet. Then I'll be absolutely happy."

Olga pulled a chair up to the gas-heater and began to untie her shoes.

"Shall I help you?" asked Myra, eager to help.

"I never heard of such a thing!" said Olga, provoked. "Why, I wouldn't let my maid do such a thing for me!"

"That's another matter," said Myra, smiling slyly. "It's a distinction that one does not confer on maids."

"You're certainly insane!" Again a sudden deep flush pulsed into Olga's cheeks.

She had pulled off her thin silk stocking and was holding her bare feet toward the flame. She raised her arms and slowly ran Myra's brush over the hair that fell in heavy black curls about her neck. Now the flush came over Myra.

Myra jumped onto the chair as their host had done and turned out the gas-light.

"Now," she said with a short laugh, "you can have a painting made of yourself, or a chromo and frame it in gold and hang it on the walls here. Title: *Au coin du feu*, or The Witch, or Firelight, or something just as good. How can anybody be so shamelessly lovely?" Myra's pulse was up again, as it had been when she had fled Uncle George's.

"Well," said Olga dryly. "Now you've done it! We haven't any matches – we'll"

"There's light enough for me," said Myra, seating herself on the floor in the ruddy firelight. "And we can always get a light from this. If we can't find anything better, we'll use a hundred mark note. We have plenty of them. Oh darling, what a marvelous foot you have! But so cold, they're always like ice!"

Myra had cast off all her reserve. It was just the two of them now, here, in this hotel room, together and alone. It was as if no one else existed, save the two of them. She clasped both hands about Olga's foot. It was as nobly shaped, as beautiful in line and color as if a master hand had chiseled it out of marble. But it was as heavy and as cold as stone. Myra endeavored to warm it in her hands, but then she could not resist temptation – she set her lips upon its cool, smooth, white skin.

Olga flushed, then broke away from Myra's touch. She sprang up and ran through the dark room to the window.

"Olga!" cried Myra, suddenly alarmed. She rose, hesitant. "What's the matter? What's wrong with you?"

Olga did not respond. Myra went over to her. But when she reached the window and stretched out her hand toward her, Olga dodged as if hunted, creeping along the wall. She stood, cowering, in a corner, Myra barring her way. Her lovely pale face gleamed pale and strange in the dark. Her face looked stricken and seemed both frightened and threatening, like that of a wounded animal that sees itself surrounded and prepares to defend itself. She seemed desperate.

Myra shrank from the expression of those beautiful lips, now pressed together tightly, and those darkly glowing eyes. Timidly, gently she laid her hand on Olga's arms, which were folded over her breasts, partially exposed through the kimono.

Olga jumped a little and shrank deeper into her corner.

"Go away!" Olga hissed through clenched teeth. "Leave me alone!"

"But you cannot stand in your bare feet on the cold bare floor." Myra was on the verge of tears. What had happened here? They had been so close – now this. Myra tried again. "You'll catch your death of cold. I don't want you to do anything but sit by the heater. I can sleep in the hall, in front of the door, or I can take another room, or I can jump out the window. But come out of that corner, I can't bear to look at you a minute longer like this."

Myra seized Olga by both shoulders, but Olga shook her off.

"Leave me alone!" she said angrily, all look of fear replaced with simmering anger. "Can't you see you're torturing me to death? How can anybody be so stupidly cruel?" Her voice broke and suddenly her face was covered with tears.

Myra could no longer control herself. Her eyes, too, brimmed over with tears.

"I don't understand," Myra said, lips quivering. "If I repulse you so much that you run from my touch, even on your foot, then why are you here? Why have anything to do with me? No one can be with a person whose presence is a torture to her. But I know why you can't stand me…"

"Why is that?" Olga asked, astonished.

Myra shook her head in silence, too choked with tears to speak.

"Why do you think I can't stand you?" Olga demanded more urgently. "Answer me! I want to know."

Myra avoided looking at her. "Because I love you too much," she said, her voice filled with   bitterness and sadness. "It must be dreadful to be loved by someone whom you do not love back. Almost disgusting."

"Oh, you are such an idiot!" Olga whispered. Suddenly she stroked Myra's hair very tenderly.

"Oh, don't," said Myra, her heart full to bursting. She disengaged herself from the hand she ached to kiss and fondle and feel all over her – her hair, her face, her breast. "There's no use forcing yourself."

Olga let her arms drop. She sighed.

"One must force one's self," she said, breathing softly, but with an effort. "If I did not force myself, I would so smother you with caresses that you'd be frightened to death and run away."

Myra felt her blood run hotter, the pulse in her neck throbbing so that she could scarcely breathe.

"I would neither be frightened nor run away. But I might go mad with happiness." Myra's words were soft, whispered. She reached out her hand to Olga, who clasped it tightly. Then Olga slowly raised both her slender white arms and laid them on Myra's shoulders. Myra felt their powerful, delicious pressure grow tenser and tenser. Olga pulled Myra close, closer. She could breathe in her every scent. Since Olga was barefoot, they were the same height, eye to eye. They looked into one another's eyes, unflinchingly, while they felt in every vein the intensity, the pulsing of their hearts.

Myra could not look away from her beautiful, exquisite Olga. She could feel the warmth of her body, the softness of her skin through the flimsy silk of the kimono. She ached for her lips, her touch, the pressure of her breasts against her own. They stared at each other for a long while, then they bent toward one another, like two thirsting souls, and laid lips upon lips.

They did not, could not, let each other go. They kissed more and more covetously. They walked through the room, nuzzling close to each other, their fingers intertwined, their lips never far from the other's. Then they sat on the edge of the bed in one another's arms, their kisses turned to touches, the heat of their bodies suffused the cold room with a scented warmth. Their clothes slipped from their bodies almost on their own and lay on the floor. They were naked and warm and their skin glowed in the burnished flame of the gas heater.

The coarse sheets were chill and damp as they pulled away the covers and slipped beneath. Yet they hardly felt the chill, so overheated were they from the desire that had stalked them for such a long time. Their youthful bodies pulsed with passion and heat and soon they were intertwined in the hotel's big bed, kissing, touching, lips everywhere, fingers and hands moving over each other in a frenzy of heat and desire.

They pressed into one another as if they wanted to become the other, to be merged, be one. Their slender, supple limbs wove into each other. They did not speak. But like a murmuring music, they heard the furious pulse of each other's hearts, and the breath that came quicker and quicker.

Their bodies seized each other as wild beasts seize and shake the bars of their cages. They buried their nails in one another's flesh, bit their teeth into their tensed muscles. Their lovemaking had been so long in its fruition, now it seemed too quick to reach its climax. And so they resumed again, mouths and hands and arms and legs all throbbing and pulsing together.

Afterward they lay nestled against each other, while their lips brushed eyelids and cheeks as gently, as softly, as a butterfly would a swaying flower.

"Oh my darling," breathed Olga, her voice rich and mellifluous. "My beautiful, beautiful one."

"My dear," Myra rejoined. "You are a miracle, something from heaven. What are you really? Are you a wild creature? A goddess? The spirit of a white orchid?"

"I don't know," said Olga, appearing to muse on the question. "I believe I am a goddess. But an hour ago I was a poor tortured creature. Are you not proud, little girl, to be able to work such miracles of transformation?"

"I wish I could work miracles," said Myra longingly. "You would be mine forever."

Olga laughed a hard laugh. "Then you'd change me into a man!" she said.

"God forbid!" cried Myra, pulling her tight in both arms. "Never! Never! Never! But if I could work miracles, I'd never let this night end. I would make it last forever!"

The red glow of the copper behind the gas flame filled the room with a warm light. The little pointed flames trembled gently, and the bright spot on the worn carpet flickering.

Olga leaned on her elbows, supporting her head in her hands. Her hair was tousled and, to Myra, immensely enticing. Between Olga's white fingers her black curls peeped. In her pale face, her clear dark eyes glowed like twin stars.

"Forever!" she repeated softly. "Do you not feel that this night belongs to God? Time is an invention of the Devil. Satan invented the passage of time in order to make man apostate to God. But God remains eternal. Satan invented much else, besides, sickness, pain, vermin, and money. Above all – money! But time came and the passage of time, and could never be dispelled again. Now they are a part of every invention of the Devil. But what is God's is eternal. New happiness always effaces old pain as if it had never been. And happiness endures. No pain can efface it. I would die of shame if I thought that only the nerve-endings in our skin vibrate. Don't you feel that something has happened to your soul that will supercede even death? Don't you feel that this, this moment between us has changed you beyond everything, even death?"

"Yes," said Myra. "And more than any birth. I was born today – tonight – with you, not twenty years ago. Now I can say to myself for the first time ever – 'I'm alive!' For so long I have both felt dead and wanted to be dead. Now..."

"No darling, we are alive!" Olga pulled Myra to her. There was an exultation in her voice that was like the jubilant cry of a wild bird rising in flight.

"We're alive, sweetheart! Forever, and ever, and ever, we're alive!" With that they began to kiss once again, their lips heating the rest of them and soon they were in each other's arms again, and more, and more.

* * *

In the morning they had breakfast in their room. Then Myra wanted them to go out for a walk in the glittering snow and sunshine.

Olga had other ideas. "First, you must write to your father," she said, gravely.

"Yes," said Myra, making a face at her beloved. "I know. You don't want to accept any responsibility for us – for me – being here."

She sat down and wrote a long, carefully crafted letter. She described the incidents at Uncle George's with as much humor as she could. She told her father where she was staying, and begged her father to let her remain here where she was happy. She begged him also to believe that she was a mature and intelligent woman and knew what was best for her. Then she begged him to pay back the money which she had "borrowed" from Uncle George. Finally, she asked him to support her for the short time until she turned twenty-one, or else give her an advance against her grandmother's legacy.

She left out one detail, however. She wrote nothing of Olga, and that she was not only not alone, but with the love of her life.

Together they took the letter to be mailed. When the letter had dropped with a soft sound into the blue box, she breathed more freely, and took Myra's arm. Tightly.

"Come, darling," Olga said, "what had to be done, is done. In three days you may get an answer. But let's enjoy those three days. Let's revel in them, in our time together."

Myra bristled. "Do you suppose that any power on earth could compel me to return home? If they won't send me money, I'll hire out to do washing or sewing, or I'll run up debts."

"I don't know," said Olga, "I only know that as long as that letter is on its way we are safe. No living soul knows where we are – that's a glorious feeling – as if we were safe behind walls and moats. But once that letter arrives, the drawbridge will be lowered. What will happen then, I do not know. I know nothing, nothing, nothing! But it's always possible that we'll be torn into little pieces by everything out there." She waved her arm in the direction of town.

"Then why did we lower the drawbridge?" asked Myra, stopping. "Why did you force me to write?"

Olga smiled, darkly. "Because I refuse to accept responsibility," she said, attempting to joke. But they both knew otherwise.

* * *

The next day they went to see if there was a letter. Olga was relieved to find none.

"This blessed postal service," she said. "The mail comes here only once a day."

Myra shook her head. "I don't understand you. I shan't really be able to rest until the answer comes. Until then we're always on the qui vive, sitting on a volcano or some such thing. Once we know where we are, then we can make plans. Eventually, I'll have to write to the attorney who is my grandmother's executor. He will surely advance me some money on which we can live for the six months until I'm of age. But I wish I were finished with all these things."

Olga played with the fringe of the tablecloth and smiled.

"Why do you keep smiling?" asked Myra.

"Because you make such elaborate plans. You father will write, 'Come,' and you will go."

"You know very well that is impossible," said Myra almost angrily.

Olga rose with a shrug of her shoulders and walked to the window. "Perhaps I will send you," she exclaimed, her voice harsh. And then she walked to Myra and took her in her arms and all was well, for the time.

* * *

That afternoon they took another long walk across the fields. The early nightfall surprised them, and they did not reach the hotel until dark.

They trudged along the highway, struggling hard against the wind, and saw the lights of the town beginning to twinkle in the blue dusk.

"Strange," said Olga, "we're going home. There is a town ahead of us whose name I had never heard of three days ago. And yet it is home to me. There is a hotel room in which some salesman may have slept three days ago, a room in which there is not a picture, not a book to attract me – and yet I call it home. When I think of our gas-heater and its reflection on the worn carpet, I feel so warm that I scarcely notice the wind. How happy a person must be who really has her own home, and loves each chair and the color of the carpet and the light of the lamp and each picture and each cup."

"You could have that," said Myra.

"I? No, never!"

"But you can," Myra said, somewhat timidly. "If you have the patience, in six months I will give you everything you want."

Olga burst out laughing. "Darling," she cried and hugged Myra's arm tighter. "My dear, sweet, wonderful little creature! In six months! Where will you be then, and where will I? You will be married perhaps, and I – dead." Myra's heart thudded. They walked on.

As they entered their room, something white was lying on the dark table cover. Myra seized it and ran to the window. The lantern outside shed a faint light.

It was an urgent telegram. "Turn on the light, please," she asked in a rather shaky voice. She tore the message out of the envelope, and read it in the dusk by the window. She read it again by the bright gas light. It was no different:

"Your father has suffered a stroke. End expected hourly."

Without a word, Myra handed the open telegram to Olga, and walked past her to the heater. She held her hands to the flame and was filled with a strange and painful sensation. She did not know how she should act. Inexplicably, no feeling welled up from the depths of her being, darkening every thought – neither grief nor fear nor love. She had only ugly thoughts: "Now I'll have to go away and arrive too late anyhow. So that it's quite useless for me to go at all. If he really is going to die, why couldn't I have just received word that he's dead, instead? Then no power on earth could drag me away from here."

She cast a furtive glance at Olga whose back was still toward her. "She'll wait for me to do something," Myra thought. "I'll have to say something. The most natural thing for me to do would be to cry. But I simply can't. Of course, it's dreadful. But it's nothing to weep about. What would Olga do in my place? Strange, how little we actually know of one another! I don't know what she would do. And I don't know what she expects me to do."

At last Olga turned, laying the paper on the table with a beautiful and extraordinarily discreet gesture. Her face was calm, but very pale.

"I'll go ask about the trains," she said and went out quietly.

This would be their last night together, this would be the last night in each other's arms before…

* * *

At home the smell of sickness and death permeated everything. The maids sat about drunk with lack of sleep, with swollen eyes and stupid faces. Everywhere lights burned. Not bright, cheerful, radiant lights, but individual lamps casting a faint glow in one or two rooms. The doors stood open or ajar so that one could see that it was not night in this house, that no one was sleeping, that people were constantly hurrying to and fro. And through the open doors, too, came the monotonous rattling in the throat of the dying man. It filled all the rooms.

Aunt Emily's owlish eyes were wide in her puckered face. "You came too late!" she said with icy triumph as she confronted Myra. "There is no more hope."

Myra felt as if something dreadful ought to happen to her, and the sudden consciousness of being so depraved, so unfeeling that nothing could happen to her, that even this woman's immeasurable hate implied too high an opinion of her, brought the tears to her eyes, for she was tired and anxious.

Aunt Emily, of course, could not divine these thoughts. "Your tears are too late, too!" she said with all her viciousness.

Each of the twenty hours that followed had a thousand minutes. Myra paced, or sat now in one chair, now in another. Everywhere she felt out of place, in the way, and observed by eyes that despised her. She was worn out in every limb and felt the need, if only for an hour, to lock herself into her room and throw herself on her bed. But she lacked the courage. She knew they expected her to stand flooding repentant tears or to sit by her father's deathbed, or better yet, to kneel. She endeavored to control the horror that made her shudder, involuntarily, and went in. The heavy air smelt of medicine and rotting flesh. In the drift of white pillows lay a small, strangely bony skull with closed eyes, an alien, distorted mask, whose yellowish lips moved gently as it gasped.

Myra sat for a while beside the bed, terrified in case that dreadful rattle in the throat should stop suddenly, terrified still more should that strange being in the bed suddenly open its eyes and begin speaking.

Doctors entered, conferred in whispers, bestowed sympathetic glances on her, and went out again.

The maid spread the table at the usual time and urged her to eat something. Aunt Emily left all the connecting-doors open, listening intently while she ate, for any change in that monotonously rattling throat.

It was all Myra could do to swallow without choking.

The twilight set in early and again the lamps were lit.

Myra picked up a book, but encountered so furious a glance from Aunt Emily that she laid it down again, and folded her hands spiritlessly in her lap.

Toward evening the terrible rattling grew feebler. The bridge of the nose stood out sharply against the tiny shrunken face. The doctor who came at night did not go away again. Now there was one more to sit in silence or pace noiselessly to and fro across the thick carpets – waiting.

The rattling grew more and more feeble. Then a louder, grating expiration of the breath, twice, with short pauses. Then suddenly – silence.

And suddenly, too, as if it had just begun, they heard the ticking of every clock in the house.

The doctor bent over the bed, then drew himself up and walked over to Myra to give her his hand. Aunt Emily dabbed her dry eyes and the maids outside sobbed.

Myra saw and heard it all as if through a dense fog. She thought she might faint.

The doctor saw how sickly she herself looked and laid his hand on her hair. "Go lie down, my child," he said gently. "You can be of no further use here. You have sad days behind you and before you. Youth needs sleep."

Myra was glad to be in her room. But she did not think of lying down. When, after an interval, she heard the doctor go, a nameless dread seized on her. She was so tired and yet equally afraid to sleep, fearful that horrible dreams would torment her once she allowed herself to think.

If her heavy eyelids shut for a moment, she saw the dying man's distorted features, or Aunt Emily trying to seize her with her claws to strangle her, or Uncle George raising his arm to strike her with an enormous bunch of keys that would crush her aching head.

Myra reached out longingly for another hand that would clasp hers warmly and firmly, for Olga's warm and lovely hand to bolster her through this. But her cold fingers remained empty. Finally, she could not endure her terrors any longer. Slipping into her coat, she stole down the rear stairs and out of the house.

In the cold night air, she awoke from her trance. She ran through the streets to Olga's house. The house was locked. Myra stood for a while, undecided over what she should do. Perhaps someone who lived there would be coming home late, or the watchman would unlock the door for her for a tip.

She waited for what seemed an interminable time. She was shivering with cold. At last she woke up the doorman. But at the top of the first stairs, she hesitated again before she dared ring.

She sat down on the steps and laid her forehead against the doorjamb. She tried to will Olga awake, to summon her by ardent entreaty, by the fierceness of her will. From time to time she thought she heard her light step approaching the door and she listened breathlessly, only to realize that she was mistaken.

At last she decided to ring. It was a long time before a very sleepy, half-dressed girl opened the door. She told some tale of having just come from the train and of being unable to go home because she had left her key with Miss

Radó. She laughed awkwardly as she talked and had the sense that the girl thought her positively demented.

She groped her way along the familiar hall, fearing, for some incomprehensible reason, to strike a light. Perhaps she was afraid that the noise or the illumination would wake someone, or perhaps she had some unconscious dread of being seen, and felt herself safer in the dark.

As she stood in front of Olga's door she felt suddenly, and with a painful intensity so strong that she thought it must be premonition, that Olga was not alone – that this dreadful day was to have a still more dreadful close.

She leaned against the wall, not daring to knock or lift the latch. A voice, which she seemed to hear speaking distinctly outside her, said, "What do you want here? What right do you have to force your way in here? How do you dare to feel at home here, to feel that the woman beyond that door wants you here as much as you want to be here?"

The door opened noiselessly and a feeble ray of light appeared. In its glow stood Olga Radó, the beloved and beautiful Olga, tall and slender in a kimono, one hand on the latch, peering sharply at Myra.

"Myra!" she exclaimed softly, and closed her eyes a moment as if frightened. "I knew it! What has happened, darling? How did you get up here?"

Myra did not walk, she staggered. She went into the room, looking at the soft light of the shaded lamp on the papers, on the desk, on the backs of the books, on the silk cushions. Colors and shapes were a marvelous exhilaration. She let herself slide to the floor, laying her head against the easy chair, and saying between tears and a laugh, between waking and sleeping, "Let me stay right here, on the floor, like this. It is so good, so lovely here, with you."

Olga raised her, undressed her as if she were a child and laid her in the bed. As the cold sheets touched her body, horror set her trembling again. Once more she was wide awake, and sat bolt upright in the bed, striving to control the chattering of her teeth.

"Lie beside me," she pleaded to Olga. "I'm afraid to be alone. I'm so dreadfully frightened."

Olga did not answer. She bolted the door, she set the lamp behind the bed, spread another silken veil over the light and let the kimono fall from her shoulders – all with a sad smile and slow languid movements as if she were preparing for a sacrifice. Then she put her arm under Myra's neck, tucked the coverlet more tightly around her and stroked the tangled hair from her forehead.

And as Myra felt the warmth of her beloved, the strong pulse of Olga's heart, the silken memory of her flesh, she began to weep, quietly, released from her intolerable pain. Now she was safe, she was not alone, she was with the one person she could love, who loved her. She cried herself to sleep in the naked, silken arms of her lover.

* * *

Deep in sleep, Myra heard a violent ringing. Then she woke up: doors were slamming, steps approaching, excited voices raised.

She opened her eyes. Olga stood beside the bed, already fully dressed. She was very pale, her eyes dark and blazing. "Get up, Myra," she commanded in a voice that was breathless with something Myra could not discern. "Get up for God's sake and dress!"

Myra threw on her clothes as quickly as she could. Meanwhile, the pounding on the door intensified. Olga immediately went to the door, unbolted and opened it a crack.

"Who is there?"

Loud, excited voices in the hall, excited faces trying to force themselves through the crack.

"I'm sorry, I can't permit you in my room at this moment," Olga said with icy courtesy.

Some voices began to shout louder than the others, Aunt Emily and Uncle George. Also the girl who had admitted Myra that night.

Myra's hands were shaking. She could not button her dress. She was aware only of a dreadful desire to be invisible or to jump out of the window or to sink into some vast unconsciousness.

Olga's voice rose above the clamor, deep and calm, but as cold and sharp as polished steel.

"Does this conversation have to take place in the hall?"

Then suddenly, a soft, gentle voice: "May I offer the use of my room. I'll be glad to step out." The voices withdrew next door and a few moments later – Myra had thrown on her dress – Peterkin, Olga's neighbor, stole into the room.

"Can I help you, Myra?" he whispered. His eyes were troubled.

At the same moment, there came a sound from next door as if a stick had been smashed across a table.

"I'll have you thrown into jail!" thundered Uncle George.

Myra wanted to rush in, but Peterkin restrained her, imploring her not to go. "Don't, don't!" he begged. "Fix your hair quickly! Put on your shoes!" While she smoothed her hair, he knelt before her and buttoned her shoes. She let him. She could not rush next door in her stocking-feet, with her hair unkempt, to the immense pleasure of all the people leering through the cracks in their doors.

When Myra did go down the hall to the next room, she was quite calm, standing erect, and sustained by a strong, brave, hot and almost joyous determination.

At the end of the hall stood a strange man with his hat and overcoat on. He looked at her, his eyes piercing through her.

"Straight from her father's dead body!" cried Aunt Emily with high pathos.

"Detectives in a decent house, as if it were a place for criminals," lamented Frau Flesch, the landlady. "Never in all my life have I had anything to do with the police!"

Myra pressed down hard on the latch. Her heart was pounding. For an instant the thought flashed through her mind: Perhaps it was best that this happened. Perhaps it was a good thing that she now would have the courage to take her place beside Olga and say, "I belong to her and will never leave her, even if you tear her and me into little pieces. If you have the courage and the right, use force on me, for I'll never go one step with you of my own free will. This is where I belong, here, with her, my beloved."

As Myra entered the room, she saw Olga standing, leaning against the table, her arms crossed on her breast, the fingers clasping her elbows. Aunt Emily rushed to Myra with a choking cry, "Here is the unfortunate child!"

Myra stood for an instant as if numbed. For a moment she felt as if she were among lunatics or had gone mad herself. With a hasty glance, she thought how very becoming to Uncle George were his stern manner, his steel-blue eyes and his iron-gray mustache against a face crimson with rage.

He came up to her and said in a deep, rough voice that trembled with something like emotion, "Myra, my child, what are you doing here? We're burying your poor father tomorrow and you're here!"

He laid his heavy hand on her shoulder.

Myra did not look at him. She was looking at Olga.

Anna Elisabet Weirauch from *The Scorpion*

"This is my home, now," she said. She meant her voice to sound vibrant and firm, but she could not manage it, and it sounded soft and tremulous. She repeated what she had thought as she had walked down the hall. "If you think you have the right, go ahead and use force on me, for I'll never go one step with you of my own free will."

It was hard, very hard to say that. Very hard to say it while Uncle George's face was distorted with rage and sorrow, while Aunt Emily blinked her little bird-eyes, while Frau Flesch's spongy face was fixed in a repulsively avid grin. Hard to say it in front of the strange man and the maid, who were listening in the hall.

Yet now it was said. And now everything would be all right. Now Olga would come and take her in her arms, would press Myra's head against her breast so that she need not hear or see anything more, would, with one of her haughty and imperious gestures, show all these strange and horrible faces the door, would point her revolver at these intruders and drive them out with a single word…

Olga turned her head without changing her position, and looked at Myra. Everybody thought she was looking at Myra and gave an involuntary start. But actually her eyes were merely resting somewhat past Myra, taking in only Myra's forehead, eyebrows and hair.

Myra strove to catch her eye, but could not. Olga's gaze was fixed on a line above her eyes.

"My dear," said Olga with a gentleness that was oddly icy-cold, "your sense of dependence on me is touching, but I have done nothing to merit it. If you feel about me as you say, you ought to go with your relatives, behave like a rational creature and spare me your visits in the future. You must see that they occasion me nothing but misery!"

Myra hesitated for a moment. "Something has to happen," she thought. "She must look at me, she must give me some sign, a glance, a gesture, that this is all a facade, that I must trust her, believe in her, wait for an explanation…"

But nothing happened. Olga remained silent, resolute.

Myra racked her brain for something terrible with which to shatter the stony mask of Olga's face. Could she not say, "You made me come, lured me, forced me and now you deny me?" No, she had no right to do that. But could she not think of some abusive word, something that would pierce, would wound, something cruel? How could Olga – after last night, after all those other nights, pretend in this grim daylight, straight from her bed – their bed – that Myra meant nothing but an inconvenience to her?

Myra turned over various silly childish epithets in her mind: "Slag," she thought. "Harlot." That was not what she was seeking. It seemed to her as if she must search for the one sharp word she must fling.

Suddenly, she felt as if she had stood there for an eternity, her arms hanging, her eyes vacant, mouth open.

She stood straight and attempted a smile that would be at once proud and affable. But she felt as she was doing it, as if madness were just beneath the distorted muscles of her face.

Her voice was cold when she spoke. Stone cold, as if she were speaking from beyond the grave. "Will you telephone for a taxi, Uncle George?" she said. "I am too tired to walk."

She went to the door. "I just want to gather my things. I won't be a moment."

She went into the next room, put on her hat before the mirror very carefully, threw on her coat and looked for her bag. She did not hurry at all. She still hoped that Olga would slip in and whisper something to her – where they could meet, where she should write, when she could explain it all to her. But Olga did not come.

As Myra opened her bag, she noticed a little wad of tightly pressed bills. – What was left from their trip. She took them out, laughing bitterly. Probably she would never again need money as long as she lived.

She raised her hand and opened it, letting the bills flutter down on the bed, still in disarray from their lovemaking the night before.

Then Myra went out, past the strange man, past the maid, downstairs and out of the house, without once looking back.

Sidonie Perrault
A LITTLE INDISCRETION (*L'Indiscret Petit*)
1925
Translated from the French by Victoria A. Brownworth

I had gone away to school that year, away and into a wholly new and, I
hoped, fully adventurous life.

I would not be disappointed.

How to describe my first days away from the restrictions of my old life,
the life I had decided must be cast off forever? It was like a breeze that comes
through the curtains after a hot day in a closed room – I was free in a way I
had never been and I had planned to take full advantage.

I had wanted to go away two years before, but Mother had disallowed my
departure, thinking still, dear sweet and deluded woman that she was, that I
would marry instead. That if I sat at home dreaming and floating about the
place in a state of aggravated torpor, I would fling myself into the arms of the
first man who would have me.

My forbearance overwhelmed her desires for me. Or should I say, rather,
that my desires overwhelmed her forbearance against me?

That is how I came to be at the school where I would learn all the things
that had long been in my head and heart and soul. An old maid of twenty, but
the bloom was not yet finished: I would find myself in fullest flower there, as
I knew before I had ever arrived. I would find myself immersed in a world of
my own choosing, whatever that choosing was. And I would revel in it, for as
long as that world would have me.

* * *

It was a brisk September day when I first met Arlette. I was running
across the lawn, books in hand, and tripped over a root, landing splayed
at the feet of a young man – at first glance I had thought Arlette to be a
young man – reading at the base of the sprawling plane tree. My embarrassment was quickly overtaken by bedazzlement as Arlette looked down
at the disheveled person – me – before her.

What a handsome creature! As I tried to right myself, skirt and books and papers all askew, Arlette put forward a hand to steady me and I felt a frisson of unmistakable pleasure at being touched, even so informally, by this person so clearly of my new milieu.

"May I help you, mademoiselle?" Arlette's voice was deep and low, a voice I would forever – I believed even then – associate with sensual pleasure.

I could feel the flush in my cheeks as I took her hand and allowed her to pull me from the ground. My heel caught, yet again, and I nearly stumbled backward, saved with unerring grace by the strong arms of Arlette.

So there we were, of a mid-day, the carillon chiming behind us, in each other's arms, her breath hot against my face and I unsure of what it was I had just discovered in her casual embrace.

Time did indeed seem to stop, just as the poets warn. So as she held me, for so brief and long a moment, I stared direct and undemure into her eyes, which were of a sea-like color, neither green nor gray, but stormy and unreadable as the roughest seas might be. And yet that sea-like color bore no warning that I might soon be cast upon the rocks, broken like so many ships that had passed this way before my own small swoon.

Her hair was very dark and bobbed – shorter, actually, even than that, and she wore no skirt but trousers and a jacket, which made her look even taller and leaner than she was, for when she stood she had seemed at first to loom over me. The shirt beneath her jacket was like a man's as well, with an open neck where a man might have a cravat. Her throat was white and lean and I could see the vein pulsing there as she held me fast and set me aright.

I had the most intense urge to kiss her and did so, flat upon her cheek, thanking her as I did with a murmured "merci" and "merci beaucoup" for saving me from worse trials than a torn stocking and bruised knee. She let me go, but the reluctance was evident in her gesture and I yearned, just as I had yearned to be in this very place for two long years, to have those strong arms stay fast about me.

"I have gone and missed the lecture now, I fear," I stammered as I knelt to retrieve my scattered belongings. Arlette bent down to help me, her hand brushing mine, with purpose, I was certain, as she handed me this paper and that. Yet still she had said nothing more, and I wished to hear her speak again – her voice had caused me to tremble far more than had the fall.

Rather than speak, she reached out to touch my hair, pulling a leaf from what I knew would be fairly mussed tresses. Her fingers lingered there, extending the removal of the leaf far beyond any necessity.

"Your hair is quite lovely." The low murmur set the flush to my face again and my hand flew involuntarily to meet hers at the curled tendril she had twirled upon her finger – the pretense of the leaf.

I had heard this appellation before from suitors whose attempts to woo me had gone unremarked. Was it her voice that made this compliment so dear? Another whispered "merci" was all I could manage. I was coming over in a schoolgirl crush mere moments into our meeting and this, I knew, was a silliness that might not be borne, either by myself nor by the charming Arlette.

So there we were, hands hovering near each other's, looks stolen upon each other. We were behaving as if we were *tu* rather than *vous* and had been so for some time – we had yet to even introduce ourselves and already I was stung with an unpronounceable and impossible – I say impossible, because time told otherwise soon enough – desire.

Like any young man would have done, she introduced herself once we were safely on our feet, some small distance spanned between us. She extended her hand – another excuse to touch and be touched in return – and I took it, glad of the excuse as she, I prayed, was.

"Arlette," was all she said, to which I replied, "Gisele."

* * *

It takes so little time to become lost. A wrong turn in the forest, a milepost passed on the roadway. There is never any turning back, only further disorientation. And that is where we were – past the signpost or the marked wood. On a clear path into darkness in which we would both stumble along as I had before the plane tree and with the same irrevocability.

How to explain the loss of one's virtue in the span of so brief a time? How to explain that desire is a careening locomotion all its own and there is no stopping it and there was no stopping it for us. We knew what we were about as I fell so literally into her arms and I regret none of it, nor shall I ever, even if scandal precedes us wherever we go, as likely it shall, for scandalous we are and ever will be, I fear.

I would like to aver that it was weeks or even months that I resisted her advances. I would like to be able to assert that I was taken without my consent. But neither would be true nor fair to say since it was a mutual desire that overtook us and I was not mere willing participant, but led her as fast to our dereliction as she might have led me.

We were of the same age – twenty – but Arlette was worldly in ways I have yet to become, experienced things I know I never shall. Orphaned at fifteen, she had lived on her own, almost as a man – a boy – on the streets of Paris for several years before she had been able, through a benefactor, to attend the college where we so serendipitously met. As she explained it to me the first night we spent in each other's arms, the first night I slunk back to her one-room flat and sank onto the battered cot that served as bed and divan and table and desk, she had spent those years as nothing less than a gigolo. She had begun by passing herself off as a young man in need of work and been taken in by older men who had not discerned her sex until they had come to her rooms for payment and found something other than what they had sought. *Pas de fils.* No young man of tender flesh and still more tender private areas, but a girl, *a jeune fille* of no desire to them whatsoever.

And so it was, as Arlette explained it to me between kisses and the lightest, most torturous and exquisite fondling of my breasts and hips, that she came to be patronized by women.

It had begun one night on the Rue de — when she had fallen into a boîte and seen her previous benefactor with a Madame T–. Monsieur H– was quick to discern that where he had lacked interest, or rather Arlette had lacked the necessary pieces for there to be a match, Madame T– would indeed enjoy the small treasures hidden beneath the boyish exterior of Arlette. Thus they had begun. The older woman had bought Arlette a meal and they had shared a bottle of wine followed by Pernod, and then Madame T– had invited Arlette home for the night to rest and bathe.

As with her previous benefactors, payment had come due by the third night. But in this regard, Arlette was prepared and – as she described it to me as she stroked my thigh while we lay flush against each other on the tiny cot – even eager to comply. For it was women she desired, and Madame T– was a woman of singular attractiveness and tremulous sensuality. She was also, as Arlette recounted, a woman of insatiable desires.

How had Arlette pleasured her? I wanted her to tell me everything. And as she did so, my education began in earnest. My mother had been right to want to keep me close. That one night of listening acutely to my raconteuse led me down a path that tripped me as fully as had that fateful root of the plane tree.

Have I said that Arlette was handsome? If not, let me reiterate: Arlette impressed all as a handsome young man – tall, lean, lightly muscular, with a flange of nearly black hair and eyes the color of a stormy sea. Her skin was ruddy – not burnt by the sun so much as lightly sun-kissed, as if she had worked a field for a long day and then retired never to do it again, but the memory had forever imprinted her body.

It was this handsomeness that Madame T– desired to display as much as possible. Her young man, her handsome consort, her unabashed paramour on her arm to the theatre, to dine, to the opera, to the salons of friends. Always Arlette, known to Madame T–'s friends as Alain, would be dressed like the fine young man he was presumed to be. Madame T–, a raconteuse herself, had invented her own tale about her Alain and his origins. But all could see that despite his youth and her *l'age certain*, there was a sweetness between them, that he indeed was more than a fop, or a prop for her vanity –they were indeed a couple in love.

For months they strutted about Paris and then set out to Avignon for the Provence season. Alain had a talent for entertaining and Madame T–'s friends and entourage were suitably charmed.

But no less than Madame herself, for Madame T– had become enthralled to her young lover and insatiable in her desire for "Alain."

As Arlette told me her tale, I had become all-over flushed. Heated up from the inside out I was, and I felt a trifle faint and oddly eager for more details, salacious details, I realized, and inexplicably without embarrassment I requested more. There was a pulse I had never remembered feeling, a beating that was neither heart nor temple, but elsewhere and Arlette – or rather "Alain" – had begun its throbbing. Arlette would put her finger to that pulse later, and soothe it, but not as yet. Not as yet.

As I heard of the fruits of Provence, the countryside, the long, lazy days of salonierre and slight drunkenness and over-feeding, I saw Arlette holding back a bit as if testing what she could and could not share with me, so new a confidante. No *tu*, really, and yet hardly a *vous*. We were indeed already something to each other and so her tale was an expiation of sorts, a confession, and for me, insolently, a titillation, for as I truly was not *tu*, I felt no shard of jealousy stab at my already opening heart. I felt only a sense of pride in Arlette's accomplishments and sensual subterfuge.

I wanted to know the substance of the insatiability that Arlette continued to reference. And so I boldly asked that she tell me.

Arlette stood in the small garret and paced a bit. She had long since discarded her jacket and boots. Now she wore only her man's shirt and trousers and I yearned, I knew, to have her shed them also and come to me as the lover she had so appointed herself as with Madame T– and, I was to discover, Madame T–'s own confidantes.

It had long ago grown dark and the light was dim in the room – the amber glow only of the lamp in the corner and a candle for romance nearer to our little cot. The window was open just a bit and on occasion I felt the chill of the autumnal air as it spread languorous, suffusing the room. Arlette saw me shiver and mistook my involuntary action for disdain. She rushed to me and covered me with her body, begging me not to disavow her so soon. I pushed at her a little and told her it was not that – for I was truly in a dream state, the surreal quality of the tale and my own desire far more shocking to me than any single thing she might have told me. And then I kissed her. Not as I had done by the plane tree, my apologetic kiss of remorse for my own clumsiness. As I searched her darkened eyes and flushed visage I put my hands to her hot cheeks and pressed my lips – my own now-errant lips – against hers and felt that pulse renew itself and I pressed yet harder against her lips, her lean body, her masculine "Alain"-ness that I so yearned to experience as I had never yearned for any of the suitors my mother had so diligently found for me.

"Continue," I breathed in her soft ear, "Tell me all Alain did for Madame T–. Tell me all Alain will do for me, as well. Tell me all, for I truly know nothing of this life and I have come here for an education and you are to be my first teacher, of that I am certain."

Arlette loosed herself from my embrace and stood by the little bed. She reached for my hand and pulled me up beside her. I was in dishabille by now, my stockings and skirt askew, my sweater in a twist as well. She motioned to me to hold my arms aloft and as I did so she stripped my sweater off and tossed it aside. There I stood in my skirt and chemise, my heart racing and my breasts heaving just a bit beneath the lace and silk.

I was asked to remove my skirt and then the chemise. I stood, near naked in my stockings, garters, step-ins and brassiere. When Arlette dropped her trousers, first with the sensuous rasp of the zipper, I was close to swooning again. I had a thought of what it would be like to lose my virginity here and now in this little over-cold garret with this handsome boy who was no boy at all. My mother had warned of men and what their desires and needs were and I had heeded her, never crossing that line between what is acceptable for a lady and what is not.

I wished to cross that line now, I wished to leap fully into the chasm and words like "fornication" and "dissolution" came and went in my head as I watched Arlette stand in just her linen shirt, open at the neck, and knew I had to be told more of the tale of her benefactress if I were to know what to do beyond the kiss and the stroking that I had already done.

Arlette began by leading me back to the little cot. She pulled aside the duvet and the worn velveteen quilt and we slid beneath the cold covers and I felt the warmth of her long legs beside mine and I slipped my leg between her two and she pulled it up a bit, so that my knee was touching her there, was against her, and I felt the shudder as she pulled me onto her and I was unsure if I should stop her and make her tell me more, or if I should just let the wave of her sea-colored eyes and her smooth, sun-kissed skin carry me wherever it was we were to go. For I was lost – utterly and shamelessly lost and I knew there was no coming back from where I was going and yet I didn't care. There was no trepidation, only desire, and that desire was in part the need to hear her whisper things to me in the semi-dark and in part the need to feel her take me as none of my mother's so carefully chosen suitors had ever done or even tried to do, I was that cold to their advances.

I was not cold now. A stiff breeze had come up and the curtain billowed a bit over the little window and sounds came up from the streets below, but I was suffused with the heat of Arlette and the intensity of my own emotions, not to mention hers, and we were just heavy with it – the whole lush cushion of emotion we felt in the little cot, pressed up against each other and ready, but I still did not know for what.

Arlette began to talk to me again, low and urgent, as if delivering a message that had to be got just right or ships might sink or planes fall from the sky. And so I learned that on those over-heated afternoons of wine and food and sunny climes in Provence, Madame T– had asked her lover to perform publicly for the group.

Madame T– had traveled much, Arlette explained. To places I had only heard of and could barely imagine. It was in those places that Madame T– developed a taste for the insouciance of public displays of sensual expression.

Madame T–'s friends were of similar character. They liked a show and as the afternoon lagged toward tea-time and the heat of the day rose to uncomfortable pitch, the group would retire indoors, to the veranda-like expanse of the open drawing room and there each would collapse upon the divans and over-stuffed cushions that littered the floor like casualty beds.

There were perhaps ten in all – three couples, married but bored with each other and needing spice. There were Madame T– and "Alain," and then two gentlemen, one of whom knew Alain's secret, one of whom did not. They were themselves a pairing and it was the knowledgeable one who had introduced "Alain" to Madame T– with the admonition that looks were indeed deceiving, but that she would be pleasantly surprised.

As the story continued and Arlette's urgency was punctuated by a rhythmic stroking of my inner thigh, I felt an uncontrollable tingling begin between my legs and go deep, and deeper still. I yearned to know what it was the group did removed from the outdoors, in the shaded and perverse shadow of the drawing room at Madame T–'s villa.

The activity began with the shedding of dresses, trousers, shirts and vests – everyone down to their undergarments. Skirts, trousers, shoes and stockings – all were discarded in neat little piles beside the wearer. Music played muffled from behind them. And then Madame T– began the action by grabbing up one of the errant wives into a little dance which ended in kissing her hard upon the mouth as if she were a man and a lewd man at that. Her action was like the first dance at a promenade. Once Madame T– had enjoined the group to follow her lead, they did so with alacrity, each passing around the wife or husband of the other, so that there were several groups engaged in sexual acts of differing kinds. The two men had drawn another, curious one, into their coupling, two wives found solace in each other, whilst their husbands were servicing Madame T– .

And what of Alain/Arlette? "He" was always garbed in the characteristic linen shirt, open at the neck, covering the sexual particulars, which were presumed to be male. It was expected that Alain would be partially dressed while the others were in dishabille. The excitement lay in not seeing what treasure lay beneath the white linen the boy wore.

Alain was requested by Madame T– to service both a man and a woman of Madame T–'s most intimate acquaintance. Sometimes a couple, sometimes not, but always an eager and receptive duo. In both instances Alain was to pleasure Madame's acquaintances as a man and all the jaded group were most eager to witness this event which inevitably led to passions of their own as the excitement rose with the voyeurism.

On a given afternoon, thick with heat, the man to be pleasured would stand, providing the erect penis to be fondled and sucked by the lovely mouth of Alain until almost ready to spend and then – the group waited and watched as the man finished himself off dramatically as a display. The eroticism was flagrant and infectious.

And Arlette? Arlette loved having this sensual power over the group, the knowledge that it was she alone they came to see and that each time some nuance would arouse them further, satiate them more, make them ever more eager for the next visit, give them a post card of intimate memory to carry home to their bed to infuse their lovemaking anew. Arlette reveled in her role as Alain and felt the most intense eagerness for the performances. Afterward she and Madame T– would retire to their own boudoir and pleasure each other with great intensity. The performances excited Madame T– immensely and her excitement in turn thrilled Arlette, who had never enjoyed being pleasured as much as at the accomplished hands and lips of Madame T–.

This introductory excitement with the man was followed by a similar seasoning of the woman. Alain would lay her flat upon the pillows and ask her to raise her legs in the air. Alain would delicately open the flower with her fingertips and display the bloom for all to see. It was decadence personified, and Alain moved as if in a dream or a newsreel or both and would fondle and caress the woman until Madame T– could see the pleasure becoming unbearable and instruct Alain to slip inside the flower and stroke until the woman spent on the pillows, her cries echoing through the hushed silence and everyone in a state of suspended eroticism.

Such a tale should have shocked me utterly, to the very heart of my being. I should have grabbed at my clothes and raced from the room, never to return. I should have felt impure just at the recounting of such decadence and the knowledge that the woman I lay beside had done such things with such a variety of persons, as close to a prostitute as I could imagine a woman being.

And yet I was neither shocked nor revulsed. I was as the entourage at Madame T–'s. I was mad with it, with the desire for more, to experience the nuances Arlette described, to fill myself with the sensations that each of them in that room had experienced in that sultry and surreal atmosphere of decadence and demimonde. No sense of shame nor revulsion had overcome any of them. Why should it me? – I who was enfolded in the very arms each and every one of them yearned for, drove a day or more to see and hoped to be the chosen one on that day, but if not, at least experience the wealth wrought by Madame T–'s most profound voyeurism. For each had seen Alain perform, if not been the given the gift of the performance upon his or her own person. And so the yearning was always fulfilled to some extent. I wished my yearning to be fulfilled now, as it was growing to an ache in my center, an ache that could only be satisfied with touch and sensation. I would not be appeased by a voyeuristic performance. I wanted to be fully an actor in this staging.

As I say, I knew my shock should have registered in some fashion and that it did not should have shamed me, and yet... And yet I yearned to be the receptor of this accomplishment of Arlette's. But first I needed to know more. What of her lover, Madame T–? What did her benefactress do after the guests had spent themselves? I wanted a recounting of their pleasures.

It was when the others had retired to their rooms, spent or eager to experience what they had just witnessed for themselves, Arlette explained, that the tables were turned and Alain became the voyeur. The two retired to their own boudoir and Madame T– began her particular ritual. Like Arlette, the woman did not strip down for the others, but rather clothed herself in a thin kimono, brightly silken and embroidered and very sensuous. This garment was always open, flowing away from her voluptuous body, always giving a hint at the treasures beneath: the skin still supple and smooth and amazingly white despite the Provence sun. The breasts still high as a girl's and rounded – the size not of melons but of small grapefruits adorned with dark, erect nipples like early blackberries.

Madame T– had her ears pierced in the French way, but she also had a more delicate extravagance, courtesy of a trip to a Moroccan palace and a night of delirium with a former lover who wanted to have her for himself only and keep her unique pleasuring abilities always by his side. The long petals of her flower were, as Arlette detailed, pierced with a thick gold hoop through which Madame T– would guide a silken tether and have Arlette pull it tighter and tighter when the critical moments rose between them. Madame T– had told Arlette that her former lover had tied her to his bed by the little hoop, so she could not leave without literally tearing herself open. But she had learned to pleasure him with the hoop, rubbing it against the head of his penis once it had escaped its sheath, and tantalizing him with it. He would remove the hoop to enter her and then replace it when he was finished. He would hold it in his teeth and slither his tongue against her persimmon bud. She had come to find the hoop a central aspect of her sensual pleasure and now could not do without it.

I had images of this Moroccan idyll that had turned so sinister. I saw billowing curtains and a huge bed covered in netting and all around outside nothing but desert and this woman – this woman who was my only competitor for the beloved Alain, the virile creature who held me fast without hoops or tethers – strung up on the bed, a swarthy man with an immense penis coming toward her and she writhing beneath him in a combination of pleasure and pain.

The images were of nothing I knew nor could know, put there in my mind's eye by my Scheherazade, my instructress, my new beloved. Alain/Arlette, the consummate actor of this sensual stage.

I slipped my hand beneath the linen shirt. I felt, rather than heard, the intake of breath as I ran my hand along the silken thighs of Arlette – was I to call her Arlette or Alain? Who was she to me at this moment – the boy lover or a lean young Atthis?

I could not know what I was doing, mimicking only the Arabian-style tale with its lurid and profane descriptions that she herself had told to me. I knew I would find no penis when I shifted my hand upward, yet I did find a clitoris that protruded far more than my own, as if it were indeed a penis, a quite small one that I knew I must stroke to completion.

"Gisele." My name resonated in my ear as I slid my body down to kiss Arlette's flesh beneath the linen shirt that seemed a part of her. My lips were hot and dry and I ran my tongue across them and she caught me in a look – those storm-tossed eyes with their sensuous, siren depths! – and grabbed me up and kissed me intensely enough to take my breath completely away and I felt her hard against me, turning me over onto my back, spreading my legs with her knee, pressing up, up, hard and harder still against me, against the place that only I had ever touched. I was inviolate and yet open, ready for her to take me in whatever way she chose and she chose quickly and gently, but with an urgency that set my pulse to racing and took my breath from me.

Her leanness belied her strength and muscularity – she was indeed the girl/man that Madame T– had trained her to be and it was that creature that

I longed for, that I opened myself to. For her I took my virginity – so long-cherished – and tossed it aside as I had tossed aside my sweater and skirt and childhood all at once when I had entered her bed.

And there we lay, she lowering herself onto me like a groom on a wedding night and me with only the barest flutter of fear and deepest shiver of longing and desire. My thighs were damp with wanting her and I reached out to take her clitoris in my hand as if it were a penis and stroke it ever so slightly until it became the stiff small thing it was, the thing I wanted to feel pressed against my own, if that were possible, and Arlette's murmurs and breathy exclamations told me that it was.

There was much *tu toier* between us then, as she gave herself over to the passion she had always been divorced from on those debauched Provence afternoons, when the scents and tastes and secretions of strangers had enveloped her. Now there were just we –the two of us, sans hoops and tethers and the ennui of those past true loving, those only seeking new ways to shock themselves to life, shock themselves from their torpor, sensual and other.

I had felt torpor myself, I knew what it was to yearn and dream and slake one's desire again and again with vapid conversation and endless pretense and restive hopefulness. But I had fled that world. I had sought newness and embraced it when it first presented itself to me at the base of the plane tree. And now here I was, *Gisele a l'ecole*, as it were, being tutored in ways that my mother could never know, yet would be bound to know one day. Just not this day. Nor the ones soon after.

"*Dites-moi,*" I demanded of Arlette. "*Maitenant!*" I added my own urgency, needing to know all that had happened between her and the benefactress so that I could proceed. Proceed with my knowledge, virgin that I was, and also purge myself of any desire to replicate that previous affair in my own with Arlette. I wanted us fresh, new, an unwilted bloom. I wanted desire and passion, sans tawdriness. And I knew in Arlette's life as the kept man Alain, there had been tawdriness, yet I also knew that it had to have been thrilling, too, and there had to have been some feeling there, between them, her and Madame T–, and perhaps even among the entourage as well.

Arlette had not told me how they parted, only that they had. I did not imagine more hoops or tethers, but I could not imagine Madame T– wanting to relinquish the creature with whom I now shared this tiny bed in this cell of a room so divergent from the villa I envisioned in Provence.

It was time. Arlette lay over me, her body covering mine and I could feel, or imagined I did, the slight pulsing of her clitoris against me and I ached to have her enter me, ached to have her, to be virgin no more at her hands, her fingers, her swollen and pulsing clitoris. But first there was the disposition of Madame T–. I listened as Arlette whispered the rest to me.

The summer had dragged on, too hot, and the afternoons had begun to take on a level of extremity that Alain had difficulty navigating. The men were fewer; women were almost the exclusive guests by late July and Alain had begun to feel stifled not only by the unremediated heat, but also by the demands of the women who seemed to view Alain as the gift their husbands would never give them; Madame T–, covetous as she was, promoted this idea at Alain's expense.

Then, finally, it was at an end. One blazing August afternoon Alain did the unthinkable and simply walked to their bedroom rather than perform for the guests. There would be no more blooming of long-dead flowers nor sparking of ill-defined passions in a haze of heat and decadence. It was over for Arlette and she began to pack what she thought she might take with her, what she felt was due her for services so acutely rendered over such a long and difficult season.

Madame T– was never one for histrionics. She strode into the bedroom as one does into a stable – ready to take the reins and have done with it. But Alain had no hoop and would not be tethered and Madame T– was above begging and pleading. Pride was her refuge; she had done no such thing before and she would not stoop to it now. Still, she managed to exact her own recompense from Alain. A final round of passion between them, sans guests, sans all accoutrements, with just their own still innate desire for one another.

Arlette had already described their lovemaking as skilled and enticing and unlike anything Arlette had experienced. In their bedroom, Alain was the young boy in training to be a man and Madame T– would do as I had done: take the swelling clitoris and pull and stroke it until it grew still larger. Except Madame T– was a woman of the world and of the demimondaine and she had visited places where things existed that neither I nor Arlette nor, I trusted, even her guests knew.

Madame T– had learned to affix her little hoop to her lover's little cock and they would work each other together, the action making Arlette wild with desire and Madame T– equally so. Madame T– would execute the swift moves of her limber body to climax Alain and each time, Arlette told me, the intensity was more, the pleasure more exquisite, the desire reprised more acutely.

As she told me this, I put my fingers around the stiff thing that now seemed larger because she was above me. It protruded between her legs and I could feel it, and grasp it, and with each intake of her breath I knew I was invoking pleasure that was not a replication of Madame T–'s, but a new and different love-making that was purely and intimately our own.

That day they had worked each other to a lather with teasing and the knowledge that Alain would soon disappear, never to return. It was heady, the excitement, and it crested them both again and again. Madame T– was open and wet as a summer flower and this time Alain yearned to sex her like a man more than ever and expressed frustration at not being able to plunge deep into her and feel Madame T–'s delicate and silken sheath close over her own hardened self.

Madame T– had arisen, then, naked and voluptuous, in a state of intense desire. She had gone to the closet and there had pulled from a box what Arlette could see was a replicate of a penis. She ached to have it, to use it, but did not know how. Madame T– showed her and the two were enmeshed until dark in their new-found passion.

Still, it was not enough. Arlette stayed the night and in the morning felt compelled to enter her lover once more, deeply, thrusting faster than she thought she would be capable of and bringing Madame T– to a resounding climax that left her breathless and panting, her legs wide and wound tight around her young lover's back.

The leave-taking was neither smooth nor easy. They had each discovered something new in the ending of their love affair and neither was fully ready to relinquish it. Madame T– suggested Arlette return to the city and stay at the house. Arlette relented. And for another two weeks there were occasional nights of extreme passion, with Arlette feeling the simulated penis pressing against her own small organ as she plunged again and again into Madame T–'s provocative, ever more intoxicating sheath.

And then she simply left, knowing that if she didn't, the seasons would change and her anger by day would evaporate into unquenchable desire in the night, nights spent between her lover's bountiful thighs, and it would go on unendingly until her resentment drove her to something desperate. And yet the desire was still there, she said, until tonight, in this bed, with me.

I wanted her to open me up then, to spread me wide and open and enter me the way she had entered her other lover and reach into me with her desire and take us both to another place from this small bed. I knew I had to tell her I was a virgin, but that I was ready to relinquish what now seemed more burden than gift. I ached for her, I knew I wanted her now and always, that I would never tire of those storm-cast eyes or her strong arms or the small stiff thing I had felt between her legs that teased me so. I knew I wanted to do this again and again and that it would feel as it did now – not quite real and yet fully real. And I knew I wanted it, and told her so.

We were lost in each other then, all else receded as we sank into each other with a slow but building abandon. All those years of aching solitude at my mother's house, all the afternoons and evenings spent with dull and duller men who wanted to possess me all faded into an appropriate oblivion. That world was lost to me forever, and I would miss it not a whit. This, this tiny cramped room with its chill breezes and threadbare coverlet and ill-worn sheets – this was what I had wanted those years I spent like a wraith floating from room to room looking for what was not there and could never be there.

It was all here, here with Arlette. Her affair with Madame T– was but the training for her romance with me. She had learned every small nuance of lovemaking that she would in turn teach me, her willing and fresh student. I ached for her instruction and she gave it readily. Just as eager to impart her knowledge to me.

There were long, fervid kisses that heated us and the small chill room. There was the clinging of our bodies, close enough to become one with each other, the scents of us commingling with our mutual heat and damp. She nipped lightly along my neck, she sank her teeth into the hollow of my throat and held it, taking my breath away. She held my shoulders down, she pressed herself into me, she whispered my name again and again as she kissed me all along my body, moving downward, her lips and tongue hot against me. I felt as if in a dream state and yet also at the edge of a precipice, as one feels right before sleep or death.

I held tightly to her.

Her tongue was agile and adept and as she opened me up, as her warm mouth enveloped me, I was transported over that precipice, yet not into an abyss, rather into a state of rapture. My legs tightened involuntarily around her as I felt an intensity of sensation that set me to writhing beneath her expertise until I was spent and near to weeping from the immensity of the pleasure.

But it was just the *hors d'oeuvres*, the precursor to the full complement of her skills. In moments she was above me again and I could feel a pressure between my legs, a pushing, a sharp sting of pain, and then she entered me.

The slow, then more strident thrusting was unlike anything I could have imagined. I opened my eyes and stared at Arlette, her strong, lithe body so attuned to mine and saw she watched me, seeking my response, and so I gave it to her, entwining my arms around her neck, kissing her deeply, urgently, moving my hips to meet her every thrust and wondering how I had come to be in this place, with these sensations that threatened to cast me into a state of agitation that I feared perhaps I would – could – never escape. I would be, like Madame T– tethered by a hoop of my own making, and should I attempt to leave, tear myself asunder in the extrication.

Yet I did not wish extrication. That I knew.

It went on like this for some time, the heat building between us and Arlette's excitement growing – I could see it in her face, feel it in her urgent stroking. I wanted to give her all that Madame T– and those Provence guests had provided, but I was so unschooled in these ways of the demi-monde, I was unsure how to satisfy her fully.

Her breathing had begun to quicken and she was thrusting at me faster and so deeply that I had started to feel something close to real pain and yet the sensation remained acutely pleasurable as well – I felt filled to the brim with her and wanted her to feel the same. I spoke, shattering the reverie that had enveloped us both.

"*Dites-moi,*" I whispered, "*dites-moi tu desire?*" What, I pleaded with her, was her desire, what would satisfy her completely?

Arlette slowed and then stopped her intercourse with me. She lay for a moment upon me, her fingers pinching my nipple, making me shudder beneath her. Then she slid off me and lay, legs splayed, in the tiny cramped bed on her back next to me.

"Come close," she murmured and I curled my body, my hot and not-quite-sated body, next to hers. Then Arlette explained what it was she wanted.

In the midst of our love-making I had not known exactly what it was she was about when she had risen from the bed and gone to a drawer in the low chest in the corner. The room had dimmed as she had turned off the lamp and there was only the low flicker of the candle to light us and the errant glow from the street beyond the window. There had been some ministrations, but I had not noted what they were. In fact had presumed I was not to know, but to wait and then slip into the same reverie she had prepared for us both.

And this I had done. I had not for a moment thought of Arlette as a man, but it was how she had taken me – as a man would – except, I knew, with a gentleness and a ferocity that no man could have laid claim to.

What Arlette wanted from me now was what a man would have wanted. She wanted me to stroke the thing she had pierced me with, stroke it in a way that would bring her pleasure. Put my lips to her thighs and put my delicate hand around the faux penis and pleasure it and in doing so, pleasure her. For beneath the thing that protruded was her own hardened clitoris, stiff and aching for the same release that those men in Provence with their erect penises had ached for and she had given with such practiced skill.

I was, however, determined to make this moment our own and something about her request was all too reminiscent of the tales of Madame T–. I didn't want to be an understudy in their intimate drama. I wanted to soliloquize our love-making for myself. And so I slipped down to her waist, undoing the thing fastened there and moving it aside. I heard her sigh of regret, of longing, but I ignored it. With the sureness of the novice and the alacrity of the neophyte, I knew I could replace that regret with deep and abiding pleasure.

I began by kissing her smooth, boy's thighs. She was indeed Atthis in her lean muscularity. My lips were hot, my mouth hotter still. I remembered what she had told me of her performances and I could still feel her own mouth upon my sex. My tongue slipped from between my lips, my fingers teased along her inner thigh, snaking along the path divined by my tongue. And then I felt it, the hard and protuberant clitoris of my lover, and I took it in my mouth as I would have done a man's penis, were I a married woman and not whatever it was I had become instead.

Arlette cried out with surprise and pleasure, yet placed her hands upon my head as if to move me away. I did not relent. Rather I took the whole of her between my lips, lightly tracing my teeth along its length, and then sucked the hard bit into my mouth as if it were the ripened fig it so resembled.

Her pleasure was unmistakable – her cries intensified and she gripped my shoulders and entwined her fingers in my hair and pleaded with me to continue, continue, not to cease what I was doing, and I was gratified by her excitement in a way I didn't know was possible. Her pleasure was my pleasure and I was incited anew by this discovery – that I had this power to make her shudder and thrill beneath me, a neophyte, a novice at this game of sensual love.

And then I felt it – the clitoris stiffened between my lips and I felt a pulsing as if I had my lips round a metronome or some other vibrating object. It was brief, but exacting and she cried out in a series of indiscernible words of love and pleasure and then her body loosed itself and I knew she was spent, the climax ended. I took my swollen lips from her, the taste of her resonant. I crept up next to her and we held each other. She stroked my hair and gazed at me and told me she had never felt that thing before, what she had felt with me, and that she would want it always, want it and me, together, in her bed.

The rush of sentiment and sensuality suffused me and I was deeply, sweetly content. My own body still pulsed and I yearned for more of her skillful touch, but I knew more would come, soon, and it would build to new crescendos each time.

The candle guttered out and a thin line of smoke rose up beside us. Outside the night was black and enveloping and we held each other tight against the dark and our own errant longing.

* * *

In the days and months and long time to come I would not regret my choice to leave my mother's house and come to the city for my education. It was not what my mother would have wanted for me, perhaps – I have no doubt she would be scandalized by my desire and my choice of lover – yet I knew I had chosen well. Arlette was my beloved, I had given myself to her, my sleek young Atthis, and I would not leave her. We would make some life together, of what sort, I remained unsure. Yet still I knew that we were indeed star-crossed and that in the night, any night, that knowledge would be a comfort, no matter how deep the darkness that surrounded us.

Isadora Atwood
A FLAPPER'S BEADS
1926

They went to early mass that Saturday, Dolores and her brothers Hector and Albert, then went home and changed for the speakeasy. Dolores was of half a mind not to go, but Albert talked her into it. Christmas was coming up, and they'd all worked hard, and it was time to have some fun. So the three of them walked across town to the Litwak's speakeasy.

The town was Freeland, Pennsylvania, a little dot built next to a coal mine on the map of the Pocono Mountains. Immigrants, all of them: Irish, like Dolores, or Italian or Polish or German or Lithuanian. They all got along. They all worked at the mine, no point in not getting along. Dolores was an assistant milliner, and walked seven miles each way to her job in Hazelton, or sometimes got a ride with Mr. O'Shea on his milk truck. Hector and Albert worked in the mine, came home every day covered in black soot, and would shed their clothes and pump up buckets of water at the back of the house after work. Albert was vain and hated that his fingernails never seemed clean. Hector, who lost his left index finger in the Great War, worried less about his fingernails.

So here they were, the three of them, walking across to the Litwak's place. The Litwak was a friend of their late father's, and was actually named Victor Akunas, and they had gone to school and played with his children, yet the moniker "the Litwak" stuck, and Mr. Akunas did nothing to discourage it. His eldest son, Bobby, let them into the speakeasy, shaking hands with Hector and offering him cigarettes. Bobby too had been overseas in the war, and he and Hector, both grown into silent men, had an easy camaraderie. Baby, the Litwak's daughter who had gone to school with Dolores, was behind the bar and waved to the three of them. She brought over whiskey and water for the boys and a ginger beer for Dolores.

"Oh, look at that cloche," she said, admiring Dolores' hat. "Did you make that yourself?"

Dolores smiled, and took off the gray hat and offered it to Baby. "Blocking felt is a pain in the neck, but I was determined to do it."

"You look like a right flapper, you do," Baby said enviously. "Bobbed hair and all."

Dolores stood up. "Put it on. Come on, let's go to the bathroom and look at you in the mirror."

Admittedly, the hat looked better on Dolores: her bobbed brown hair and narrow face lent themselves to the flapper style – Baby had a fat, round face framed by errant curly locks.

"I could do one for you, cheap," Dolores told Baby. "But it would have to be after Christmas. Mrs. Kendricks is full up with orders."

Baby gave the hat back to Dolores. "Pa would shoot me if I wore a cloche and bobbed my hair," she said with a sigh.

Someone banged on the bathroom door, and the girls opened it. It was Gloria Montrose, an older girl. "Quit yer pow-wow," she said, tossing a cigarette end into the toilet. "I gotta fix my lipstick."

They let her past them, and walked back into the speakeasy proper. "She's had a bit much to drink tonight," whispered Baby conspiratorially. "A bit much every night, actually." The two girls giggled together.

Albert had his arm draped around the shoulders of Anselm Montrose, Gloria's younger brother. "Hey, Dolores. Anselm knows of a party over in White Haven. There should be dancing. You should come too, Baby."

"White Haven is a bit of hike, Bertie," Baby said flirtatiously.

"I've got my father's car," said Anselm with a quick smile. "It's just a house party at Dom Ruggerio's, but he's got a swell gramophone, and there'll be plenty to eat and drink – his family owns a delicatessen."

Gloria reappeared behind them. "Don't listen to him, girls, he's just sweet on Valerie Ruggerio, and doesn't want to be obvious by showing up alone."

Nevertheless, it was decided, and Anselm and Gloria and Hector and Albert and Dolores and Baby and Baby's brother Billy and Billy's best friend Freddie all piled into the Montrose car, and headed down the snowy, crystalline road to White Haven. Freddie sat next to Dolores and insisted on holding her hand every time the car lurched, which was often, and Dolores didn't mind much, although she did notice the coal grit beneath his fingernails.

The party was swell. The gramophone was out on the glassed-in porch and the dancers all had steam trailing out of their mouths, and no one seemed to mind dancing in the cold without a coat. Baby started dancing immediately, and Albert with her, but Gloria dragged Dolores into the house and upstairs.

"God, I hate these parties," she said as she led Dolores to a bedroom in the back. "Valerie? You up here?" she called, and stuck her head in a doorway.

Dolores had never seen Valerie Ruggiero before. She was tall and thin and had short curly hair the same shade as midnight. Her dress was dark blue, the color of a stormy sea. A long string of pearls – the ultimate flapper regalia – hung down to her waist. She smiled at the new arrivals.

"My brother is downstairs panting for you," remarked Gloria as she strode into the room. "Blessed Mother, tell me you have something to drink up here." She examined a bottle of gin sitting on a dressing table. "Is this watered down?"

"Don't mind Gloria," said Valerie to Dolores. Her eyes were a crystalline gray, almost devoid of color. "I'm Valerie. Would you like some gin?"

"Why, yes. I'm Dolores. Dolores Leary."

"Well, come on in, Dolores Leary. Have a seat."

Dolores sat on the edge of Valerie's bed, and Gloria brought her a glass of gin. Gloria kicked off her shoes and reclined on the bed. "God, 'Lores, you're dull," she slurred.

"Am I?" asked Dolores, who had never considered the question.

"Posi-lutely," declared Gloria.

Anselm stuck his head in the door. "Is this a girls-only party, or can anybody join?"

"It's girls-only," Valerie told him, "but Dolores and I are going downstairs to dance." She put the bottle of gin on the floor next to the bed. "The gin's right here, Gloria," she announced.

They went downstairs and out onto the porch. Anselm danced with Dolores and Billy danced with Valerie, then they switched partners. Billy said, "Your Albert has been dancing with Baby all night."

"Well, they've always got along. She probably feels safe with him."

Billy grunted. "True. You could never say that the Leary boys take advantage."

Dom Ruggiero cut in on him, a broad but slim short man with a straight nose and glittering blue eyes. "So you're Albert's older sister, the hat-maker," he said. "Could you make a hat like the one you're wearing for my sister?"

"Sure," said Dolores, "but not until after Christmas."

"Swell," said Dom. "She's got a red coat she loves – I'll bring it to you, maybe you could match the color." He grinned, and reminded Dolores of a stocky Valentino. She found herself smiling back. He was a good dancer.

They danced until Dolores' fingers turned numb from the cold, then went inside for warm punch. Hector sat on a loveseat talking to girl Dolores didn't know. Dolores helped Dom put out more cold cuts.

"Running a delicatessen may not seem like much," he said. "But it's the people I like. I get to talk to all kinds of people." He smiled at her. "I imagine you get a lot of stuffy old ladies in your line of work," he said.

"Well," said Dolores conspiratorially, "Mrs. Kendricks does cater to a certain lack of style…"

Dom laughed loud and hard. "You're all right, Dolores," he said smiling. "And you dance great."

Valerie came into the kitchen. "Don't monopolize the girls, Dom," she said, winking at Dolores. "The punch needs refreshing." She linked her arm through Dolores'. "Did Dom tell you we have a maze?"

"A maze?" asked Dolores.

"Out back. Made out of fir hedges. Or some member of the evergreen family. My grandfather planted it. Come, I'll show you."

She pulled Dolores out the back door. Their shoes crunched on the thin crust of snow. In the moonlight, the long yard was a silvery white, with a tall, snow-capped hedge at the back of the yard.

"There's always a secret to a maze," said Valerie. "Usually, it's that you should always turn right, and you'll end up in the center." Dolores followed her into the maze, the dark green hedges high over their heads. "So my grandfather decided he'd be different. Here, if you keep turning left, you end up in the center," she said, turning left. "My grandmother said that left is the direction of the devil, and that the maze is cursed."

They emerged into the clear center of the maze. Valerie led Dolores to a marble bench. "Stand up on this. If you stand on your tiptoes, you can see how the maze is laid out."

Dolores obeyed, and realized that the hedges weren't as tall as they appeared, and that the maze was actually small. "Who keeps the hedges cut?" she asked, stepping down from the bench.

"I do, usually, although Dom helps out. I work at a florist's two days a week, so I'm often bored." Dolores shivered in the cold. "Let's go back in. Gloria is probably out cold."

They went inside and up the back stairs to Valerie's room. Gloria was asleep on the bed, snoring. Valerie gently put a blanket over her. Dolores looked out her window at the maze.

"It looks just like a hedge from here," she said with disappointment.

Valerie stepped up behind her and rested her chin on Dolores' shoulder. "That's because the outer walls of the hedge are taller than the inner walls. Grandfather was very sly. And he could smoke a ham like no one's business," she said with a smile.

It felt, to Dolores, like a moment from a book, the two of them standing there, so close, the cold white outside. She wanted it to continue, not to end.

Valerie reached out and stroked Dolores' cheek. "You have such soft skin," she murmured. "Why on earth did they name you Dolores? Sorrow is not a proper name for a young woman."

Dolores turned and saw herself mirrored in Valerie's grey eyes. As she opened her mouth to speak, Valerie lifted a finger to her lips.

"Such soft lips, too," she said, and then leaned forward and gently kissed Dolores, a long kiss. She leaned back, looked at Dolores, and then leaned forward to kiss her again, and Dolores found herself kissing back, tasting the tart tang of punch on Valerie's tongue.

Soon Valerie's mouth found the hollow of Dolores' throat, and Valerie gently ran her hands along Dolores' breasts and down to her waist. It was nothing that Dolores hadn't had done to her before by any number of boys. But this felt different. Her stomach felt like it was flipping itself over and her knees felt rubbery and Dolores didn't want Valerie to stop touching her.

She leaned back against the window frame as Valerie slid her hands up under Dolores' dress and into her knickers. Before Dolores could imagine what might be next, Valerie had parted her sex and was gently stroking it with her finger, a stroke that made Dolores sigh. Then she leaned forward and began to lick Dolores' sex, a slow, deliberate motion like a cat grooming itself. Dolores found her fingers gripping Valerie's dark curls, swooning with the intense pleasure.

When Valerie moved her tongue away, Dolores wanted to protest, but Valerie hushed her and slid a finger, then two, into Dolores' sex, stroking hard and fast until Dolores felt a wave, a tidal wave, course through her whole body. She leaned into the window, stunned and weak.

Footsteps sounded up the stairs, and Dom knocked on the doorframe. "Dolores, I think your brothers are ready to go," he said.

"What... what about Gloria?" she asked.

"Oh, Anselm left ages ago." He turned to Valerie. "Somebody told him you were in the maze with another boy."

"Oh what rubbish," said Valerie. "It was just me and Dolores." To Dolores she said, "She can stay here tonight – Dom will get her home in the morning."

Albert came bouncing up the stairs. "Hey Dolores, are you ready to go?"

"Just let me get my coat."

Dom held her coat for her. "I'll visit you at the shop, Dolores," he said with a wink.

Valerie kissed her cheek. Then, as Dolores was almost out the door, she called her back, and took off the long strand of pearls, and arranged them around Dolores' throat. "Really, it goes perfectly with your dress," she said. "Now you have an excuse to come visit, so that you can return them." She smiled.

"All right, Valerie," said Dom, "let the guests go home." He saw them out, making them promise to come again soon, party or no.

"That damn Anselm Montrose," said Hector as they all walked back along the cold road to Freeland. "Eight miles we have to walk in the middle of the night."

"Oh, it's good exercise," said Baby, always a sport, holding Albert's hand.

Billy offered Dolores his gloves. "No thank you, Bill," she said softly. She kept pace next to him, but all the way back she fingered Valerie's pearls. They could have been a rosary, except that there was something about them. They shimmered like the moon outside of Valerie's window, and Dolores kept turning them over and over in her hands. They were the perfect flapper's beads.

Edwina Leonard
SILENT STARS
1929

When she finished school, Rose had two choices: nursing school – rolling gauze for bandages – or marriage. Yes, Ben had asked for her hand; he'd told her he would wait if she really wanted to go to nursing school. But Rose didn't really want to go to nursing school. Nor did she want to marry Ben and be stuck forever in this tiny New Hampshire town. Really, there was only one thing Rose wanted to do: be a movie star.

Rose had no illusions about being an *actress*: she knew she couldn't possibly remember lines and speeches and stand on a stage in a theater full of people. But movie stars didn't need to do those things. Mostly they had to look pretty and gaze pensively at the leading man, or occasionally fling their hands up in distress. Rose was pretty, with bright green eyes, milk-white skin, and delicate hands perfect for expressing distress, and she liked to pose before cameras, so she thought, yes, I could be a movie star.

So Rose and Mabel, her best friend, who yearned to be a dancer, took the train to New York City. They stayed in a small, stuffy hotel for women, one that catered to typists and clerical workers who went home on the weekends. Rose and Mabel could only afford one small room with one small bed – Mabel assured Rose that it wouldn't be for long, that they would soon have work. That first night, Rose lay quiet in the bed close to red-haired Mabel, listening to the sounds of the city rising from below, and wondering if it would ever be quiet enough for her to sleep. Mabel stirred, moving closer to Rose, and leaned over and kissed her softly. "My parents say that you should always kiss goodnight," Mabel murmured, and curled an arm about Rose. "Rose, your lips are so soft," said Mabel, who kissed her again.

Rose had been kissed before, chaste kisses from cousins and more intense, if equally uninteresting, kisses from Ben. But Mabel's kisses were different. Mabel's kisses lingered softly, her dark lips parted, the tip of her smooth tongue gently brushing Rose's lips. Rose wanted more, more softness, and Mabel happily continued kissing. Rose didn't even protest when Mabel ran her hand up the back of Rose's demi-slip – it seemed so normal, Mabel holding her and kissing her. After all, Mabel was her best friend. Then Mabel pulled slowly away and tugged off her own slip; Rose saw no reason not to follow suit. In the half-light of the hotel room Rose saw Mabel's naked form, the swell of her breasts, the red patch of hair between her legs. She reached out and touched one of Mabel's nipples, surprised as it hardened beneath her fingers. Mabel moaned and pulled her close, rubbing her breasts against Rose's. Then, starting with Rose's chin, Mabel ran her tongue down the front of Rose's body, pausing momentarily above the delicate bud of her sex, and then sliding her tongue slowly against Rose's vulva. Rose recoiled, shocked and shocked by the pleasure she felt, then quickly moved her sex back to Mabel's mouth. Soon she found herself rocking to and fro against Mabel's mouthing, moaning, twitching. Mabel withdrew her mouth and, just as Rose began to protest its absence, slowly slid her fingers up into Rose's sex. Rose froze, then found herself pumping up and down with Mabel's fingers and then, although she did not know the term, orgasming. Mabel held her as she shook, then slowly withdrew her fingers, and lay Rose back against the bed.

Rose lay, sated, soft-witted, and Mabel straddled her prone body. She grasped Rose's hand and rubbed it hard against her sex. Then she slid Rose's fingers into herself, and Rose found herself entranced by the hot, soft, wet feel of the inside of Mabel's shell, by the way Mabel's sex contracted rhythmically around her fingers. Mable leaned down to bite Rose's nipples, then reared up and moaned with her own orgasm, her breasts heaving, her freckled body magnificent, her eyes dark and glittering.

Finding work in New York was easy. Finding work as a movie star was not. Rose was able to model for illustrators, but sitting still for hours on end with a box of Bright Bubbles Laundry Detergent bored her and she found her mind wandering, usually back to Mabel's body and the fun she had with it almost every night. Rose ate at drugstores, hoping to be seen by a movie scout, but her breakthrough was so much more prosaic: she took a train to Metuchen and walked to the Biograph movie studios. The man in the office eyed her tiredly, asked if she had any acting experience, offered her a cup of tea, and prepared to send her home when his secretary came in saying that Miss Dorothy Gish needed a girl for the film she was shooting. And so Rose was taken to meet Miss Dorothy Gish.

Miss Dorothy Gish was short, with sharp, intelligent eyes. Less famous than her ethereal sister Lillian, she was dark-haired and hazel-eyed. She eyed

Rose up and down, pursed her cherry-bud lips, and sent Rose to the costume department. Moments later, Rose was standing behind a movie star – a movie star! – as the star emoted over a man dying on a sidewalk. Rose wept real tears, albeit tears of joy, and was told Miss Gish was quite satisfied with her and that she should return the next day. She was given an envelope with a full dollar's pay in it.

For the next two months, Rose went to Metuchen twice a week to act, usually for Miss Gish. Miss Gish was sweet and warm and did the Charleston to amuse the actors while the cameramen fiddled with their lenses and magazines. Sometimes she would declaim speeches from Shakespeare, a reminder to all that she had been brought up on the stage. Rose liked Miss Gish, and although she had no desire to learn Shakespeare, she found herself with a distinct desire for the lacework collars that Miss Gish favored, and even for the alabaster neck that the collars laid against. Rose was not yet a movie star. But she saw her goal not far off.

One day, Miss Dorothy Gish announced that she would be shooting her next film in Los Angeles, and she asked several actors to join her, including Rose. So Rose packed up her one suitcase and boarded the transcontinental train with the others. The actors all had sleeping berths, except for Miss Gish, who had a compartment. The first night on the train, a pajamaed Miss Gish asked Rose into her compartment. She offered Rose a gin blossom. Rose, unused to strong drink, soon found herself laughing and talking about herself and, before she knew it, sitting naked in Miss Gish's lap while Miss Gish rubbed her face against Rose's breasts. Overwhelmed, Rose took Miss Gish's hand and brought it to her mouth, licking the delicate fingers. Miss Gish took her hand back and thrust it into Rose's wet sex, and Rose rode Miss Gish's subtle hand to the rhythm of the train until she reached satisfaction.

Rose tried to reach into Miss Gish's silk pajama top, but Miss Gish softly batted her hand away and said, "Soon, tadpole, soon enough." Miss Gish helped her into her clothes, kissed her once on each cheek, and sent her off to her berth for the night. Rose let the motion of the train and the memory of sitting in Miss Gish's lap lull her to sleep. She was awoken by Gertrude, one of the make-up girls, sliding into the berth next to her. Gertrude threw off her robe, complaining of the heat, "but oh how delicious it is to be going to California," she cooed. Gertrude smelled of freesia eau de cologne and rubbed up against Rose and Rose, in a fit of pique at having been sent to bed by Miss Gish, slapped Gertrude across the face. Rose was amazed by how much she had enjoyed slapping Gertrude, the sharp sound of the smack, and so she slapped her again, and again. She rolled the stunned Gertrude onto her stomach and, not caring who heard her, began to spank Gertrude's firm bottom, taking distinct pleasure in the faint red marks her fingers left and in the percussive sound of each smack. She slid her fingers into Gertrude's waiting sex, and pushed roughly as Gertrude moved her bottom up to meet her. Finally, Rose pushed her clitoris against the back of her own hand as it shoved into Gertrude, and they rutted that way for long minutes, until the sleeping car bounced on the track and Rose found her entire hand curled up in the pink, open flower of Gertrude's sex. Gertrude moaned as Rose twisted her hand, and suddenly they were rutting again, with Rose pushing harder and harder until they climaxed one after the other.

When the train arrived in Los Angeles days later, it was early morning, and Rose was struck by the brightness of the sunlight, how it lit up all the outside like a klieg spotlight. They all went together to their hotel, except for Miss Dorothy Gish, who went to the bungalow she shared with her mother and her sister Lillian. Rose wandered about the city, looking at the sandy soil and shading her eyes from the sun. She and Gertrude went to the studio lot and walked around the street sets – so huge compared to the small, dark sets they used in New Jersey. She went back to her hotel and napped, the sunlight an unrelenting red behind her closed eyelids, the heat shimmering in the air.

The cast and crew had supper at the hotel, and both Misses Gish and Mr. D. W. Griffith, the famous director, joined them. After dinner Mr. Griffith left and Miss Dorothy Gish invited Rose back to the bungalow to meet their mother. Mr. Griffiths had worn an old-fashioned suit, but the Gish sisters both dressed as flappers, Dorothy a shorter, darker version of her tall, ghostly sister, each with the same pert pout to her lips. In the car, Rose sat next to the delicately moon-faced Miss Lillian, and was struck by the sad look in her pale blue eyes, and by her soft, sad smile.

When they arrived at the bungalow, Mrs. Gish was out playing cards, and Miss Dorothy brought out the gin and put a platter on the gramophone. The three of them drank and danced, and finally Rose found herself being supported by the two sisters as they guided her to a quiet room with an enormous bed in it. The sisters laid her down, and started to slowly undress Rose, periodically shedding their own garments as well. Off came the silk hose, off the slips, off the corsets. Rose quivered, and then moaned, as Miss Lillian bit Rose's lips with her tiny, animal-like teeth, her tongue exploring Rose's mouth, while Miss Dorothy's tongue caressed her sex. As Miss Dorothy's fingers dipped into Rose like a hummingbird into a blossom, Rose grabbed at Miss Lillian, running her hands up and down the actress's body, rubbing Miss Lillian's sex hard with her hand, until Miss Lillian grasped Rose's hand and moved it inside of her. Soon Rose's hand in Miss Lillian moved with the rhythm of Miss Dorothy's hand inside of her, and Miss Dorothy pulled Rose's knee up and rocked rhythmically against Rose's leg. Neither sister spoke. For a brief moment Miss Lillian's eyes seemed luminescent in the darkened room, and she could have been either an angel or a vampire, her fine pale hair framing her face – Rose could see a pulse beating in the hollow of Miss Lillian's throat, and thought of a majestic warbling bird about to take flight and soar. After all were satisfied, Miss Lillian leaned over and kissed Miss Dorothy on the mouth, saying, "You've done well," and then turned to Rose and smiling her famous quick smile, said, "You've done well, too, tadpole." Her smile faded as quickly as it came, replaced again by the sad, lost look.

Rose was just beginning to bask in the shed light of the two naked, iridescent movie stars when Mrs. Gish returned home. She stood in the doorway of the bedroom, wearing widow's weeds and a string of pearls. Glaring at her daughters, she shouted, "I will not stand for this!" stamping one delicate, booted foot. "Will I have to sleep between the two of you for the rest of my life?!" As Mrs. Gish continued to rage, the sisters pulled Rose to her feet and gently helped her dress, almost as if they were dressing a cherished doll, patted her hair in place, then walked her to the waiting car. Each sister kissed her on the cheek, and then, hand in hand, they returned to the house, where the lights went out one by one.

Rose stayed in Los Angeles for four years, working in the movies, until the talkies came along. She never became a movie star.

Editor's note: Mrs. Mary Gish, herself a movie actress, did indeed sleep in a bed between her two daughters until the end of her life, in 1948. Dorothy Gish died in 1968 at the age of 70; her older sister Lillian died in 1993 at the age of 99. Both sisters had careers in the talkies.

A. N. Graeme
THE ARTIST'S MODEL
1933

Only a few weeks remained in the term. Ava Scott walked slowly from student to student, wandering throughout the big, drafty studio checking each easel with her practiced eye, lifting a brush here, patting an arm there, murmuring encouragements and gentle admonitions. She liked this group of students, all of them true painters, not mere illustrators, or worse yet, dilettantes. Yet, although most of them were quite talented and all were driven, Ava knew that fine arts had ceased to be a field for men and had never been one for women. These were not Renaissance times, they were lean, scrabbling times. Her students, with their fresh faces, bright eagerness, and passionate, late-night discourses about art and politics at the local boîte shouted over cheap wine and Gitanes, were destined for the illustrator's factory. There simply was no place for a real painter any more, save the small hell of studio portrait painting or the indignities of tourist croques on the Rue de Chartres.

Ava strode to the window and looked out briefly at a darkening, autumnal sky. She could paint this gorgeous Parisian vista, romantic as it was realistic, in her sleep, but no matter. There were no buyers, not now, not when even the rich were pinching pennies. Which was why she was here, teaching these young hopefuls (she herself had been one of them not so long ago) to dream a dream she had – if she were brutally honest with herself – all but relinquished.

A little trill of notes came from behind an easel across the room. *Elise.* Lithe and languorous, Elise stood in a comically large white smock, a caricature of an artist, singing to her canvas. The girl regularly broke the painterly silence by bursting into an *a capella* rendition of some tune with her clear, sweet voice. Ava had objected the first time it had happened, but she'd come to welcome the outbursts. It lightened the air, Elise's voice did. Sometimes Ava could actually see the atmosphere lift from the brief spate of notes. Sighs rose with Elise's singing and receded from the studio when she ceased her little concert as suddenly as she had begun.

Yes, Ava's group knit together well, buoying each other up as the term wore on and nerves frayed with worries over what would be next, what the world outside the long, unreflecting windows of the studio held for them.

As Ava studied the progress on what would be their final assignment, she realized with relief that each of her students would pass, which made her job that much easier and made their futures that much more promising, if not actually secure. These paintings, all of Keiko, the model who now lay stretched and naked on a wooden dais at the front of the room, had captured the distinctly unique beauty of this mysterious Oriental girl. Keiko, with her astonishing ability to hold a pose for long, languorous minutes as if she were indeed marble. Keiko, who resembled Manet's odalisque, with her simmering and inchoate sensuality. Keiko, who was unlike any woman Ava had seen before. Her Japanese beauty, foreign and enticingly exotic, charged the room with an electricity when she posed. Fleshy, smooth, pale beyond believability, strikingly beautiful. *Lush*. That is how Ava thought of Keiko whenever the model posed for her classes. *Lush*. Ava had chosen Keiko for this last assignment with careful deliberation. It wasn't simply that the Oriental presented such a fine composition for the life class, with the stark ivory of her skin, her coal-black eyes, and long, shiny, blue-black hair. There were other, compelling features that Ava was drawn to. The first time Keiko had slipped off her kimono, a wave of whispers had rippled through the studio. On her back – the whole of her back – were tattooed an intricate series of scenes, scenes of complex Orientalism, some singular as a cresting wave, others detailed sensual exposés, in which Ava had even spied a man's penis entering the widespread labia of a woman.

Ava had found herself intensely aroused the first time she had discovered the scene, when she had brought the students up, in groups of three, to admire the work of the artist who had executed these remarkable tableaux upon the canvas of Keiko's perfect back. There it was, just above her tiny waist: a man, fully clothed in Oriental regalia, his penis huge and erect, held in his hand like either a sword or a flower, a gift he was to offer his beloved. Before him, the woman, beautiful and petite, her black hair pulled back in an ornate dressing, her neck and throat elegantly exposed. The woman's kimono was open, showing a perfect apricot breast, like some Renaissance painter might reveal a blush of nipple above the décolletage of a woman's gown. This Orientalist nipple was crimson, and the man appeared excited by its appearance. But the more arousing still was what lay below. The woman was cross-legged on a pillow and her thighs were sleek and spread and her labia was open, a flower fully bloomed. There was no hair – the area was clean and bare as a young girl's pudendum. One could see the clitoris, erect as the man's penis, standing away a little from the cerise slit. Exposed and open, waiting for touch, waiting for entrance.

"Her name is Izanami," Keiko had explained. "It means, she who invites you to enter."

After Keiko said this, Ava had wondered how many parents had named their baby girls Izanami once that sensuous connection had been made, or if it had become a popular name among geisha only. For when Ava had first seen the replication of the sexual scene on Keiko's bare skin, she had been stunned. Rarely at a loss for words, Ava had been swept with a wave of sensual longing which she had needed to quell in order to continue her dispassionate lecture. She had glanced furtively at her students. The men were clearly as aroused as she, she saw hands covering the fronts of trousers, men shifting uncomfortably as they do with an erection. Among the girls there was a more subtle responsiveness. Each had been moved by the scene on the naked Eurasian's exquisite back, but there were no bawdy titters, only a somewhat shocked silence. Nevertheless, like Ava herself, it was clear each was pondering the art, the artist, and the surprise of a living, breathing canvas.

Keiko, her head turned and peering over her own illustrated back, had caught Ava's eye. Ava had been unsure what it was in the look Keiko had given her, but it had inflamed her, and she had felt her cheeks redden with the sort of blush she equated with sexual arousal – her own sexual arousal.

She would not become enticed by a model, however. Ava promised herself this. She had been tempted when still a student, but in recent years she had watched the love affairs happen with these models and her friends, men and women. The volatile nature of these girls was well known. One day in your bed, the next in your best friend's. These girls, she knew, were not to be trusted. Ava had witnessed more than one flaming affair burn down to ashes and had also seen one too many scandals erupt. She could not afford such a scandal, nor did she want to risk a bloodied heart.

And so she had turned away from Keiko's beautiful stare, but not before noting a hint of a smile – welcoming? enticing? – flit over the girl's exquisite, perfectly painted lips.

On this day, Keiko had her gorgeous back to the class and her head demurely cast down, a look of sadness or intense contemplation on her lovely face. Ava never knew if these were poses or natural states of being. Was the girl unhappy or simply feigning unhappiness to match the students' endeavors?

Ava tried not to think too much of Keiko, as the girl had come to her thoughts far too often, unbidden, and Ava knew she had to keep her distance. Still, her yearning overcame her at times. One evening a few weeks back, Ava had found herself in bed with a prostitute she had met near the Spanish Steps, a girl she had chosen because she wanted no morning-after tears or whimpered regrets, but also because in the half-light after a few drinks she had seen the girl's long dark hair and envisioned Keiko.

She had taken the girl back to her flat and had posed her on the little bed, and then drawn a crude version of the sexual scene, Izanami and her suitor, upon her back with pastels. She had gazed upon that scene and the girl's long, silken hair as she had made love to her over and over, her arousal intensifying each time as she imagined what it would be like to slip a penis into Keiko's crimson slit, as she wondered if Keiko's clitoris was taut and erect as the one she herself had drawn on the back of the girl in her bed, and what it was she would do with the Oriental's tantalizing lotus bud.

Ava had done many different things with the girl she had bought for the night, whose name had been Felice. Felice was shaven, like the woman in the illustration on Keiko's back. It had been a surprise, a welcome one. The nakedness of the girl's labia had incited her all the more, made her voyeuristic. She had wanted to gaze upon her, this new model, and she even drew a few sketches of her. Lurid, obscene sketches that she would look at later. She had posed the girl against the wall for a time and asked her to spread her pink lips with her fingertips and expose the slit.

Ava had used a deep crimson to draw what it was she saw, what it was she wanted to see. She had refrained from putting her mouth to the exposed bits; yet she imagined doing that to Keiko as she drew Felice's opened slit. When she had finished sketching she had come over to Felice. She had held her shoulders against the wall and kissed her hard, then fingered the little clit until Felice came, making the girl cry out in what appeared to be real, not feigned and paid for, pleasure.

The girl had taken over then, shoved Ava back onto the little bed and undone her trousers, but not before she had pushed her manicured hand against the place where, had there been one, Ava's penis would have been stiff and aching for release. Felice was a practiced girl and had discerned what Ava wanted even before she herself had. The girl had kept on her garters, stockings and shoes, but let all else be removed. Felice knelt over Ava now, her shaven bits spread across her and Ava caught her scent, light but heady, as she opened herself over Ava.

Felice did it to her then, rubbed her clit roughly, her hand slipped through the trousers, frigging her as if she were a man, hard, in a way Ava had not known she'd wanted it until she too came, as much from the images that ran through her head of Keiko in this and that pose like frames of a newsreel as from Felice's practiced and expert touch.

They had smoked together then, in silence, the harsh aroma of the Gitanes commingling with the scent of their love-making. Ava's arm lay casually over the girl's shoulders as if they were lovers, rather than client and patron. Felice had given Ava a good deal of pleasure and she was grateful beyond the payment, which now seemed paltry given the headiness of the pleasuring.

The two had a brandy, then another, and Felice did what all girls who sell themselves do, she started it all up again. The illustration was still clear upon her back and she knew this was the enticement for Ava. She sat at the edge of Ava's bed and slowly turned herself, exposing the drawing. Then she bent forward, her well-shaped derriere protruding toward Ava. She lifted it further upward and then shifted on her knees, opening a space between her legs where Ava could see the shaven slit, glistening in the burnished glow of the lamp beside the bed.

Ava had come up behind her and run her hands over the smoothness of Felice's buttocks. She undid her trousers then and took them off and stood in only her shirt, close to Felice's raised bottom.

She got onto the bed behind the girl and held her hips fast. She slapped Felice lightly on the raised part and the girl cried out, involuntarily, more from surprise than any bit of pain, for the slap was light, and mostly playful, although Ava did not feel playful, she felt a wave of obsessive longing and an urge to be rough rather than tender.

There it was – the pictorial on Felice's back, the welcoming slit of Izanami and the wide open slit of Felice. Ava slid her fingers along the girl's dampness and played with the little bud, pulled at it and pinched it a bit until she had the girl writhing in earnest. She pulled the girl back, as if onto her lap and she felt the hot, round buttocks splayed against her own arousal and she wanted to feel it spread over her.

Ava turned the girl around, so she was straddled by her dampness, soft thighs and eager wanting. This would be good, just as the other bit had been. Ava was deeply aroused. The room had gone hot from the sex and the smoking. Music wafted up from the floor below her flat and the whole thing had the atmosphere of a Hollywood film, smoky and sensual and just a bit dangerous.

She took the girl's hand and put it between her own legs and asked the girl to rub her again as she had before. But this time Ava was frigging the girl at the same time, playing with the little slit as the girl rubbed her own piece roughly, getting it fully hard and ready for orgasm.

She held the girl tight against her lap as she fondled her, pinching her nipples and pinching her clit in equal measure until Felice grabbed Ava's hand and held it between her legs and pushed it back and forth over her slit, fast and faster until she took in her breath very deep and Ava could feel Felice squeeze against her and knew she was fully spent. It took little more of the girl rubbing her to make her come as well.

Ava had rarely felt such supreme pleasure. Most girls she'd been with had always held themselves too primly, held themselves back, as if acknowledging either their own or her pleasure was to admit to something base and low, acknowledge something animal in themselves that they associated with men, not women. They had moved prettily in her bed and there were little stifled cries, but nothing like the intensity of the passion she had felt with Felice. She tried not to think of how she'd wished her other women had been whores, yet there it was – the languid prostitute knew what she wanted and gave it, apparently willingly. And apparently was what she needed right now.

At twenty-nine, after many a dalliance, some more long-lived than others, Ava could say with a bittersweet clarity that Felice had pleasured her best of all, had somehow known what it was that Ava wanted, and given it to her without judgment or demur. The price was hardly steep and, for Ava, worth more than what had been decided upon for the night.

And there were the sketches, besides. The sketches over which she would stand but two nights later, one hand firmly on her desk, the other fingering herself through her trousers just as Felice had done, only to far less satisfaction. Still, it gave her pleasure —both the lewdness of the drawings and memory of the lewdness with Felice.

Ava had contemplated asking the girl back, ached to do so, in fact, to make it a regular engagement. But Ava feared exposure or blackmail. It was not unheard of. The girl knew what Ava wanted, that was apparent from the manner in which Felice had frigged her, had found her desire and plundered it. In the end she decided to make one more date, for the same. She wasn't sure if it would replicate what she'd experienced that night, but she knew even a lesser round of the same would be worth both price and risk.

The girl had left before dawn, after Ava had washed the drawing from Felice's back. Left despite Ava's urging that she stay and be bought breakfast. She and Felice had agreed upon another night the following week, and Ava knew she'd think of the girl – or at least what had transpired between them – a good deal between now and then, the memory heating her up easily and to completion more than once.

Ava thought of that night with Felice now, as she stood before Keiko's tattooed back, tapered at the slender waist. Her back with its sensuous portraiture, so delicate in comparison to what she had fitfully drawn on Felice. Each time she gazed at Keiko – her ethereal beauty spread out before her, a visual feast – she could not help but become aroused. She was certain Keiko knew her feelings, sensed her arousal. Whether or not Keiko returned those feelings, she certainly played upon them with her extravagantly languorous poses and looks.

Ava immersed herself in that visual feast of the hours in which Keiko's inert form was laid out before her. Was it voyeurism if she and her students all looked at Keiko as if she were fruit and flowers laid upon a table, like any classic Dutch still-life? Or was it simply the job at hand? Ava glanced furtively at the men in the room to see if she could discern whether or not they were aroused by the beautiful body before them still as she continued to be, but each appeared intent solely on the work itself, ignorant of the enticements of Keiko's sensuality, where once they had not been.

As she strode through the studio, Ava could see her model evoked with great intensity and passion in each painting. Lucy focused on Keiko's beautifully shaped head cradled in the crook of her extended arm, her long, shiny black hair displayed like a peacock's fan behind her on the dais. Bill, his bold use of white and black with just the slightest slashes of brilliant color outlining this or that feature, had brought Keiko's voluptuous curves into the foreground with such drama that Ava caught herself as she reached toward the wet canvas, then lifted her eyes from it to the girl who seemed to barely breathe on the platform before her.

Ava passed along from easel to easel, sometimes taking the brush to explain how a line would better flow, sometimes just miming it above the canvas with her finger. She felt a rush of contentment at the depth of her students' work and something else. She knew what it was, but feared the definition. With this assignment ended the weeks of Keiko on display before her. Keiko whom she watched slink into the room for each class, her body clothed in demure, muted outfits, her hair pulled back in a thick and unfashionable chignon. Unlike other figure models who came to the classes wearing a kimono and nothing else, changing in the room off the studio, Keiko frequently came into the studio in her street clothes and undressed at the edge of the dais as if alone. Seated, like one of Degas's dancers lacing up her ballet shoes, Keiko would begin the undoing of buttons and unzipping of skirts. She would stand and slip off her skirt, which would fall from her perfectly rounded hips. She would shed her sweater or jacket, her hair would be loosed.

It was then she looked most like one of Toulouse-Lautrec's fleshy girls from the Moulin Rouge, in her pale pink chemise, black stockings and short laced boots. Once nude, her black hair cascading in shimmery waves over her shoulders, strikingly dark against the whiteness of her torso, Keiko would turn away from the class, exposing the incredible Orientalia of her tattooed back. On these occasions when Keiko disrobed before the class, Ava would be incited to touch her and at times would grab a brush and grip it tightly, anything to compose the hands that ached to place themselves on Keiko's voluptuous body.

Ava had long ago abandoned wondering if, as Keiko pulled a kimono from her bag – either vermillion or teal – and fluttered it over her body, if Keiko did this matter-of-fact strip-tease on purpose. Not as a tease, per se, but as a query of sorts, a question about her students' knowledge: how many painters are represented on my back and from what periods?

This day, as was true of every day Keiko posed for her, Ava was struck by Keiko's rich, textured presence on the dais, in her studio. Oddly, she felt no sense of possessiveness over the girl, despite her obsessive longing. Yet at the same time, she could hardly bear the thought of the girl leaving and never returning.

Ava had never painted Keiko herself and now, as the hours grew short, she suddenly longed to do so. She had recorded every movement, every nuance, every turn and gesture, every subtle shift in shadows of Keiko's body in previous classes. She knew she could paint Keiko from memory, but she wanted more than memory. Even with Felice memory had been poor substitute for the girl herself.

Outside the long rectangles of window which ran nearly floor to ceiling throughout the big, whitewashed room, the sky had flushed a deep magenta. Indigo spread along the tip of the horizon, purpling beneath. A peal of five bells from the carillon of the cathedral nearby sounded plaintively through the late autumn afternoon, accompanied by the more muted sounds of traffic and the occasional cacophony of taxi horns.

As the bells rang out, her heart fluttered. The time was up, the class had ended. There would be no more with these students, save their final presentation. And no more Keiko, either. This part of their link was broken.

"We're finished, now. Time to pack it in." Ava's voice broke through the concentrated hiss and scratch of brushes on canvas. Sussurant voices – murmurs of relief mingled with a few of disappointment that more hadn't been accomplished in these hours – soon became the banging and scraping sounds of their leave-taking. From the dais Keiko rose languidly as if from a late-afternoon nap and stretched her luminous arm to reach for the pool of silk kimono that lay on the floor nearby. As she sat forward, Ava glimpsed her legs spread briefly, caught the quick flash of vermillion slit, while her arms raised themselves into the arms of the robe. Ava caught her breath and called goodbye to the last student. They would return in a week with their final presentations.

Ava reached in the pocket of her black trousers for the one cigarette she always kept there. Ava had barely smoked since that night with Felice. She generally bought one pack of Gitanes a week, but always put a cigarette in her mouth after each class. She never lit it, just let it loll on her tongue, hang from the corner of her mouth till she left the studio. She would light it as she went on toward home and her flat where the many small drawings of Felice were tacked to a corkboard, studies for a painting she knew she would never make – too lewd – but handy for the arousal they continued to engender.

Ava could feel her stomach flutter, and something else, as she turned toward Keiko, who sat, as immobile as if the students were still working, at the edge of the dais, kimono not completely closed over her small, full breasts.

Ava stared directly at Keiko, then strode to the door, her long slender legs liquid with something akin to fear. The sharp click of the lock reverberated too loudly in the cavernous studio with its high ceiling and concrete floor. The snap of the shade being pulled over its small window sounded like a hand slapping flesh. Ava turned, braced herself against the door and looked directly at Keiko who stared back with equal intensity, but intensity Ava could not fully read.

Ava clicked off every light but the one illumining the dais.

"Do you want to paint me now?" The model hadn't moved, yet now she too held a cigarette, unlit, between her brightly painted fingertips which were deeply red, and shimmered, like her hair.

"I can stay all evening." Keiko paused, looking at Ava full-on. "If you want," she added, her voice suddenly lower.

What was in that pause? Muriel still held a paint brush in her hand. Small, sable-tipped, soft. It had never actually touched paint. Merely a prop, a teaching tool. Sometimes she used it, other times she used a pointer. She held it out toward Keiko the way an artist does, gauging size and perspective. Keiko now stood slowly, dropping the unlit cigarette to the floor and ground her pale, bare foot against it. The room was chill and Ava felt her nipples harden suddenly beneath her heavy chamois shirt. Her clit throbbed just as suddenly – or so it seemed. Yet she knew the wetness between her legs had begun much earlier and was merely building to this moment, this moment when she was going to trace the outlines of the body she had seen in her mind's eye over and over, that she had mimicked on the back of the girl, Felice. She held the brush tightly as she imagined tracing Keiko's illustrated back with her fingers, her tongue, and the very brush she gripped so hard in her hand.

"Yes, I want to paint you. I always want to paint you." Ava, too, discarded her cigarette, slipped it back into her trouser pocket for when she would need it, later. She ran her hand through her short auburn hair and bent toward Keiko who stood directly before her, the white and illustrated body barely covered by the kimono.

Ava put her hand to Keiko's elegant, silken neck, lifting the heavy drape of hair. Keiko leaned away, sat back down upon the dais, said nothing. Now, so close to the Japanese beauty, Ava could see that she was breathing quickly, could see the flutter of the pulse in the ivory neck, could see deep into eyes dark as the night soon would be.

"Paint me, then." Keiko's voice, sudden as it had come, startled Ava. Her voice was lush and fleshy, like her body, and silken, like the kimono she now slithered from as she took Ava's hand, the one with which she held the sable brush, and began to trace the soft taut fur of the tip over her breasts, down her stomach, onto her lovely shaven mound and into the crevice between her thighs.

"Paint me," Keiko breathed as she pulled Ava down onto her upon the chill, white platform where she had lain like a beautiful corpse for three hours, barely moving, barely seeming even to breathe.

"Paint me," she whispered into Ava's ear as she kissed the artist's throat, pushed the brush hard into Ava's grasp and spread her legs wide beneath her. Ava lifted herself off Keiko. She lay beside her, stroking her with the brush, her tongue running along an ivory arm, teasing a dusky-pink nipple. Keiko turned toward Ava, the liquid flow of her body cantilevered on the edge of the dais.

Before Ava she lay, the eternal artist's model, the girl she had watched so furtively, rising from the dais like Boticelli's Venus. Keiko. Ava ached to paint her, to immortalize her, suddenly understanding as she never had as a student or even in the years she had taught her own students, what it was that led painters to obsessive mania over their models, what it was, she now realized, that led to brilliance, to greatness and, inevitably, to destruction.

Keiko lay still before her, immobile as she always was, except when she took off her clothes for each class.

"Dress."

Ava's voice was harsh with longing for Keiko, desire pumping through her thick and hot as her own blood. Keiko sat and began the reverse of her striptease. When she was ensconced in her Moulin Rouge camisole and slip, Ava knelt before her, pushing her knees apart. Black stockings to the thigh but nothing else. The shaven labia looked damp to Ava, Keiko's scent barely discernable over linseed oil and paint. Ava ran her brush up Keiko's white thighs and dipped its sable tip into the dampness she had seen. Keiko shuddered, but didn't move.

"Paint me, more," was all she said, her voice barely audible.

As Ava's fingers pushed into Keiko's silken slit, her own clit throbbed hard and pulsing as any cock. She leaned Keiko back, pressed her knee between the model's legs, her fingers stroking deep and long, in and out of her. Ava's fingers were slick with Keiko as she moved quickly, rhythmically, feeling Keiko's soft flesh trembling beneath her, small animal sounds coming from the back of her throat.

"You are every painting that ever took my breath away," Ava whispered in the model's ear as Keiko's sheath tightened over her fingers, her thighs squeezing against Ava's knee even as she tried to keep herself still, maintain the pose at which she had become so expert.

"I can't stop looking at you," Ava murmured. "I see you when I paint, I want to draw you all the time."

Keiko's lips were all over Ava's neck and cheek as she came, hard, her gasps echoing softly in the studio, her breath hot against Ava's skin.

Ava collapsed on the dais next to Keiko, her fingers gleaming wet in the luminosity of the spotlight. The little sable brush lay in the small space between them. Keiko sat up, pulling off her camisole and tossing it aside. She picked up the brush, its tip still damp, and traced the outline of her nipples. Ava squeezed her thighs together, her gaze rapt at Keiko's exquisite face, now flushed for the first time with color. Keiko leaned her lush breasts over Ava's taut body, straddling her, black-stockinged thighs gripping Ava's slim hips. Ava could feel the heat of Keiko's slit on her thighs and pulled Keiko's hips down onto her. Keiko held the brush-tip against Ava's lips, ran it down her neck, the space between her breasts at the opening of her shirt. She turned the soft end into her hand and ran the handle between Ava's legs, pressed it hard against the clit thick and throbbing against the crotch of Ava's pants. Tip positioned against her own clit, wooden handle stroking hard against Ava's, Keiko moved as deftly as she had always before remained so still. Ava closed her eyes, images of paintings, each featuring Keiko, flashing like a slide show as her breath came faster and faster, as she pushed her swollen clit up toward this painting-come-to-life leaning into every part of her, this girl she had watched with studied voyeurism, week after week.

Keiko rocked her hand and the paint brush hard against them both until Ava came, explosively, in wave after wave of pent-up orgasm. Then Keiko opened her lips wide with one hand as she flicked the brush back and forth over her clit with the other.

"Watch me paint," she commanded Ava in a low voice.

* * *

The bells pealed again out in the now-dark evening. Keiko kissed Ava softly on the lips and neck, then finished dressing, finally winding her hair up into its chignon. Ava stood slowly, taking up her brush and Keiko's discarded kimono.

"I'd like to paint you again," she said, not touching Keiko, holding the brush, its moist tip between her fingers, close to her lips.

"I am an artist's model. I pose when asked," Keiko replied, her voice still heated. She took the kimono from Ava's hand, touching it lightly against Ava's cheek and walked toward the door. Ava heard the lock click open, and the door shut behind the girl. She sat down on the edge of the dais and closed her eyes. She saw Keiko's illustrated back, her crimson slit, her apricot breast. She saw Izanami, she who invites you to enter. She lifted the brush to her lips and touched the tip of her tongue to the dampness there. Then she rose, took the cigarette from her pocket. She had an appointment to meet with Felice later.

Ava walked slowly through the canvases one last time, then she turned out the light, grabbed her coat, slipping the brush into the pocket, and left, walking purposefully down the stairs and onto the street. She stopped and looked out onto the Paris street. She lit her cigarette and turned toward home.

Gale Wilhelm
from WE TOO ARE DRIFTING
1935

Those seeking blatant sexual explicitness will not find it in these excerpts from Gale Wilhelm's extraordinary novels (see also *Torchlight to Valhalla*, also in this volume). What they *will* discover is a potent and simmering sensuality with some overt sexual references. Wilhelm's discourse on the sexual aspects of relationships between women is so ahead of its time that it will astonish readers, as Wilhelm delineates lesbian relationships more powerfully than many lesbian writers are doing seventy years later. The sexual tension between the women in Wilhelm's writing is tantalizing.

–Victoria A. Brownworth

Jan opened the car door and said, Get in, I'll drive.

If you like, Madeline said.

I want to go home, Jan said. She went around the car and got in.

All right, Madeline said. She gave Jan the keys and tucked herself down beside her. Couldn't we take a little drive first, darling?

No, thanks, Jan said.

Madeline tucked herself closer. Jan thought how wonderful it would be to be starting off somewhere with Victoria, Victoria who loved to drive at night, Victoria with her hair whipping up in lovely curling wisps. She looked up and saw the stars scattered and clear in the early dark and Madeline said, Darling, please don't look so black about it. I'm not going to be silly. She lifted her head and said gently, Jan does she really mean so much to you?

Yes, Jan said. She turned into Post Street and wanted to be standing with Victoria in Post Street and fog over the street and people hurrying past.

You never were that way about me, Madeline said. This is something you think you can't do without and you knew all the time you could do without me very nicely, didn't you?

Jan looked at her. What do you want to say?

Madeline looked up and said, I love you so terribly. You don't seem to think of that at all. Am I just to snap my fingers and say, There it's over? You don't think of me at all. Jan, remember the time at Highlands? Jan glanced at her and she said, I wish we could drive down there tonight and do that again. I mean everything, just as it was that time.

Are you crazy? Jan said.

I'd love to be if you'd be too, Madeline said. Jan, that morning in the park when I saw you with her I wanted to kill her and then I wanted to die, Jan, and then I wanted to hurt you terribly. I don't mean with the scorper or whatever it was but...

I know, Jan said. Let's not talk about it.

No, what I mean is I don't mind your being in love with her, she's so terribly sweet, but, darling, why couldn't you...

Are you crazy? Jan said.

When you changed that way almost overnight, darling, Madeline said, you can't really blame me, can you?

Jan drew in along the curb and slipped the motor out of gear but didn't cut off the ignition. Sit up, Madeline. Look at me. You knew damned well it was all over months ago, didn't you?

I knew you thought it was, Madeline said, but you've never treated me nicely for more than a day at a time and, oh, darling, it's so silly. She took Jan's hand and held it between her hands and said, Darling, if you'll let me come tonight I'll promise you anything. I'll give you my word.

Without any warning Jan felt the dark swift pain and it darkened her face and she knew it was there still. She hated it and knew it was there and it sickened her. Madeline felt it in her hand and she said, I'll give you my word, darling.

Jan stared at the back of Madeline's hand covering her hand. You haven't any word, she said, but she knew it was there in her and it sickened her, but it was there.

Madeline locked the car and took the keys. Jan stared at her hand black against Madeline's hand. Come on, darling, Madeline said, and she opened the door and got out and Jan got out and Madeline drew her hand up under her arm and they went up the steps and Jan opened the street door and they went inside. Going up the stairs she knew it couldn't be true that they were going up the stairs like this together again. But she knew they were going up the stairs. She was terribly aware of Madeline and she hated it and it was sickening but it was true. Then why didn't she stop, why didn't she stop Madeline? Her throat was small and tender, why didn't she kill her? If she killed Madeline it would be all over and finished. Why didn't she? Because it was in her and deep, it had been acting asleep but it was there and hating it didn't matter. She unlocked the door. It the dark room she stood with her back against the door and something was dying in the room, something was dead.

They were awake and still in the morning light and when Madeline could see Jan's face clearly she said, Darling, please don't look so black and lost, wasn't I nice? You were darling. She pushed back Jan's hair and kissed her forehead and closed her eyelids with her lips and kissed them and kissed the hollows that seemed deeper under her cheekbones and said, Darling, I know what you think, but it's not true. I give you my word. She looked closely at Jan's thin dark face, searching for some sign, but there was none. The eyes were still and the gray deeper and darker, but there was nothing there. She put her lips in the cup at the base of Jan's throat and tasted salt and said, Darling, please don't look so lost about it. She looked closely at Jan's face and she knew suddenly and finally that this blankness was the invulnerability of absolute indifference and she said, Oh, darling, I can't believe it means so much to you.

She gave this moment, this knowledge a few tears. Jan gave it nothing.

Lois Lodge
from LOVE LIKE A SHADOW
1935

I

The two girls walked quietly over to the window, and watched the car leave. The elms were so bare, they could see it weave to the far end of the campus, to be swallowed up in the black ambiguity of the town streets.

Jean Moorhead was the first to turn away. Impatiently she tossed her evening wrap toward the Morris chair beside the study table. It slid neglected toward the floor. "So much for that," she said. Her voice was squeezed and dry. Her head was turned broodingly away from the other girl's.

"Didn't you enjoy it, darling?" Alice Jennings retrieved the wrap, smoothed the white fox neckpiece, hung it so that the metal cloth cleared the rug. Her eyes studied the svelte flawless figure of her roommate furtively, a part of a covert never-ending appraisal. "It's the last Thanksgiving Prom *we'll* ever go to."

"I thought it was foul. Why must men make a dance the stuffiest thing in the world? I feel filthy all over. – Dirtied. – Unclean." In tense agitation, she moved her lovely hands up from her waist to her neck, and then let them slip down to caress the soft outswell of her young breasts, beneath the crumpled orchid gown that had been such a fresh unworn pride to her, five hours before. "I feel as if I'd been in the gutter... in a pigpen."

"Anything especial happen?" A furtive remote gloating appeared in the older girl's shrewd eyes.

"Oh, nothing. I got pawed, that was all. I got mauled. That was enough," her tone low and rasping. "That little shrimp from Amherst, Ed Scribner, isn't it? – He tried to kiss me, when we were out on the porch for a breath of air. He wouldn't stop. And the tall Pointer – you know, the football one – he tried to make me swallow a drink; heaven knows he'd had too much. He could hardly stand... And then Roddy – " The color slowly deepened in her young cheeks, "he was the worst of all, Al. I don't care if he is your cousin, he's a beast! He got me out in a car, and he – His hands…" She shivered, she grew suddenly silent. "Of course, I didn't let him touch me. I mean, really. But he tried to. They all did. Look at this waist," cheeks rosier in her angry embarrassment. "I feel slimy, where they touched me. I'm going to take a bath," with bitter finality. "I won't feel clean for a week." In swift anger, her deft fingers lifted the skirt of her dress, and moved it delicately up, until she could slip out of it.

Alice watched her with warmer eyes, forever appraising, weighing. Her tongue moved once around her mouth. She swallowed unobtrusively. "Come on over to me, darling."

She had never seen any girl as beautiful as Jean. Everybody in Chadwick said so. They would ask Jean to lead the Daisy Chain—they would have to! Once Alice had hoped for this. But not now. She had had lovely roommates the three preceding years, but none like this tempestuous Southern beauty. She could understand what moved behind men's hot and lidded eyes, when she looked at Jean. The girl had a figure that could have been used by God to model his angels from. She had the body of the Cnidian Aphrodite, and a head poised as proudly as that of Artemis leading the chase. And no man had ever known her yet… no man had ever known her yet! Please God, no man would ever have her! Alice's tongue moved hotly within her mouth once again, again she swallowed unobtrusively. She had seen the full splendor of her roommate's body time after time; she could never tire of it. The thrill of it made life sing. In her dress, or as now in the tantalizing lacy loveliness that curtained the shrine, she was a constant and infinite temptation to Alice. She wanted to rip the silk and the lace, and bare the full flower again. But the time would come. The time was bound to come.

Jean came softly over to her. Her eyes were gentler now. "What is it, dear?"

"Throw your arms around my neck." Alice's voice was queer and oddly strained. "Kiss me. Tell me you love, and nobody else."

"But you already know it already, dear," in soft surprise.

"Tell me – *now*!"

There was ineffable adoration on Jean's face, as she let her arms cling tensely around the other girl's body. "I love you, dear." It was a whisper. The color deepened in her rose-sweet cheeks.

Even as her lips were parted sweetly to finish it, Alice's lips closed hotly, conqueringly, over them. They clung hotly, moistly, leechingly.

Senses a little dizzy, Alice let her go at last. "I'll take a tub too." Her tone was hurried. She half turned her back, and began to slip out of the slinky black lame she was wearing.

Laughing a low little song, Jean went ahead with her disrobing. Off came the magenta slippers, the deep-toned silk stockings, one by one. She stretched her cramped pink toes, one by one, in relaxed serenity. "If only men could kiss like that," she meditated aloud. "I adore it, when you kiss me."

"Men try to." Alice had her dress and underthings off, and hovered uncertainly above the exquisite other girl, eyes still devouring her. "Roddy kisses pretty well."

"But it isn't the same thing." She smiled up at the other girl, as her slim fingers undid the brassiere, and began to remove it. "I've never liked it. Mother once told me never to let a man abuse my mouth. – I never want to."

"But she didn't say anything about *girls*." Alice's addition was a little song of triumph.

"Oh, that's different. There couldn't be anything wrong in my loving you." Her whole soul was serene.

Covetously Alice watched the unfolding of each blossom of a breast. "You have the most beautiful body in the world, darling. Just made to be loved and oh, so tenderly!"

"That was one of the things made me so wild with Roddy." The color was still high in her cheeks. "When he was mussing me. He slipped a hand inside, before I dreamed of what he was doing, and… Why, he must have left bruises, Al, he squeezed so hard!" She studied herself ruefully.

The other girl shivered, and knelt protectively lower. "I'm going to kiss the hurt away."

Jean's soft hazel eyes rounded in surprise. Her tone was faintly thrilled. "Why, if you really want to, Al… Isn't that what that lecturer was talking about, in the Y? – Things like that?"

"We love each other, darling; that's all that matters." Never before had Alice summoned up courage to suggest a thing like this. She had wanted to, for more than a year, now. She had to rein her emotion in, now, to keep from revealing how frantically she wanted to clench the other girl. "It can't be wrong." Reverently she let her lips descend. There was a prayer in her soul, as she closed her eyes and let her lips see instead.

"People would talk," her voice a bit uncertain. "Teachers, and all…"

The room was quiet for a long sweet time. Alice sat up at last, her fingers weaving restless harmonies on the velvet flesh. "I never told you, but my freshman year, one of the teachers kissed me… That way. I had a dreadful crush on her, even before… Peggy. They're human, too. When one's living in the house with you, as monitor, and all… She taught me how. It drove me wild." There was a calculated hopefulness in her eyes, as she watched the other girl's face. "You – you *like* it, darling?"

Jean shivered a little. "It does things to me. I – I like it," color still high. "No one ever has," eyes still vaguely troubled.

"The other," imperatively, huskily.

Jean relaxed quietly, staring with strained happy eyes at the ceiling.

Alice spoke at last. "Did he touch only your breast?" Her voice was hushed almost to silence.

"N-no," flushing with remote anger. "I couldn't stop him, Al! Honest. He – he touched me all over. I pushed him away, and got out, and ran. I wouldn't stay out the dance with him. I swear I couldn't help it."

"I worship you." It was a prayer, this time.

Jean lay dreamily where the other girl had pushed her. The hush in the room was pulsing.

"Let's take that bath." Alice rose. She did not look at her roommate. Her eyes would have been too eloquent. "Time for little girls to go to sleep."

They were in bed together before she started speaking again. "Men can't love, the way a woman can." The voice was confident. The uncertainty was hidden.

"I couldn't let a man touch me, that way." In sweet honesty, Jean let her restless fingers pat the other girl's shoulder gently. "I'd die, if a man even saw me, naked. It's no more than being with myself, when I'm with you."

"Because I can understand." Alice's own body was singing in a key too high. "Take Roddy. I like him. I suppose, if I didn't have you, I might learn to love him. He says so. But it couldn't be the same thing. Never. When you've been raised with a boy, even if he *is* only a second cousin… He's swell, in lots of ways. You know, he made his Y in track, this year. And he's president of Dramat, and on the News board, and all. But he can never understand," with finality.

"Why do they talk about girls?" Jean wrinkled her forehead in the intimate dark. "Lectures, and all. Anything sterile is wrong. That's what she said. But that's silly. A statue, a painting… They don't have to have babies."

"They've got to have something to talk about. Morality is just older people, who're too old really to love, trying to keep others from being natural. They say lots worse things about being with men."

"I don't see why he bothers with me, at all. He wants to marry you." The overtone of resentment was still there.

"That's the way men are. All of them." There was no uncertainty now. "A man can't be what a woman is – sensitive, intuitive… He can't be really subtle. – Like the male after the queen bee. He's got only one idea, and then he dies. They're like bears, or big chows: they rush barking at you, and want to knock you down, and jump all over you, licking your hands, your face, anything. And it doesn't mean anything. Except that they're just like a dog with a – lady dog," the voice stiffening to primness. "That's not real love. It's just something they want; and, once they've gotten it… A girl is never like that." Her voice was confident again. "It's forever, with girls. Girls can understand. A man can't."

"I can't understand girls that do like them," in a puzzled wondering voice. "It seems so… low."

Alice nodded. "Look at 'Liss Metcalfe, with Tony. And Mary Castleman, and Hilda, and little Skeets Bowman. Everybody in college knows what they do. They go the limit. They won't deny it. Everybody knows it. And it's all so furtive, and disgusting. They can't even see the boys, except on weekends at home, or at the dances or something like that. If the faculty ever guessed… Or their people… You remember what happened to Mildred Whistler, only last Easter. It means disgrace. I mean," she made it clearer, "merely if it's found out. – Expulsion. And that isn't the only disgrace, sometimes, darling." Her tone grew more significant. "Mildred Whistler had a baby. Zoe told me so, and she'd roomed with her. They hushed it up, of course; even her family. It got adopted. They had to. But think of how dreadful! – No, *that* wasn't sterile."

"It's utterly disgusting. I can't understand how a girl would let a boy touch her." Jean spoke as firmly as the other girl, now. "I never liked boys, that way. Back home, even when I was a kid, I never liked to play with them. They're nice enough, for boys. But there's a difference."

"They're that way, in Baltimore; Southern boys are kind of nice. – On the surface, anyhow. Out West, they're not even that. Not only Cleveland; everywhere out there. They're… they're beasts, Jean: what you said. Jean, they'll force a girl, if they can't get her any other way. You know that. And what you're always reading about in the papers… Can you imagine a woman forcing another woman – or anybody? It's the whole difference between the sexes. That's what men really are:" Alice was struggling to phrase it perfectly. "They can never put themselves in the position of the other person. Selfish; nothing but selfish. You know," a faint exulting flush stained Alice's unseen cheeks now, "what you let me do, tonight, I've wanted to do, from the first night we roomed together. – Just to kiss your breasts. I never even breathed it to you, before tonight. I would have died before I'd have done anything you didn't want me to. But that's the way girls are. Men…" Her voice trailed off.

"Out West, it's anybody. Men," Alice said with disgust. "—But I can love you," like a song it came forth, "morning and noon, and all day and all night, and all the time, and we can live together and everything, and everybody knows it's all right! It's more like a real marriage."

"I suppose it is. I'd feel slimy, if I let a man touch me." Her voice grew more intense.

There was a long silence. Each girl lay, taut in her own thoughts.

"You never let a man touch you, did you?" Alice's voice was small and very far away.

"Heavens, no! Except… – Like tonight."

"I have."

There was a silence.

"—Roddy?"

"Yes," even more quietly. "They want me to marry him. I was raised with him. I don't mean all the way," in swift self-defense. "I'd never do that, with a man. But that's what's so awful about men. It was Christmas week last year. We were on a house-party. It was a stuffy crowd. He knows I can't drink. So he kept on feeding me out of a flask. Then there was egg-nog, and I suppose everybody got a little high, even the hostess. I didn't know anybody on the party very well, and I – Well, they were all just stuffy. And he was my cousin, and all. So when he slipped up into my room with another bottle, after everybody had gone to bed, I didn't chase him out. I suppose I was lonely for Ruth."

"And he did it, then?" in an awed voice.

Alice sighed. "I didn't know what was happening, at first. I must have been out. Blotto. Then suddenly I knew. Of course, I made him stop. But I'd found out," in a melancholy voice.

"You mean…" The voice was timid. You didn't talk things like this out loud.

"I don't know what just happened. I felt all nice, all over: as if I were on fire. As if the fire was over. I suppose that's what made me come to. It's a blessing I did! I could have killed him, for it!"

Jean lay tenser. She could hardly bring herself to talk. "You didn't like it!" It was an indictment.

"If it had been a girl, I would, darling. I – I know," voice hushed. "But what I meant was, a man can make you feel that way. Never the way a girl can though." Restlessly her fingers stroked the unseen velvet beside her.

Jean could hardly bring the next question out. "Do you suppose he went… all the way?"

"Oh, he didn't, that way. I'm sure of it. He didn't have time. It would have been so different, with a girl." Again and again Alice came back to it. She had already found out that her exquisite passionate roommate was an infant still, in all these things. She had to learn, some time. Somebody had to be the teacher. There was nothing in life that Alice wanted more.

"I've never let anyone touch *me*." It neither asked nor denied.

"A man can," returning persistently to it. "But you don't ever have to let a man touch you, to find out. I could show you."

"I'd be afraid," with a little shiver.

"You love me, don't you, darling?" Her voice throbbed.

"More than anything in the world."

Alice took the other girl in her arms. "I worship you." More than her words spoke.

Jean shivered away. "No. It wouldn't be right."

"If you love me, it is."

Jean's voice was panicky. "Nobody ever has."

"You ought to *know*."

"I suppose I'll find out, some day." Postponement was comfort.

"—For your own protection." The argument was plausible. "So no man could ever do it, to you."

"I'd die, if a man tried."

"I worship you," ever with more insistence.

"Darling, I can't let you!"

Her very uncertainty was a banquet for Alice's desire. The time would come. The time was bound to come. No need to hurry it. "But you do love me."

"You know it! I'd die for you!"

"For Christmas," Alice's voice was very low, "you're going to let me pick my own present, you said."

"Anything you want, sweet."

"Anything I choose?"

"Of course!"

"You swear it? On your sacred word of honor?"

"Why, of course!"

Alice drew in her breath until she thought it would strangle her. Slowly she let it out. "May I tell you... now?"

"Why, of course, dear!"

"You're going to give me yourself," in a low quiet voice. "It's what I want. It's all I want."

"Oh, but, darling—"

"You promised," passionately at last. "We can't go on like this. I lie here beside you night after night, and sometimes I can't sleep all night, for thinking of you – of how heavenly it would be to hold you in my arms, the way I want to! I'll love you forever, nobody in the world can ever come between us! 'Let me not to the marriage of true minds admit impediment—' " The sonorous line rolled out like an epithalamium. "We're married already, in soul, dear. You know it. Let me love you, with all of me!"

Tensely, defensively, Jean had her clenched hands crossed across her breasts. "You know I didn't mean that!"

"—Whatever I wanted," in quiet exultation. "—On your word of honor."

Jean was sobbing, now, soft racking frightened sobs. Alice had her protectively in her arms. But she did not relent. "You promised..."

"I m-meant it. Whatever you wanted." And somehow the other girl's kiss made her forget to cry.

* * *

"I think you're all perfectly disgusting." Verna Stanton eyed her four classmates with level scorn, as they sprawled in undignified dishabille over the bed, the davenport and the big Morris chair, in the room occupied by Jean and Alice. The two inseparables were reclining, as close together as they could get, on the heaped up pillows at the head of the bed. Melissa Metcalfe, slow and blonde and lushly voluptuous, sprayed the length of the davenport. Tiny Skeets Bowman was lost in smiling complacency in the center of the huge chair. To emphasize her attitude, Verna sat stiffly on the edge of a plain Windsor. "Isn't there anything but sex to talk about?"

"Tony isn't sex," drawled 'Lissa. "He's just my boyfriend. You were the one started raving about him. You'd think I was the scarlet woman, or a courtesan like Phryne. I'm not, honestly, Simple. He'll make a good woman out of me, if I'll let him. Whenever I want him to."

"It's none of your business what I do, with Walden." Skeets' eyes flashed fire. "If you snoopers kept your noses in your own business... What business of yours is it, anyhow, *what* Jean and Al do? They've got their own lives to live. Nobody's asking you to live it for them."

"It's all you four talk about," said Verna, vehemently as before. "It's all everybody talks about. We aren't animals. Honestly, the conversation in this college sounds like lady cats yowling. In heat. It's the most disgusting thing I ever heard. If your mothers and fathers knew what you did with your time..." Her prim austere features mottled with morbid shame. "And boasting of it, the way you do!"

"What else is there to talk about?" Alice Jennings hugged Jean closer. "—That's important, I mean? Studies?" Her lips curled downward, her nostril crinkled.

"What do you suppose college is for? Lab work in petting? But that's not all," self-righteously preempting the burden of the conversation. "You'd think you didn't know there was a whole world around you, with a million interesting things to learn – with things happening every minute. Look at the experiment in Russia! They're probably all wrong, but what marvelous things they're trying to do!"

"—Nationalizing women," grinned Alice wickedly. "So you want to go *there*, do you?"

"Look at Italy—"

Jean baited her impishly. "—Tax on bachelors, extra pensions for every baby a woman has, erotic literature forbidden – They never heard of sex there, I suppose! And when Italy was really great—"

"Even a country like Germany—"

'Lissa Metcalfe smiled blandly. "I see that Hitler's just jugged six hundred pansies. So he could get a convenient census of them, I suppose. With telephone numbers."

The one Puritan flushed angrily. "You dirty everything your mind touches! Don't you realize you're in life for a purpose? Is there no such thing as virtue or morality left? What about religion?" triumphantly. "If you went to the Y more, and to petting parties less –"

"You know," there was a dangerous glint in Alice's eyes, "I have my opinion about girls who are too pure. You've been doing all the lecturing. What about yourself? Do you think you're better than we are? Do you think your moral code is higher, or your moral practices more worthy to be open for public inspection? What about making this a sort of confessional – a mourner's bench, with you as the first repentant sinner?"

"I don't know what you're talking about," frosty fire in her eyes. "I'm sure I don't let men paw me, or girls either," with an accusing look at the two girls on the bed.

"No, you don't," said Alice agreeably. "But what do you do? You've got a body, the same as we. You've passed puberty. Your body cries aloud for satisfaction, like any girl's. What do you do with it? Deny the natural demands of it, and call that virtue?"

"There are higher things than mere animal instincts. 'Be ye pure, even as your Father in Heaven is pure.'" She quoted as if that settled all argument.

"Mm-hmm. At that, he did pretty well, as the Holy Ghost. But that's not what you do, Verna Stanton."

"I don't know what you mean." But her face mottled more angrily.

"Oh yes, you do," savagely, tensely. "You roomed with Mary Carter last year, and she's rooming with 'Lissa now. And she's told us plenty, hasn't she, 'Liss?"

"I'll say she – "

"It's a lie, whatever she said." The girl rose nervously, as if to end the discussion.

"Just a moment, before you get out of here – you and your namby-pamby goody-goodiness. You're pure, aren't you? You're sweet and virtuous and unstained, aren't you? But what do you do, Verna Stanton, when you're in bed alone with yourself?"

"I refuse to listen to such dirty insinuations!" Stormily she made for the door.

Alice was off the bed, and before the door, quicker than the other girl could get there. "You'll listen, before you go; you made us listen to your low vulgar insinuations, and now you're going to listen to one simple fact, that everybody in college knows, by now. – The way all you Y sharks get your kick, I suppose. You don't play with girls, and you don't play with men. But Mary has told us, and everybody, what you did by yourself."

"It's a lie, and you know it!"

" 'Be ye pure,' " jeering openly. "And I'd even prefer being with men, much as I detest them, to that sort of sterile amusement, Simple!"

"I'm going," cheeks flushed in hot exasperation. "You dirty everything your mind touches, all of you! I won't waste my time on you—"

"Tony has a nice classmate from Williams – a regular sheik," 'Lissa grinned unrelentingly. "He's coming down next weekend, looking for a hot date. If you want me to teach you how to qualify—"

"Maybe you think there isn't a hell," she threw her head back, eyes gleaming fanatically. "You'll find out, when it's too late! Playing with fire—"

"At least, it isn't our own fingers that get burned," said Skeets, with acid relish.

Verna slammed the door after her.

"Of all God-awful things on earth, I hate a priss most," said the lush blonde. "There isn't a man would look at her. That's why she's so pure," the scorn on the surface.

"You were hard on her," Jean spoke in soft reproof. "She can't help being homely. Even Mary Carter never liked her. I'm sorry for her. I do wish she wouldn't stick her nose into everybody else's business… 'I am so glad that Jesus loves me' – it must be an awfully lonely life."

"I'll be sorry for her, when she leaves you alone," Alice said in loyal indignation. "—And the rest of us. That's what's wrong with the world – silly fools like Simple trying to reform everybody, except themselves. She's a fine one to be giving moral lectures to anybody! She makes me sick! Say, I've got a bottle of wine," eyes bigger. "If anybody can rustle up some cigs…"

"One mo'." Skeets flashed away, and was back as soon as the glasses had been set out. "I always make Walden leave a box or two of Pall Malls with me. – To remind me of him, in between times," with her typical impish grin.

"We don't need to be reminded." Protectively Alice let her arm come to rest around Jean's waist. "That's one of the things wrong with boy friends."

"Don't think the whole world's like college," 'Lissa nodded sagely. "I'll see plenty of Tony, after June. You can't marry your Jean, remember."

"We could live together," said Jean soberly. "I wouldn't be happy if we didn't."

"It isn't so easy." Skeets shook a determined mop of dark hair. "People say things. What'll your people say? It's different with a man. He's supposed to give you a rush. And you can get married, and all. Not that I mind," swift to note the distress on Jean's face. "I've had my crushes, when I was a kid in Miss Garners' – even my freshman year here. But you have to grow out of a thing like that. It takes a man to make love." Her lovely little face grew dreamy for a moment. "You'll find out, some day," she concluded in tempestuous certainty.

"You can't love a thing you're not like." Jean's eyes were far away. "You couldn't love a mushroom, or a flamingo. It's that way with men. You couldn't even really love a man out of your own class. There would be too many differences: everything would clash. Of course, when a man has the same background, that's nearer the real thing. But they never get over being different. No, the real love, the highest love, is when you love something like yourself. Like your own better nature. 'Like calls to like,' " in dreamy complacency. "It's the only ideal mating."

"Pity the world doesn't agree with you," an impish flash of Skeets' eyes going with it.

"Babies – I want babies," smiled 'Lissa indolently. "Oodles of 'em. Tony does, too. When you've got enough nurse and things, they're no trouble at all. And, unless you're going into a profession, or something – And all I'm fit for is to be somebody's wife." She smiled proudly.

"What did that pill say about animal instincts, my child! Any hen can hatch more chickens than you can have babies in a dozen years. And quintuplets won't come into general style, until women get breasts like a lady dog. I'll be no baby incubator, thank you! I want to love and be loved; I don't want to spend a lifetime changing diapers." Alice snuggled closer to the girl beside her.

"No babies for me," Skeets giggled. "But a man – Oh boy!"

"Disgusting," smiled Jean. Her face sobered. "If they didn't paw so! But, if you happen to like it—"

"And how! This is good wine, Alice. Needn't ask if your boy friend gave it to you," with a knowing smile.

But Alice raised her eyebrows at 'Lissa. "It was Roddy. Of course, he's my cousin…"

"And can he pet!" Skeets sighed deliciously. "Boy, if I didn't have Walden, I'd go after Roddy Jennings on roller skates! You don't know what you're missing, Al!"

"You don't know what *you're* missing," in profound thankfulness, from Jean.

The lights seemed more golden, when the two visitors had gone. Invitingly Alice changed to a satin negligee, and with her eyes lured Jean to attire herself more intimately.

"They do seem happy," Jean wondered aloud. "I can't understand it. Of course, 'Liss is just a cow – a very attractive cow, but about as bright as a puddle. But Skeets is different. She has a mind."

"I suppose some girls are just built that way, darling. I couldn't be happy, without you." She had dropped her reserve of demeanor, now. When other girls were present, and most of all when parents or teachers were around, you didn't dare show what you felt. When the two of them were alone, it was all different.

"Two more months," Alice continued, dreamily. "Time just seems to vanish like smoke. It hardly seems yesterday, our Christmas eve." She flushed proudly, looking meaningfully at the girl she adored.

"I think about that night, more than all the rest of my life put together." Jean's voice was low, like silver bells heard over a hill. "I was so frightened… It was the finest thing I ever did in my life, darling. You have to take your courage in your hands, and do things; or life just passes you by. And, oh, my dear, how lonely the two weeks that followed were, down in Baltimore! Everything happening – you know what they do in a Southern town, when everybody's back from college… Dances every night, teas and things every afternoon… And all I could think about was you, and mad I was to lie in your arms all night long! It wasn't so bad, Spring week. I had more to remember, then. I knew, by then, it wasn't all a dream. I knew you were real," her hands stroking the dark hair of her roommate affectionately. "But that Christmas holiday, I thought sometimes that it was all a dream: that it hadn't happened, at all. Just a marvelous dream I had had, that I could never dream again. Oh, my dear, my dear, you've made me so happy!"

"I thought I knew what love was," in reverent thanksgiving, as she snuggled down on the floor at Jean's feet. "Never, until I met you."

A far fugitive shadow crossed Jean's face. "You won't let them separate us, will you, darling?"

"Who?"

"People like Verna Stanton. The world, that envies happiness like ours. We'll room together, after Commencement?"

"I'd rather do it, than anything else in the world." But there was a queer uncertain brooding that Alice could not conceal.

"You will, won't you?"

"I don't see why not. – Not in Cleveland, of course," more decision in her voice. "Mother'd never stand for that. She's heard things." She shivered a little. "I think it was Roddy. Some girl must have blabbed to Roddy. Just gossip. I don't think he even believed it. But he teased me about it, before Mother. And maybe he talked with her. She's... she's said things, Jean. –Things that hurt."

"Not in Baltimore, either," said Jean in a small panicky voice. "They could never understand it, in the South. We could go to New York," in far hopefulness. "I'm going to write plays. Prof. Herndon says I really can. Of course, it'll be slow, at first... But I've got an income from Grandfather; not enough to live on, but enough for a start. I couldn't *live* without you, darling."

"I don't know what I could do," Alice sounded desolate. "Of course, majoring in history, there ought to be something... I wish I knew. There's nothing but my allowance, of course. –Roddy talks about marrying me." She brought it out almost with a gulp.

"But you wouldn't do *that*! Honey, I'd die!"

"It's the last thing in the world I want to do." Her hands fondled the sleek satin, and the warm shapeliness beneath it.

"A play makes a lot of money," in a confidence not fully felt. "All you've got to do is land your first one... They can't separate us now," in a despairing tone. "You're simply everything in the world to me, Al. Everything in college means nothing, compared to you."

"A girl couldn't love a man like that," in a firmer tone. "And that's how I love you too, dear."

"They make it hard for us," in a far away voice. "Everybody talks about your graduating, and then getting married. They take it for granted, down home. There's not a man in Baltimore I'd look at a second time."

"They talk about Roddy, all the time." Alice stared off into the murky night outside. "—As if it were settled. Of course, he's only a second cousin. He's going right into his father's business; he won't have any trouble. But I couldn't love him, after you. There's something coarse about a man; about the finest man." She was on firm ground, at last. "No, it would drive me crazy, if I had to."

"They couldn't make you. We'll just get a little apartment, in New York... And then, for a whole sweet lifetime..."

Alice's tone was lower. "I don't deserve your love, darling. You're the most marvelous thing in the world!"

"Let's go to bed." There was a sudden husky throbbing quality in Jean's voice. This was the best way, she had found out, to forget all doubts, all troubles. In Alice's arms, nothing else mattered, in the whole world. "You yawned."

"—Thinking of Roddy," with a grin. "One nightcap, darling – we'll empty the bottle." She halved what was left. It filled each glass a third full, almost. She raised hers bravely, clinking the rim of the other glass. "Here's to us, together forever!"

"The only toast I'll ever drink!"

They stood, as they drained what was left in the glasses. Wide-eyed, Jean slipped over to the bed, and watched Alice latch the door, and pull down the window for ventilation, and turn to blow a kiss to her as she stood with the light chain in her hand.

She pulled the chain, and darkness rolled into the room. As if it came from the room itself; as if it grew there – For there was a moon there, a soft April moon, peeking in through the wind-teased curtains. There was spring outside, and the soft rustle of young baby leaves, and the drowsy notes of a few night birds, and most of all the silver pour of the moon.

Flesh in the moonlight is ivory, and a little hill can be as tall as heaven. It was brighter outside, but it was warmer inside.

* * *

"And so tomorrow's the great day!" Roddy Jennings smiled down at his cousin and her lovely roommate, that pitying superior smile that a handsome man gives to the rest of the world. This very week the ballots had been announced, and his classmates had selected him as Most Popular Man and as Most Likely to Succeed. You couldn't ask much more than that. He knew that his fishtail was sartorially perfect, and that he might have stepped out of a Twyeffort advertisement. Compared to him, even the two girls who had led the Daisy Chain should be flattered by his noticing them. "And then, you go out to conquer the world, and you begin to get educated!"

Jean smiled happily at him. "Perhaps that's what Yale teaches its prodigies to expect; our demands are much simpler. We're quite content to go on living, enjoying life to the fullest. Of course, I intend my plays to get on, finally; and Al isn't going to write historical studies merely to read them herself. But we're not asking the world to salaam. We know just the kind of little place we'll have in New York, probably in the fascinating Village... Some huge living room in an old-fashioned *pension* facing the Square – I can picture it already, to its last detail. You must drop in and see us, if you ever come East."

Alice stole a frightened look at her roommate. But Roddy's eyebrows curved up in supercilious scorn. "It sounds extremely romantic, almost Cocteau. But there's only one little flaw in your daydream, Jean. You'll have to find some other birdie to share your nest with." There was a sardonic gloat on his handsome features.

"But I don't know what you mean! Al and I –"

His voice purred on. "Alice and I are going to live in Cleveland, after our marriage." He knew how crudely he had phrased it. He had meant it to be as crude as the crack of a lash.

Jean sat stiff and still. The color slowly drained out of her cheeks. Her hands were clenched so tensely that they seemed hempen cords knotted together irrevocably. Her eyes burned anguish toward the other girl. "He's teasing, Al." She could hardly make it as loud as a whisper. "You're not..."

Alice's face was the color of putty. She stared in horrid fascination at the callously nonchalant young man. "You said you wouldn't tell, Roddy. You promised—"

"But you didn't mean Jean, darling. She has a right to know. – Your closest friend, and all..."

Jean seemed to shrink still smaller. Her head stood stiffly up, as if the blow had not quite been able to subdue it. "Tell him he's lying, darling!"

There was something dead in Alice's voice. "I was going to tell you tonight, dear. We're being married at the end of this month. We're going to live in Cleveland. You'll come and visit us –" tempestuously, with a glare almost of hatred at the man.

But here was Jean's escort for the Senior Dance at the door, grinning at the three of them. "Sorry I'm late, children," he breezed easily in. "Taxi had a blowout. All set?"

She couldn't talk, with an outsider present. Jean had to try twice before she could speak at all. She rose, like a thing so fragile that a tiny puff of zephyr could have blown it over the wall and into the sky. "I'm ready," she said. She looked only at her escort. "You've met these people, Mr. Scribner. Shall we go?"

"See you later, children!" Proudly he caught the arm of the beauty of the college, paying no attention to a pallor on her face that no powder could have given. "Boy, I'll bet this will be a big night!" He escorted her almost pompously down to the waiting taxi.

You had to have a man escort you to a dance like this. It was expected. Everybody who was anybody did. Three days before, Jean had insisted to Alice that she much rather not go, if there had to be men there. But she finally admitted that Alice was right: people would talk, and you simply couldn't start gossip. It burned too much.

She was glad, now, that she had decided to let the Amherst senior take her. He was harmless, brainless, and entirely acceptable. His worst fault was trying to make a girl kiss him once or twice during a dance. He never even noticed what a girl was wearing, or how she was feeling, or anything: he had a good time himself, and that was all that mattered. He actually went through the long dreadful hours that followed, without dreaming that the girl he was with might have been dead, for all her interest in what was going on.

Jean showed it as little as possible. She smiled just as fixedly, she acknowledged introductions and went through the motions of enjoying the dances, she answered wisecrack with wisecrack, she played the role of queen on the last night before her abdication with mechanical perfection. But something within her had snapped finally, she knew it. She marveled that she could keep on her feet.

It couldn't be true. It *must* be. Roddy would lie; but not Al. They were going to be married at the end of this month. They were going to live in Cleveland. Tonight was the end of the world... *Last* night was the end of the world. It had already ended.

She forgot to fight back, when Scribner, when two or three others, pocketed her off for a brief tête-à-tête, and insisted on a kiss, or tried to insist on more. "I wish you wouldn't." That was all she could say. She said it so tonelessly, they paid no attention to it, as a protest. But the kisses were no fun at all. Her lips were like marble in a frieze, her body was stiff as if stuffed with sawdust, or limp as a soft pillow. There was no warmth in it, anywhere. She was no fun, tonight, they decided promptly. Better try some other skirt...

He didn't even try to get her to take a drive with him, after it was all over. There was a snappy little waitress at the hotel, who had given him her room number, and said she'd be in. He drove Jean back to the dormitory, and told her goodnight formally.

"It was a swell dance." He put as much enthusiasm in it as he could. Most of it *had* been swell.

"Thank you so much." She shook hands formally with him, as if bidding life adieu. She walked down the hall and up the stairs and into her room, as if to the guillotine.

She did not put on the light at all. She sat collapsed in a chair by the window, not even crying. There was no use to cry. There was no use in anything anymore.

She saw Roddy's car drive up, hours later. She heard the low intimate laughter just below her window, the tense silence, faint sounds that jeered in a way silence could not. She heard Alice come down the hall, and enter the dark room. Suddenly the light flooded everything.

"Oh!" A startled gasp. "You're here, darling! I thought – no light... Waiting up for me? How long have you been here?"

"I don't know." The tone was drained of everything but sound.

A half dozen questions were on Alice's lips. She dismissed them, one by one. They didn't mean anything. She stood staring at the crushed doe, dry-eyed and listless. She hung up her own wrap, and busied herself in the bathroom. She came out after a few moments. Jean had not moved. It hardly seemed that she had breathed.

Still Alice did not know what to say, how to begin. It wasn't her funeral! She took off her shimmering evening gown. She flushed guiltily, eyes suddenly on Jean. It was not the first time she had taken off this gown, tonight. But the other girl was not noticing.

Well, if she wanted to act *that* way! Callously, as if she had been alone, Alice stripped off the two remaining garments. She slipped on a negligee, and stood in the middle of the room, biting her lips, as she stared down at the unmoving figure.

"Aren't you coming to bed?" Alice was almost bitter.

Jean stirred lethargically. "I suppose so." She rose, staggering faintly. Her head seemed whirring around. She steadied herself, face still putty. She did not speak, until methodically she had removed her garments, slipped on a negligee, slid out of it beside the bed, and tucked herself between the sheets. She looked at Alice now. Her eyes were embers.

"Why did you do it?" There was the ghost of emotion in the question.

"You've got to believe me, darling," in increasing panic. "I had to. There was no other way."

"You'd given me you sacred word of honor…" Deep down within her soul, something wailed in agony. No hint of this, in the leaden tone.

"I was going to tell you, tonight. To explain everything…"

Jean considered this for a long chill silence. "It doesn't make much difference now, does it?"

"But you've got to understand," almost hysterically. If only Jean could see it the same way that she did! She came closer and closer to Jean's bed – heart, soul, body aching to comfort the other girl. "There was nothing else that I could do. He made me. Oh, darling," she plunged her head into the fragrant softness of Jean's shoulder, "I love you so, I adore you so, I worship you so!"

"And so," in icy scorn, "you're marrying him."

"You've got to understand!" She sat up, with frightened tragic eyes. "Jean, he knew all about us! He'd found out – from dozens and dozens of girls! Even the Claiborne girls and Mae Hynes, from Cleveland. Girls that all my people knew. He was going to tell Dad and Mother! Beth Claiborne had said she'd go with him. It would have spoiled everything. Of course I could never have seen you again, as long as I lived! They'd have stopped my allowance, and everything. They –" the panic grew in her eyes, "—might even have done something about it. He talked about a place for delinquent girls, or something. Oh, he was dreadful! I wanted to kill him, right then and there! But he had decided to get what he wanted, and he wouldn't stop at anything."

"But you're marrying him," in a tone as dead as before.

"I hate him!"

"Oh, no, my dear. You must love him. People love the people they marry, don't they?" There was a world of weariness in the tone, now.

Like a storm Alice flung herself prone on the other girl's body, and lipped and mouthed her neck, her cheeks, her lips frantically. "You must believe me! I've never loved anybody but you, since the day I met you! I wanted to love you forever – And I simply despise Roddy! Stuck-up beast…"

"You always said you liked him," toneless again.

"But not since I met you, darling! Oh, I like him, I suppose, in a way… We *were* raised together, and he is my cousin. But not after what he did," shuddering. "I could never love him, after that!" She clenched the other girl more tensely. "I don't want to love anybody but you, as long as I live!"

Jean had responded not at all to the other girl's passionate endearments. "And yet you're marrying him."

Hysterically Alice ignored the interruption. "It was last night, after the alumni dance. He's not even staying in town; he has a room in a hotel in Springfield. I know why, now." Her voice was melancholy. "He made me go there with him. He told me all this, and what it would mean. – To both of us, darling! I had to agree to do what he said, or it would mean disgrace for both of us. He said he'd have me branded as a … a moral pervert, a degenerate, all over Cleveland, and here, and all over the United States! It would break Mother's heart – he was right, there," in tragic hopelessness. "I don't care so much how Father would feel; though he has been a swell sport always, as decent as could be. Of course, no allowance; and how could I live, darling? I had to decide, right then and there. When I thought of how Mother would take it… And of you disgraced… There was nothing else I could do." Her voice froze slowly, until the words barely trickled forth. "Even what he did then I couldn't mind."

Horror was in Jean's strained hazel eyes. "You can't mean—"

Alice nodded, hot moisture in her reddened eyes. "That's why he had the room in Springfield. Nobody would dream who I was, there. Yes." She could not meet the other girl's eyes; her cheeks were ruddy with anguished embarrassment. "He made me, then. –Or he'd have told."

"You slept with me," in anguished horror.

"It was all worthwhile in life," in humble pleading. "I thought it would wipe out the stain. What he'd done to me."

"And… tonight?" in a ghastly monotone.

Alice nodded, wordlessly. She sighed as if the last faintest breath left her body. "There was no way to prevent it. He had the room still. That was why. He said he did it to make sure. Oh, darling, don't you see? He wanted me. He found this out. He's making me marry him, he made me do what he did to be sure I would have to – to save you from disgrace!"

Jean sat up in bed, and stared at her friend, as if seeing her for the first time. "You've ended everything." It was a dirge.

"Oh, but don't you see, darling, I haven't! It was the only way. This way, nobody'll ever know," her voice stormed hysterically ahead. "You'll visit us – you'll come and live with us! Once I'm married to him, I'll make him do what I want him to! I can't live without you! Nothing's ended…" And slowly her voice died away, at something in the eyes of the other girl. "I would have let them crucify me, Alice Jennings, before I did what you have done. Let them tell—let anybody tell: what difference could that make to me, as long as I was true to *you*? Why, you were more to me than all the world: than all the world! Let them tell my parents – Roddy or anybody: what difference can that make to me?" Her hands suddenly clawed through her chestnut hair, as if to lift the load from off her pounding brain. "Other girls – your parents – the people of Cleveland, or here, or anywhere – let them see with their own low eyes, let them look on the most beautiful thing in life as vulgar and degrading, if that's the best that they can do—What difference can all that make? I know I'm right! I know our love was the one pure and unstained thing in the universe! Pervert… degenerate… They're degenerates, for being low enough to let a man make love to them! They're perverts – they pervert everything good and fine and true in life, to soil it with their own dirty minds. Like Verna Stanton: to her, everything was dirty. I would have let them crucify me, before I would have betrayed *you!*"

"But I haven't betrayed you – I've protected you," her whole soul in the plea.

"What difference could it have made?" Her tone was mournful, now. "Suppose the whole world knew of it – would you be ashamed of that? Was Sappho ashamed? Were the great women of history who have loved other women ashamed? Let my parents learn – I'd go myself and tell them, if it would do any good. If they can't understand what's true and beautiful, that won't make me dirty my soul and my body, by living down to their low standards? Oh, Al, Al... You were my wife." Her head was back, chin high, eyes staring off into the unseen high heavens, like a very Cecilia. "You were more than my wife. I was your wife. We were married. For life. And now you've proved yourself recreant to it all. You've promised to go through the farce of a marriage to a man, you've given yourself – yourself, that belonged to me – to him, for him to foul and dirty and—" She lifted her two clenched hands in impotent agony.

"But, Jean! There wasn't any other way—"

There was a haggard wildness in Jean's eyes, a frozen horror. Her voice was thinner, smaller. "You came to me straight from his adulterous arms, as if to make me share the stain too! And now you want to live a lie before the world – to go through the mockery of marriage to him, the soilure, the ordure of it all – and secretly, furtively, hypocritically, sneak away to my pure bed, for stolen rapture, when ... Don't you see you've spoiled it all? I'd have given up everything for you – friends, family, everything – if only I'd have you. This way, I'd never have you: I'd have only the fragments that he left, the mouthed and spotted fruit, the mired crumbs after his banqueting. Oh, dear dear Al, it was so clean, so fine, so high, before you did this! Why didn't you see what you were doing, and kill yourself before you stooped to this ignominy?" The very excess of passion would not let her say more.

Alice watched her sullenly. "Jean," she snapped it out suddenly, "you're being a fool. This is theatrics, not life. I haven't fouled anything, dirtied anything. We've got to live, both of us. We've got to live with other people. We've got to be careful of what they say about us. Of course, our love is the finest thing that ever happened to us. But I never saw you like tonight," more tensely. "You seem to have gone out of your mind. There was nothing else I could do. We can still be as close as we ever were..."

"Never, never, while life lasts." She looked with infinite pity at the other girl. "If it all means that much to you – the world's opinion, and all, well... Why, then, I just didn't understand you, that's all. I can only know how *I* feel about it! I'll never stoop! I'll never compromise! I'll never pretend one thing, and do another! I could never stoop that low. There's no double-dealing in me. I couldn't stand it. – You married to him, and me visiting you! It's dreadful, all the way around. No. This is the end." The solemn bell notes tolled relentlessly to the end.

"You've got to be practical," said Alice with stubborn anguish.

"Not at the expense of everything noble, everything fine, in life."

"It would break Mother's heart." Her own thumped frighteningly.

"You must be yourself, or you are nothing."

"You don't realize the public disgrace of it all!"

"If others could die for their faith, why not me?"

Alice sobbed openly. "You mean everything to me, darling!"

"But not quite enough." It came with mournful finality. "So tonight will be our last night... Our goodbye."

"Jean, you can't be that cruel!" She clung desperately to the other girl's waist. "Life won't be worth living, without you!"

"But people won't gossip about you, this way." There was no pity now in Jean's soul. "No, dear. You had the choice; and you took what seemed to you the best way. I would have done differently. You – you're going back. To Cleveland. To be married." There was not even scorn now. "I'm not going back. Ever. Not to Baltimore, not to my family, not to anything they stand for. I may go on alone, till I die: but I can always stand up straight, I can always look my own soul in the face."

"You mean," in timid sorrow, "to New York, and all? The way we planned?"

"Of course. You've got to have a soul of steel, in this world, Al. You make up your mind, and you do what's right, though they break you for doing it. What else in life is worthwhile, but being worth your own self-respect? I'm going on. And this is goodbye."

Alice felt as if her soul was wrenched apart. She burrowed tensely beside the other girl's unyielding body. "This last night, then, darling..."

"No. That's all over. It was my fault – I love you so, I never saw... I never saw..."

"You never saw – what?"

Jean faced it at last. "How you would bend. How you could stoop. How practical you were. But I loved you once, dear, and I'll never forget that. And some day, please God, if I can ever get over this... If I can ever find a girl who's soul is steel, like mine..."

Nothing would change her. It was a cold night, for both of them. Alice lay awake, and looked at herself as little as possible. And Jean saw things dancing in the darkness before her all night; and she tried to see as little as possible of Alice there, and what darkness danced beside her and in front of her.

||

"Come in." Marian Maitland opened the door, and radiated welcome. "You'll have to forgive these pajamas. On a day as sweltering as this has been, my sole object in life was to close up the shop and fall into a tub as soon as possible. I thought Texas was warm; but New York in August can blister the pants off it."

Jean relaxed into a chair. "I wish I had my own on. My dear infant, if you think this is hot, just try Washington some nice July or August afternoon, about three o'clock. I've fried eggs on the Capitol steps myself – it's not a Ripley, it's a fact. Heat! – But today has been a scorcher. My, you've got a lovely place here!"

Marian considered the plunger cocktail mixer, and the bowl of ice cubes. "What'll it be?"

"What have you got?" Jean giggled.

"O-oh, Dubonnet, or dry Martini, or Presidente, or almost anything."

"This is a Dubonnet day. Dubonnets and Tom Collinses seem to go with August."

"It's a lousy place," said Marian, as she measured her liquids, and plumped them in on the ice with professional celerity. "Honestly, it gives me the jitters, every time I survey it."

"Why, I think it's lovely, honey!"

"You aren't a decorator. Verni Martin table with Duncan Phyffe chairs – and lousy reproductions, at that! An Aubusson rug, made in Newark, with chintz curtains! And a Murphy bed, to cap it all! I have nightmares all night from it. God, how I long for a place of my own, where I can do things!"

Jean smiled softly. "You're too deep for me, there. I didn't major in Chippendales at Chadwick. I should think, as a decorator, you'd have your own place."

"It's the old budget, pet. I'm half owner of the dump, you see, and I can't take out as much as I'd like. And, besides, a place by yourself isn't so calorific. One of these days," her eyes dwelt in slow appraisal on the other girl, "I'll find me a buddy, and then you'll see an apartment that'll knock your eyeteeth into your tonsils!"

"I'm not sure that would be pleasant," Jean drawled, chuckling with amusement. "Where would you locate this paragon of apartments, if you had it?"

"There's only one place with any color in New York – the Village. Not one of the obvious streets – nothing north of Waverly, and certainly not on the Square. But Washington Mews, or Charlton, or Gay, or Bank – a miracle could be worked there, if there was somebody to hold the wolf's tail, while I held his front paws."

"That's funny," Jean meditated on her part, "that was where I intended to live, when I first landed in this great metropolis – these are absolutely delicious, darling. You have the knack."

"*Bartendera nascitur, non fit.* Which is, being interpreted, a bartender has got to be born with a toddy in one eye and a mint julep in the other. Well, why didn't you?" Her mind galloped ahead much further than her words.

"A census of Americans shows ninety-nine and nine-tenths per cent of them think a cocktail is a highball with a fancy name, and that Tom Collins wrote a book about looking at life and letters. The cause is simpler than that. I had planned to come down from Chadwick with my roommate. She upped and got hitched. I didn't give much of a damn, then. Some friends of mine were coming here, so here am I." She could say it casually, now.

"Girls have such funny tastes." Marian's voice was aloof. "You've had a couple of beau lovers, I've noticed. At least, that big Pierce has called for you twice; and then there's the Arrow Collar ad in the Buick."

"It's the firm," with a sigh. "Mr. Underwood has the big car, and his daughter Janet is a big problem. Fourteen years old, with the sophistication of Tallulah Bankhead and the habits of a baby in a crèche. He's a widower, and he is a dear. The Buick is Hal Garner, thirty, and still trying to find out what life is all about. They're darned decent to me – they pay me fifty a week now, and heaven knows I'm not worth fifty cents. Barring that, my record is pure."

Marian Maitland studied Jean with slitted eyes. She rose and refilled the glasses, and then slumped down again in one of the Duncan Phyffe chairs. "Men are a mess," she announced suddenly.

"You're telling *me*?" Sometimes Americanisms said more than a volume.

"I haven't gone out with one, since I've been East."

"Oh, these were harmless enough. We merely quote the New Yorker to each other, Hal and I. And Mr. Underwood regards me as a sort of Pestalozzi. What have they done to you?" shifting to the offensive.

"Plenty." Her lips clamped in a straight line.

"Tell mamma?"

"There's every reason why I shouldn't. So I will," said Marian in rebellious sudden determination. "A burnt girl dreads the fire."

"You've had a past." She held her glass up silently toward the Texan. "I forgot the capital P."

"Oh, just the sort of thing that happens," in callous distaste. "I guess it will do me good to shoot it. You know, things that *really* hurt you ought to be led out into the park and given the air, every now and then. Otherwise, they mess up the house an awful lot. Until it stinks." Her tone was coarser. "The only healthy way is to out with it. When I was thirteen, my uncle, my mother's brother, took me driving with him down to Cuero. That's the turkey town, down toward the gulf. He drove the car into the mesquite about a mile, and told me to take off my clothes, or he'd kill me. I was so frightened, I believed him. He was thirty-five; it was the day before his birthday. So I did. I was rather bloody, when he got through. He didn't mind a little thing like that. He got back on the road, and went down and finished his business. I didn't cry, until I got home. I cried for a week, then."

Jean's heart was torn. "Didn't they find out?"

"Of course. He told 'em what had happened. He said he'd had a bottle of mescal, and had gone cuckoo. He came right out with it. They all knew."

"Didn't they kill him?" in agitated horror.

"There were three of us, all girls." Her tone was colorless. "I was the youngest. They seemed to think it was my fault. I was disgraced, in everybody's eyes. Even Mother's. They thought I was going to have a baby, of course. You couldn't disgrace a member of the family. I was too young to get married off. They sent me to a school on the Hudson, to get me as far away from home as possible. Father let him take one of my sisters to Cuero, the next time. It was all in the family." Her tone was acid.

"It's the most dreadful thing I ever heard!"

"Well, I've heard worse," in cool, aloof tones. "So that's my past. They wanted me to go south again, after it had all blown over. A couple of years later, I wrote them they could all go to hell. I finished at the school, and came down to New York and took a course in decorating. Dad did send me an allowance, for quite a while. And then 1929 came, and I was on my own. And so I'm what I am today." She ceased talking, and blew lazy smoke rings toward the ceiling. "I've never been partial to men, since that day."

"You poor darling!"

Marian shook her head. "I figure differently. I had to find out, sooner or later. I got my lesson early. Maybe it was a harsh one. But it stuck. Baby, it stuck! I haven't had much use for men, since then."

"Girls?" Jean's heart pounded at her own daring.

"I'm telling this all to you, aren't I? Women are cats, a lot of 'em. It's what men have made 'em. But you – I guess you're different."

"I am." Jean considered her for a long time. "Why don't you find somebody to room with? To have your apartment with?"

"Will you?"

"If you want me." Her heart gave a great bound upward.

"I do."

"If I can afford it. I'm only making fifty a week…"

"I'm a swell manager, baby. I've had to learn to be. I can do the decorating for almost nothing – a thousand dollar job, too, I mean. They'll do favors for me. Like modernistic?"

"What little I know of it. Radio City," apologetically.

"You'll like what I do with it… Stripped utility, and the sheer beauty of line and mass, with no gewgaws of any kind. Tomorrow's Saturday. Shall we find the place, then?"

"You bet!"

And they did. It was on Washington Mews, the first place of Marian's choice: a delightful little duplex, with balcony and everything, just made to fit their dreams. It was empty, and they had the lease dated the first, to give Marian every chance to have it ready in time. And Jean felt happier than she had been since arriving in the city.

When she actually saw what Marian had done with it, she capitulated completely. There was a soft cool beauty in even the tiniest end table, grown out of the use of some metal like aluminum and a great deal of glass. The chairs, the larger pieces of furniture, had the easy curving grace of great machinery; and, where wood was used, the argent glow of polished holly wood appeared, decorated with redwood burl. It was a triumph. And it was more comfortable than it was beautiful.

The bedrooms – there were two that she had finished, leaving one for a sort of storeroom – were dreams. Jean's had been done in honey-colored inlays, with tones of blue for the upholstery. The bed was low and full double width: the very sight of it was seductive. And the dressing table was so exquisitely beautiful that Jean cried when she saw it. Not Frankl, not Urban, had ever designed anything so exquisite. Marian's own was more somber, with night-dark inlay, and upholstery that smoldered from dull burgundy to flame curtains. But it was as effective, and the dressing table was almost as lovely.

"My dear, it's a palace! I didn't dream anything could be so lovely!"

"Yours is the heaven room, and mine the hell room," smiled Marian. But I like them equally."

"But why hell, for you, dear?"

"I don't know. I *do* know, too. I had quite a hell of a time of it, you remember, when I was thirteen. I've had rather a hell of a time of it, ever since." There was stark unhappiness in the firm, fine-chiseled features.

"I haven't had an easy time, darling…" Jean stared at the dark smoldering beauty of Marian's bedroom.

"Don't tell me *you've* been raped, my dear. It doesn't happen to everybody."

"No man has ever touched me. Except things I couldn't prevent – at college, you know – petting, and that sort of thing, that they started and I stopped at once. Not from men, no. I never liked them. I mean, not really. I guess I was built to like girls and women. Father's very Southern, you know." Her tone curled ever so slightly. "A Moorhead, of Maryland. There's the whiskey-drinking, slave-owning, nigger-beating South in his face. He was a gentleman," her tone curled more ominously. "The Civil War took away his slaves. He had to have somebody to work it out on. There was Mother." Her tone was dangerously quiet. "She never could understand him. It wasn't only that he drank too much, especially at home… when there were guests, or anything, he was the pink of politeness, even to her. But when they were alone… I didn't count, of course… My dear, if he had used daily the Chinese torture of flaying the skin off the living body, it would have been kinder. Instead, he peeled the skin off her soul, with every word he said. She would writhe in anguish by the hour; she would have screamed, if she had not been a lady. That was at home. He's even had his mistresses there," in quiet horror. "I slept in a little room next to them. I saw him in bed with one of them once. They were both a little drunk, I'm afraid: a dreadful cheap woman, all flash, who Mother would never have invited in socially. I was about fifteen then. It was Christmas Eve; they had been decorating the tree for me, when they sent me to bed. Mother hadn't expected any guests; Father had just picked her up somewhere. They must have left Mother downstairs with the tree. The door was open: I could see everything. It woke me, what they were doing. Utterly disgusting things to each other, both of them. I didn't dare get up and close the door…"

"You poor darling!"

Jean shrugged. "They left, finally. I couldn't go to sleep. Then the worst part of it happened. The door was still open. Mother came up. She begged Father to let her go to sleep, she was tired. And, of course, she must have known what had happened, though she didn't say a word: she never dared say a word to him about the women he had, everywhere. He didn't let her go to sleep, until he was ready. I saw it all. On the same bed where he'd had this other woman, an hour before. I don't know: I suppose I saw my father in all men, from then on. I never forgot it. Though I locked my door from that night on."

"I don't see how your mother stood it!" in wild indignation.

"Women do. It's a part of marriage, I suppose. He had a right, a legal right, to beat her. He said he did, anyhow. With a stick no thicker than his thumb," in fierce, stabbing hatred. "It was old English law, he said, and still good in Maryland. I think I'd have killed him, if he'd ever tried it! Luckily, I went to Chadwick that fall. I spent my summers with friends," quietly. "I've never been back, except for holiday weekends and things like that. I came on to New York. I'd *never* go back home!"

"You loved your mother." It was not a question.

"More than anything in the world. Then." Jean glanced covertly at the other girl. "I've loved other people more since."

"Men!" in shocked disbelief.

"No. A girl. At college. My roommate, senior year. I loved her, as if I'd been married to her." Jean's eyes studied the other girl's fine face with absorbed eagerness.

Marian weighed this a long time, before answering. "You mean it?"

"Yes."

"I… I've never loved anybody, I think."

"But you've wanted to." There was a low, rich huskiness in the confident tone.

"Yes."

"I thought I'd never love anyone again." Jean kept her tone low. There was a fire at its heart. "She got married, you see. After swearing she never would. She wanted me to be her friend still – to visit them, and all. Maybe to live with them. I couldn't do anything underhanded."

"But if you loved her," in wondering uncertainty.

"No. I felt that way about it, when I came to New York. I don't know, that part has gotten duller, now. You can't live in the past. And I'm not through with love." There was faint far exaltation in the voice.

"No one has ever loved me." Marian's tone was low and faintly questioning.

"I think I wanted to love you, from the moment I saw you first, Marian. That was why I was so glad, when you suggested living together. I know I love you now." She stood still and quiet in the center of Marian's room. She made no move to come nearer to the other girl.

"You'll be disappointed." The tone was somber. "I've been pretty much of a wreck, since what happened to me."

"No. You can't live in the past. You're young – younger than I. A year younger. Forget all that. I – I love you." It was a young wind sighing over the first bank of jonquils.

"I – I love you, too, dear. I'm going to love you. I know it. I — I'm almost afraid to. I was so sure I never would, with anybody."

"Never be afraid of life… You've made a real heaven out of this place. Externally, I mean. We can make it the other sort of heaven. From the inside."

"I never want to see a man here." Marian shivered.

"Except on business, neither do I. Remember, they were both members of the firm."

Marian stole quietly over beside the lush flawless beauty of the other girl. "I want you to kiss me, dear. Show me you love me! Nobody ever has."

Only then did Jean turn toward her, a silent psalm of thanksgiving in her heart. It was only the lips: but they spoke like bugles, like trumpets blown at sunrise.

Marian's breath came in quick, happy gasps, when it was over. With passionate intensity she clung tight to the other girl's hand, to make sure she was real, to hold her. "We'll celebrate tonight," she whispered. "Just you and me. Our own little housewarming. We'll splurge – dinner at the Brevoort, then back together, just you and me."

"We'll need nobody else. From now on!"

* * *

It was not until Christmas Eve that Jean and Marian became more than inseparable friends. Both of them shrank from the irrevocable step. Jean could not help remembering Alice Jennings. She had been so high with hope, during all of that: she had been so cruelly wounded, at the end, that she did not want to risk such a torture garden again. The most they had done had been to lie side by side on the davenport, or on one of the exquisite beds; to kiss, morning and night and during the evening, long and passionately. Marriage was for life. She had made her mistake, once. Whom love had joined together, man's world had separated, and the scar on her soul was still unhealed. And so she played nightly with dreams of what life might be with Marian, and did no more than dream. And the other girl was afraid, no matter how much her body burned. She did not know what to do. She did not know how to start. It was heaven, this way. She had someone to love, someone who loved her: that was enough. The love blossomed as slowly and surely as a tardy spring over desolate winter-stripped fields.

But each day brought them closer and closer to the realization that this could not go on forever. Jean had had her baptism into the actual fires of loving – fires that did not char, but in their ending; fires that lifted and purified the soul, and burned it clear of all slag and dross. Marian only knew that the time was nearing, and had come, and was more imperatively upon her, when nothing that the other girl asked could be refused.

It was on Christmas Eve that it happened. Days before, Jean had known something would happen this night: that something must happen. It was her anniversary: her anniversary of the one real love of her life. The one real physical love: and all other loves were tepid and pallid, compared to that. Her love for her mother had been a protective love for a cripple, a soul cripple, a woman scarred and flayed and tortured out of all recognition by man's world. It was a love of the anguished past. But the other love had been love of the present and the future: and only her fault in building on sand instead of rock had kept it from lasting forever. But Marian was different. She had been burned in the fire too, her soul was already forged steel. It had to come. By some queer whim, Jean postponed it until this anniversary night.

Marjorie Dawse had been down, with her daughters, for dinner and the evening. Moira, the golden-haired one, was six, and little Sheila almost nine. They were quietly beautiful children, and exquisitely well-behaved. They had investigated the details of the lovely apartment methodically, serene in their own play. The dressing tables especially had fascinated both of them. Moira insisted that, when she grew up, she would have a room exactly like Jean's; and Sheila had been just as positive that she would have a room like Marian's. They were in and out of the living room too, and their mother did not subdue the frankness of her conversation, even when they were in the room. But most of the time they were in the bedrooms, with permission, if they were careful, to use the fascinating perfumes and make-up paraphernalia on the dressing tables. It was like being in fairyland, to them.

The mother nodded her head vigorously. "I've been married – you girls haven't; and – I know. I have two lovely daughters out of it, two. But it can never be a success. Men can't talk our language to us. Harry was as nice as he could be. But there's a strain of coarseness in every man. Some women have it; men have taught it to them. They use it to keep men, to hold them; and what are men but meal-tickets to them? Either as husband, or as a man keeping a woman, or men who pay cash for one night, and let it go at that. It's the same, no matter what name it's called. You never heard of a woman buying another woman's love! No. It's the only perfect mating."

"Of course, you're right." Jean's voice was low. Her eyes were on Marian. "I've always known it."

"You don't need to *persuade me*." Marian was as definite. Then it was a mistake, your getting married, Marjorie?"

"I wouldn't say that." She considered it carefully. "I'm a poet. I suppose I owed it to myself to find out about everything. Even – this. Besides," her cheeks flushed, "there would be no girls, if there were no marriage. We have to use men, or there could be no perfect lovers – no perfect matings. Until the time comes when a woman can merely meet a man for that purpose only, and not have to live with him – until marriage is abolished – I suppose it's something women have to go through with."

"To make more Lesbians." Marian used the word with a little shiver still. She had learned it as a word of reproach. She was beginning to think of it as an order of merit.

"There's no other way, yet."

"You don't really mean that, Marjorie." Jean studied the older woman earnestly. "Your two little girls, now – your two little beauties – surely you wouldn't want to let them become what you say you are, without making their choice for themselves, I mean."

"There's where you're wrong, Jean." She leaned forward hotly. "I want them to understand life. I want to save them from my mistake. If they must get married, let them understand what a dreadful thing it is. Of course I'll teach them that the only perfect love is between girls. I've already started," in tumultuous exultation. "I wouldn't mind what they did with a girl, no matter how young they are!"

"I can't believe that." Jean's face was puzzled; she was too close to her Baltimore background. "Mother would have died, before she'd have let me..."

"I wouldn't care if they love you two, right now!" There was a hysteria almost fanatical in her tones. "I'll call them in." She rose tensely to her feet. "Sheila! Moira!" They came in. The mother stood there, a queer glitter in her eyes. "Moira, you love Aunt Jean. Get in her lap, and give her a big kiss, and tell her so. And Sheila, you tell Aunt Marian." She stood watching, breasts rising and falling in frantic excitement.

Little Moira clambered brightly up. She laid her soft rose-petal cheek against Jean's, and then kissed her full on the lips. "I love you, Aunt Jean," she whispered.

Sheila was no more backward with Marian.

"O, but I'm proud of them! That's why I don't mind getting married. I'll pay Harry back, for what he did to me! O, it wasn't anything specific," shrugging more resignedly. "Only, he never considered my feelings at all. Only his own. At first, I let him; I thought he'd get over it, that he'd have to show consideration some time. Not him," almost fanatical once more. "Not any man! He turned what might have been a thing of beauty into a hideous mockery, with me the victim. That's what wives are – the victims of their husbands. Do you wonder that I'd die, before I'd let my two girls grow up to be tortured as I've been tortured? That was why I left him."

"Are you divorced?" Jean was listening tensely to every word. The mother noticed that she paid no attention to little Moira. But Marian was different. She was stroking little Sheila's hair, she was rubbing the slim boyish grace of the girl; from time to time she nuzzled her head in the youngster's neck, apparently relishing the sweet clean fragrance of her body, where the perfumes from the dressing table had not been applied.

Marjorie shook her head. "He wouldn't let me. He wouldn't give me the evidence; and, naturally, I wouldn't have anything to do with a man. He caught me once with a girl," her eyes flamed indignantly. "It was then he talked about taking the little darlings away from me. You know," her voice became curiously quieter, "you can't divorce a woman, for that, in New York State."

"I suppose you can't." Jean was unusually thoughtful. "I'd never thought of that."

"Adultery means with a man. So I'm tied. A lot of good it does him! I know he has other women, but I'm not going to stoop to spy on him. But it makes all the difference in the world to me. I feel clean, since I left him. He said things about me to some of my friends, too." Her cheeks were still stained. "About the girl I liked so. Most of them didn't mind. It isn't the way it once was, my dear. People are growing more intelligent, more civilized, all the time."

"I hope so." But Jean thought about Alice Jennings, and wondered.

The guests left at last, and the two girls were alone together. The talk had been unsettling to both of them. Especially to Jean. Christmas Eve, she felt, meant something especial in her life. It had been on Christmas Eve that she saw through the open door of her bedroom what had scarred her soul for life. It had been another Christmas Eve when she had first found what happiness could be. And now a year had come around, and it was her night again.

They had a nightcap together, of heady cognac from Carmel. Marian went to her own room, and busied herself preparing for bed. Jean heard the bath running, and then the shower. She was ready for bed first, and stood like a marble from Paphos in front of the pier glass of the dressing table, studying her own Echo mirrored on the revealing quicksilver. It was not good for woman to be alone... She went to the closet, and selected a lacy blue froth of a nightgown. There was a queer frightened smile on her face as she shook her head and hung it back in place. She chose, instead, a negligee of sky blue crepe de chine, with a marabou collar. She draped it slimly around her svelte figure, and studied herself again in the pier glass. It would do for a trousseau.

She walked quietly into Marian's room. Each night they kissed a parting kiss, before sleep divorced them. Marian stood toweling herself briskly, just inside the bathroom door. Jean felt that her own body must shine like flame.

"You know, dear," she said softly, "we don't have to sleep alone."

"Oh." Marian studied her, with lidded eyes.

"My bed's double. And your bed's double."

A smile like sunrise woke in Marian's face. "Either will do," she said, simply.

* * *

They never slept alone, after that first night. The day, even with the most interesting problems at Jean's office, or the most appealing task of decorating at Marian's, became merely an irritating interruption in the real business of living. For a time, they even begrudged having friends over in the evening, or going out at all. Jean could have kept on this way forever.

"You know, darling," Marian clenched the other girl tensely one night, long after they had gone to bed, "I could never be jealous of you. I love you too much."

"I love *you* so much, I'm dreadfully jealous," Jean giggled happily.

"I mean it. I know your soul is mine; I couldn't possibly object, if you wanted to thrill another girl as you thrill me. It would be more of a compliment to me, when you came back to me." She felt restless and dissatisfied. She worded it in this magnanimous way.

"Oh, but needn't worry, darling; I never could!"

Marian persisted. "I'm always thrilled, when I read about Sappho and those other great lovers of antiquity. They weren't jealous, or selfish. At times, they had real orgies, darling – dozens of lovely girls, in love with each other or with the divine Sappho herself, intertwined in a passionate Bacchanalian revel, with death to any man who intruded. My, but I'd have liked to have lived then!"

"And me lost three thousand years later," in a low unhappy voice.

"Oh, but no, darling! You would have been the Sappho to all of us. It would have to be you," with warm loyalty. "And who knows, one of these days," eyes half closed, voice dreamy, "we, you and I, might have our own little court of love, like hers!"

Jean's face was twisted with unhappiness. "No. Not that, Marian. It's you I love, and not anyone else. That was what was wrong with Alice. Not that it was another girl, there; but it's the same thing, really. I feel, dear," she stroked the warm pulsing flesh softly, "that I was your wife-husband at the same time:

that we were united by a bond deeper than any marriage I ever heard of. You can't play with a thing like that. It's too sacred. You can't share it: any more than you can share your faith in God with other gods. It would be infidelity. It would be as bad as adultery."

"I wish you didn't feel that way, darling." Marian's face was troubled. "I love you so much, I think you're so wonderful, I want others to know how marvelous you are. I'm so proud of you, I wish the whole world – the whole world of girls, I mean – could worship you as I do."

"No." Jean's heart was twisted. "I couldn't stand it! I'm yours, and yours only. Till death do us part."

There was only one answer to be made to this, and Marian made it.

The next afternoon, just after lunch, Marjorie Dawse phoned to the decorators' shop, and asked for Marian. "I wasn't doing a thing this afternoon, sweet, and I wondered if you wouldn't like to drop by for cocktails." There was a tense restlessness in her voice that was not lost over the wires.

"Not a thing." Marian felt something hot and leaping within her, in response to the voice of the older woman. "I'd love to."

"How early can you be free?"

"You're asking Jean?"

"She'll probably be at the office till six. I knew you could get away."

"Any time," in a hot breathless voice. "I can get away right now. I'm just warming a chair here. Are you at home?"

"Yes. Come right on over." There was a feverish note in her voice. "The girls are at school. The nurse will take them for a walk, afterward."

Marian went over at once. She did not go blindly. She knew what she wanted. She had given Jean her chance, and the very suggestion of any spreading of her love had shocked the other girl. If she was built that way, it was not for Marian to object. But Marian was not built that way. She had an insatiable curiosity about the garden of girls, which had barely awakened. She felt as if she were at the top of the longest, steepest toboggan slide in the world, with a strong, powerful toboggan beneath her, yet held back from plunging down into the giddy frantic delight of the magnificent downward slide. It was silly, when the narrowing path below beckoned so. She knew why she was going.

"I was terribly thrilled, talking to you Christmas Eve." Marjorie's voice was huskier than usual. "I've hardly seen you since. You two seemed all tied up, every time I called."

"Jean's been pretty busy at the shop." It was an evasion, and she knew it.

"It was you I was interested in, my dear. I noticed how well you and Sheila got along together." She licked her lips nervously. "I saw how wrapped up you were in Jean. But there was a restless look on your face."

Marian did not tell the other woman why it had been restless, that night. Her cheeks flushed a little. "I am restless," she admitted. "I don't know... I want everything that life can give me. Except men."

The poetess stood silently beside her, as close as she could stand. "I'll be awfully good to you, my dear."

Marian did not turn away. "I know it."

"I've wanted to kiss you, since I met you."

"I want you too!"

Somehow they were out of the living room. There was a sudden panic in Marian's eyes. "She must never know! It would kill her!"

"You can trust me. I wouldn't hurt her for worlds. But I've been wild for you."

It was more than an hour later before Marjorie suddenly laughed. "Good Lord, what a hostess I am! Here I invited you over for cocktails, and I've clean forgot them!"

"As if it mattered!"

Lilyan Brock
from QUEER PATTERNS
1935

The final curtain had fallen, and backstage hands were busy striking the set and disconnecting the powerful lights in the wings preparatory to placing them against the back wall for the night. Only a few moments ago these dull inanimate objects with their metal frames containing colored sheets of gelatin had been alive. Their vari-colored beams had shone brilliantly on the shimmery gowns that seemed to be molded on the exquisitely formed bodies of stately show girls... on the filmy costumes of swaying dancers... on the handsome figure of a young man in white military uniform and the beautiful fair-haired, dark-eyed girl he held in his arms. Now the theatre was empty – void of the gay audience and its appreciative applause that had marked another successful evening. The heavy velvet curtain had been raised, disclosing rows of lately vacated seats bathed in the rays from a large bench light set downstage to flood the house.

Sheila Case walked wearily toward her dressing room, seemingly unmindful of the confusion around her. She had given a good performance, one that had been most graciously received, but now she was tired: tired of the theater, tired of the shrill, high voices of the chorus girls as they laughed and chattered gaily while they removed their make-up, tired of the noisy actors as they talked merrily on their way to their dressing rooms. Arriving at her room on the other side of the stage, Sheila saw Philip Rowan standing at her door waiting, the coat to the uniform he wore in the show hanging over his arm.

He was a handsome man, tall and dark, with a slim, well-built body that fitted perfectly his role as leading man.

"Tired, Sheila?" he asked solicitously as she came up to him.

"Dreadfully so!" The words came forth with a sigh. "I feel as though I could sleep a week."

"Your work was great tonight." Philip's clear-cut features were wreathed in admiration. "You had them in the palm of your hand right from the beginning."

Sheila smiled wearily. "They were nice to me, weren't they?"

Philip came closer. "Sheila, I know you're tired, but don't you think you'd feel better if we go someplace for a bite to eat and then drive through the park?" He hesitated – "I'd rather hoped you would. I want to talk to you. Besides, the air will do you good – make you sleep."

"You're a darling, Phil – always looking after me. All right, we'll go – I shan't be long."

"Good! I knew you would. I'll take my make-up off in a jiffy, get the car, and pick you up out front."

Sheila's eyes followed him as he strode rapidly across the stage; then, turning, she walked into her dressing room. Seated before her make-up shelf she gazed steadily for a moment at the lovely features reflected in the smooth silvery surface of the mirror: large, velvety brown eyes, full, sensitive mouth, and dainty chin. The yellow of her fine waving hair caught the light and held it captive in a golden prison. Thoughtfully she brushed it back from her high forehead and with slender tapering fingers applied cold cream to her face to remove the grease paint.

Philip was so thoughtful of her, she reflected. Why – why couldn't she return in some slight degree the deeper emotions he felt for her? Dismissing the troublesome thoughts from her mind, she hastened in her dressing and a few minutes later passed through the stage door into the street. Philip's car rounded the corner and drew silently up to the curb.

"Waiting long, Sheila?" he asked as he leaned over the wheel and opened the door of the roadster.

"Not a minute, Phil — I just came out."

"Good. Now where do you want to go for something to eat?"

"If you're not too hungry, I believe I'd rather drive first; I think I need air more than food – the theater was frightfully stuffy tonight."

"Your word is my command, your majesty," Philip replied with mock solemnity. "We drive."

It was good not to be alone, Sheila decided, as the car threaded its way through the traffic. Somehow tonight she felt the need of his understanding companionship more than ever before. Always it seemed she fought the desire to belong to someone – to have someone who loved her by her side. Sheila knew that Philip loved her with all the strength in his virile young body. Repeatedly he had asked her to marry him, but always in her heart had been something that had warned her that marriage was not the answer to her longings. But later, as they drove through Central Park, Sheila found herself thinking that perhaps what she felt for Philip was, after all, all there was to life and love. He had been most considerate, scarcely speaking, but allowing her to lie back in the deep cushions and rest. The night air felt cool and refreshing on Sheila's face as it gently caressed her cheeks, almost lulling her to sleep.

Philip's voice roused her: "Shall we park for a moment? I want to talk to you."

Sheila nodded assent, and Philip brought the car to a stop at the side of the drive. Switching off the motor he turned, and putting his arm around Sheila's slender shoulders, drew her to him.

"Sheila, darling, you know how mad I am about you – how I love you and want you! *Won't* you marry me? Somehow I can't see anything ahead unless we can go on together. There is no future without you. Please, dearest, say you will."

In answer to his earnest plea, Sheila raised her head, and pulling him down, gently kissed him. "Yes, Phil. I think… I need you too – I am so alone."

Philip's arms closed tightly around Sheila; he kissed her tenderly. Then, "You've made me so happy! I've dreamed so long that one day we would belong to each other. Can't we be married soon?"

Sheila thought for a moment. "Well, we'll close here this week, then we'll have a week's layoff before we open in Chicago. I'll tell you – why not take that time for our honeymoon?"

"That's a great idea; we'll do it," Philip exclaimed. "I know just the place where we can go. I shan't tell you where, but it's a favorite spot of mine. I manage to get up there every now and then between shows. I want you to see it."

* * *

Sheila and Philip were married in the "Little Church Around the Corner" with only a few friends from the company attending their wedding. Sheila was lovely in the black velvet suit she wore, with its luxurious silver fox collar making a beautiful frame for her blonde beauty. Philip had sent her a corsage of white orchids, which she wore on the soft fur. As he looked at her at the altar he felt certain that there had never been a more beautiful bride, and in his heart he thanked God for having placed her in his care.

That night at the theater, after the last act had ended, the company gave a wedding supper for them. This came as a complete surprise, for when the performance ended there had been no sign of the elaborately laid table that they saw later upon coming out of their dressing rooms.

There was much gaiety as the company gathered around to express good wishes and drink to their happiness. Even the newspaper men who attended seemed to think it the ideal marriage of the season.

A few hours later, amid the noisy goodbyes and good-natured wishes for continued happiness from their friends and fellow performers, Sheila and Philip left the theater. As they got into the car and started toward their hotel, they were both very close to tears – the unexpected thoughtfulness of the company had touched deeply. It was good to know that they would see them all again the following week in Chicago.

They had decided to leave New York early the next morning and Philip's luggage had that afternoon been sent to Sheila's hotel, where they would spend their wedding night.

During the short drive Sheila found herself wondering what it would seem like to share her privacy from now on with a husband – to give not only part of her room but herself as well. How could she reconcile the strange being within her to that? Her thoughts were broken by Philip's voice: "Do you realize, darling, we're actually married, and now you're all mine?" Not waiting for an answer, he went on, "I've dreamed that one day you would be – but now that it's really happened I can scarcely believe it."

"It is like a dream," Sheila's voice was low. "I keep thinking I'll wake up and find it was one."

Philip's heart beat faster at the implied happiness in Sheila's answer.

He drew up in front of the hotel. "I'll put the car away and then I'll be right up."

When a few minutes later she heard the door of the room close behind him, she had just stepped out of the shower. The cool needle spray had felt stimulating and had brought the blood tingling to the surface of her young firm body – a body made for love, from the soft, rounded pink-tipped breast to the firm alabaster white of promising thighs and slender limbs… a fitting shrine for passion and its fulfillment.

Sheila finished brushing her hair, turned to put on the ivory satin gown that hung in graceful folds on the inside of the door; then sliding her feet into a pair of dainty mules, walked into the room where Philip sat impatiently waiting.

He rose when she entered and crossed the room to take her in his arms. His hungry mouth claimed her own, then deserting it, wandered over the smoothness of her throat and shoulders. "I shan't be a minute, darling," he whispered huskily... "I want you so."

Philip's words rang in Sheila's ears as she lay waiting. Over and over she asked herself why they had sounded so formidable. Why did not she too feel the anxiety of them? Why did the effect which she so perceptibly had upon him arouse no reciprocal feeling within herself?

The door of the bathroom opened and Philip's pajama-clad figure emerged.

Sheila tried desperately to speak. The words simply would not come... the tiny bed lamp was extinguished... a form slipped silently into the space beside her... strong arms drew her close to a warm, trembling body... the stranger within her protested... vainly.

* * *

The faint flush of the morning found them driving out of New York. The city was just beginning to stir from its deep slumbers, preparing to doff the velvety black robes of night and don in their stead the brighter one of pale violet shot with gold threads of the rising sun. An occasional party of late revelers in evening clothes hailed taxis that came to screaming stops. In vivid contrast were the plodding laborers in their shabby clothes, dinner pails in hand as they hurried homeward from all-night shifts. A milk truck rumbled by, closely followed by a larger vehicle loaded with fruits and vegetables bound for one of the many restaurants. A stray dog, bedraggled and dirty, nosed about in some refuse. A human derelict charted a weaving course along the pavement. Broadway was beginning to take on a busier air. Everywhere were signs of the preparations necessary for a new day.

Soon the waking city and its activities lay far behind them. As they drove along the highway, Philip thought he had never before been so perfectly at peace with the world, for beside him sat the lovely creature who was so necessary to his life if it was to know complete fulfillment.

Sheila, on the contrary, tried in vain to solve the riddle of her emotions.

Was this love, and if so, why did it leave one feeling so strangely unmoved, so apart from it, as if one were standing aside and looking on, but in reality not a portion of it? Why did it repulse one?

Philip was precious to her, so gentle and tender in his love for her; yet why did the thought persist that it was not herself who lay in his arms the night past but a stranger – a woman she did not know? Who was this being inside her who could not find completeness? What were her desires, her unspoken longings? Why must she grope blindly for the light that would awaken her soul? Where was that light? What was it?

* * *

The show opened in Chicago with the theater filled to capacity, with one of the most enthusiastic audiences of the season.

Weeks sped by. Sheila appeared happy with Philip, while at the theater her popularity grew nightly. Yet, notwithstanding the gay, busy rush, away from the footlights she seemed once again to lapse into her old state of yearning and loneliness. The thread that thus far had outwardly conformed to the rest of the pattern was definitely beginning to twist and warp.

It was during the last week of the Chicago engagement that Sheila heard of a new play to be placed in rehearsal in New York that fall. Friends in the company with her stressed the fact that the story, from what they had heard, seemed made for her, and besides, they knew she had always wanted to do a play – something heavier than the frothy musical comedy roles in which she was usually cast, something in which she could use the great emotional work she was capable of doing.

* * *

Philip sat talking earnestly to Sheila at a quiet corner table in a small café near the theater.

"But darling, don't you see? This is the big chance you and I have talked about. You should at least interview Nicoli about the role – it's foolish not to. Don't you see, Sheila," Philip argued, "This is a marvelous opportunity for you to do something big – something you've always wanted to do. I simply will not stand for your sacrificing yourself because of me. Think of it, Sheila; you'd be a huge success in a play, and I'd be so proud of you. You must at least try, in fairness to me – I want you to."

"But Phil –" Sheila voiced her protest – "suppose I should be fortunate enough to sign for it. We'd be separated a whole season, and that wouldn't be fair to you."

"Nonsense! I should probably be playing right in New York in something else and the only time we should be separated would be during performances."

Sheila sat thinking. She did so want at least to make an effort to get the part. A play of Nicoli's was the goal a great many actors and actresses set for themselves. Many an unknown had risen to stardom due to her clever lines and brilliant direction. Yes, she decided, she would arrange an appointment as soon as they arrived back in New York. She announced her intentions.

Philip received her decision with a smile of satisfaction.

* * *

Nicoli: a woman outstanding in her place on Broadway; a woman whose plays in previous years had enjoyed tremendous successes and upon whom critics showered praise not only for her ability to write but for the genius with which she directed her pieces. In the annals of the theater she occupied a unique place: there had never before been such a woman. Her writings seemed to sound the very depths of the soul of humanity.

Sheila was nervous about her first meeting with this great personage, and so carefully and painstakingly groomed herself for that hour when she was to see her. Philip thought that she had never looked more beautiful, more appealing or more glamorous than when she came into the living room of their suite where he was sitting reading. Smartly gowned in a brown street frock and tight-fitting brown hat, her loveliness was almost dazzling. She was almost too beautiful to be anything except a beautiful picture. Philip, gazing at her, was more keenly conscious than ever of the magnetism that emanated from her always. Her statuesque figure made her outstanding even in the crowds that thronged Broadway.

Sheila glanced at her watch. "I'm leaving now, Phil – wish me luck!"

"I do, darling, all the luck in the world. I'll be waiting here, so come back as quickly as possible and tell me what happens."

"I will," Sheila promised. The door closed behind her retreating figure.

Her footsteps were light as they rose and fell on the deep carpet of the corridor. Her heart sang as the elevator bore her downward. She – Sheila Case – actually had an appointment with the great Nicoli.

It was almost unbelievable. She recalled her conversation with Nicoli's secretary. No, the part had not been filled. Nicoli would be glad to see her and talk with her. She was already familiar with her work.

One – two – three blocks. Sheila turned into the entrance of the building that housed Nicoli's offices. Up – up the elevator car carried her. The door of the cage closed; the car started its descent.

Sheila stood facing a large glass door. On it she read "Nicoli." She opened her bag and produced a mirror. She studied her reflection in it a moment, gave her hair a final pat or two, then, satisfied, returned the glass to its place. Her hands grasped the doorknob and turned it.

A girl at the switchboard looked up.

"I'm Sheila Casc," she told the girl. "I have an appointment with Nicoli." To herself her voice sounded breathless.

The girl turned back to the board. "Miss Case is here to see you. Yes, I'll send her right in. Nicoli will see you now, Miss Case. First door to the left."

Sheila passed through the little gate beside the girl and into the hall beyond. Why was she so nervous? she asked herself. Where was her usual composure? She shook herself slightly, then opened the door marked "Private" and walked in.

Behind a massive glass-topped desk sat a woman whose deep gray eyes at the moment were upon her.

"Nicoli, I'm Sheila Case."

The woman's low, vibrant voice when she spoke fascinated Sheila. "Come in, Miss Case – I've been expecting you."

Nicoli motioned her to a chair before her desk. Sheila seated, she continued: "I believe it was about the part in *The Woman Alone* that you wanted to see me, was it not?"

Sheila's eyes met those of the woman before her. "Yes, it was. Your secretary said you hadn't signed anyone yet. I was hoping you would give me a chance to read it for you."

Sheila trembled under the direct scrutiny of Nicoli's intent gaze. Why did she feel so shy? Why did her heart pound so? Why couldn't she say all of the things she had planned to say?

"I am already familiar with your work, Miss Case, and from what I've seen of it, you shouldn't have any great difficulty with the part. Then too, you're the type I had in mind."

"I'm so glad!" Sheila exclaimed happily. "You see, I've always wanted to do something heavier than musical shows – and I've always hoped that some day I could work under a really great director, the kind who would make a girl do things she didn't know she was capable of doing – the kind... you are."

Sheila's eyes spoke of the wealth of admiration she had for this woman whose genius had placed her in the enviable position she occupied. They took in the details of Nicoli's appearance: strong yet beautifully cut features; well-shaped head and short dark hair with its sprinkling of silver; then her gray eyes and their depth. What was behind them? Sheila was surprised to find herself wondering and really wanting to know.

Her speculations were brought up short by Nicoli's question: "You're married, Miss Case, are you not?"

Sheila nodded an affirmative. Nicoli went on.

"I merely spoke of it because my cast is filled with the exception of the lead – I couldn't use a team."

Sheila replied quickly, "We've agreed to work singly this season if you should decide on me for the part."

"That's splendid," Nicoli announced abruptly, "because I have decided – I do want you. Now then, let's get together on salary."

After a short discussion, Sheila prepared to leave. It had been agreed that she was to come the following day to sign her contract.

Reluctantly she bade Nicoli goodbye. The desire to remain and engage her in conversation filled her brain. What was it that made her feel as if she had known Nicoli always? Why in such a brief period did she feel so close to her? What was it in her voice that made her heart leap when she spoke?

During the short walk to the hotel, thoughts of Nicoli persisted – disturbing thoughts.

Over and over she felt the urge to go back and talk to her again, about what? It didn't seem to matter.

Philip noted the time on his wrist, then resumed his reading. Sheila would be along shortly, no doubt. Perhaps the steps in the hall now were hers. The door opened and Sheila entered, her face flushed with the exciting news she brought.

"Phil, I have it! The part, I mean. Nicoli said I am just the type – I'm signing the contract tomorrow!"

"Darling!" Philip grasped Sheila's hands. "I *knew* you would! Come here – sit down and tell me what happened."

* * *

Work on the play commenced. Sheila's eyes flashed with enthusiasm as she worked untiringly at the theater, and spent hours at the hotel going over scenes and studying. Philip sensed a change in her, the presence of something intangible that he was at a complete loss to explain, though he racked his worried brain for the solution. At night when he held her in his arms, telling her over and over of his love and his passionate longing for her, he seemed ever aware of a tautness in her warm body as it lay close to his own. It was maddening to accept her surrender when always he sensed that he possessed only a part of the emotion she was capable of displaying. What could awaken this wealth of hidden passion? What matter of love did her soul cry for?

As days sped by, Philip was more and more in darkness. Sheila was plainly beginning to strain against the vows which held her to him. Each day lengthened the distance between them, which he began to fear he could never span. They had changed their suite so that Sheila might be alone in the privacy of her own room to better concentrate on the part which seemed to be her whole existence.

After several weeks of this enforced separation, Philip took her into his arms and implored her to remain with him that night. But in the ebony blackness of the room, he knew that the woman he held in his arms was only a part of the lovely wife he so adored. The tenseness that so often before he had sensed was still there, but a new element was manifesting itself. Sheila seemed to be actively repelling his caresses, endeavoring to keep him from possessing even a part of her. Truly this was a new Sheila… a Sheila he was at a complete loss to understand.

Finally he held Sheila in his arms with her head pillowed on his shoulder while she slept, unaware that his tortured mind kept him awake until the first gray streaks of dawn were visible through the heavy curtains as they hung slightly parted. His brain still grope helplessly about, trying to find the reason for Sheila's indifference. Why did he feel the presence of something he could not name? What was the power at work?

The answer came quickly. After several attempts to regain the woman he had known, his harassed mind had failed to find a solution to his problem, and he had simply pleaded with her to give herself to him. It was on this night that Sheila told him that never again could she submit to his desires.

She had said simply and in almost a child-like manner, "Philip, I'm sorry, genuinely sorry to hurt you – but our lives together must come to an end – we can't go on – my life and my love belong to –" she hesitated over the name – "Nicoli. In her I have found what I know now I have been looking for, without realizing what it was that I really wanted."

Philip had his answer – an answer of which he would never have dreamed. But suddenly with searing clarity he saw that Sheila was one of the twisted threads of life which had finally found another like unto itself, and that together the two would form their part of the design of Life.

* * *

Weeks of work on the new play followed. For the first time, Nicoli was working with a divided mind; working in daily contact with the woman who was slowly consuming her every thought, becoming more and more of her being... days when in the theater she encountered more and more difficulty in controlling her once amenable mind... forcing herself to work, yet ever conscious of her growing love for Sheila... telling herself that it could not be, that Sheila belonged to Philip Rowan, and even were that not true, she probably would not understand Nicoli's feelings toward her... warning herself that she must forever force the strange longings out of her heart and out of her life... telling herself that she must forget Sheila Case except as a puppet to be moved about the stage under her direction... that for her she must never be anything else but clay to be moulded by her skillful hands into the character she wished portrayed. Sheila must cease to be a woman, a warm, breathing, lovely woman whom she, Nicoli, had grown to want so madly. Never again must she allow the promise of her lips to fan the flames of desire within her, driving out all reason.

Then there were nights when Nicoli would drive for miles alone, her short hair blowing in the night wind as she drove aimlessly on – or, stopping along the road, she looked heavenward and asked God why in His otherwise perfect universe He had created women such as herself, with the impulses and desires of men and the bodies of women. Certainly this was one of Fate's cruelest jokes: to love so completely that which the world denied her. Why should it be irreconcilably wrong for her to adore Sheila? Surely no man living could love her more tenderly or hold her more sacred.

Unceasingly Nicoli fought this battle – until the day came when in directing she found it necessary to demonstrate a piece of technique to the actor playing opposite Sheila. She walked over to Sheila and, trying desperately to master her emotions, held out her arms, folded her close, and kissed her. For a moment her senses reeled as she felt the warmth of Sheila's mouth and the unbelievable trembling of her body. Was her mind indeed running rampant, or had Sheila's kiss been a response to the wild longings within herself?

Somehow Nicoli finished the rehearsal and dismissed the cast. She then gathered her manuscript and notes together and walked over to where Sheila stood putting last-minute touches to her make-up before leaving the theater.

"Tired, Sheila?" she asked in a voice that seemed oddly unlike her own.

"A little, Nicoli; but I think I'll get over it as soon as I get out in the air."

"You've a right to be fatigued. We worked an unusually long time today. I thought I never would make Mr. Sands understand what I wanted in that scene with you in the second act."

At the mention of the scene wherein Nicoli had taken her in her arms and kissed her, Sheila's cheeks flushed. Had Nicoli noticed the trembling of her body, of her lips against her own? Had she guessed the presence of the unusual feeling that had swept her soul? Had she guessed that in that moment in her arms she had seen revealed to her wondering brain the reason for her strange longings? Had Nicoli tried to tell her in that kiss what she felt for her in her own heart?

Sheila made an effort to answer calmly. "I think he understands the piece of business now, Nicoli. Tell me, aside from that, how did you like the way rehearsal went?"

"Splendid – the whole thing is shaping up nicely," Nicoli told her. "I see no reason why we can't open on the date I set originally."

Her cosmetics replaced in her bag, Sheila prepared to leave.

"I'll see you at ten in the morning, Nicoli. You said ten, did you not?"

"Yes. I thought we'd start an hour earlier, so I wouldn't keep the cast so late again."

Nicoli hesitated. Should she ask Sheila the question that persisted in presenting itself? Yes, she would, she decided – she must.

"By the way, Sheila – I intended to drive out a way to a place I know for dinner. I'd love to have you go with me – unless of course you have to get back to the hotel."

Sheila spoke up quickly. "Not at all. I haven't a thing planned and I'd like very much to go."

A voice within Nicoli warned her. She thrust the warning aside.

"That's fine; then we'll walk over and get my car. I always store it near the theater – only a block or so. Shall we go?"

Life teeming with pleasures, sorrows and mistakes lay all about them as they drove away in the gathering dusk. Lights were beginning to flash on over the city. One by one they came on, changing from drab pieces of glass to scintillating forms that seemed almost alive – like souls being awakened into the glorious realization of living. The last bit of daylight gave way to their glow and the city lay behind them bathed in light, flooded with the warmth and brilliance of thousands of gleaming globes.

The steady stream of automobiles moved slowly onward; pedestrians hurried homeward, and Life and Fate moved relentlessly forward.

The broad ribbon of open road ran through the heart of nature, speaking softly of the peace she held for tired mortals – yet Nicoli was not attuned to that peace.

Neither spoke much in words, but Nicoli sensed the tenseness of the air about them that seemed to be charged with something dynamic… charged with words which were struggling tempestuously for expression, with passions which were wailing for escape. Sheila reclined apparently relaxed in the cushions of the car, very much as a child who, worn out from play, sinks comfortably into a welcoming chair – there was no outward sign of the inward chaos she felt.

They stopped for dinner along the road at a charming, restful inn surrounded by large old trees. Low on the horizon rode a mellow autumn moon and through the trees just over the rambling roofs hung the evening star, glinting clear and radiant, reminding Nicoli in its pure fire of the purity which was Sheila. Forever after, as she saw the evening star, she was to remember with exquisite clarity the first moon and starshine she had shared with Sheila.

During dinner a stringed orchestra played softly, its romantic melodies designed to warm the hearts of its listeners. To Nicoli as she listened to the plaintive strains came a frantic desire to flee away from the dreamy tender eyes of Sheila and the music that threatened to burst the floodgates of her soul. Still, when they left the inn, she wanted sorely to suggest riding on into the night. Then the side of her that for so many years she had compelled to dominate asserted itself and she turned the car toward the city – driving rapidly, seldom speaking on the homeward journey, fearing that something in Sheila's voice would cause her to abandon her resolutions. Arriving in town, she drove Sheila home, not trusting herself to linger and talk, but with almost feverish haste speeding away from her.

In her mind, as she drove blindly on, she recalled Sheila's expression while talking with her that evening: was she wrong, or had her eyes held a new light, a new look of tenderness? The desire to drive back and ask Sheila to come with her – anywhere – was consuming.

The perfume of this precious person still lingered in her senses, causing her heart to beat madly, her blood to pound in her temples as if seeking an outlet…

Another day of the struggle within Nicoli had come to a close. Slowly but surely Sheila had stolen into her daily life until Nicoli could not visualize life without her. The Weaver in weaving had somehow caught their threads together and twisted them into a single strand.

The next day found Sheila nervous and unable to concentrate at the rehearsal until Nicoli, in desperation, after several attempts to straighten her out, called her aside and quietly said: "I think it would be a good idea, Sheila, to take these scenes tonight and get them set in your mind before tomorrow. I can't take time to work on them now. We can come here, or –" she hesitated – "better still, we can work at my apartment; it will be more comfortable there."

"Yes, I think so too," Sheila replied. "I'll be glad to get the extra time in – I do want to get the right interpretation. I don't know what possesses me today, Nicoli – I seem to have gone haywire for some reason or other. I'll try not to cause you any more trouble… I'm sorry."

Nicoli smiled at the earnest face. "No trouble at all. Will eight o'clock suit you?"

"Any time is convenient; you see, Philip went out of town today, so I shall be perfectly free to work as late as we may want to. By the way, Nicoli, where is your apartment?"

"I'm at the Shidan-Plaze, on Riverside Drive," Nicoli told her. "Apartment 11-A. I'll expect you then, around eight."

Eight o'clock: Sheila emerged from the elevator on the eleventh floor.

"First door to your right," the cheery voice of the elevator boy informed her.

The door of 11-A opened as she approached it. Nicoli greeted her: "I heard the elevator and thought perhaps it was you. Come in."

Broadly spacious rooms greeted Sheila's eyes as she stepped into the apartment. Rooms splashed with light. The floors were wax-like, and upon their gleaming surface stood decisive, virile, cleanly angled furniture. Everywhere was the touch of Nicoli's own inimitable style, truly a fit setting for her dynamic self.

"Nicoli, it's lovely," exclaimed Sheila, looking about. "It is just the sort of place one would expect you to have. It even looks like you. I believe I should have known instantly that you lived in it."

"I've lived here among these things a good many years, Sheila; they are like old friends—" then in a voice tinged with sadness, "they are my only close companions." Throwing off the fleeting mood, she continued, "But here, young woman – we have work to do, and a lot of it, too. We'd best get started."

As they sat on a huge divan under the glow of a lovely old lamp, Sheila studied the woman who sat so earnestly, manuscript in hand, discussing the scenes. Nicoli was wearing a smartly tailored robe which suited her type perfectly, and under the mellow light her closely cropped hair looked peculiarly beautiful with its scattered sprinkling of silver.

It was difficult for Nicoli to keep her eyes on the papers before her and, as the evening wore on, they strayed more and more often to Sheila's lovely face, until Nicoli felt certain that she too must feel the magnetism in the air about them. Surely she must sense the presence of the force that seemed to be drawing them together, urging them into each other's arms.

The resonant voice of Sheila repeating the lines of the play began to beat rhythmically in Nicoli's brain... over and over... over and over... until her blood seemed to be coursing through her veins attuned to that same strange rhythm. Her emotions eddied in a mad whirlpool, striving to free themselves from the brain that impeded them – until at last they burst their bounds and she took Sheila into her arms. Her lips sought Sheila's, loosening the wealth of passion she had fought so long to conquer. Her exploring fingers wandered over the flame-enkindling curves of the lovely body... her warm mouth moved hungrily downward over the firm young throat and on to the smoothness of the velvet-like skin of Sheila's breast. Her voice was low and husky when she spoke:

"I love you so, Sheila," she whispered hoarsely. "I've tried so hard not to, but I do. You've been in my thoughts every moment since that first day – I haven't been able to think of anything else – I've wanted you so."

Sheila's arms tightened around Nicoli. "I've wanted you too, darling – I've wanted you to love me as I love you – I've wanted you to kiss me and hold me close to you forever."

Nicoli's eager mouth claimed Sheila's feverish one. Their souls merged into one, and all of the desire and longing of the weeks past had its fulfillment at that moment.

Later, wrapped in Nicoli's close embrace in the silken blackness of her bedroom, Sheila found a love that was forever to set her apart from the world and bind her always to that world of shadow and shade whence there is no escape.

In the darkness her restlessness and loneliness were silently spirited away, her search came to an end, and the dense fog of longing and yearning that had hung over her being lifted and vanished in a vaporous mist before the brilliant sun of revelation.

Peace and calm came at length to pour oil on the passion-tossed waters of her soul. Sleep descended to carry her away to a land of heavenly dreams – dreams of Nicoli's love… her arms… her long, fervent kisses.

Nicoli stirred slightly, her hand instinctively reaching out to touch Sheila. She awakened with a start at finding herself alone, and sitting up quickly, she called "Darling!" Her voice sounded through the empty rooms. Plainly Sheila was gone.

Why did she leave? Nicoli asked herself. Then glancing at the disheveled pillow beside her, she saw a note. What does it mean? She pondered, as she ripped it open, afraid to read it lest it tell her that Sheila had torn herself from the spell that had bound them so closely. Her eyes scanned its contents:

Nicoli, darling,

How can I tell you what last night meant to me? It is as though I had always known your love. I have been seeking so long the thing you have given me – striving vainly to solve the riddle of my being – wondering, ever wondering what it was that made me an outcast from the lives of others.

When I return to you I shall have broken all ties that might have kept me from being wholly your own.

—Sheila

* * *

Nicoli recalled the ensuing weeks. They had taken up their lives together, there in her apartment. The very atmosphere of it had taken on a new meaning: everything seemed to have become permeated by Sheila's influence; her presence could be felt even during her absence at the theater when Nicoli sat reading or writing alone in their rooms. These had been utterly happy days for them, filled to overflowing with their newly found contentment. *The Woman Alone* had opened, and critics and showmen had pronounced it the greatest thing Nicoli had ever done. They had been lavish in their praise of Sheila Case, saying there was a new life and fire to her work that raised it above all past performances. The glamour that had always been hers was enhanced by the flame that burned so brightly within her. A new dramatic star had risen in the realm of the theater and everywhere the public acclaimed Sheila Case.

Weeks and months passed and still the play went on, until the capacity attendance was the talk of the entire show world and the phenomenal success had become almost a legend on Broadway. Sheila's every move was recorded in the papers, depriving her of all privacy. Everywhere she and Nicoli went, they were immediately surrounded by admirers anxious for a glimpse of the star of the moment.

They had been happy – supremely so – living each day for each other, each night for the love that was theirs; thanking God that He had brought them together, praying Him ever to keep them so; vowing never to part until death should take one from the other. Yet, wrapped in each other's arms, they had been fearful of their sublime happiness lest something destroy it and send them back to the solitude each had known.

* * *

"When will you have to leave?" Sheila inquired anxiously as they sat in Nicoli's office.

Nicoli's eyes dropped again to the cablegram she held in her hands.

"As soon as I can get a boat. Vance says it's urgent that I get there before the opening."

"That isn't but two weeks off, is it?"

Nicoli glanced at the calendar on her desk. "Just exactly two weeks. I can't imagine what the difficulty is – I thought until this arrived that the show was all set."

"Well, it seems to me that as familiar as Vance is with the script he should be able to get the show in shape to open without you." Sheila's voice was petulant.

"You're absolutely correct, darling," Nicoli agreed. "If I had known that he couldn't handle it himself, I never would have allowed him to persuade me to produce a number two show."

"Still, from a financial standpoint, you would have been foolish not to, but – " Sheila's hand reached out to Nicoli's – "this separation is going to be dreadful. I don't know what I shall do without you!"

Nicoli's strong fingers gripped Sheila's slender ones. "It is going to be beastly, my darling, but it's too late now to do anything about it – I'll just have to go."

Sheila sighed resignedly. "Well – there's one thing about it; with you over there, the first night is bound to be a success."

"Let's hope so! I'd hate to leave you only to see a failure."

The telephone on Nicoli's desk rang. "Yes?"

"You can sail tomorrow night," her secretary's voice informed her. "Shall I make reservations?"

"That's fine," Nicoli replied in her usual clear decisive manner. "Go ahead and make them."

She replaced the telephone. "That's that! I won't need much time to pack. I'll leave the office early tomorrow and throw a few things into some bags. I shan't need many clothes."

"I'm so glad – I don't believe I could stand to see many of your things leave the apartment." Sheila's words were tinged with the anguish she felt at losing her beloved Nicoli for even so brief a period.

* * *

In the speeding taxicab on the way to the docks Sheila sat close to Nicoli, her arm linked through hers.

"I can't bear to let you go," she whispered. "I don't see how I can stand having you away from me."

Nicoli's arm slipped about her waist, pressing her closer. "There isn't anything we can do – I have to go – but I'll be thinking of you and loving you every moment of the time. Nothing can keep me from doing that."

"Promise me you'll cable me the minute you arrive," Sheila pleaded. "I have to know you're safe. I have to have some word from you."

"I promise, darling…"

Conversation was brought up short by their arrival at the docks. Pier 47 was crowded and a motley throng wended its way up the gangplank and onto the decks of the departing liner. Messenger boys laden with flowers and elaborately packed bon voyage baskets hurried about seeking their respective destinations. Merry groups in faultless evening attire talked and laughed gaily as they pressed through the crowd, eager to find departing friends with whom to share a farewell drink or two. A woman recognized Sheila and turned excitedly to inform her companions, "That's Sheila Case, the actress!" Immediately Sheila's receding figure drew all their eyes as she and Nicoli followed a steward to Nicoli's cabin.

Comfortably settled there, they spent the remaining minutes talking, each endeavoring to direct the conversation away from Nicoli's impending departure.

In just a few moments the luxurious liner, bearing her human cargo, would slowly pull away from the shore and begin her long journey across the great body of water, only to glide gracefully up to another pier and its noise and confusion.

The ship's clock ticked away the fleeting time.

"All ashore that's going ashore." The words drifted into Nicoli's stateroom, followed by the deep musical tones of the gong.

Sheila rose unwillingly from her position on the lounge. Bravely she strove to keep her voice cheerful. "I must go, or I'm afraid they will be taking me along." She made a valiant attempt to smile.

Nicoli gathered her into her arms. "I wish they would, darling! I don't know what I'll do without you."

Sheila's hands caressed Nicoli's face. "I love you so, my darling." Her mouth came to rest on Nicoli's. Her kiss was long and fervent. Reluctantly she released her and with an uncertain voice bid her a hasty goodbye, then hurried from the stateroom – along the crowded deck – down the gangplank – her only bridge between supreme happiness and abject loneliness. With eyes blinded by tears, she watched the narrow strip of water widen relentlessly between the shore and the huge white glistening ship. With an aching void where her heart had been, she turned away… her Nicoli was gone.

The following days Sheila felt horribly alone. Alone in a city where so many would gladly have given anything to share even a moment with her. But people meant nothing; their applause left her strangely untouched, for no matter how appreciative her audience was, when the final curtain fell and the noise and confusion of the theater were left behind, all that remained for her were four walls and her utter loneliness.

"How empty fame is, after all," Sheila thought. "How little it is worth compared to the precious moments it costs in separation."

Three weeks. Nicoli's long-awaited cable announcing her departure for home came at last. Hours dragged by – hideously slow hours – as Sheila in her mind followed the steamer mile after mile across the expanse of water. Then the gala day... Nicoli, her Nicoli, was coming. Sheila sang gaily as she dressed to go to meet her. Long before the steamer slipped into its berth she stood waiting. Finally it arrived, and Sheila pressed forward through the crowd to the gates.

At last her eager gaze caught sight of the familiar figure coming down the gangplank. "Nicoli! Nicoli!"

During the drive home Sheila talked excitedly, loosening a flurry of questions, allowing no time for answers. "Did you have a pleasant crossing? Any interesting people on board?" And repeatedly the query, "Did you miss me? Are you glad to be back?"

* * *

As time went on they were happier than ever before, blissfully unaware that slowly a mighty force was gathering that would tear their lives from their foundations.

Broadway was beginning to talk. The gaunt, ugly spectre of Gossip stalked the brightly lighted street, trailing slimy fingers dipped in the filth or rumor and scandal, leaving a viscous trail in its wake along the path it trod. Its fetid breath seeped into the minds of friends who struggled vainly to deny its presence and into the already corrupted brains of people who were only too willing and anxious to acknowledge its existence there and further rank its progress.

In a short time the habitués of the White Way were divided into two warring camps: those who fought to disclaim the malicious charges, and those who offered what they contended was ample proof of their validity. The defensive faction pointed with pride to Nicoli's position, her years of work unsullied by even an atom of scandal, to Sheila's artistry and her exquisite femininity. "Is it not quite natural," they asked, "that these two should be close companions? Sheila Case is the finished product of Nicoli's unbounded genius – hers is the love of a great artist for the masterpieces she has created."

"Lies – all lies," jeered the offensive. "Physical attraction – baseness – is the bond that holds them so firmly together. They belong to a group of people who have no acknowledged place and never will have because of the vileness of their natures. What can they know of love – they who do not even know the meaning of the word? Their sort should be stamped from the earth – eradicated completely – so that normal minds would not have to witness their degrading escapades."

So the battle raged, while the insidious gossip gained momentum everywhere. In the nightclubs, restaurants, and theaters people talked. Actors whispered choice bits; stage hands passed them on to onlookers and they in turn to their friends.

Unsavory fragments drifted to Sheila's ears. What could she do? What must she do to protect Nicoli? She was sensitive, Sheila told herself, but not nearly so much so as Nicoli. How could she stand idly by and see her lose friends of years' standing – see her lose caste among the people who now reverenced her name? See her outstanding independence of mind slip away – see her lose her most valued possession, her self-respect? And at last to see her marked by the world – a failure. How could she bear to know that it was she who had ruined her life – her career – and finally stripped her of everything her years of untiring effort had built up?

When that day should finally come, would her love be compensation enough for the great loss Nicoli would sustain? Could she, Sheila – would she – accept such a sacrifice? If she did, what surcease could she possibly find from the pain that would come when she gazed into Nicoli's deep eyes and saw the hunted look and sorrow hidden there?

Hourly Sheila sought the answers to her questions; hourly one and only one solution came to her weary brain. Always she fought bravely to cloak her fears and mental turmoil with laughter and carefree chatter, yet ever she carried the burden of knowledge that sooner or later she must bow to the tyranny of public opinion and man-made conventions.

Nicoli too sensed the situation and tried desperately to conceal her own misgivings. Was this not the very reason, she asked herself, that for years she had gone on alone, steeling herself against the unusual desires of her heart – starving her inner being of the love that she knew was so essential to its happiness – working hours on end in order to still, through sheer weariness, the pleading cry within her? Had she not always known that she could not bear the onslaught of public opinion? Not against herself – she would not let that matter – but how could she tolerate having people who could not hope to comprehend, make of their love a cheap, tawdry thing? How could she reconcile herself to the coarse references made to that love by persons wholly unsuited by nature to grasp even in the slightest degree its true meaning? They deemed it unnatural, and so it was to them, unnatural – but deeper and sweeter for the very nature of its unnaturalness, and God-given to the few to whom He had given understanding. Yet, notwithstanding her apprehension, Nicoli thanked Him fervently in her dark hours for His heavenly gift and determined anew each day never to relinquish the untold joys and peace of Sheila's love, no matter what the world might demand in payment. She would give willingly to the unseeing masses anything they might demand save Sheila and her love for her. These she would keep forever locked safely away in the innermost recesses of her heart, sheltering them always – protecting them ever.

* * *

Weeks passed with Nicoli and Sheila both trying bravely to hide from each other the disturbing knowledge that had become such a burden. They became more and more retiring. Sheila pleading fatigue and Nicoli devoting the hours away from her office to her writing: neither of them wished to subject themselves to the curious, wondering gaze of people who still strove to meet them.

It was late in May when Nicoli gave the show the two weeks' notice that announced its closing.

In a few weeks most of the legitimate houses along Broadway would be in darkness for the summer months; the warehouses would begin to fill, as wardrobe and scenery were carefully stored away. Theatrical offices would be quiet until August, when the call for performers would again be heard. Actors who were affluent at the close of the season would be leaving New York for vacations and much needed rest; others not so fortunate would congregate in the various clubs and on the streets, talking of the break that was sure to come when the new season should open, while in the meantime they spent sparingly of the meager savings that were almost certain to have vanished before rehearsals should begin again.

Nicoli and Sheila were both tired after the grueling months of work, and the closing night found them eager for the rest the following weeks would yield. It would seem a real treat to have every evening free to lounge about their apartment.

It was comfortable, delightfully so, Sheila thought, the first evening she was at liberty to enjoy it. The lights were so soothing, so mellow, compared to the bright searching lights of the theater. Yes, it would be nice to be lazy, if only… Nicoli's words interrupted the disturbing thought.

"I've been thinking, Sheila, that perhaps it would be a good idea for you to rest a few days before we try to make any plans for a vacation. In that way I can finish up at the office and you'll be feeling better to go away."

"That's perfect, darling. I'm too tired now even to think about where I'd like to go." Sheila's voice, usually resonant, sounded hollow. Why must Nicoli speak of their trip together, when her heart was so torn by indecision? Aloud she continued:

"I think I'll shop tomorrow, Nicoli – it's been so long since I've had time for that sort of thing – and then I'll have all that behind me, with nothing to do but rest and wait for you to come home at night."

"Too tired to do a little shopping for me, darling, while you are at it? You know me – the only time I care about shopping is when I am buying something for you."

"Of course I am not too tired for that, Nicoli," Sheila answered reproachfully. "I'd love it."

Later in the evening Sheila lay stretched out lazily on the sofa with Nicoli reclining on the luxurious fur rug beside her. Her graceful fingers wandered lightly through Nicoli's hair as they listened to the soothing tones of the radio. The throbbing notes of a mighty organ filled the room – the organist was playing "Always."

Sheila's hand pulled Nicoli's dark head closer. "Darling," she said softly, "I want you to know what I've been thinking just now."

"What is it, sweetheart?" Nicoli looked up.

"Well…" Sheila hesitated. "I know it sounds flowery, but I've been thinking that no matter what the years may bring to us, and no matter how things may seem, I want you to believe and know that I'm always yours, Nicoli – that I'll always be loving you and wanting you—" her voice dropped to a fervent murmur – "always, my lover, always."

Nicoli looked long into Sheila's earnest eyes. "I've always known you were completely mine, darling. You could never be anything else, any more than that song could ever belong to anyone other than you in my mind. I never hear it without remembering the way you sang it that first time I saw you. I think I must have loved you even then…" The words trailed off, lost in the enveloping warmth of Sheila's kiss.

The following night Nicoli came home early. All day long she had heard no word from Sheila. She had called the apartment twice during the day, but then she remembered that Sheila was shopping. Perhaps she had been too tired to come by the office as she had so often done before.

"How silly for me to feel that something is out of order," she told herself shortly. "She is not a child who has to give an account of every moment of her day."

She rang the bell to their apartment. Sheila was not yet home. She took her key from her bag and unlocked the door.

On the floor just inside the door lay a letter addressed in Sheila's familiar handwriting. A nameless fear clutched her. Hastily she tore the letter open, her eyes flashing across the pages… eyes that gradually dimmed with tears as she read the words that were forever to remain in her heart:

My darling—

I need not try to tell you how cruelly difficult it is for me to write this. You must know what you mean to me, and how I feel. I have known for months that although you love me dearly you have been unhappy – unhappy because of outside influences over which you and I have no power.

You are fine and good, my sweetheart, and it is unfair that you should suffer the pain of our being the subject of so much discussion. I know that you have tried desperately not to worry, but in spite of your efforts you have worried. You cannot, must not be allowed to go on trying to fight a losing battle, one from which neither you nor I can hope to emerge victorious.

Our love is not an accepted one, darling, and sooner or later the constant onslaught will have its deadly effect, and it will become torn and broken. I could not bear that, my Nicoli – it is too perfect, and so I choose rather to keep it always in my

heart as it now is even though many miles and many years may separate us, and many tears mark their passage. I love you, my own, and always will be
—*Your Sheila.*

* * *

M onths passed... months of desperate silence for Nicoli; days and weeks of torture and effort to keep herself from the endeavor to find Sheila and implore her to return; nights when in her agony she cried out to God, asking Him to ease the sorrow and longing in her heart; sinking into the furthermost depths of grief – struggling vainly to erase from the impressionable canvas of her memory the exquisite picture of her life with Sheila.

Yet... in her mind she was ever conscious that Sheila had been right. It was best to sacrifice their love now that it might live eternally in its entirety, unsullied by further contact with a ruthless world. Yes, it was best so – to let it go while it was yet perfect; to keep it always enshrined in their hearts away from human power to harm its gloriousness; to protect it ever from the fires that eventually would destroy it and reduce it to ashes.

Dorothea Krivatsky
from THE SCENT OF NIGHT
1936

My brother Bill had left a note at the mental hospital telling me he'd paid my rent and left some of his clothes for me at the boarding house, to check the inside pocket of the suit jacket for some cash. He'd told my mother I was in again for the junk, but I'm sure she knew better. So I took the trolley into town, went to my boarding house for a bath and change of clothes, and to ponder what I would do next. My hair was getting long, but the barber could wait till tomorrow. Bill's worn chinos felt good against my skin, and with a white shirt and jacket I almost felt like myself again, not some inmate in the Ladies Ward.

I decided to stop by Joe's garage before eating. Joe always gave me work when he could, knew I was a good mechanic, knew not to ask questions. I found him doing body work on an old Ford, slow careful work. He smiled when he saw me.

"Frankie! Where you been?"

"Hey Joe. In the hospital for a spell."

"You okay now? Need anything?"

"I'm good, just looking for work."

"It's slow here. I barely have enough work to keep Bobby on. Hey, come back to my office for a minute."

Joe's office was a desk, a clutter of catalogs and invoices, a telephone. He shuffled through a stack of business cards, finally pulling one out, eyeing it, and dialing the number on the telephone.

"Mrs. Baxter? Joe Doolittle here. Are you still looking for a driver?" He nodded at the phone. "I've got someone you might like. Clean, polite, good mechanic. Name's Frankie Polonski. Yep. Thank you, Mrs. Baxter, I'll pass that on."

He hung up the telephone and smiled at me.

"West Chester. Rich beyond belief. So rich the crash didn't affect them. Wants a driver. She'll see you tomorrow at two." He wrote down an address on a strip of paper. "Get a haircut. Do you need money?"

"No, Joe, I'm good." I grinned at him. "Thanks."

He shooed his hand at me, all gruff. "G'on, get outta here."

* * *

Driver. For a rich woman. Probably middle-aged, fat, pretentious. I contemplated driving while the barber trimmed my hair. Shouldn't be too bad, at least for a while. Get some money together, think about going out west. Keep my distance from the servants.

She eyed me for a long time, but said nothing. She could only be a few years older than me, her blonde hair bobbed, her blue eyes ice cold. She had a fine thin scar that stretched from the outer corner of her left eye to the top of her ear. Finally, she snuffed out her cigarette.

"You'll do. Mrs. Waddington will give you the address of the tailor to get your uniform from. Can you start tomorrow morning? Good. Bring your things with you and spend the morning getting settled."

I looked at her, surprised. She smiled faintly.

"Didn't Mr. Doolittle tell you? It's a live-in position. There's a flat above the carriage house."

* * *

Mr. Baxter drove himself, a new Ford. He was rarely at home. Mrs. Baxter's car was a Bentley. She spent her days lunching at the houses of other equally bored rich ladies. While I drove her from one place to another, she jotted in a small diary. I knew better than to ask. She was a remarkably silent woman, methodical, seemingly without pleasures. Her relations with her husband were cordial – one could see that there was some anger rippling under the surface when they dined together. They had separate rooms, as I learned when I was instructed to take his suitcase to his car.

The servants were hers, the house was hers, but the money was his. She was bored – she spent her afternoons reading or working in the garden. One afternoon she wandered into the carriage house while I was changing the oil in the Bentley. She sidled up next to me and peered at the engine. "Combustion?" she asked.

"Pardon?"

"The engine – it's a combustion engine?"

"Uh... yes."

She looked at the engine a moment longer, then reached over and touched the bulge made by a carefully rolled sock at front of my uniform pants. I wasn't expecting that, and shivered. She smiled, and looked back at the engine.

"How long does it take the oil to drain?"

Her coolness stunned me. "About twenty minutes."

"Hmmm. Enough time to go upstairs." She walked casually over to the stairs that lead to my small apartment. At the foot of the stairs she stopped and turned. "Come along," she commanded, and I followed.

Each of the 12 steps to the flat was misery. I couldn't think of a way to keep my secret from being found out, which of course would mean the end of this job and the quiet, rent-free flat. When I reached the door at the top of the stairs, Mrs. Baxter had already stripped off her shoes and dress.

"Don't be shy, Frankie," she said as pulled me to her. And so I did what any other woman in the same situation would do: I kissed her hard, then peeled off her slip and tore my way through bra, garters, and hose, and ran my hands, still dirty with grit, all over her porcelain white body before pushing her roughly onto the bed and running my tongue over every inch of her. She was still gasping for air as I lowered myself onto her and started licking her nipples, slowing working my way to her mound of Venus, then taking her clitoris between my teeth and rubbing it hard with the tip of my tongue. She squirmed with pleasure and pleaded with me to take her, but I held back, savoring the taste of her in my mouth. She pulled at my fly, but I slapped her hand away and instead thrust my fingers deep into her, and rocked her to climax with my right hand. She stifled her cry of passion in my pillow. As she lay still on the bed, fingers still clutching my sheets, the sound of the engine of Mr. Baxter's Ford came clearly up the drive.

"Stay here," I said softly, and went quickly down the stairs, so that I was in place and peering at the Bentley's engine when Mr. Baxter pulled the Ford into the garage next to me.

"How are you, Frankie," he asked as he left the car, not waiting for my response, but hurrying into the house by way of the kitchen.

Moments later Mrs. Baxter appeared. I handed her a pair of shears from my workbench. "Go through the back garage door and cut some flowers before you go back to the house," I said. Her lips curled as she took the shears from me and disappeared. I stood in front of the Bentley, sucking the taste of her off my fingers, wondering what to make of it all.

* * *

After a month, I decided that it had been an aberration on Mrs. Baxter's part, and that it would not occur again. I contemplated spending my nights off in the city, but had my own reasons for staying away. I kept myself to myself. One late summer afternoon, as I was driving Mrs. Baxter home from a luncheon, she instructed me to pull down a winding side road that brought us to an apple orchard at the foot of a hill. "Frankie," she said softly, almost in a whisper, "turn the engine off and come sit back here with me."

I joined her in the back seat, and we sat quietly for a moment. "I must be careful," she said softly. "I can't get pregnant. Charles—" she bit her lip "—Charles is sterile." She turned her pale blue eyes on me. "What you did that afternoon – up in your flat –" her hand reached out, caressed my leg, moved dangerously close to the inert sock in my pants "—do that again."

She wore a matching skirt and jacket and I had those off her in a trice. Her blouse and her brassiere came off quickly too, and I took my time examining her full round breasts, the pale pink of her nipples. She slid out of her slip and garter belt, and suddenly I felt greedy, pulled her soft bottom up against me, and slid my fingers into her without preliminaries. She gasped hard, but pushed back against me, and I thrust inside her with a ruthlessness I didn't know I possessed, with a sudden anger over the situation she had put me in, and I felt my already-wet clitoris hardening, and knew I was in over my head. That was the moment she reached back to caress my member, saying in gasps, "But Frankie, you're not even hard," and I thrust against her harder, until she came, her cry hoarse and deep, unstifled.

She turned to me, as I sat there, fully clothed in my immaculate uniform, and eyed me appraisingly, in the same way she had on that first day when I came to see her about the job. She straddled my knee, rubbing herself against the coarse cloth of my trousers, caressing the rolled sock, which stayed as inert as ever. "You're an odd fish," she said angrily, and as she started to move away, I lifted my knee, and she moaned with pleasure and lowered herself back against my leg. "Kiss me," she commanded, and reached out and pulled my face to her. And everything stopped.

My heart thudded with a deadly slowness as she sat back and looked at me, then felt my cheeks and chin with trembling fingers. "You—" she said, her eyes wild, "you – you're a *woman*!" And she slapped me hard across my face. After a shocked moment, she started to move away, but I quickly pinned her against the seat, her legs beneath mine, her hands together in my left hand, high above her head. I figured that this job was over now, so I might as well take my time. I nuzzled her throat, then carefully licked her breasts, sucking on her nipples, which hardened in spite what she must have been thinking, and slowly eased myself south to her soft, downy womanhood. I let go of her hands and began to lick her clitoris, felt her pulse quickening, then she had her hands in my hair. She pressed her mound hard against my mouth, and I entered her with a full hand, pushing slow and hard inside her until once again she cried out in delight. Then I gently took my hand from her, stepped out of the car, and closed the door. I gave her time to dress and then started the engine and headed homeward.

* * *

That night, I packed my one bag, put my books in a box, hung my uniform neatly up on the back of the door. Best to wait for the occupants of the house to turn in for the night, and I'd walk into town, hitch a ride from there. I took a last bath – if I headed west it might be a long time before I had another chance to get clean again.

When I came out of the bathroom, she was sitting on my bed.

"Mrs. Baxter—" I started, but she looked up angrily.

"For God's sake, we're alone, you can call me Helen. Unpack your bag, you're not going anywhere, Frankie – or whatever your name actually is."

"Frances."

"Frances. Of course, how obvious." She looked up at me in my towel. "You'll forgive me for being shocked. You pulled it off quite well. I never would have known." She looked down at her shoes, frowning. "I haven't done anything like this – with a woman – since boarding school. Not that I suppose you know anything about that." My anger flared, and I beat it back – how would she know that her chauffeur had indeed gone to the best schools in the country?

"The main thing," she said, turning to me, "is that you don't go quitting. It would only make Charles suspect something unsavory. The key is to carry on as always." She stood, as if to leave. I blocked her path. She slapped me again, hard. "God damn you, you have no idea…" I slapped her back, letting the towel fall to the floor, and pushed her on the unmade bed. She didn't resist as I undressed her quickly, as I pressed myself up against her. Still, her passivity angered me, and I took her hand, and guided it up and down against my clitoris. She drew in her breath sharply when I pushed her fingers inside of me. I pushed her back on the bed, and rode her hand hard, finally letting myself go. Then I settled down on top of her and this time, as I caressed her skin, she returned the caresses, licked my neck, explored the softness of my breasts.

"How do you," she began, as she teased one of my nipples with her fingers, "how do you make yourself look so flat-chested? And the broad shoulders? You don't look anything like you do in uniform."

I have to admit, I found that pretty funny, and stopped to light a cigarette. "I bind my chest with linen bands," I said softly. "And the broad shoulders, well, that comes from padding that I had the tailor add."

She chuckled with me, took a drag from my cigarette. "And that thing in your pants?" she asked. "A piece of garden hose?"

"A rolled-up sock."

There was no more intimacy that night, nor for the next few nights. She was capricious in her desires. She spent a week in New York City with Mr. Baxter and brought me back a book bound in red leather. "A peace offering," she said as she gave it to me. It was a volume of Sappho. "She was a Greek poetess," she began, and I stopped her.

"I've been to college," I said softly. "I don't know much Greek but my Latin is still pretty sharp." She looked surprised. "I live like this because I'd rather be a chauffeur or a mechanic than have to be some rich man's wife," I said evenly.

"But what about your family?"

"Well, my family… when my mother found out, she had me committed to a mental asylum."

"Oh my god," she said softly, and pulled me close.

* * *

I wasn't sure I liked Helen. I knew enough to know that I didn't love her. But I did like having a steady lover, I liked unwinding the linen and wearing just a t-shirt, I liked not having to pretend all the time.

Helen liked – well, she liked to get away from the house, the respectful servants, her respectable life. Sometimes she would come up to my flat and stretch out on the bed with a novel while I worked at the typewriter. What the servants thought of this I never knew, and after a while I ceased to think about it. Helen told me that they all thought I was studying up to go to college to study engineering.

Sometimes she would feel restless and she would pace back and forth, cigarette in hand, as I wrote. Sometimes she would read through whatever pages I had left on my desk, sitting very straight and prim in the spare ladder-back chair. Her concentration could be unnerving. She would read the pages as they came out of my typewriter, pacing with impatience for the next page to be finished.

"You are wasting your life, being a chauffeur."

But I was free. The bargain was worth it to me.

* * *

We spent autumn afternoons at the apple orchard, on an old quilt or, when it rained, in the back of the Bentley. I still worked on my novel at night, but I found myself settling into a quiet routine, with quiet assumptions. I ate my meals with the rest of the house staff, but spent most of my time in the garage, tinkering with the Bentley or with the old truck that Earl, the gardener, used. Once she learned I was writing a novel, Helen brought me books from Mr. Baxter's library. Christmas approached; I heard in the kitchen that there was to be a big party, that the Baxters were going all out. And then I was sent to Awbury.

The only thing that distinguishes Awbury from any other small country town is a girls' boarding school, and it was there that I was sent to pick up Helen's niece Audrey. Audrey was 18 and looked like Helen in a schoolgirl's uniform, right down to the blue eyes and bobbed hair. I held open the Bentley's door for her, then put her valise in the trunk. As I started the engine, she said, "You're new, aren't you? Aunt Helen goes through drivers so fast. What's your name?" and on, a nonstop list of observations and questions until four hours later when we arrived home.

That night Helen came late to my room. "I hate the holidays," she declared sternly, "all these people coming and going. How is one supposed to fuck the chauffeur with all this ruckus?" Her attempt at humor fell flat. She sighed, and sat down next to me.

"You might have told me I was picking up your daughter," I said. She turned to me, alarmed. "I know, she's supposed to be your sister's daughter. But really, Helen, she looks exactly like you, and I'll guess she looks nothing like your sister."

"Well, my sister Gloria and I looked remarkably alike. I had Audrey the first year Gloria was away at college. Gloria died of pneumonia a month after Audrey was born, and so it was easy for my parents to say Audrey was Gloria's child. It would have been better if she had been put up for adoption, but Charles was dead set against it."

"Charles?"

"Oh dear. Charles had been trying to marry me since I was 15. I wasn't interested. Even when I got pregnant by another man, he didn't care, he was ready to marry me right then. But I refused, and that was that. Then Gloria died. Charles joined the army and fought in France. Prohibition came along, and Daddy had to close his distillery. We came very close to losing everything, had sheriffs ready to sell off the household goods when Charles arrived with his stock market money. At that point I was no longer proud. I married him." She leaned against me, and I stroked her hair. "I'm trapped here, more trapped than you are." She kissed me. "I can't see you as much during the holidays," she said. "Don't be mad at me."

Indeed, I spent most of the holidays picking things up in town and bringing them back to the house, meeting guests at the train, and even splitting logs for firewood. But I didn't mind. I've never liked Christmas, and all the activity kept my mind off my family. Bill surprised me late one afternoon – he'd caught a ride in from town with Earl. He had a big square box with him, and a smaller paper parcel. The parcel contained three shirts with detachable collars. The square box contained a typewriter he'd bought second-hand from a company that went bust. I drove him back to the train in the Bentley. I felt that perhaps my life was finally coming together.

* * *

Boxing Day was more hustle and bustle, but in the evening Mr. Baxter went off to his club. Helen left Audrey listening to music on the wireless and came up to my flat. "Frankie," she said softly, "I can't stand any more of this." I helped her take off her clothes, and we caressed each other in the chill room. "Please, Frankie," she begged softly, "Take me now." I slid my fingers into her. "More," she said, and soon my fist was inside her, and she squealed with pleasure, wrapped her legs around my neck. I licked her clitoris as I thrust inside her, and her squeals became moans. My heartbeat matched itself to the pulse of my fist inside her. When it was over, I rubbed my face against her mound, sat up and smiled at her. I reached for a cigarette and saw something in the corner of my eye – at the head of the stairs stood Audrey, stock still. As I opened my mouth to speak, she raised a finger to her lips, shook her head, and retreated silently down the stairs.

* * *

It was two days before I saw Audrey again. The Baxters were at a party, and I was in the quiet garage, polishing the chrome on the Bentley. She bustled through the side door, announcing she was bored. What could I possibly say to her? She had witnessed me in my true form, making love to her mother. She was 18, and I couldn't imagine her keeping her mouth shut forever. I knew she would be my undoing, so I kept quiet and continued my polishing.

"I notice," she said, "that you didn't tell my mother." My eyes flicked up her referring to Helen in such a way. "Oh, don't give me that. We all know she's my mother." She leaned against the Bentley. "You know, I'm even older than she was when she had me." I didn't rise to that bait, but kept my eyes on the chrome. "What do you thing would happen if Uncle Charles found out that his wife was sleeping with the chauffeur? Or that the chauffeur was actually a woman? Or both?"

I straightened myself, put down the polishing cloth. "What is it that you want, Miss," I asked, fighting to maintain an oriental inscrutability.

"I want what every woman wants, well, every woman except maybe you," she said coyly. "I want you to do to me what you did to my mother. Right here, right now."

"You're a child!" I protested.

"I'm 18 and I have everything my mother has." She opened the back door to the Bentley, slid onto the leather seat, and began to undress. I heard footsteps on the gravel outside, and quickly shut the car door and pretended to polish. Earl came in, fired up the truck, and drove out. I shut the garage door behind him.

When I opened the Bentley's door, Audrey was naked on the seat, fingering her clitoris. She had so little hair, and her nipples were taut in the cold air. I reached out, and grasped her left foot, caressed it, bit her big toe. "You are going to get dressed and get out of this car and go back into the house," I told her. "I am going to drive this car to pick up your aunt and uncle. I don't think they want to leave their party to find you naked in the car."

She sat up and glared at me. "You think I'm just a little girl. You think no one will listen to me. Well, you're wrong there. I'll have you in jail so fast—"

I slapped her hard, across the mouth. Her nose started to bleed. She scooted away from me on the leather seat. I sat down next to her and shut the car door. She sniffled. I leaned to her, quickly, kissed her hard, full mouth, and slid two fingers into her vagina. She was a virgin and I confess I liked the feel of her hymen tearing at my fingertips. She whimpered, but my fingers continued to explore her, and my lips found their way to her small bud-like nipples. Did she climax? It was hard to tell. There was blood on my fingers when I pulled them from her. Disgust welled up in me. I left the car, and went upstairs. I packed the one bag, put the books and typewriter in a box. When I brought them downstairs to the car, Audrey was gone.

I pulled open the garage door, and set off on foot down the snowy driveway.

Gale Wilhelm
from TORCHLIGHT TO VALHALLA
1938

She sat low on the divan with her shoulders and neck bent sharply against the back cushion. The wind roared in the chimney and the acacias beat against the house under the windows. If you sit like that, Fritz used to say to her, you'll grow into a concertina. She lifted herself a little. She had been looking into the fire so long her eyes ached with looking. Darkness knelt in the room, though it was still the time before sunset. The rain came in spasms, beating at the windows with small vicious knuckles. She was waiting but when she heard the other knocking it was in her ears only a variation of the same theme and she didn't move. Then it came again and this time the sound penetrated and she went swiftly to the door and opened it.

She stood silent and without moving for so long Toni finally laughed and stepped inside unasked. She took Morgen's hand off the door and closed it herself.

When you laugh like that, Morgen said, you're all silver and crystal.

Toni laughed again and began to unfasten her raincoat.

Let me help you, Morgen said. Oh, you're so wet!

You're getting wet.

There, Morgen said. Let me take it.

I might have taken my gloves off first, Toni said, smiling.

Morgen looked at her hands coming out of the wet gloves. I thought you'd never come, Toni. I went up to your house.

Aunt Lida told me. I meant to come earlier but I didn't know I was going to the library.

They smiled at each other and Morgen took the dripping coat and hung it beside hers in the bathroom and Toni made cautious footsteps across the floor to the hearth. Morgen came back with a bath towel and a pair of straw scuffs. Toni smiled at them and sat on the divan and unbuckled her small thick-soled shoes and Morgen, sitting on the hearth, took them one after another out of her hands and put them to dry. Toni slipped her bare brown feet into the scuffs and Morgen gave her the towel and, smiling, still saying nothing, she sopped her short hair and then, letting the towel drop onto her shoulders, looking like a child just out of its bath, she leaned forward and said, Brunnehilde circled with fire.

A stillness went around them and Morgen leaned across this stillness to touch the hands and face she loved. That was a moment made wholly of tenderness. She withdrew from it gently, sitting erect again but not alone. You're so known to me, she said slowly. It isn't possible for one person suddenly to be everything like this, but you are. Her voice sank and she smiled and after a moment she said, I was waiting. I didn't know what I was waiting for, I didn't even know I was waiting, but when I saw you I knew.

* * *

She knew when Toni left her. She lifted herself a little and thought, In sleep you seem almost not to breathe. Where do you go? And then her thoughts became formless and liquid. She lay separate and awake, looking at the silhouette of Toni's head on the pillow. She heard the campanile chime three o'clock. The sound of the wind and rain had softened into silence but the darkness had a voice and it spoke insistently. Finally she said, Toni?

Toni turned her head. Yes?

I had to say your name.

My heart and I are sleeping, Toni said.

You did sleep a little, Toni. I watched you.

With cat's eyes, Toni said smiling. You say my name as if you'd given it to me. There's no other way to say it.

Didn't you sleep, Morgen?

No, Morgen said. She felt Toni slipping away from her again into sleep. She lay listening with her fingertips and heard the heart slow and the soft beating go deep and then without waning breath and pulse and nerves caught and turned in her and she turned.

She woke Toni again but so gently waking was like dreaming.

* * *

When Toni opened her eyes she saw a strange room bright with light. She lay in space touching nothing. Then she turned slightly, finding herself, and her ankles moved against Morgen's. In sleep they had drawn apart all but their ankles. She turned her head and saw Morgen's hair on the pillow and she saw her face, pale with soft fringed shadows under the eyes, her long curved throat. She held her breath. She wanted to melt and pour herself around Morgen like wax.

Violet Black
SHOP GIRLS WANTED
1938

Autumn afternoons in Manhattan were always bustling, that's what Rose thought as she pulled her coat a little tighter against the chill October wind and clutched her pocketbook in front of her. Hustling and bustling, as her mother would say.

Rose was glad of the hatpin as the small gusts pushed at her beret while she fairly shoved her way up the subway steps, flat against the flow of people on their way home from work. *What had she been thinking of, coming into the city at the end of the day for a job interview?* The sun was beginning to set and soon it would be fully dark. Rose shivered involuntarily.

Of course, Rose knew what she had been thinking. She'd been thinking like any other girl would be thinking right about now. She was desperate, that had been what she'd been thinking. She'd been doing a little of this and a little of that for Mrs. Dombrovsky at the tailor down the block from her little flat in Brooklyn, but the rent kept coming due faster than she could keep up with it and she needed something, well, more substantial and less demanding than Mrs. Dombrovsky standing over her smelling of sausage and cabbage and making her rip out more stitches than she put in. Times were very hard, and she had come to New York for work, so she could not just leave Mrs. Dombrovsky. But, she thought, as she glanced at herself in a shop window as she fairly ran to the appointment, if she kept stinting herself as she had been doing, she was going to lose her looks, and that just wouldn't do. She knew her looks were the one thing she could count upon.

Rose stopped for a minute, turned full face to the window and straightened her hat, smoothing the waves of her hair as best she could. She pulled her gloves a little sleeker over her slender wrists and put her pocketbook over her arm a little more gracefully. She wanted to make a good impression, after all. She bent down and straightened the seams of her last good pair of stockings. A newspaper boy jostled her as she turned back toward the street and gave her a wolf-whistle, "Nice gams, sister," and trotted off.

Rose blushed.

* * *

Peau de Soie Salon catered to elite Upper East Side women with lots of time and even more money. As soon as Rose entered the place she knew she'd never get the position. Her clothes were wrong, for a start, and so was her very look. Rose was a big-breasted, milk-fed girl from the Midwest, with deep blue eyes surrounded by long lashes, peaches-and-cream skin, a few freckles where no one would ever see them, and a thick cascade of wavy auburn hair that she just couldn't bear to cut into a more fashionable style than the swirled chignon she wore at the base of her neck.

At twenty-two, Rose was tall and almost graceful, but she looked young – too young, she thought – and naive. Her tight little gray twin set and tweed skirt were more clerical than soignée, she realized as she strode toward the sleek black, kidney-shaped desk at the front of the shop. Everything in the room was fancy and rich-looking. Everything, that was, but Rose.

"Yes?" The tone of the well-dressed woman behind the desk matched her expression, which was of immeasurable disdain. The severe high collar of her black silk dress set off her short black, marcelled hair. Marcasite earrings adorned her small lobes and a marcasite choker emphasized her slender throat. There was no wedding ring on her well-manicured hand. The woman reminded Rose of the wicked stepmother in *Snow White*, and Rose involuntarily stepped back.

"Good afternoon, Ma'am. I'm Rose Blakemore. I'm here to see a Madame Frederique Odile about a position here. My appointment is at five."

It was 4:45 pm. Rose hadn't wanted to appear too eager nor slothful. She was lucky to have made that train, or she'd have been late. She let out a little breath. Her lips remained slightly parted, a look the woman across from her could not help but register as inadvertently sensual.

"I'm Miss Adams. Muriel Adams. I'll let Madame Odile know you are here."

The woman – Miss Adams – stood and Rose saw that she was tall and swanlike, with the body of a ballet dancer and the grace of one as well. She moved swiftly toward a door Rose hadn't noticed before, opened it and closed it behind her. Rose heard a soft sussuration of voices.

She looked around her. It was difficult to discern just what it was *Peau de*

Soie provided. There were no clothes, no jewelry, no signs of beauty products nor anything at all for purchase. There were the wide windows with a soft fold of blue-black drapery at the sides, several blue and grey velvet-covered chairs, a small love seat in the same clean style that Rose knew from magazines was French, the kidney-shaped desk with a ledger of some sort open on it, and a black telephone. On the walls were what Rose knew to be Erté prints, from that same style as the furniture, and a few softly glowing sconces. It was all pretty spare in a rich sort of way, but Rose had no idea what service it might be that *Peau de Soie* provided.

She clicked open her purse and pulled the advertisement from it. All it had said was "shop girls wanted." The advertisement had specified that the girls had to type, which she did, be personable, which she'd been told she was, and be attractive and able to model clothes in sizes two through eight. Rose was a size six.

Miss Adams had not yet returned and it had grown dark outside. Rose watched the flow of people on the sidewalk, all clearly engaged in the business of getting back home. And here Rose stood, feeling foolish, knowing whatever it was *Peau de Soie* offered, she would be unable to provide it.

Perhaps she should just leave, she thought. Save herself the embarrassment of being chided and rejected by Miss Adams, with her perfect model's figure and her chill demeanor.

Rose turned to go, annoyed with herself for wasting the subway fare to get here when it was too late to even apply at other shops now she was in town.

The door opened behind her and Miss Adams' curt voice proclaimed, "Madame Odile will see you now. Please come with me."

Rose blushed involuntarily at being caught slinking away like a cur, and went meekly to Miss Adams' side, following her through the door.

The room beyond was darker than the other one, and appointed quite differently. The style of this room was more opulent, of a different character altogether. Along one wall stood two deep velvety chairs, dark red, and along the other, a long claret-velvet divan of the sort Rose had seen in the pictures. Catty-corner to the divan, where a window should have been, thick claret drapes hung like a theatre curtain. Sconces with softly glowing gas lights dotted the wall at regular intervals above the furniture.

Off to the side was a small antique writing desk, on which an inkwell, some papers and other items Rose could not distinguish were arrayed.

223

Behind the desk sat a petite woman who even in the semi-dark Rose could tell was quite beautiful, if older – perhaps even forty.

The small woman stood and Rose was surprised to see she was dressed in what appeared to be a man's smoking jacket, man's tailored shirt, and man's trousers. The jacket was a deep bottle green, the shirt white, and the trousers black. At her throat, Madame Odile had a green paisley ascot. Like Miss Adams, Madame Odile's hair was short and sleek, but hers was not marcelled, just swept back, like a young man's would be. Her ears were obviously pierced, in the French way, and two points of red glowed from each lobe. Rubies, Rose guessed.

"Hello, my dear," the woman's voice was low and movie-star sultry, and she had a slight, but not pronounced, French accent. "How good of you to be so prompt –promptness is quite important in our business. My apologies for keeping you waiting."

Madame Odile stepped from behind the little escritoire and extended her delicate hand to Rose, who hastily pulled off her right glove and took it. Frederique's hand was cool and silken, but her handshake was surprisingly strong.

"You are a very pretty young girl, Miss Blakemore," Frederique noted approvingly, before Rose had even murmured a "Pleased to meet you, Ma'am."

"*Tres, jolie*, isn't she, Muriel? Oh, I think our clientele [this she said with the French pronunciation – clee-uhn-tell] will be delighted with you!"

Rose glanced warily at Miss Adams whose demeanor had abruptly changed from severe to welcoming. Suddenly, the look of disdain Rose had engendered upon her arrival had been replaced by a look of avid interest. Rose was confused.

Frederique took Rose's arm and steered her toward the divan. "Come dear, sit over here with me and tell me some things about yourself. I believe you are what we are looking for, at present. Why don't you remove that jacket and your hat and let us see your lovely figure. You understand there is some modeling of apparel involved in the position?"

Rose found herself lulled by both the warmth of the room and the mesmerizing sound of Madame Odile's voice. Perhaps she had misjudged things and she would get the position after all. Whatever the position was.

She perched herself on the edge of the divan and unbuttoned her jacket, took it off and folded it carefully over the edge of the sofa. Then she reached up and took out the blessed hatpin and removed her beret, putting it on her jacket. Her pocketbook lay across the jacket as well, along with her gloves. She involuntarily smoothed her hair.

"Muriel, get us some tea, *cherie*, would you? Cream and sugar or lemon, Miss Blakemore? Oh, and some biscuits – we are coming onto Miss Blakemore's dinner hour and we don't want her faint from hunger. Get me a glass of sherry, too, please." Her voice was low and forceful and yet infinitely warm. Rose found herself staring directly at Frederique. She'd never seen anyone like her outside of the pictures. She actually felt as if Madame Odile were indeed a film star, a mysterious and foreign one, like Greta Garbo.

Muriel left the room through yet another door Rose hadn't seen and Frederique turned to her, giving Rose her full attention.

"Now my dear – may I call you Rose, such a lovely name – what we do here is we pamper women. You know – the spa treatment. European. And a little more. For women who just can't get away for a vacation to the Continent, especially these days, but they need a lift, need a little relaxation for an afternoon or so. Our clientele are wealthy women who need to get away for a bit from the drudgery of their lives. You know – the children, the husbands, the entertaining, the dinners, the charity events, the balls. It can be very exhausting for them. So we take them under our wing, Muriel and I and our girls, and we give them what they need. A treat, pampering, something special. You understand."

Rose had relaxed a bit as Frederique spoke and had barely noticed as Frederique took her hand and began to stroke it while explaining the workings of *Peau de Soie*. Rose let out a soft sigh – breath she didn't realize she'd been holding practically since she'd entered the room with Muriel.

Frederique noticed the sigh and turned her gaze toward Rose, meeting her gaze full-on. Her eyes were dark – almost black. "I had hoped we had put you at ease, my dear, but it seems you are still, well – nervous."

Frederique leaned closer to Rose and now took the hand she'd been absently stroking between both of hers, then held it to her lips and kissed it, the way Rose had seen men kiss the hands of women in the pictures. She felt the color rise in her face and felt something else she couldn't quite place. A fluttering somewhere.

"Forgive me, Madame Odile," Rose began.

"Call me Frederique, cherie – you will be one of my girls. At least I hope you will be." Frederique's black eyes looked searchingly at Rose and again she felt that unsettled feeling, the fluttering. She felt unaccountably warm.

"Frederique," Rose began again. "Forgive me, but I don't yet understand what it is I would be expected to do. I've worked in two shops before, back in Indiana, but they were certainly not —" she waved her hand to take in the room — "like this. And of course I don't even think we *have* spas out in Indiana. And we surely don't have them in Brooklyn, where I live now." Rose thought of the difference between Mrs. Dombrovsky and Madame Odile and prayed a silent little prayer for the job. Madame Odile smelled of something spicy and sharp, like cinnamon or cloves, and Mrs. Dombrovsky with her sausage breath and her constant criticism… Somehow Rose knew that even Frederique's criticism would be welcome.

She settled a little more comfortably into the velvet recess of the divan and felt Frederique shift almost imperceptibly toward her. Muriel had yet to reappear.

"As I said, we are in the business of relaxing women. Making them feel as if they have not a care in the world. Free, you know, to express their tiredness and the needs that they cannot express at home. They are looking to be pampered. In there —" Frederique inclined her head toward where Muriel had disappeared — "we have a series of small rooms where we give massages, facials, and some other little niceties the ladies cannot get at home." She stopped, looked at Rose and put her index finger, on which flashed a small ring of silver and onyx, to Rose's lips. "What a pretty mouth, you have dear. Very pretty. Kissable lips, as we say in Paris."

Rose didn't blush this time, but felt something altogether different. She raised her hand to touch Frederique's. It was involuntary, but she saw that it was somehow the correct and welcomed response. Frederique took Rose's hand and held it against her own mouth. Rose's breathing quickened and she felt an unmistakable longing, one she hadn't felt very often, to be kissed.

"This is part of what we do here, *cherie*," Frederique murmured in her low, accented voice, her lips warm and soft against Rose's fingers. Frederique leaned toward Rose and took her chin in her small hand and kissed her. Rose slid a little closer to Frederique, leaning into the kiss, unaccountably hungry for it and trying not to think that this person — this Frenchwoman in man's clothes — was indeed a woman kissing her the way she had only been kissed a few times before, back in Indiana and then once by Mr. Dinelli, the butcher near her flat in Brooklyn. Mr. Dinelli had flirted with her every time she came in the shop and always gave her better cuts of meat than she had paid for, and then one evening when she had rushed there after work, just before closing, he had grabbed her and kissed her before he let her out of the shop. He had tasted clean and sharp and she had let him kiss her several times after that, but they had never spoken of it and he had not asked her out. She almost never thought of him when she wasn't at his shop. But she thought perhaps she would be thinking of Frederique more often than she had thought of Mr. Dinelli.

The kiss was not of a sort she'd experienced before. Frederique moved her hand from Rose's chin and placed her fingers on Rose's lips even as she was kissing her, touching her lips and kissing them at the same time. Rose felt liquid against her.

Frederique touched the tip of her hot, moist tongue to Rose's lips and outlined them lightly. Then she pulled back and Rose was afraid there would be no more kissing.

"So my dear, do you think you can do that again?"

Rose was confused. Kiss Frederique again? Kiss this strange, exotic half-man, half-woman again? Yes, she could indeed, and wanted to, unaccountably, even as she thought she had better leave this place, that she really didn't understand what was being asked of her.

"Yes, yes of course," Rose fairly stammered, her voice unsteady as herself.

"Well, dear, this is what we do here. We kiss the ladies. We stroke their skin, we put our fingertips to their faces, and we kiss them, long and hard as I just kissed you. And then we do some other things for them as well."

Rose knew she didn't understand, but was afraid if she asked a question, she'd never experience that kiss again.

Suddenly, the door opened and Muriel came in, a tea tray in her hands. Rose let out a little gasp.

Gone was the severe, black-silk dress. Now Muriel wore a diaphanous peignoir, also black, and through its gauzy folds Rose could see a black brassiere, black garter belt and black stockings. Muriel wore no panties and Rose could see a triangle of dark hair where the panties should have been.

"Thank you, Muriel, put it down, please. And come here. I was instructing our new girl on her duties." Frederique turned to Rose. "You *are* our new girl, aren't you? You will be paid handsomely, of course. Handsomely enough to move from Brooklyn—" Rose saw Muriel involuntarily shudder at the thought of Brooklyn — "and handsomely enough to manage quite well, I believe."

Rose sat still, aware that she was nearly lying on the divan when she should have been sitting. But the sense of unreality that had overtaken her kept her from righting herself. *Yes*, she thought, *I do want to be the new girl. I want to be Frederique's new girl.*

She came to and answered, as she had to Frederique's kiss. "Yes, I am your new girl, if I am hired, of course. Ma'am."

Muriel let out a brisk laugh and strode over to Rose, standing before the prone girl who could now see how very naked she was. The triangle of hair was right before her now and Rose could not help but stare at it.

"Look, dear, something tells me you've only ever seen one of these, your own," and with that Muriel pulled her peignoir open and the little triangle was there in front of Rose and she could see that it was clipped somehow, dressed like Muriel's other hair, sleek and combed so Rose could see all the particulars. She felt a little faint.

"Kiss me, dear. Kiss me there." Muriel took her well-manicured fingers and opened the part beneath the hair. Rose could not look away, fascinated, just as she had been by Frederique's kiss. But Muriel was no creature between this and that. Muriel was a woman, likely only a few years older than herself.

"Here—" Muriel added, "Frederique will show you how." Muriel stood, her beautiful, elegant body above Rose, and spread her long legs wider, standing akimbo before Rose and Frederique.

Frederique turned first to Rose and said in the tone of a patient instructor, "Watch me, *cherie*, this is very important, this is what our ladies come to us for."

With that she took her fingers and lifted apart the petals of Muriel's sex and Rose could see the darker bud beneath. Frederique's tongue shot from her mouth, quick and fluid as a snake. She flicked it at the little bud and Rose blushed as she watched. What was she doing here, what kind of job was this? There it was, *Peau de Soie*, right on the street, a handsomely appointed street in one of the wealthiest parts of Manhattan and no one ever suspected that any of this was happening beyond the sleek accoutrements of the anterior room. Except, obviously, these ladies that Frederique and Muriel spoke of.

Wealthy ladies with children and husbands and charity events and a desire to have a girl kiss them and touch them and put her lips to the place where only their husbands should be and in the dark, no less. Was this something rich people did? Rose could not be sure and again she was afraid to ask, more afraid still to put her lips to Muriel's dark flower.

"I think we have begun too quickly for our Rose," Frederique said, and reached to stroke Rose's flushed cheek. "A girl from Indiana might not know of these things, am I correct, *cherie*? Have you seen this before?"

Rose couldn't imagine where it would be that she would see such things and blurted as much to Frederique. Muriel laughed her brisk laugh and Frederique smiled what Rose knew was a patronizing smile.

"Yes, well, American tastes tend to be rather plain," she said, not unkindly. "But I have found, you see, that once they get a taste for something new… well, then they just cannot get enough of it. Our ladies cannot get enough of our girls."

Muriel had begun to do something Rose had herself done, but only in the darkest night and all alone. Rose watched as Muriel's long, slender finger brushed over the dark bud of her sex again and again. Rose could see that it was wet from Frederique's tongue and that there was a light but intense scent, like a garden at night, or the seaside. And she could see that Muriel was flushed and her lips were parted and she knew what it was Muriel was feeling, as she had felt it herself. She reached up toward Muriel and put her own finger atop Muriel's to feel the rhythm, then Muriel slid hers away, moving it up to her breast and inside her brassiere. Rose could see the dusky pink nipple hardening like the bud Rose now had beneath her fingers. Rose took up the rhythmic stroking, feeling a dampness begin between her own legs and a pulsing there as well. Frederique leaned over and kissed her, then put her arm around Rose and held her tightly as Rose stroked Muriel's hard, hot little bud. Frederique whispered her sultry, foreign voice into Rose's ear.

"You want to pleasure her fully, Rose, you want to keep doing it a bit harder and a bit faster as you see her excitement grow. This is what the ladies want, you see. It's very relaxing. And they rest afterward, very happy, like a little cat."

Muriel made a sound — a sharp, sighing sound and pressed her hand hard against Rose's now-wet fingers. "Fast, fast," she whispered in a husky voice

Rose had not heard before and Rose obliged, wishing that Muriel or Frederique might do the same for her and leaned harder into Frederique's arms. "Press into me, now, with your fingers, two of them, push, in, now, yes, like that, stroke, fast, fast, yes…" Rose folded her fingers together and entered Muriel's sleek sheath.

Muriel was breathing fast, shallow breaths like sighs and now she had both hands on her breasts and her legs trembled against Rose. Rose could feel Muriel's silky sheath tighten around her fingers and pulse for a few seconds and then release her. She pulled her hand away and Frederique took it and licked her fingers. "They might want to see you do this, too, dear. Or they might want something else entirely. Could you stand up?"

Stand up? Rose thought she might faint, the headiness of it all had so overwhelmed her. She needed that tea. She said so. Muriel poured her a cup of tea, now a bit lukewarm, and Rose drank it gratefully. She put the teacup down and stood before Frederique. Muriel took her place on the divan.

"What shall I do now, Ma'am?" she asked in the slightly sultry, slightly obsequious manner she assumed she would ask the same question of women who might visit *Peau de Soie*.

"You are a quick study, *cherie*, I like that. I like *you*." Frederique patted Rose's hand indulgently. "I'd like you to take off your twin set and skirt and show you a few more things, and then Muriel and I will make you something to eat and the driver will take you home. We cannot have you walking the streets at some late hour all alone."

Rose was reeling and disquieted, even as she knew she had already accepted the job, accepted this odd new set of circumstances and accepted – with some relief – that Mrs. Dombrovsky would soon be a part of her past. Her inelegant past. She pulled off the sweaters slowly and carefully, folded them neatly and unzipped her skirt and stepped out of it, placing it beside the sweaters. She stood in her best slip – an ivory silk with a lacy bodice – and turned toward Frederique.

"And now, Ma'am?"

"That hair, *cherie* – can you take it down? I would like to see it on those lovely white shoulders." Frederique was staring at her approvingly, leaning forward on the edge of the divan as if she were about to pounce on Rose. Rose wanted her to pounce, ached for her to pounce.

"You must be a little excited from this evening's events," Frederique noted.

Rose nodded. "You must want a little —" she paused — "relief." Again Rose nodded.

Muriel exited and returned with what looked like a velvet pillowslip. From it she took an object Rose did not recognize, as well as a satin sheet. The sheet Muriel spread over the divan where the three had sat. The object she handed to Frederique.

"We have six girls here, Rose, plus Muriel. And now, of course, you. I do not teach all my girls. I leave most of that to Muriel. But you – you're such a fresh pupil and so very, very pretty. I've taken quite a fondness to you already, as I think our clientele will also."

A soft sigh came from Rose's barely parted lips. She could feel the dampness between her legs, on her inner thighs. She wanted to touch herself as Muriel had done. She smoothed the sides of her slip and her hand involuntarily fluttered near her sex.

"Yes, *cherie*, that's right, that's what you want – to touch it, now, don't you?" Frederique's voice was mesmerizing, it was like a thing itself and Rose wanted it, wanted Frederique's voice in her ear and her lips on hers again, and that tight, small, wiry cat's body that was half-man, half-woman atop her own.

"See, the ladies will want to see that – that you are excited by being with them, by touching them, and relaxing them. They will want to see you relax yourself, or perhaps they will want to relax you. Come, *cherie* —" Frederique patted the divan and Muriel moved across to one of the chairs and sunk into it, her eyes half-lidded, yet avid, watching the other women.

Rose moved to the divan and knew she was to lie down, and did so. She felt slightly awkward and stiff, and abruptly sat up again. Frederique turned toward her and pushed her back down, holding her by her shoulders. There was a quickening in Rose's sex and she felt intense heat there. Her nipples hardened as Frederique's arm brushed against them.

"Are you a virgin, dear?" Frederique was speaking to her in a stage whisper – Muriel was meant to hear every word and from the periphery Rose could see that Muriel was pleasuring herself again, slowly and languidly this time, without the urgency of earlier, without the urgency Rose felt now.

"Yes, Ma'am, I am a virgin." Rose blushed, unsure if she should be proud or ashamed of the revelation. She heard Muriel gasp slightly, but knew it for a gasp of excitement, not shock.

"Is that something you want to be, my dear, a virgin? For if it is, we can leave it that way. But if it is not, Muriel and I would like to, well, explore other possibilities."

Rose saw the object Muriel had brought in Frederique's hand, but she did not know what it was, yet felt a small chill overtake her. Frederique stood, opened her jacket and unzipped the fly of her trousers. She inserted the object and stood before Rose, leaning down and turning Rose's pretty, flushed face toward her and the object in her trousers.

When Mr. Dinelli had kissed her at the butcher shop, he had pulled her against him and Rose had felt the hardness in his trousers, like a thick roll of sausage. He had pressed himself against her and the hardness had moved slightly, right against where her own sex was and it had excited her and she had been drawn to touch it, to put her hand against that part of him, against that hardness in his trousers. They had stood there and he had kissed her harder and harder till she could barely breathe and she had rubbed her hand against that hardness which had pressed against her own sex through her skirt. They had stood there like that in the butcher shop for some minutes, her hand on his hardness, the part where it stopped right against her own pearly bud.

Rose had thought about it later in the dark – not Mr. Dinelli, but the hardness pressing next to her and the sound of his breathing faster and faster as he kissed her mouth, her neck, her earlobes. She remembered the sound that had come from him as he had grabbed her buttocks and pulled her as hard against him as he could, held her tightly, and then let her go. And she had pleasured herself more than once as she thought of it, later. He had kissed her lightly and sweetly as he had let her out of the shop after they had done whatever it was they had done and when she had walked outside, the air had felt cool on her hot cheeks and she had been surprised to realize that there was a dampness between her legs.

Now, here, with Frederique, she wanted to feel the sort of feeling she had felt with Mr. Dinelli as he had grabbed her buttocks and pressed her against the white tile wall of the butcher shop. She wanted to be pressed up against Frederique that way.

"Touch this, Rose, stroke it." Frederique had her own small, well-manicured hand around what looked like a man's penis to Rose, but which was the object Muriel had brought in the velvet pillowslip. Rose shuddered involuntarily, but was unsure if it was a shudder of excitement, fear, or revulsion. She put her fingers to the object and pressed them against the tip. Frederique's gaze turned glassy and her breath altered just a bit. Muriel shifted in her chair, then stood and came toward the two.

"Let me show you, Rose, what Frederique wants. There are two ladies who like this and they will want to see the new girl." Muriel's voice was matter-of-fact, yet tinged with excitement. Rose propped herself up on one arm and watched as Muriel took the object and wrapped her long delicate fingers with the red-lacquered nails around the whole of it and moved it up and down. Her other hand played along the inseam of Frederique's trousers and Rose could see that these two things were creating an intense excitement for Frederique. This – whatever Muriel was doing – seemed to be the one thing over which the Frenchwoman had no control.

Suddenly Muriel stopped the motion and Frederique let out a small sigh of frustration. Muriel slipped the peignoir from her shoulders and stood in just her brassiere, garter belt, and stockings before Frederique. She unclasped her brassiere and let it slip down, exposing small, tight breasts with large, dusky-pink nipples. She pulled at one nipple with her fingers and then bent down a bit and rubbed it against Frederique's lips. The older woman took the nipple into her mouth and then put her own hand on the object and pushed it against Muriel's sex. They stood like that for a minute – the sucking of the nipple and the object slipping into the crevice between Muriel's legs – and their breathing was synchronous, rising and falling with the movement of the object.

Rose could no longer contain herself. She sat up on the divan, swinging her legs over. She moved to the edge of the sofa. She slid her slip up over her milky thighs and pulled it off swiftly, slightly mussing her hair. She sat in her ivory brassiere, garter belt, and panties. There was a small ladder in her right stocking, now, and she involuntarily ran her finger down it. Frederique bent over her and plucked at the ruined stocking.

"We will have to get you another pair of these, Rose," she murmured. Then she kissed Rose again, lightly, softly, and asked, "Would you let me touch you, Rose? Would you let us both" – she glanced at Muriel – "touch you?"

Rose spread her creamy thighs apart in silent assent and the two women sat on either side of the girl. Muriel ran the lacquered nails down Rose's thigh and Rose felt a sensation that made her shiver and flush at the same time.

"I find this is most relaxing to our ladies," Frederique murmured low into Rose's ear as her small, warm hand traveled up Rose's inner thigh. The frisson was immediate and Rose grabbed for Frederique's hand, only to have Muriel pull it away. Muriel leaned forward and began to kiss Rose, as Frederique stroked the girl's thigh, maddeningly close to, but not actually on her sex, lightly teasing the flesh around the elastic of her panties, but not entering her yet.

That was left to Muriel, whose long, beautiful fingers slowly slipped beneath the panties and finally found the little bud between the petals of Rose's sex. The desire was now so strong Rose could barely wait for the touch. She could feel herself pulsing under Muriel's expert fingers as she stroked and pulled at the pearl in ways Rose herself had never done, never thought to do. Her thighs began to quiver and Frederique slid her hand up under the back of Rose's brassiere, unclasping it with one swift motion. Rose's breasts were full and large, the nipples such a pale pink as to be almost imperceptible against the creamy skin.

"Your breasts are quite lovely, my dear," Frederique whispered as she lowered her lips to Rose's nipple. "Our ladies will love the freshness of your skin – you are a darling girl, truly you are."

Rose had never felt so wet and hot between her legs. She had never experienced such a hunger to be touched. Suddenly she knew she wanted the object – Frederique's object – inside her and she reached for it, making the older woman sigh as her hand gripped it and moved it up and down as she had watched Muriel do.

Muriel turned Rose toward Frederique, never taking her hand from between the parts of Rose's open shell, and Rose moved her other hand beneath the object, along Frederique's thigh, which felt strong and somehow masculine beneath the trouser fabric.

Frederique whispered something in French that Rose didn't understand, but Muriel heard and took her hand from between the girl's legs and stood, then pulled the girl up. "Watch," she commanded in husky voice, as Rose stood, helplessly ravenous for completion, as Muriel spread her lovely long legs over the Frenchwoman, opened her own flower-like petals with those long fingers, the red lacquered nails flashing briefly against the dark pink of her sex, then slowly sat herself upon the object as Frederique leaned back against the divan, moving her hips upward as Muriel spread herself over the object and took it inside herself.

The scene was more than Rose could imagine, could ever have imagined. There she stood, nearly naked with her auburn hair cascading over her white shoulders, her large breasts exposed, the pale nipples stiff, watching what she knew was some variation on what men and women did together. Married couples did together. Her last beau, Johnny, had shown her some dirty pictures once, back in Bloomington, pictures he had found hidden in the barn, pictures he said belonged to Hank, his father's farmhand.

In those pictures there had been women in various states of *deshabille*, some in panties and brassieres, and some completely naked, but without their nipples or sex visible. There had also been men with unbuttoned shirts and open trousers with their large penises – well, she had thought they looked very large – protruding from the fly. Other men wore only shirts and were naked below. Some of the pictures were just of women in different poses, their backs arched, their breasts full, hands demurely placed over their nipples. Other pictures showed the men holding their penises against the women, near the sex of the women, and two of the pictures had been of the men with their penises inside the women. One showed the woman on all fours, her backside to the man, who was kneeling. His penis was inside her from behind and his hands were on her hips and her face was turned back toward him with an expression that looked like surprise. The other picture had the woman on her back with her legs up and wrapped around the man's back. Rose didn't remember what her face had looked like.

Johnny had been very excited by the pictures and he had talked about them to Rose in detail with "Did ya see this?" and "Did ya see that?" She hadn't known what to make of the pictures at the time. She was only nineteen and she'd gone steady with one boy in high school and dated several others since, but she hadn't gone very far with any of them. Not like her best friend back in Indiana, Betty, who had let two boys put their hands in her panties. Betty had told Rose the things she had done with the boys and Rose had been shocked.

But that day in the barn when Johnny had shown Rose the pictures, Rose had let Johnny lay on top of her, the pictures scattered on the hay nearby. She hadn't let him do anything to her, though, except kiss her and rub her breasts through her sweater. It had been oddly unpleasant, with the scratchy hay

235

beneath her and his rhythmic rubbing of her breasts and his hardness against her thigh. Nothing like what she had felt in the bright, white butcher shop with Mr. Dinelli. And nothing at all like what she was feeling now.

Rose thought about those pictures. That was what Muriel and Frederique were doing, now: "married love," her mother called it. What Muriel and Frederique were doing didn't look anything like those pictures, which hadn't excited her at all, in fact they had both frightened and repulsed her – the expressions on the women's faces either bored or something else she couldn't quite discern.

The expressions on the faces of Muriel and Frederique were exciting to her, Muriel was saying things to Frederique in French, things that Rose didn't understand, but could tell were things that Frederique wanted to hear. Muriel was moving very quickly up and down on the object between Frederique's legs, almost bouncing on Frederique's small lap, and the older woman was sighing deeply and jutting her own hips up to meet Muriel's. Suddenly Muriel let go a little cry of pleasure and Rose saw her squeeze her thighs tight against the other woman's. Frederique took Muriel's face in her hands and kissed her hard on the lips.

Rose wanted to be part of what they were doing, although she was unsure if she wanted to do exactly what Muriel was doing. She leaned closer to the two of them as they kissed and ran her fingers lightly down Muriel's thigh as it moved against Frederique. She slipped her hand in between the tightness of the two women, slipped it down so she could feel the wetness on the object and the wetness on Muriel's inner thighs.

The other women slowed what they were doing and Frederique turned toward her. Rose sat, pressed close to Frederique, then she stood and removed her panties, standing before them in her garter belt and laddered stockings, her brassiere discarded when Frederique had removed it. She walked behind Muriel and put her arms around her from behind, and touched the small breasts. She pressed her own breasts against the other woman's slender back and reached her hands around to pinch Muriel's nipples as the other woman sighed.

"Shall we play with Rose, now, Muriel?" Frederique asked of her assistant.

"I think it is she who is playing with us. Like a cat with some mice," Muriel replied, her voice still husky from the sex. "She seems to have learned quite a bit in a very brief time, don't you think?"

Rose wasn't sure what it was that she heard in Muriel's voice – a bit of accusation? Jealousy? She couldn't be sure. All she wanted now was to be part of this wild scene before her. Whatever she was doing was a tune played by ear – she had no idea what either woman wanted, or even what it was she herself wanted. What she did know was that the pulsing between her thighs had become too intense to bear and she wanted to be touched, to be kissed, to be held down and rubbed against and possibly even entered with the object that she now saw wet and slick between Frederique's legs as Muriel stood and passed by her, going to the desk and taking a small box from a drawer. Rose saw her light a cigarette and breathe it in, deeply. Rose turned to Frederique.

"Do you want me to leave?" It was not what Rose had meant to say and certainly not what she wanted to say. She didn't want to leave. Whether or not there was work here past this evening's dalliance, she wanted this scene to play itself out. She wanted to feel Frederique, this strange, sensual half-man, half-woman, to do all the things to her she had seen her do to Muriel.

When Johnny had shown her Hank's pictures, she had at first been aroused, excited by the foreignness and strangeness of the unknown women and men in those most intimate poses. But Johnny had mistaken her excitement for a different kind of interest, the avidity he himself had felt when he'd first seen the pictures. He had told Rose how the photographs had made him think of her, and how he had pleasured himself thinking of her as one of those women.

She had expected to be either insulted or excited by what he had said, but she had been neither – the photographs had been of interest to her only in their freakishness, their strangeness and newness. They had not made her think of when she and Johnny had been in the back seat of Jim's car, with Jim and Betty in the front seat, everyone kissing and steaming up the windows. That had been different. She had been watching Betty's face as Jim had rubbed her breasts under her jacket and the slight sound she had made – a sigh, a small moan – had made Rose pulse between her legs and she had laid her hand casually in Johnny's lap, and felt the hardness there and let him press her hand against it and rub it a little. But all the while she had been watching Betty, had heard the sound of Jim's zipper being slowly undone by Betty's deft hand, had seen her moving her right arm up and down as she kissed him and did something to his penis that had made him throw his head back against the seat and moan. Then Betty had opened her eyes and looked right over the seat at Rose and winked at her, and made a little kissing face, and Rose had had a crazy urge to lean forward and kiss Betty then, kiss her instead of Johnny and somehow she had felt that Betty had wanted to do the same. But neither had ever said anything about that night except, "Wild, huh? Those boys!"

"Do you want me to leave?" Rose asked again and it was Muriel who answered. "Frederique doesn't want you to go, dear. Frederique just likes to make me jealous – don't you, lover?" Muriel's tone had shifted to one that was a little acid and a little hurt. Rose turned to look at her, but Muriel's expression behind the veil of smoke was inscrutable.

"Don't be silly, Muriel. You will always be my special girl, always, as you know." Frederique's voice was consoling, not condescending, and Rose suddenly understood what people meant when they said someone wanted to 'have their cake and eat it, too.' Frederique wanted her Muriel, for sure, but she also wanted to try the new girl on for size, as well. And she, the new girl, wanted it, too. Wanted it badly. Ached to have it.

"I think we all need a little drink before we try anything else, don't you, *cherie*?" Frederique patted Rose on the thigh, but she was looking at Muriel. "What about a small aperitif, darling? Nothing too heavy. Would you get that for us, *cherie, s'il vous plaît?* Muriel put out her cigarette, pulled on her peignoir and left the room. Frederique turned to Rose.

"Come here, pretty girl, and sit next to me." Frederique patted the divan and Rose obeyed, sitting next to her, close, feeling the heat of the other woman's thighs through her trousers. It was surprisingly warm in the little room and Rose felt slightly woozy from the events of the last hours.

Then Frederique pushed Rose down on the divan, holding her by the shoulders and kissing her so hard it took Rose's breath away. Rose involuntarily opened her legs and Frederique lay on top of her, a small lock of hair falling over her beautiful brow, which was nothing like a man's, Rose could see that now, as she stared into Frederique's face. She wrapped her legs around Frederique like the woman in Johnny's photo had done. She felt the hardness prick at her sex and the sound that escaped her lips was an animal sound, a sound of desire – and it was desire she felt. She slipped her hand down between her legs and rubbed her pearl hard for a minute, her desire like an ache between her legs. The bud was wet and slick to her touch and as she rubbed it she felt the hardness of Frederique pressing against her fingers, her bud, her sex. Pressing, insistent, and Frederique's breath hot against her face, that sharp, aromatic scent closer to her now as Frederique nipped lightly at her earlobe and ran her hands down Rose's naked torso, grabbing at her naked buttocks. Frederique ran her fingers up the crevice of Rose's buttocks and played along the edge of her shell, opening the petals gently, the object so close, ready, it seemed to Rose to enter and pierce her at any moment. The thought made Rose shiver with anticipation and fear.

"I desire you, Rose," Frederique breathed into her neck, into the side of her face. Her accent was more pronounced now, with her arousal, and the foreignness of her voice and everything that was happening to her made Rose want to swoon or cry out. She wanted something to hang on to, something solid. She gripped the edge of the satin-sheeted divan with one hand, the other in Frederique's hair at the back of her neck.

What was to become of her?

"I desire you, also," Rose replied, and meant it. She had never desired anything more, even though she wasn't at all sure what it was she was desiring. If she let Frederique enter her, would she still be a virgin or not? She was past caring, the pulsing in the whole of her demanded attention and Frederique was ready to give her that attention.

"I want you to take me," Rose whispered, unsure where it was she had heard those words before – maybe Betty had told them to her, told her it was what boys, men, wanted to hear, even if you stopped them before they did take you – whatever that was, exactly. "Please."

It was all Frederique needed. She put her small hand around the object and guided it slowly between the lips of Rose's sex, rubbing the end of it lightly against her hard bud until she wanted to cry out, cry out Frederique's name into the small, hot, room.

"Yes, *cherie*, now, *cherie*," Frederique whispered as she kissed Rose's flushed cheek and bit her lightly on her already swollen lips. Rose felt a pressure, a hardness, a glancing pain and then the most intense sensation, so intense that this time she did indeed cry out her pleasure – or was it pain? – and Frederique kissed her hard then, and she began to tremble from the inside out. Rose wrapped her legs tighter around Frederique as the Frenchwoman's penis thrust in and out of her, shifted her hips and angled them up to take in more and return the thrusts, which were both painful and immensely pleasurable. She felt a warmth suffusing her entire body. Her nipples had hardened when Frederique had first entered her and she had winced slightly and Frederique had asked if she were all right, if she should stop and Rose had murmured *no*, had not wanted it to stop, this madness, this wild intensity. Images of the evening flashed before her like a newsreel and she felt like she was in a kind of dream state, with this strange foreign creature taking her and talking to her in a language she didn't understand, except that she knew it to be the language of love and sex and desire.

The heat began to overtake her. Rose felt it building between her legs and she writhed under Frederique, moving back and forth against her penis, rocking onto it and slapping her buttocks against the damp, satin sheet. "Faster," she pleaded, and slid her hand down between her legs to grab hold of Frederique's hand to urge her on, to give her the pleasure she had been waiting for all evening, waiting for in Bloomington, and Brooklyn, and now.

And then it happened. She felt a shivering all over, a tightening inside her and what felt like a heartbeat between her legs, a pounding, pulsing sensation that overtook her and she kept murmuring, "Yes, now, yes, now," into Frederique's lips as they kissed.

She was spent. Utterly and completely ravished. Frederique slipped off her and lay next to her, her hand caressing Rose's skin as she whispered how lovely Rose was and how sweet and delectable a flower. Rose looked at Frederique and saw her face was flushed and even more beautiful, the lock of hair fallen over her brow reminded Rose of an actor, she couldn't remember who. Frederique folded Rose into her arms and kissed her lightly on the lips and cheeks.

"You were very lovely, my dear, so very lovely. I shall never forget the pleasure you gave us both. Your pleasure was my pleasure. Now you must rest a bit, *cherie*. It's quite a lot the first time."

Was it all over? Rose wasn't certain what would happen next. She felt sleepy and drained and slightly chill. She shivered, then closed her eyes. Rose felt Frederique pull something warm and silky over her, a coverlet of some sort. And then she slept.

* * *

Rose heard a sound she couldn't place. She started awake and sat up abruptly. Where was she? Then she took in the room and remembered *Peau de Soie*, Frederique, Muriel. What was the sound? The room was nearly dark and Rose turned almost imperceptibly to see Frederique and Muriel in the chair catty-corner to her.

She wasn't sure what it was she was seeing. The room was lit only by the sconces above the chair where the two women were. The ones above her, which had been lit earlier, were out. Muriel was sitting in the chair, but not quite sitting. Sprawled was a better word, yet too inelegant for how Muriel looked. Languid, Rose thought. Still, she knew languid wasn't a pose. Yet that was how Muriel looked – she was sprawled languidly in the chair. Kneeling before her in a manner that was anything but supplicant, was Frederique. She had taken off the smoking jacket and Rose could see the ascot draped across the arm of the chair. The white man's shirt was untucked from the trousers and Frederique's face was between Muriel's legs. She seemed to be kissing and licking Muriel's sex and the other woman was sighing deeply – the sound that had awakened Rose – and whispering words that Rose could not quite discern.

She watched the two women, fascinated by what she saw. Was this the same kissing that the two women had shown her earlier when Muriel had stood before her? It looked different to her now and she wasn't sure why. Then she saw that Frederique had her hand, her small, delicately boned hand with the short manicure, inside Muriel's sex. She was moving her arm the way Rose had remembered Betty moving hers with Jim that night. Quick and rhythmic, in time to some internal beat that only the two participants understood.

Muriel's excitement was growing and she was lifting herself a little off the chair with her long, slender arms. Whatever it was Frederique was giving her, she wanted as much of it as she could get.

Rose felt a tingling between her legs as she watched the two women and listened to the sounds of their lovemaking. The sighs and murmurs, the indecipherable words were infinitely exciting to her. Rose watched the scene as if from inside a dream. She turned quietly onto her stomach, propping herself up on the shoulder of the divan. She watched them, her own hand slipped down between her legs, the dampness from earlier still there, every part of her sex tingling and ready for yet more enticements.

Then Muriel cried out and flung herself forward into Frederique's arms. There was kissing and cooing between them and suddenly Rose felt very separate from the other two women, as if all that had happened earlier had been no more than fantasy.

Rose thought it was time for her to go home. She stirred slightly on the divan and Frederique turned toward her.

"Ah, you are awake, *cherie*. How do you feel, my dear?" Frederique strode over to the divan, her walk much more that of a man than a woman. The lock of hair still fell across her brow and Rose saw again how beautiful – or was it handsome? – she was.

Frederique sat beside her and Rose heard the door close behind Muriel as she left the room. "Would you like a nice, hot bath, dear, and something to eat? And then we will have the driver take you home. But I think a bath would be the thing, right now, don't you?"

Rose wasn't certain what the thing should be right now. She felt so disoriented, so adrift on the divan, in the little room. She ached for something, but was unsure what it was. An image of her friend Betty flashed before her mind's eye and she realized, with a start, that what she wanted most was to be held and cooed at the way Frederique had done with Muriel moments before.

"Yes, I *would* like a bath, thank you," Rose demurred, "but I would also like you to help me bathe."

Frederique had been gazing slightly past Rose, into the space where Muriel had been. Now she turned and stared at Rose. She let out a little laugh, warm and pleasant. Rose felt the sound wash over her.

"Muriel was right – you are indeed a little vixen. I do hope you still want to work at *Peau de Soie*, Rose. I think you will be much in demand." Frederique patted Rose on her naked buttock and then held out her hand.

"Let's go, dear. Bathe you I shall. Then I shall feed you and ride home with you in the car. On the way you can tell me more about yourself and what else you might bring to *Peau de Soie*."

Frederique stood, extending her arm to the naked Rose. The young woman rose from the divan and leaned into Frederique, who held her tightly for a moment, her arms encircling the beautiful young body. Rose pressed her breasts against Frederique, pressed all of her against the other woman. Frederique tilted Rose's pretty chin toward her and put a finger to her lips, then kissed her – a deep, passionate kiss in which Frederique's tongue entered Rose's mouth and Rose felt Frederique filling her up – with desire and longing.

The kiss ended and Frederique put her arm round Rose and led her toward the door to the other room.

"Let us go, my dear. I want to see you slip into the bath, I want to see you relax in the hot water, while I wash you all over. You are a sweet and lovely girl, Rose. I hope you will be with us for a long, long time."

Frederique opened the door to the other room and held it for Rose, who walked into the other room, into yet another wing of *Peau de Soie*. Frederique looked back into the little room – Rose's clothes folded neatly on the divan, her underthings scattered across it – and then she turned toward Rose, smiled and closed the door behind her.

Felice Swados
From HOUSE OF FURY
(REFORM SCHOOL GIRL)
1941

At eight o'clock the girls went upstairs to take their baths. They ran up and down the slippery floor of the hall, knocking and jostling to get into the bathroom. Girlish voices shrilled above the flow and splash of water while steam drifted from the open door, soap perfume, and the odor of rosy wet bodies.

Jeff stood near the bathroom trying to shove them along. I'll go nuts before I get them to bed tonight, she thought. Her greatest trouble was with Tony and Daisy, who remained in their rooms. "Get a wiggle on!" she called. "You're always the last. One of these days I'm gonna dump you in the wash-tub and scrub you with laundry soap."

Despite her fear and worry she was still amused at the girls going to their beauty ritual, and thought: they're the same everywhere; they come from different places and yet they do the same things, just like the girls I knew in high school, spending three hours waving their hair and always making mouths at themselves in the mirror.

Clouds of steam rose from the two old bathtubs, made of enameled iron with claw feet and set in doorless cubicles; steam rose from the showers, too, which had heavy canvas curtains and wooden drain floors set over cement. On the benches which bordered the room sprawled girls, naked or draped in towels, patting Epsom salts on their legs, languidly kneading the loose flesh of their thighs. Some who looked trim in clothes were wobbly and dough like; others who ran around in baggy overalls all day emerged at night clear as marble.

Mabel poured a cup of bath salts in a tub, bending her head over to sniff the geranium tang. After binding her hair in a towel she turned her back to the door, slipped off her kimono, and slid down into the water. "Ah-h –" she sighed, as the heat spread up her legs and waist. Lying with limbs afloat, loose with weariness yet buoyed up like water wings, she dreamed of the sea in her childhood, the sun sinking pink, the water calm as milk, and the weight flowing out of her body into the water.

Doll came into the cubicle, wearing a blue flowered gown, her hair piled on top of her head. "Hurry up, slow-poke." As she sat on the edge of the tub, with the bath mist wreathed about her face and strands of hair clinging to her forehead, she let the wrap slip down over her shoulders to her waist, clasping it around her hips in one hand with lazy modesty. It fell in folds around her childish legs, almost reaching to her feet. She might have been a little girl, were it not for her full, heavy breasts which fell wearily, heavily over her narrow ribs, wearing maturity like a burden almost too heavy to bear.

Meantime Daisy stole into the bathroom, almost tripping over a long bathrobe that Mabel had given her, clutching it tight around her. She moved near one of the old soapstone sinks, her eyes cast down, afraid and ashamed to look at the hot, foggy cubicles, the splashing showers crowded with naked girls. She sank down on a bench, still gripping the bathrobe. If only Tony were there! She did not stop to think that the girls were too busy to notice her as they pushed and crowded each other around the big full-length mirror that hung above the sink. Some were winding their hair in curlers, others creaming their faces, plucking their eyebrows, shaving down off their legs, squeezing imaginary spots off their noses till their faces were all red and splotched.

Pat sat down on the toilet, and a friend who worked in the beauty parlor began to set her hair, molding every strand into perfect undulations but complaining all the while. "They need cutting," she said, her mouth full of hairpins. "I can't do a thing with them."

Little Violet stood before the mirror, her lips drawn apart in a thin grimace, her eyes screwed up. "Look how pale my gooms are."

The girls commented freely on their own bodies and the shape of everyone who came into the bathroom. When Doll stepped out of her bath and sat down on a bench a skinny girl next to her said: "How much you weigh?"

"Hunderd an' six."

"Go way, you look smaller 'n me. Why I weigh a hundred one."

Doll cupped her breasts in her hands and held them a moment as though weighing them. "I take it all in here," she said.

Mabel sat next to her in a glow of cleanliness, rubbing her hair.

"If I was home now," she said softly, "I'd jump into bed just like I am…"

"Don't say it," whispered Doll, shivering with delight, "you'll drive me crazy… Gee, look at the legs on that girl there…"

"Well, my own ain't nothin' to brag about. Guess Alice is gonna have 'em too. Though you can't tell with a baby; they all look fat." She poked her thighs till they quivered like soft pudding. "Look at that."

"A woman has got to be soft," she continued sagely. "Who wants to be tough like a man? Straight up and down and hard as a piece of leather."

"Don't say it!" cried Doll. "Don't you talk like that."

Everybody laughed.

"Well," continued Doll, talking loud above the laughter, "Negroes have got big muscles just like men. They even walk like men too. Ever see 'em when they're out on the ball field?"

"Yeah," said Pat eagerly, "it's funny how their legs all bend in at the front. Like you can hardly tell which was front and which was back…"

Doll nudged her. "Shut up. Here comes Jeff."

"Why should I shut up? Jeff knows all about it."

Jeff came padding in on bare feet, her shirt unbuttoned and hanging loose around her waist. "What's that?"

"I don't chew my cabbage twice," said Pat.

"I guess you were talking about me," Jeff began, so mad she scarcely knew what to say. The words tumbled out of her mouth like burning coals. "You're all mixed up and you're trying to mix everybody else up too. What do you know about friends? You haven't got any. You don't know how to make friends…"

The girls were listening, eager, intent. Do they care what I'm saying, thought Jeff, or do they only want a fight?

"*You* know all about friends," said Pat, "actin' like a Girl Scout all these years. Where d'you go every night, little Jesus?"

Jeff took a step forward. "I'll tell you this," she said; "a swell girl is a swell girl if she is red, yellow, black or white. You don't have to be stuck-up about being white. Personally I think you're yellow, but maybe not everybody can see it. If a white girl is friends with a black girl because she likes her, because they have a lot to say to each other about – about how they feel and life and everything – why shouldn't they be? Why do you have to be evil-minded? Get your head out of the gutter. I know how you're talking about me behind my back and I have only one thing to say: if you could be such good clean friends with any girl in this house as I am with – with Bonnie Johnson – why, I'll give you up my room and keys and everything and tell Mis' Haddon you can have my job."

She finished breathlessly, feeling the girls' eyes focused bright upon her as though they were taking her picture. They said nothing.

Jeff looked at their empty faces. It was useless to talk: they just wouldn't think.

"Well, what are you hanging around for?" she snapped. "Go take your baths."

She felt she could hardly breathe. The atmosphere was so charged with excitement. If I should light a match, she thought, it would explode. And then a warning flashed into her mind: never snap the light on when you're wet. In a second you're stretched on the floor, dead. All that electricity, all that tremendous power released by one wet hand.

She looked around. "Where's Tony?"

No one had seen her.

I'm getting sick of this, thought Jeff, focusing her anger on Tony. She always tries to get out of taking a bath, she stalls around and holds up the whole works. I don't know what's wrong with her. She doesn't fuss like the rest of them but she's certainly not dirty.

She turned to Doll and Mabel. "Go and get her, won't you? If she won't come you better drag her out. I'm going to my room to change my clothes."

Doll tossed her head but went with Mabel down the hall to Tony's room. She sat cross-legged on her bed, wearing a pair of striped pajamas that Mabel had made for her birthday, pasting pictures of baseball players in a scrapbook. She seemed absorbed in her work but was really listening to the distant sound of falling water, thinking about the time when she first came to the school only twelve years old. Mabel, with mild curiosity, had asked: "Do you wear a brassiere?" The girls all looked at her flat chest and laughed. Tony still grew hot to think of it.

"Hello," said Mabel. She walked into the room, followed by Doll, and gave Tony's cropped head an affectionate little push.

"Come and take your bath, Stinky."

Tony rubbed her fingers on her pajama leg and took up another picture.

"Had one yesterday."

"You've got to have a bath every day," Mabel explained. "Otherwise you'll smell bad."

"So what if I do? I took a cold shower this morning."

"That's different from a hot bath," said Doll, primping before Tony's mirror. "Come on, hurry up."

Tony did not budge. "Listen, you know what I read in my history last term? I told you before. You forgot it already. Well, why did Rome fall? Answer me that."

"I don't care," said Doll petulantly. "That was a million years ago. Come on, quit stalling." She pulled at Tony's wrist. Tony turned to Mabel.

"I'm just the cook," said Mabel. "I don't know nothing. Why?"

"'Cause they took too many baths. Too many hot baths."

Doll and Mabel looked at each other and shrugged their shoulders. "She's cockeyed."

Tony jumped up. "I'll show you the book."

They closed in on her from either side, pinioned her arms behind her back and thrust her out the door. Tony squirmed in their grasp, then stiffened backward. They both pushed her from the back, shoving her on her heels along the slippery floor. She giggled, thinking she could still overcome them.

At the bathroom door she wrenched herself out of their grasp and started to run back down the hall. But she tripped on a rug and fell to her knees.

Doll and Mabel came rushing up, grabbed her by the heels, and lugged her along the floor like a sack of meal, right into the bathroom. Doll kicked the door closed.

In a desperate attempt to sit up Tony flailed wildly with her arms and legs, but Doll came and squatted on her chest, heavy as a rock, crushing her breath out. A crowd of girls, damp, flushed and half naked, closed in on her. Her senses swooned at the smell of their warm flesh, dusty with talcum powder. She gasped for air.

"Let go of me, you dirty bitches," she yelled; "I'll kill you." Her face was beet-red, and a thick vein swelled on the side of her neck like a rope. She tried to butt Doll's back with her knees.

Pat stood behind her. Tony stretched her neck back and saw Pat's face upside down, her grinning teeth, the whites of her eyes, and her pupils glittering black.

"Let's strip her and throw her in the tub."

The girls tore at her clothes. "Sure, let's toss her in."

They pulled off her slippers, tickled her in the ribs till she howled with pain, pinioned her arms to the floor, and ripped off her pajama top. She felt something beat inside her skull like a drum. My head'll bust, she thought. She shut her eyes against the faces pressing in on her, devouring her nakedness. For an instant her muscles loosed as if in surrender, then she braced her heels on the floor again, bursting with enormous strength. As long as she could not see their eyes she felt covered.

I'll kill them, she thought again; they're all making fun of me. I'll kill them.

She wrenched a hand free and jammed her fist into Doll's eye. Doll screamed, clapped her hands to her eye, and sank backward between Tony's ankles. Tony bent forward from the waist, but Pat grabbed her under the arms, and holding her in a nelson, jerked her chin back.

"You'll break her neck!" someone screamed.

Daisy climbed up on her bench and, through blurred eyes, saw Tony writhing under a pile of arms and legs. It looked as though the girls would claw her to pieces.

There's nothing I can do, she thought frantically. I'm the only one. They're all against her. All?

She turned around. Where was Jeff? She tucked up her robe, jumped off the bench and squeezed out through the door.

"Jeff! Jeff!" Her voice rose to a wail.

Jeff came running out of her room, her bare arms and legs white in the dusk.

"Jeff! Make them stop!"

Jeff pushed open the bathroom door.

Instantly she caught sight of Tony's nude body – her heaving ribs, her thin shoulder blades that flashed in and out beneath the skin, and as she turned, the tender outlines of her budding breasts. The struggling figures blurred before Jeff's eyes; she felt deep shame that she must look on something she had no right to.

She shoved her way through the girls. Pat had Tony by the waist; two other girls held her by the legs, ready to swing her into the tub.

"Stop it!" cried Jeff. "Let her go!"

She saw Tony's face, her eyes, always bright, now bloodshot and opaque, seeking Jeff's own eyes in tortured appeal. At once Jeff knew; she is no tomboy to do my errands. She will never be funny any more.

The girls turned and stared at her.

"Look at Doll," Pat complained, still grasping Tony's arms though her legs dragged limply on the floor. "Tony socked her in the eye."

"I said let her go," repeated Jeff, her voice resounding loud and clear against the bathroom walls. She took no notice of Doll, who stood weeping before a mirror, surrounded by her friends, some sympathetic, some admiring.

"Go to bed, everybody." The girls reluctantly filed out – not from obedience but because the surprise had taken the edge off their fight. They looked sidewise at Tony, grumbling to each other.

"What's she proud about anyway?… Say, maybe she really is a boy… Go on, didn't you see her? Well, somethin' must be wrong with her; I never saw a girl who could fight like that… Say, maybe if you do it long enough you get to look like a boy… What, her, she's innocent, she's no percy, just runs around after Jeff like a dog…"

Tony got up off the floor, trying to pull together her tattered pajamas, and stumbled out of the bathroom, her head bent low. Jeff followed her through the door. She longed to say something but found to her surprise that her voice was all choked up. Looking at the back of Tony's neck, she felt afraid of her – there was a certain sternness about a person so utterly alone.

In the hall Jeff almost knocked down Mabel, who came dashing up the stairs, red and panting, dangling a purplish scrap of raw meat. "I snitched it out of the icebox," she explained, "for Doll's eye. Tony gave her a shiner."

"Next time don't start up with her," Jeff warned. "You can carry a joke too far. Besides, they're all on edge."

Mabel looked down at the floor. "I feel kinda bad about the whole business. She's only a kid… Say, did anybody ever tell her anything?"

"Gee," said Jeff, "I never thought of it. That would be a tough order… Oh, well, she must know. How do we all know? You pick it up."

"It's kinda hard, though," said Mabel. "Don't you remember? Me, I cried all night long."

"Yeah," said Jeff, smiling at the recollection, "I didn't know a thing. I was kind of a dumb kid. You know I thought something happened to me, thought I got hurt, or I had a disease…"

"Ain't it funny?" said Mabel. They both laughed. "I'm gonna tell my baby everything good and early. Nice too. With fishes, an' flowers, an' all that stuff."

She stopped abruptly. "Maybe I better talk to Tony. Soon."
"Yes," said Jeff. She considered a moment, then said almost shyly, "You act like a mother to her."

"A fine mother. Look at tonight."

The warning bell rang, harsh and brassy. "You can make it up," said Jeff.

"I got to." Mabel looked at Jeff with her kind, troubled eyes, then turned toward Doll's room.

Epilogue

The pieces included in *The Golden Age of Lesbian Erotica* are representative of the period, but they also – due to the constraints of the era – excise some of the passion and the fruition of the relationships between lesbians in those decades. While many of the stories in this collection are intensely passionate and some quite sensual and sexually explicit, these last stories are meant to reflect what lesbians might have written about in all their explicitness and immediacy had those avenues been open to them and had there been venues for publication of such stories.

—*Victoria A. Brownworth*

Diane DeKelb-Rittenhouse
JAZZ BABIES 1920's

Amusing, the lies society will swallow whole, the truths it shuts its eyes to, will deny to its last breath. Or perhaps I mean tragic. It is, nevertheless, a situation one must understand in order to properly cultivate the fine art of finger-fucking a girl in public, or allowing oneself to be publicly finger-fucked, arts at which I excel. At the moment, I am, or am about to become, the fuckee rather than the fucker, and the artistry consists of masking my reactions, schooling myself to appear cool and aloof when my thighs are trembling, my breasts aching, my core swollen and wet, anticipating the path one slim finger will take as it makes its way above the rolled tops of my silk stockings.

Thank heaven – or realms less sublime – for the new hemlines. So much less fabric to be gotten out of the way.

Concealed by the full-skirted linen tablecloth, a teasing touch brushes lightly at the back of my knee. I tamp a muggle into my cigarette holder and, ever attentive, Teddy immediately has his lighter ready. I lean into him, hand on his wrist to steady the flame. I squeeze perhaps too strongly as I inhale the harsh smoke, and understanding flares in his eyes as he favors Geordie with a hot-eyed look. Geordie smiles politely back, attention immediately turning back to tonight's diversion, Miss Emily Chase of the Boston Chases.

"We don't have anything like this in Boston," Miss Chase sniffs. The glance with which she favors the clientele at Lulu's cannot be said to be favorable.

"Don't you?" Geordie replies with grave sympathy, and no sincerity. We've been to Boston. The finger abandons my knee, and begins a slow and torturous journey up along my thigh.

Lulu's is one of the better speakeasies, and certainly one of the best and most discrete of those clubs that cater to a largely female clientele. The main room is large and roomy, with a good-sized dance floor and a comfortable stage that can hold a jazz quartet with no one falling off the platform. The times are, fortunately, more tolerant than they were in the past, and there are plenty of white, straight customers on hand tonight, of which our party of three apparently straight couples is supposedly a prime example. Miss Chase doesn't appear quite as uncomfortable in this milieu as she would like us to believe she is. I notice her gaze straying over a flapper in an ashes of rose silk dress and a cloche hat a few tables away. The flapper winks at her, and turns back to her girlfriend.

"Well, gosh Miss Chase," Bertie Thicke says brightly, "That's the whole point, ain't it? Mr. and Mrs. Beardsley promised that they'd show us a side of town tourists don't get to see."

I exhale the fragrant smoke I have been holding in my lungs.

"I trust I've kept my promise," I say, shifting subtly, my thighs parting invitingly wider, unbeknownst to the others seated at the table. I am hoping to entice the finger to hurry along its way. My invitation is ignored, as the finger chooses, instead, to brush back and forth, slowly and maddeningly, across the same few inches of sensitive flesh. I bring the cigarette holder to my lips, inhaling once more.

"Pos-i-lutely," Bertie's fiancée, Fanny Maxwell, beams at me, waving her own cigarette holder – containing a regular fag, not a muggle – for emphasis. Such a pretty child, dark haired and dark eyed, an egret feather in a diamond band gracing her brow, her lips a proper cupid's bow stained vermilion, a long string of pearls wound about her neck, and hanging to her waist. And so eager. I have high hopes for the Honorable Francine Juliana Maxwell. "Everything's jake."

On stage, Gladys Bentley, the celebrated bulldagger in her famous tuxedo and top hat, is giving her own rendition of Half-Pint Jaxon's "Can't You Wait Till You Get Home." I don't believe Miss Chase approves the new lyrics. The finger stroking my thigh has finally abandoned the tease and is moving higher, closer, nearer. I exhale once more.

> *Just wait 'till I get you home*
> *Wait until we're all alone*
> *I love you, Mary, goodness knows,*
> *And Mary, I love you tearing my clothes…*

"Ivy always keeps her promises," Teddy says loyally. "Don't you, darling?"

"Always, darling," I respond. "At least my promises to you." Fanny giggles, while Teddy, Bertie and Geordie laugh. Emily Chase manages a tight smile, which I return as the finger between my thighs finally finds me, slipping easily into slick wet folds.

...Lick my muff when we're alone
Do you in the parlor when we get home...

My pleasure is mounting when our waitress arrives, her uniform a bit of silk and sequins that would do Ziegfeld proud. Teddy smiles at her wolfishly.

"Hello, sweetheart," he purrs. She blushes. I admire the view, bringing my cigarette holder to my lips again, taking a deep drag, conscious of the finger inside me stroking slowly, sweetly, against my walls.

She takes our order for drinks, and coming ever closer to ecstasy, I allow myself to fantasize about running my own fingers over sequins and silk, running them under it, over pert breasts and smooth skin. The waitress speaks in the broad accents of a corn-fed Midwestern girl, and everything about her is big-eyed and ingenuous. Wherever did Lulu find you, little girl? Cornflower blue eyes, corn silk fine blond hair in a Louise Brooks bob, I imagine those bee-stung lips opening beneath mine, those dimpled knees parting, imagine rolling a stiff rosy nipple between the fingers of one hand while the fingers of another slip into a tight wet darkness.

Inside my own tight wetness, one finger is joined by another, while a thumb presses down on the tender center of sensation, the tight bundle of nerves that governs – or at least unleashes – my passions. I close my eyes briefly, then open them once more, exhaling the held breath as the world is reduced to the clever fingers inside me and the pretty girl with wide eyes and incarnadined lips waiting to take my order.

"Absinthe Frappe," I manage to get out against the escalating rapture. Absinthe has been illegal in the states for sixteen years, but what isn't illegal, these days? Well, muggles aren't. At least not here. But it's only a matter of time.

"Yes, ma'am," our waitress says dutifully, as she takes my order, then moves on to the others. I close my eyes as the fingers inside me press just the right spot, the thumb brings just the right pressure, and the world dissolves in light. I float for several moments, precious and prolonged, as the fingers inside me continue their tender ministrations, and I am able to put aside who I am, what I am, where I am...

Sadly, the world does not remain dissolved for long. It will right itself, reform, realign and bring with it the tedious business of ordinary life. I sigh, opening my eyes and lifting the cigarette holder to my lips once more.

Gladys has moved on to parody something by Mr. Cole Porter, and Fanny giggles again, delightfully shocked.

We talk of the performance we took in earlier in the evening, the performances we might take in tomorrow, the travel plans that will see Miss Chase safely back to Boston, and madcap Fanny off to Chicago, adoring Bertie in train. Soon, our little waitress is back with our drinks. I sip mine, pleased to see that Lulu's connections are still top drawer. Even Miss Chase can't fault the quality of her gin.

"Well, this juice joint sure is the bees knees," Bertie says admiringly. "I hope we can do as well by you when you come visit us."

"I'm sure you'll manage," I smile, my gaze flicking from him to the waitress who is standing by Teddy's chair. My spouse is engaging her in flirtatious conversation. Fanny and Bertie are oblivious, but Miss Chase casts me a pitying glance, which she tries to hide. I repress my laughter and return it with something suitably brave and long-suffering. Miss Chase, along with the rest of the world, takes me for the uncomplaining wife of a notable philanderer, Geordie as the cake-eater who bears me company in the face of my husband's inconstant affections. The pretense is tedious, but necessary. Not pretending… that's a choice none of us have.

Our waitress is off to bring Teddy whatever it is he asked her for, and I rise, graciously excusing myself from the table. I smile warmly at Fanny and she, dear girl, takes the hint. Geordie keeps Miss Chase occupied with lively conversation while Fanny and I withdraw.

There are two other girls in the alcove leading to the powder room, standing intimately close. Perhaps they are merely whispering confidences, but the glances they cast us are wary. Fanny looks at them with breathless wonder. I smile reassuringly. They return my smile, and go back to their conversation. The powder room only has space for one. As a girl leaves, I motion for Fanny to go in… and I push in behind her. The girls we interrupted giggle knowingly.

"Why, Mrs. Beardsley," Fanny begins, but there's a certain heat in her eyes and a throatiness in her voice that tells me this is neither unexpected nor unwelcome.

"Don't be coy, darling," I tell her, "there really isn't time."

She glances nervously at the door.

"But they'll hear," she says breathlessly.

"I certainly hope so," I say, amused. Why does she think they're hanging about in the alcove?

"Oh," she says, and "Oh!" again, as I place my hands on her lightly rouged cheeks and pull her face to mine.

I lick across lips still tasting of gin, the tang bitter, but welcome. Fanny stiffens for a moment, then the shock is over and she melts like butter, creamy and sweet, kissing back, cupid's bow mouth parted, and little hands clutching at my shoulders. My own hands dip below the handkerchief hem of her skirt, skimming the silk-clad legs. I adore the feel of a woman's calves encased in silk, so much more naked than the old woolen stockings we used to wear, and yet not quite as naked as bare flesh. Had I the time... but I don't. And so my hands simply push up her skirts, and then slide under the wide leg of the combinations that, flapper that she is, she's thankfully adopted. My fingers find her wet and pulsing with heat, and she moans as I stroke her silky folds. Fanny is half gone in pleasure, as I free one hand to pull down the low neck of her sheath dress, slip the straps of her combinations and her bandeau over her shoulders, pushing them down so that I can get my eager fingers on her breasts. Oh, my, isn't this lovely? Soft little mounds, topped with delicate, rosy nipples that respond so eagerly to the lightest touch. I plunge my tongue into the wet cavern of her mouth, sucking eagerly. She shudders, but wraps her tongue with mine. And then she's gathered the courage to slip her own hand under my skirts, under the leg of my silk drawers, into my own wetness. Recently sated, I'm quick to trigger, but she's hot and young and eager, so she's ahead of the game. It takes me less than five minutes to work the dear girl into a lather, and then she's twisting on my fingers, muffled shrieks sounding against my lips, and I have to hold her hard against the wall to keep her from sliding to the floor in a mass of silken skin and gauzy fabric. I'm so excited by what I've done to her, that my second climax of the evening is hard on the heels of hers. But, older and more experienced, I'm in no danger of falling. We rest against the wall, kisses slowing, becoming tender rather than hungry, until I've recovered enough to pull away from her. I raise my hand, still damp with her, to my lips, and slowly suck my fingers clean. Her dark eyes widen, grow darker yet, and I realize I could have her again, right now, but we've already been gone quite long enough.

"Later, sweetheart," I promise, giving a final lick. I clean my hands, straighten my clothes, and leave her to whatever business she originally had here, my own business having been satisfactorily concluded. I blow her a kiss as I close the door, smile at the girls waiting in the vestibule to use the facility, who smile knowingly back, and head, not toward our table, but to one in the back.

Lulu is in her usual place, holding court, keeping one eye on the stage and another on her customers.

"Ivy, darling." she greets me. "Didn't know you were back in town."

"Only just," I tell her. Lulu is an old-fashioned girl. None of these boyish dresses, laced bodices, bobbed hair or Eton cuts for her. A Bertha collar on her button-over tunic discretely covers the unfashionably large breasts she refuses to bind, and the hem of her skirt would, were she standing, likely hover just above her ankles. Her hair has, miraculously or cosmetically, escaped any tinge of gray, and she wears it coiled in a neat bun gathered low on the back of her neck. It would hang about her hips if she let it free of her hairpins, and a fond memory comes of running my hands through the thick black mass of it, and holding on tight, back arching off a bed, her tongue impossibly skilled as she licked me into a frenzy.

"You've gotten yourself a new girl since I was gone," I mention. "The little blonde from the Midwest."

"Ah," Lulu says with a knowing smile. "You've met our Margie."

"Margie, is it?" I say thoughtfully. Of course it would be. There really is only one, at least for tonight. "Well, darling, I'm thinking of having a late supper back at the hotel. I'll need a waitress. Will Margie be available?" Lulu's smile widens, and we quickly come to terms. I return to collect Fanny from the powder room, and escort her back to our table.

Gladys has been supplanted by a jazz band, led by an awfully good trumpet player. A few girls have gotten on the dance floor for a Charleston, knees flashing as their skirts swirl with the fast moves of the dance.

"Goodness," Miss Chase observes. "There was a time when we'd have been arrested for indecent behavior for exposing so much of our nether limbs."

"How fortunate that time has passed," I murmur, reclaiming my seat.

"Ah, there you are, Mrs. Ivy," Bertie says fondly. I can see that he has managed to down one or two drinks during my absence, and am not unduly surprised when he breaks into song. "...I know you'll be clinging, Ivy, come on cling..."

I smile as if flattered. I never could abide that song.

Teddy smirks at the boy.

"You've another admirer, my dear," he says jovially.

"One must admire Ivy," Geordie returns gallantly. "There's simply no other choice." Miss Chase smiles politely, unconvinced.

Margie has noticed that my glass is nearly empty, and hurries over to inquire if I need another.

"No, dear. But has Miss Lulu spoken to you yet?" Margie blushes, blue eyes wide. Miss Lulu has.

"Wonderful," I murmur. "Another round for my friends, dear and then we'll have the tab."

Miss Chase is somewhat mellowed by her third glass of gin, and is humming softly as Geordie escorts her out of the club and into the roadster that's been brought around for them.

"Thanks ever so much for the pleasant evening, Mrs. Beardsley," she manages just before Geordie helps her into the car.

"Good night, Miss Chase," I wave politely.

It was perhaps a mistake to let Bertie drink as much as Miss Chase.

"You're a heart entwiner, Ivy, Ivy…" he warbles, as Teddy and Fanny help him out of Lulu's.

"He's spifflicated," Fanny giggles.

"So it would seem," I reply thoughtfully. Perhaps this mistake will prove fortuitous.

The Imperial is brought round, and Teddy helps the children in, before sliding behind the wheel. I join him up front. Bertie continues to serenade us all the way back to the hotel.

Ah, youth.

Returned to the hotel, I send my maid to bed and insist that Bertie and Fanny join us for a nightcap. One more ought to do it. A quick phone call to room service. Then, at the bar, I make sure that Fanny's drink is on the rocks, more rock than liqueur, and that Bertie's is a stiff shot, neat. He passes out on the couch.

"Do help the boy to bed, darling," I encourage Teddy. He grins, and urges the young man up, companionably slinging an arm around him and steering him off to his own suite. Teddy will see him safely tucked up and will return in no time flat.

"I suppose I ought to go," Fanny says, sipping her gin.

"Oh, no dear," I smile. "I've planned a late supper, hadn't I said?" Fanny smiles and settles back on the couch. Teddy returns in minutes, Geordie not far behind him.

"Oh, Mr. Goodman," Fanny says brightly, perhaps a shade disappointedly. "I hadn't expected you to rejoin us."

"I could never desert Ivy," Geordie says with a bow.

"My dearest friend," I murmur fondly.

Lulu, true to her word, has delivered Margie to my door in time for her to serve supper. There's a knock, which Teddy is only to happy to answer. Margie stands nervously in the entrance, wearing a wrap-over coat and cloche hat, both in midnight blue.

"Come in, come in sweetheart," he says. "Ivy will know just what to do with you."

Fanny's smile slips just a bit to see Margie. She is apparently reassured by the fiction that Margie is here to act as our waitress while we have supper. Why she thinks my own maid couldn't have performed that function… well, she does think it, doesn't she?

Margie thinks so, too. She quickly demonstrates that she knows exactly why she's being paid the princely sum of one hundred dollars to dish up supper. Lulu, who understands the subtleties, has seen to it that the girl is wearing a proper maid's uniform, stiff black cotton and starched white apron, beneath the midnight blue coat. But she's also wearing stockings of real silk, not art silk, and T-strapped pumps. And, as she serves me my hors d'oeuvres, she brushes carefully close against my thigh, her hand brushes against my arm. I smile indulgently. Fanny's glass is not allowed to empty, and by the time I tell Margie to pour herself a glass, as well, Fanny's not at all surprised at such familiarity with a serving girl.

She's going to become every so much more familiar with her before the night is over.

It doesn't take long. The food, after all, is merely an excuse. None of us is all that hungry, although caviar never comes amiss. It doesn't take me all that long to get Fanny into the bedroom, with Margie assisting. After all, the girl is tired and ought to be tucked up in bed.

Geordie and Teddy wait until I've gotten Fanny out of her slip-on dress before they follow us in. Margie looks at them nervously, but I can see she's not really surprised. I do so admire Lulu's ability to find good help.

I doubt Fanny even knows there's anyone else in the room. She giggles, standing in her silky combinations, and her rolled hose, the egret feather listing terribly to one side. I remove it, and kiss her. She opens her mouth and kisses me back, a bit more sloppily than she had earlier in the evening, but I'm not one to complain. Still kissing Fanny, I hold out a hand, and Margie understands perfectly, coming in to me, unbuttoning the back of my own evening dress, letting it slip to the floor in a rustle of taffeta. She presses a hesitant kiss to the back of my neck, and I moan into Fanny's mouth. It doesn't take long to have both of them naked. Margie's skirt and bodice and apron take next to no time to remove, and her corset is quickly discarded, along with the step-ins and the bandeau. Naked, she is a slender nymph, with narrow hips and small breasts, a perfect jazz baby, a model flapper. Fanny isn't far behind, though her breasts are a trifle larger than is fashionable. I leave them in their stockings, and have Margie help me lower Fanny to the bed.

What follows after is the fine art of entertainment. I am aware, as Fanny is not, of our audience. And so it is with artful display that I pull Fanny's thighs wide, so that she is quite open and vulnerable to the watchers. Margie, not quite so drunk after only one glass, shoots me another nervous glance.

"Don't worry," I tell her. "They won't touch you."

She's reassured. I give her permission to kiss Fanny, who is not at all reluctant, while I lay to Fanny's side and begin to suck on her lovely nipples. I take Margie's hand, and lead it to Fanny's center, showing her what to do. Margie doesn't actually need my guidance, but she plays along. Soon, both our fingers are sliding about in Fanny's pretty muff, and Fanny is lifting her legs to give us better access, moaning against Margie's mouth, pushing her breast into mine. I lick my way down her body, and settle my mouth over her tight and tender button, while Margie's fingers continue to work her inside. It's too much for Fanny, who begins sobbing and thrashing as I push her along the road to rapture. A few feet a way, Teddy is panting, leaning forward in his chair so that he doesn't miss a thing. He doesn't miss it when I pull back slightly, extending my tongue so that just the tip is circling her bud. He doesn't miss it when I lash down harder, and draw my tongue down her narrow slit. He doesn't miss it when I lick my way up and back, lashing at the little bud for five excruciating minutes, while Fanny wriggles and twists, and he doesn't miss it when I bite down, oh so gently, onto the little button, and Fanny shrieks her climax.

Margie and I cuddle Fanny, kissing her and petting her until she's recovered and is kissing and petting right back. I push her back into the pillows, and order Margie to sit on her face. Teddy has his pants open by now, and has begun to stroke his cock. I still don't think Fanny is aware of him, though Margie certainly is. Margie is ordered to play with her breasts while she rides Fanny's tongue. For my part, I'm playing with Fanny's pussy once more, fingers soaking in her well-pleasured muff. Teddy's eyes are pleading with me, but I merely smile.

"Patience, darling," I coo. And, really, Fanny is such an enthusiastic learner. Margie is whimpering in her own orgasm a bare ten minutes into the game. Once she's collapsed to Fanny's side, I climb over Fanny, and rub my own wet pussy against hers.

"So, how do you like your taste of the night life, darling?" I tease, taking her mouth, eating the taste of Margie off her tongue, rubbing my thigh between her legs. Fanny bucks beneath me, her own pleasure reached; I roll off of her. There are now three of us naked and spent, sprawled across the deluxe bed in our penthouse suite. Teddy's eyes are glazed. I look at him thoughtfully.

"Fanny, darling, may Teddy eat your pussy?" I ask her, eyes riveted to those of my spouse. Fanny giggles, and spreads her legs. It's about as much as she can manage, poor dear, exhausted as she is.

Teddy gets to his knees with alacrity, grabs Fanny's ankles, and pulls her down to the bed, fusing his mouth to her soaking muff.

Leaving him to his own devices, I reach for Margie.

"There you are, darling," I purr, pulling her up against me, spooning her.

"What do you think of the show?" I ask, directing her attention to where Teddy is eating Fanny with enthusiasm.

"I liked it better when you did it," she says pertly.

"Naughty," I smirk, lightly slapping her ass, then soothe my hand over the little sting.

I don't really care what Teddy and Fanny are up to. I pull Margie close, one hand busy with her breast, the other traveling over her belly, down her hip, into her cunt. She bucks against my hand as I force a second finger in along with the first.

"My, you're tight," I whisper into her ear. "Haven't been at this long?"

"Wrong," she says, writhing. "I've been doing this with my girlfriend in Kansas for years."

"Sure you have," I say, adding a third finger. She bucks harder, moaning and twisting. I pinch her nipple and she nearly comes off the bed. Fanny is wailing away, and soon Margie is wailing right along with her. I suspect that Teddy is coming all over himself as well. Geordie observes the proceedings calmly, slowly sipping a glass of gin.

Fanny is done. The last time was too much for her, and she's already snoring lightly. Teddy manages to wobble to his feet. He's a sticky mess and I suggest he take a bath. He grins foolishly, pulls me up for a sloppy kiss, and takes himself off at last.

"Well," Geordie says, "Took him long enough." I simply smile and hold out my arms. Geordie smiles back, standing, and starting to undo buttons.

We owe a lot to the Symmington Side Lacer. Not that Geordie's breasts are all that large, but as she's supposed to be a man, any breasts at all are rather inconvenient. The Side Lacer, designed for the flat-chested flapper look, is much more convenient than the old breast bindings and wraps we used to rely upon.

Still, I can't wait to get her out of it.

"I've been waiting to fuck you all night," I growl in her ear. We've left Fanny on the bed and have moved to the bed in the adjoining room. Margie, naked and disheveled, wobbles along in our wake.

"What, my fucking you at Lulu's wasn't enough," she laughs.

"Only once," I pout. "Once is never enough."

And so she fucks me again, long and hard, getting as much of herself up inside me as she can, until I've got four fingers crammed tight and deep, her thumb busy on my clit. She's had Margie join us, and if there's anything better than having a girl's slender fingers fucking your cunt, it's having two girls' hot, wet mouths, suckling on your breasts while those slender fingers piston inside you. I reach to return the favor, but Geordie slaps my hand away.

"Later, baby," she whispers. "This is for you, for everything you put up with so we can be together."

"Darling girl," I murmur, and she presses her thumb down, hard and ruthless, and the world drops away once more as I howl in delight.

The night is young. There's time for me to pull Margie to my mouth, her lips sealed to Geordie's cunt, and Geordie's to mine, as the three of us suck and finger our way to glory. Later, I use a strap-on, Margie kneeling on the bed with her ass in the air while Geordie lies beside us, fingering Margie's clit. And, of course, there's time for Geordie to give me the black kiss, tonguing my ass while Margie sucks my cunt, so that I'm dissolving between the two of them. I'm exhausted when Margie and Geordie engage in a final bout of sixty-nine, and the three of us curl up like kittens in a heap, seeing the dawn in and finally drifting to sleep.

Experience pays off. I'm awake before anyone else, able to help a groggy Fanny back into her clothes, out of my suite and back into her own. She's back in the bed she belongs in, where Bertie will find her whenever he recovers enough from his own hangover to come looking.

Afterward, I look in on Teddy, who's asleep in the dressing room. He's curled in on himself, chilled because he's kicked off his covers. I pick them up off the floor and tuck them around him, dropping an affectionate kiss on his head.

Geordie is still sleeping, but Margie is awake.

"Should I go?" she asks.

"Do you want to?" I return.

She thinks about it.

"Not just yet," she admits. I smile and pick up the phone to order breakfast.

Margie is not interested in a position as my maid. She really does like her work at Lulu's, and she really is sure she can build her own career as a singer there, once she's been around long enough to pick up the kind of lyrics that are popular. And then she'll write to her girlfriend back in Kansas, and the two of them will move in together and everything will be just as she always wanted.

I smile. Sure it will, kid.

But I let her know the offer is open.

Margie wants to get back home. She's got another waitressing job she needs to be at in a few hours, this one slightly more respectable and, consequently, less lucrative, than the one she enjoys at Lulu's. I kiss her good-bye and send her off with the promised hundred, plus money for a cab.

"Come back to bed," Geordie murmurs when I return to the bedroom, and I do, even though Geordie is sleeping.

Amusing, the lies society will swallow whole, the truths it shuts its eyes to, will deny to its last breath. Miss Chase is content in her lie that she is a good and virtuous woman, with no evil thoughts or deeds to her name, despite the desires she suppresses, which are slowly turning her bitter and mean. Fanny Maxwell is content in her lie that she is just a thoroughly modern woman, up for a bit of adventure, and that she will be perfectly happy to settle down with Bertie, that she will be able to be faithful to him for the rest of her life. Margie is content in her lie that she has found true love, and that her little girlfriend hasn't moved on to some equally corn-fed farm boy, or that she, of the million arrivals to the city every year, is the one talented enough to make her living as a singer. And the world is content in its lie that Teddy is a faithless, if indulgent husband, and I a long-suffering wife, and Geordie a man who is too effeminate to be any real threat to my marriage.

And what it blinds its eyes to, what society will deny to its last breath rather than admit, is that love comes in many forms and shapes and flavors, and my love for one of my own sex is as normal and as right and as splendid for me as that of any dewy-eyed virgin for her handsome groom.

Amusing. Or perhaps I mean tragic.

I am Ivy and I cling only to myself and perhaps to Geordie, as I dream of a time when we may be what we are without laws to condemn us, without the need to hide, without having to pay the price of unfaithfulness, pandering to someone else's lusts, in order to enjoy what is not lust, but love to me.

But then, that is perhaps the lie in which I am content to live.

I am Ivy. And I cling.

Diane DeKelb-Rittenhouse
HARLOW BLONDE 1930's

As it had been from the first, Evelyn led and Grace followed, the tide being tugged along at the moon's least whim. Tugged along to dance classes when the friends were eight, to singing lessons when they were ten. And at sixteen, tugged away from their small home town to Manhattan's Lower East Side to pursue their dream of becoming Ziegfeld Girls.

At least, that was Evelyn's dream. Grace never bothered with dreams of her own, content to share her friend's. After all, she was certain that Evelyn's dreams were destined to be realized. With her short hair set in thick curls, her eyebrows plucked to fine lines above large eyes, her plump lips painted in the heart shape her idol affected, Evelyn was the very image of Clara Bow. Perhaps not an exact image. Evelyn was a gray-eyed brunette, not a redhead. But still, the resemblance was striking, and that alone had to impress Ziegfeld, even without Evelyn's fluid dancing and angelic singing. Grace's dancing was just as good, maybe better, but her singing voice was a shade too thin, her face a bit too plain. Although Evelyn was given a spot in 1928s *Follies*, Grace, like Norma Shearer and Joan Crawford before her, was pronounced "not up to standard" by the great impresario.

Grace's needlework, though, was second to none, and Evelyn managed to get her a job with the wardrobe mistress, helping to take care of the wonderful costumes that, even if they were now being designed by Harkrider instead of Erté, were still the talk of New York. Grace never asked just how Evelyn had managed to get her in. Although the wardrobe mistress seemed to have more than enough help already, work was somehow found for Grace.

The next two years were idyllic. Pooling their salaries, they managed a tiny apartment, and began the glamorous life of Ziegfeld Girls.

Began, but never finished.

Like other pretty girls in the *Follies*, Evelyn found herself surrounded by swarms of hopeful young men. Grace, too, discovered that even if she wasn't up to Flo Ziegfeld's standards, there were other standards she met, if not exceeded. At first, the girls enjoyed their evenings on the town, but that enjoyment soon faded. The price for being taken to the fanciest restaurants, the nicest clubs, the smartest shows was that they were inevitably subjected to clumsy pawing and heavy petting of the sort they quickly discovered they did not care for. They soon turned deaf ears to the swarming swains, preferring evenings spent quietly at their own apartment, or together at the cinema.

There were no *Follies* the next year, or the year after, but Ziegfeld had other projects in which a part could always be found for Evelyn, and wardrobe duties could always be found for Grace. It was the end of 1930 and the Great Depression was fully under way. Boys who had taken them to wild parties now panhandled for dimes, or sold apples on street corners. The girls regarded them with a mixture of pity and horror. There but for fortune...

Their own fortunes were, if not good, then at least good enough for the times. They were eighteen, and the world was as much their oyster as they could desire. Life might have continued to drift along pleasantly enough had not the moon once more exerted her pull upon the tide.

Evelyn danced two performances on Wednesdays, evening and matinee. She would come home to their apartment exhausted, complaining of her tired feet. Grace would attend her anxiously, making her cups of tea or hot cocoa, drawing her a bath. And afterward, as Evelyn draped herself across the chaise lounge in their tiny sitting room, Grace would sit beside her, massaging away the pain in Evelyn's hard-working little feet.

One Wednesday evening, Evelyn complained that the aches she felt were not confined to her feet alone, and she encouraged Grace to expand her massage from Evelyn's delicate feet to her trim ankles, the soft curves of her well-muscled dancer's calves. As Grace's clever fingers soothed away Evelyn's pains, the dancer sighed her pleasure, and declared her intention to return the favor. Grace made no demur, but happily allowed Evelyn's hands to mimic the path her own hands had taken. And she made no demur when Evelyn's fingers moved higher than her own had, brushing along the sensitive back of her knee, pushing up Grace's skirt to dance along her silken thighs.

At some point, Grace's eyes widened in understanding, and she gazed into the laughing, knowing eyes of the friend of her childhood, who, with childhood behind them, was becoming more than friend.

And so the moon drew the tide to her once again, and it seemed to Grace that she had always known, in some secret fastness of her heart, what path the moon would draw her down. She understood why she had never liked the harsh, sloppy kisses of the stage-door Johnnies, the brutish touch of their hands. Evelyn's lips were softer, her kisses more delicate. Her mouth teased and coaxed, it didn't importune, and it only made demands when those demands were ready to be met. Her hands were gentle on Grace's breasts, caressing and arousing, rather than mauling and mashing. Grace had slapped away hands that had pinched her bottom or tried to work their way beneath her skirts. Now, she found herself rubbing against hands that fondled her bottom, spreading her thighs for fingers that soon did away with her skirts altogether. Suddenly, one of those fingers went someplace that Grace's own fingers had never been. She arched upward, gasping at the sensation, breaking the kiss.

"There," Evelyn said huskily, a hint of triumph in her voice, moving her finger a tiny bit further, but gently, easily. "I can feel how wet you are there. You're ready for me, aren't you darling? You're ready for me at last."

She stared into Evelyn's eyes, which were suddenly a stormy gray, darker than Grace had ever seen them, and yet sparkling with something heretofore unknown, if wholly fascinating.

"Yes," Grace said breathlessly, helplessly. "Yes, I'm ready for you." Evelyn smiled in triumph, her finger probing further.

"Mm. So tight," she said, dropping soft kisses all over Grace's face. "And all for me." The finger pulled out a little way, then pushed back in, repeating the pattern, going a little further every time. Grace found her hips moving jerkily, trying to keep that finger inside her, where it was making her feel things she'd never felt before, had never known were there to be felt. Her thighs parted further, she wriggled closer.

"Easy," Evelyn murmured, her lips moving downward, kissing a trail from Grace's mouth to her neck and lower, to a small, firm breast with its tight, rosy nipple. As Evelyn's mouth closed over the firm peak, Grace whimpered, her hips bucking upward, driving Evelyn's clever finger deeper yet. Evelyn moaned her approval, and sucked hard on Grace's breast. Grace was in a delirium of pleasure, a delirium she had no way of knowing was only beginning. Evelyn did not neglect Grace's other breast, lavishing it with equal attention. Grace was panting, every nerve in her body, ever fiber and cell, alive and filled with gorgeous sensation, responsive to Evelyn's least touch. Evelyn touched and tasted her fill, lips moving from Grace's breasts to her belly, to someplace else, a place just above the damp heat Evelyn's finger explored, someplace hidden and unguessed at. Evelyn parted Grace's soft folds, her tongue sliding along the hidden flesh, finding something there that Grace was only too happy to discover. Evelyn's tongue savored the hidden secret, cherishing it, worshiping it, bringing it alive. Grace keened her appreciation, her thighs parting further as moisture rapidly gathered, a tidal wave of joy building deep inside. That inexplicable joy built and built as Evelyn's tongue worked faster, her finger harder, and suddenly there was nothing in the world but that joy, the joy Evelyn brought her, that Evelyn had revealed. It built to a dizzying height, from which Grace could espy a vista unlike any she had known before, and it was at the apex of that joy that Evelyn went further, a second finger and a third joining the first, pushing hard, reaching for something, some hidden prize.

Whatever Evelyn reached for, Grace found it, the world coming apart and being remade in a shower of light and heat. This was bliss, pure rapture, divine sensation, a hidden world suddenly revealed. Evelyn's attentions ensured that Grace lingered in that world for moment after ecstatic moment, ensured that when the light faded and the heat cooled, Grace had learned enough about them to desire their rapid return.

Afterward, when the world was the world once more, if seen from a different perspective, Evelyn shifted, lifting her hand away from its intimate caress of Grace, holding it up for the other girl to see. Evelyn's slender fingers shone with some thick and glistening substance that gave off the tangy sharp scent of bitter aloe. And with thin shining ribbons of blood.

"There," Evelyn said again, with even more triumph than before. "You're really mine, now." Grace laughed, and sat up, pulling Evelyn into her arms and kissing her.

"I always was."

The next year and a half, from the end of 1930 through the summer of 1932, marked their happiest time in New York. Alone in their apartment, lying on their narrow bed with its feather mattress and cast-iron frame, Evelyn and Grace curled together in a secret world of perfumed girl-flesh, languid kisses, hidden desires. Ziegfeld had mounted another one of his *Follies*, and it sometimes seemed to Grace that Harkrider was her own private genie, decking Evelyn out as various mythic creatures, allowing Grace to fantasize that she was making love to a harem odalisque, or being ravished by a mermaid. And, oh, wasn't the ravishment sweet? Tender kisses, not of lips alone, slow caresses of soft hands upon softer thighs, clever fingers prizing open locked treasures, uncovering matchless pearls. They would lie on their sides, embracing, kissing, touching, Evelyn's lips tracing paths of flame along Grace's flesh, pressing open-mouthed kisses to Grace's breasts, paying lavish, wet tribute to her taut rosy nipples, fingers dancing across the drenched little bud of sensation between her thighs, dancing lower, dancing within the mermaid's secret cavern, dancing like a wave approaching and receding, only to approach again, slow at first, but with increasing force and speed and urgency, the moon demanding the tide meet its rhythms. And Grace, the tide, was always helpless to resist the pull of the moon, and could do nothing but follow her desires, ascend with her to glorious heights, crash with her into rapture.

Grace reveled in the path they had chosen, a path that seemed to free something inside her, so that she became more herself, more Grace, and not just a quiet little seamstress. Though being a seamstress had its advantages, especially for a girl who was as good at what she did as Grace was. Grace could sometimes salvage bits and pieces of worn costumes: scraps of silk, strands of beads, discarded feathers or bits of satin. An inventive girl could get up to all sorts of things with such scraps, and Grace was nothing if not inventive.

One night the tide turned upon the moon, and Grace found herself bound to the iron bedstead with ropes of silk, a satin cloth covering her eyes. Something soft and delicate shivered along her flesh, barely tangible, light as a breath of wind. Surely, nothing so ephemeral could lead to satisfaction? And yet, the soft strokes, the shivering delicacy, came again and again, in an unending cycle of teasing temptation that could not help but rouse stronger passions. Grace writhed and moaned against the cotton sheets of the feather bed, her skin made sensitive to the least touch. Not until she begged and wept for that touch was it offered, hands moving with sure, firm strokes, fondling firm breasts and full buttocks, gripping rounded hips and lifting them to an open mouth and a probing tongue. Grace screamed her pleasure, the moon compelled to follow the tide.

They were young and beautiful and in love and they thought the world would go on that way forever. But the world had other ideas.

Ziegfeld died in July of 1932, leaving his wife, Billie Burke, with his debts.

There were no *Follies*, no new shows. The girls were suddenly without employment, and with very little put by to sustain them. They spent the next year scraping, getting odds and ends of work in the theater when they could, in the garment district when the theater had nothing to offer. Their fortunes had declined, as had the fortunes of most everyone else in the country, and like most everyone else, Evelyn and Grace often sought to forget their troubles by going to the cinema.

But unlike anyone else, they were able to find a possible way out of their troubles when they went there.

"This is it, Grace," Evelyn breathed, her hand clasping the other girl's, her expression rapt, her gaze fixed upon dozens of girls dancing with neon-lit violins as Dick Powell led them in the *Shadow Waltz*. "It all comes together here, in the movies."

"Yes," Grace said dreamily, entranced by the Busby Berkeley display. "Yes, it does."

Everything they owned was sold or pawned for the train tickets that would take them to Hollywood. Surely, one of the studios had a place for a former Ziegfeld Girl? Surely the costume departments could always use someone who was good with needle and thread?

It didn't seem so, at least not at first. It seemed, instead, that Hollywood was full of hopeful girls, young girls, beautiful girls. Some of them younger than the twenty-two years Grace and Evelyn could claim. And some of them more beautiful than a girl who merely looked like Clara Bow without Clara's indefinable *It*. Grace's luck finding costuming work was marginally better than Evelyn's at finding acting. Not enough to afford even a small apartment, like the one they'd had in New York, but enough to let them share a room at a boarding house for young ladies.

It seemed that all the young ladies were there for the same reason: to be the next Greta Garbo or Carole Lombard or Marion Davies.

But, usually, they wanted to be the next Jean Harlow.

Bow's star had faded, It eclipsed by *Bombshell* as peroxide sales soared. Evelyn considered this all very carefully. She noticed how many girls bought peroxide, observed that more than a few of them only succeeded in burning their hair, rather than blonding it, and decided not to follow that particular fashion. She was no less successful than her blonde housemates in getting occasional work as an extra for seven dollars a day. And no more successful, either.

Grace fared no better, and it began to look as if the move to Hollywood had been the wrong choice, after all.

But that was before Mary moved out, and the new girl came, the Harlow blonde.

She moved into the room at the end of the hall on the same floor as theirs, a girl who was tall, but not too tall, curvy, but not overblown, a girl with a knowing smile and bedroom eyes. She said her name was Mae.

"It was Mazie," the Harlow blonde laughed, in that low, sultry way she had as they sat in the drugstore, sipping Cokes flavored with the Angostura bitters Mae had recommended rather than their usual orange. "But, really, do you think a producer wants to put Mazie Moskovitch on a theater marquee when he can put Mae Marks?"

No, both Evelyn and Grace had agreed, a producer probably wouldn't. Although Grace privately thought that a producer wouldn't have cared what name he had to have on the theater marquee as long as he could have Mae on the silver screen.

"You ought to think of doing the same thing. Maybe Eva instead of Evelyn. Just a touch more exotic, classy. And what about Giselle instead of Grace?"

"My, that does sound lovely," Evelyn sighed dreamily. Grace smiled, but said nothing, signaling to the soda jerk and asking him to bring her a chocolate Coke.

Mae had managed to figure out the right way to use peroxide, a secret she offered to share with the other two girls. But other than the things every girl knew about high heels, girdles, and padding a bra, there were no secrets that could teach them to make their legs that long, their waists that narrow, their breasts that full, their voices that smoky. Or, if there were, they were secrets the Harlow blonde kept to herself.

But the secret she offered was treasure enough, and Evelyn soon took her up on it. Grace declined.

"Probably just as well," Mae said thoughtfully. "Golden blonde might not be as popular as platinum, right now, but it's a lot less trouble to keep up." Grace offered another smile, and kept another silence. Evelyn, who wore the new hair color well, as it made her skin seem milkier and smoother, her gray eyes larger and more intense, laughed as if Mae had said something quite brilliant.

Perhaps she had. Even Grace had to admit, there was a kind of brilliance, a sort of light, that seemed to permeate everything the Harlow blonde did. Mae's clothes were the same cheap cotton all the girls wore, and like the rest of the girls, she had only one pair of good shoes, stylish black lace-ups, for her auditions, and one nice hat. But she seemed to know the right way to tie a bright scarf around her neck to set off her outfit, make it look elegant rather than ordinary, and her shoes were always carefully polished, her hat set at an angle that managed to be both dramatic and flattering. And she always had a clean pair of white cotton gloves. In short, she looked like a million dollar baby, and if she were dressing herself from the five and ten cent store... well, weren't they all?

Grace learned more secrets from Mae than the ones being offered. After all, she was a seamstress and inventive. So she figured out ways to add a panel of lace here, or a fresh collar there, change a sleeve or a hem or a cuff, to make the dresses she and Eva wore seem newer and more fashionable than they really were. Mae smiled knowingly. Eva simply smiled. Not only at Grace.

With Mae, the comfortable pattern of their lives began to subtly shift. Grace had always gone along with Evelyn to her casting calls and auditions, even though she never auditioned herself. Now, Mae joined them, and she encouraged Grace to try out for the roles that were available.

Sometimes, it almost seemed as if she were daring Grace to audition, rather than encouraging her.

Grace took the dare.

The standards Flo Ziegfeld employed weren't the ones used by Hollywood. Neither Norma nor Joan had suffered long from his rejection; now, neither did Grace. Hollywood was filled with young and beautiful and talented actresses. But not all of them could do a time step or even knew what a ball change was, and half of them couldn't carry a tune in a bucket. There was something to be said for having been a Ziegfeld Girl, or having worked with them, after all.

And, there was something to be said for going on casting calls with Mae, as well. Maybe it was the bright scarves or the rakish hats, or the lady-like, spotless gloves, but she always drew the eye of whoever was in charge of hiring that day, and once eyes were drawn to the Harlow blonde, they couldn't help but find the other two blondes standing with her.

Their fortunes seemed once again on the upswing, enough so to put a little by for another apartment, rather than a room in a boarding house.

"We should go in with Mae," Eva told Grace one night as they lay together in bed, planning their future. "It'll be easier to split the rent three ways than two."

"Are you sure that's wise?" Grace said, drawing a little away. "I mean, she knows we share a room, but…"

"Oh, don't be silly darling," Eva said, her laugh too bright, too quick, her gray eyes not meeting Grace's blue ones. "Mae's all right. She won't mind." Grace opened her mouth to say that most people minded, very much indeed, and that what happened when they found out was never pretty. But Eva had better things to do with Grace's open mouth than let it spill out arguments. She pressed her own plump lips – no longer painted in Clara's bow – to her lover's, engaged her tongue, distracted her thoroughly from whatever objections she might have to the newest pull of the moon.

At the moment, Eva was interested in pulling Grace into familiar patterns. She deepened the kiss, pushing Grace's nightgown off her shoulders, hands fluttering over the soft mounds of Grace's breasts. Grace shivered, kissed back, allowed herself to be pushed down on the bed, her nightgown discarded, allowed her thighs to be pulled apart, allowed a finger to slip inside her growing wetness, a second, a third. Allowed herself to be tumbled into rapture, and to tumble Eva into it, as well. Allowed herself, after, to dream of a little apartment, or perhaps a bungalow, where the two of them could live. It was a dream that was taking rather a long time to come true. They were getting odds and ends of work, enough to get by, but not quite enough to build the kinds of savings they needed.

That was about to change.

Eva had been very excited about the call they were going on.

"They've got Dorothy Arzner," she enthused. "You know. The woman who directed Clara Bow in *The Wild Party*."

"Pity she couldn't save Bow's career," Mae said.

"Still, it was quite a good film," Grace offered thoughtfully.

"Yes, and maybe her next film will be good," the Harlow blonde replied. "But the fact is, she's a woman, and no studio is going to give her the best films or the biggest stars. That's why she left Paramount to work as an independent."

"So, then, that's why she'll need fresh talent, like us, won't she?" Grace pointed out. The other girls smiled.

Arzner wasn't anything like what Grace had expected, from the little she'd read in *Photo Play* and *Silver Screen*. The press showed pictures of Arzner in a dress, insisted she gave her directions in a feminine voice, touted the fact that though she was a woman doing a man's job, she remained very much a woman.

A woman, it seemed, who preferred to dress like a man.

Women had been cropping their hair for years, now, but Arzner's wasn't styled into soft waves or tight curls. She wore it brushed back severely, mannishly, and she wore slacks and vests and ties. At her side, a petite woman in tap pants and ballet flats, her light hair marcelled in neat waves, was scrutinizing the hopefuls who had assembled for the casting call with the same professional regard that Arzner had bent upon them.

In the end, Mae, Eva and Grace were hired as extras for a large dance scene meant to evoke a Parisian society ball. It was not the sort of dance number that Eva had hoped to find herself in when *Gold Diggers of 1933* inspired her to make the trip West. Neither Dick Powell nor Busby Berkeley were in sight, and there wasn't so much as a hint of a neon-lit violin. But the requirements of this dance were as strict as anything Mr. Berkeley could have imagined, for here they must portray taste, elegance and refinement through the dance.

But it wasn't the dance that fascinated Grace, and it wasn't the lavish costumes or the beautiful scenery, or any of the other kinds of things she had found on a dozen Broadway stages and Hollywood studio lots before, things that had long lost the ability to dazzle her. It was Dorothy Arzner herself. And it was the woman who stood at Arzner's side during the casting call, the woman choreographing the dance for her, Marion Morgan.

No one said anything. No one had to. What they were was obvious from the way they worked together, the way they communicated pages of dialogue to each other with a facial expression or the touch of a hand. Grace was fascinated by the attraction. Neither Arzner nor Morgan was what Grace thought of as attractive, at least from a physical perspective. Arzner's features were entirely too broad and masculine for Grace's taste, while Morgan was simply too thin and too plain. And yet, there was an intensity about each of them, a quiet focus to Arzner, a fierce, if equally quiet, passion to Morgan that showed in the work each woman did. And it was this quiet, hidden quality that gave each woman her own allure. At length, Grace thought she understood why it was that Marion had become to Dorothy what Grace had become to Eva.

What Mae, it seemed, intended Eva to become to herself.

She wasn't supposed to be home. Grace had decided that with the money they had earned for that day's work, they could afford enough fabric for a new dress apiece, and she had gone off to see what she could find. Eva had pleaded exhaustion, so Grace had left on her own. But passing the grocer's she remembered they were out of eggs, that she'd forgotten to purchase them this morning as she'd planned. And because the grocer would be closed by the time she was done her other shopping, and because she knew Eva would want eggs for breakfast in the morning, she bought a carton and hurried back to their room in the boarding house to put them away before they spoiled.

Afterward, she considered it a miracle that she didn't drop the eggs when she opened the door. Of course, she'd only opened the door to their set of rooms, not the bedroom itself. But the bedroom door was partially open, open enough that if one took a single step into the sitting room, one couldn't help but see. Grace had taken that single step, and was powerless to take another.

She hadn't been gone fifteen minutes, but it was amazing what a clever girl could get up to in even so short a time, and Mae, bless her, was a very clever girl.

Clever Mae had Eva naked, up against a wall. The Harlow blonde had pulled Eva's hands together, was pinning them against the wall with one hand of her own. Her other hand was caressing Eva's breast. Mae was naked, too, or mostly naked. From behind, Grace could see leather straps tied around Mae's hips, holding something onto her that she was using on Eva. Eva apparently liked whatever Mae was using. Her strong dancer's legs were wrapped around Mae's waist, and she was all but screaming into Mae's hungry, devouring mouth.

Grace supposed she should be feeling a lot of things at that moment. Betrayal, rage, pain, jealousy, anger, hurt. But after all, it wasn't so surprising that the moon could no more resist the pull of the sun than the tide could resist the moon. And what she felt, to her own shock, was… wet. Grace grew even wetter, watching Eva writhe against Mae, as Mae broke their fevered kisses to whisper dirty, wicked things into Eva's delicate ear. Eva liked Mae's suggestions. So did Grace. But now was not the time to act on them. Grace stood quietly, just long enough to watch as Eva threw her head back against the wall, arching into Mae, sobbing and moaning in a way with which Grace was intimately familiar. Only when the sobbing and moaning had died away, when Eva was sliding down the wall, Mae sliding with her, both girls oblivious to everything else around them, did Grace back away, quietly leaving and gently shutting the door behind her. She headed for the communal bathroom on their floor, locked the door, hoisted her skirts, closed her eyes, and let herself remember what the Harlow blonde had been doing to Eva, and how much Eva had liked it. Her own fingers would have to do for whatever Mae had used, but that was all right. Grace was just as clever as Mae.

Ruby, on the floor below, was home, and Grace asked Ruby if she would keep the eggs in her ice box, because Eva was out on a casting call and Grace had forgotten her key, but didn't want to take the time to get the super to let her in to her own apartment. And, if Ruby had flour, maybe Grace could make pancakes for all of them in the morning. Ruby happily agreed.

Grace did not go shopping for fabric, after all. She went to the drugstore, ordered a glass of iced tea, and thought about what she wanted and how to go about getting it. Grace had never seduced anyone before. Eva had been her only lover, and it was Eva who had taken the lead in their courtship. But, Grace had always been a quick study. She laid careful plans.

It took three days of work before Morgan was satisfied with the choreography for the dance scene. At one point, she stopped the rehearsal, muttering to herself as she tried a set of steps over and over. Grace watched her avidly. She was quite as clever at dancing as she was with anything else. Suddenly she stood up from where she and the other girls were taking a break, sitting on the floor, watching Morgan polish her choreography. Grace grabbed Mae's hand, pulling the Harlow blonde forward. "Just follow my lead," she whispered. Then, in a louder voice, she said, "What about this, Miss Morgan?" and she pulled Mae into her arms, led her into a quick, graceful pattern of steps. Mae smiled wickedly, allowing herself to be led. Morgan, startled, watched. Then her eyes narrowed, in concentration.

"Good," she said. "Very good. Let's see that again."

The steps were not adopted whole. Morgan polished them, smoothed them over until they fit seamlessly into the pattern she was devising. But eventually she was satisfied and the scene could be filmed.

"That was quick thinking," Mae said admiringly. They were in the crowded dressing room with a dozen other girls, changing out of their rehearsal clothes into the costumes that had just been brought over from wardrobe.

"She's always quick on her feet," Eva laughed, throwing her arms around Grace. "Aren't you, darling?"

"Sometimes," Grace allowed, "sometimes."

Mae smiled, and moved behind Eva to help her with her zipper. Grace smiled, herself, and when Mae stepped away from Eva, she turned to Mae.

"You're dress isn't hanging properly," she murmured, and twitched the bias-cut skirts into a more graceful drape. As she did so, her fingers lingered on the other girl's hips just a fraction longer than they ought to. Eva didn't notice. Mae's eyes widened and she favored Grace with a speculative look, which was met with a seemingly innocent smile.

The filming went off smoothly enough, but Arzner wasn't happy.

"It's not your choreography, Marion," the director said. "I just think I need something smaller, more intimate here, first, before we get to the ball." Arzner and Morgan conferred, and Mae arched a thin brow as Morgan walked directly to the three of them.

"Grace, isn't it?" she said.

"Yes, Miss Morgan."

"All right, Grace, I'd like you and…" she peered closely at Grace's companions, seemed to come to a decision. "I think all three of you. Come along." As everyone else was told to take a break, Marion Morgan led them to the director.

"Tell me what you want," Marion told Dorothy, "and we'll give it to you."

Dorothy ran her eyes over the young women and sighed.

"Does every girl in Hollywood want to be Jean Harlow?" she wondered. "Never mind. Here's what I want you to do…"

The scene was very short, and didn't require them to do much more than stand close together at one end of the ballroom set, beside a prop table with a fake Ming vase, pretending to gossip behind their fans. But at one point, Mae had to turn to the camera, lean toward Eva, to tell her something titillating about a new arrival to the party. Her one line was delivered in a throaty whisper that pleased Arzner immensely.

"All right, then," she said agreeably. "Maybe not Harlow so much as Swanson." She raked her eyes over the three girls, assessing them. "Come back tomorrow," she said at length. "I think I can use you in another scene."

With the ballroom scene completed, the other dancers were being let go at the end of the day. The additional work the three of them had gotten, combined with Mae's single line of dialogue, was ample cause for celebration. The girls splurged on a big dinner, and ended the evening back at the room Grace and Eva shared.

"That was smart, getting Morgan to notice you," Mae said. "Smarter, maybe, than trying to get to Arzner."

"I didn't plan it," Grace admitted. "It just seemed like a good idea."

"It certainly was," Mae laughed, lifting her teacup in salute.

"Maybe we'll all get a line in tomorrow's scene," Eva said dreamily. "Maybe we can move up from extras to walk-ons."

"Oh, yes," the Harlow blonde agreed. "I think we're on our way from chorines to starlets."

"Then we should be able to afford an apartment soon," Eva went on, brightly, sitting up in her chair. "Grace and I shared one in New York, you know," she confided to Mae. "And we want to find another. Maybe you might want to share?" Grace hid a smile as Mae pretended the idea was new to her.

"That's not a bad idea," Mae said with studied casualness. "We'd be like the girls in *42nd Street.*"

Not quite like them, Grace thought privately, if she had anything to say about it. But she wasn't ready to speak up just yet. Whispers seemed more in order.

She sat quietly, appearing to listen attentively as Eva and Mae talked about what parts of the city they should look in when they went apartment hunting, and how much they should plan on spending. In fact, she was watching the way they were watching each other, noticed the brief touches that weren't as brief as they might have been, the glances that lingered a shade longer than was usually the case. Mostly on Eva's part. She was an outstanding dancer, Grace decided, but she'd never be the actress Mae, who had herself under better control, was.

As the other girls chattered on, Grace announced she was going to brew another pot of tea, and made to push her chair back from the table so she could stand up. Somehow, the leg of her chair caught the hem of Mae's long skirt. There was an ominous ripping sound, and Mae looked at her skirts in alarm.

"Goodness! I'm so sorry!" Grace said, wide-eyed. "I can't think how I could have been so clumsy."

"It's all right," Mae told her graciously. "Just a tear in the seam. I can get that fixed."

"Oh, no, you have to let me sew it up for you," Grace insisted. "I can have it done in a jiffy."

"Yes," Eva agreed. "Grace is really awfully good with a needle. You'll never know there was a tear."

It was late, so Grace insisted on walking Mae down the hall to her own rooms, so that she could take charge of the damaged dress which she swore she could have finished by the next morning. Eva remained behind, having decided to turn in for the night. As they walked down the hall, Grace continued to apologize.

"I can't think how I came to be so clumsy," she said, with every appearance of remorse as Mae turned her key in the lock and opened the door.

"It's all right," the Harlow blonde said again, stepping into a sitting room even smaller than the one Grace shared with Eva and switching on the light. "As long as you can fix the seam, we're square." She headed into her own bedroom, telling Grace she'd be right back. But Grace followed her into the bedroom.

"Here, let me help you," she said, reaching for the zipper. "We don't want to make the tear any worse."

This seemed perfectly reasonable to Mae, who lifted her arms as directed, allowing Grace to lift the dress away from her, with no further stress on the torn seam. It was certainly reasonable for Grace to carefully fold the dress, so that she could carry it back to her own rooms. Placing it neatly on top of the bureau was perhaps less reasonable, and certainly unexpected. Finding Grace's hands on the shoulders of her satin slip, pushing them off her arms was quite surprising.

"I thought Eva was your girlfriend?" she drawled, lips curving in a wicked smile as her slip was sent the way of her dress.

"Oh, she is," Grace reassured her, expertly unclasping the other girl's brassiere and discarding it, revealing beautifully large breasts with pale pink nipples. "But as you're fucking her, I thought it only fair that I fuck you." And she slid fluidly to her knees, making quick work of Mae's satin underpants, so that the other girl was left only in her garter belt and seamed stockings, and her lovely lace-up high heels.

"Well yes," Mae gasped, as Grace's mouth found her clit, her fingers thrust into the Harlow blonde's damp cunt. "We must be fair."

In the interests of fairness, as the fingers of Grace's right hand played in Mae's pussy, Grace's left hand caressed its way upward over Mae's hip and belly, until Grace could play with the Harlow blonde's nipples, taunting the tiny bits of flesh until they were diamond-hard and Mae's legs were trembling with the effort of keeping her standing, instead of collapsing on the floor and letting Grace have her way with her. The idea had its appeal, but Grace seemed to prefer Mae on her feet, for the moment, and who was the Harlow blonde to complain? There was nothing to complain of in the strength of Grace's fingers, the skill of her tongue, the balance struck between tenderness and force, nothing to complain of as Grace's left hand reached higher, the fingers brushing lightly against Mae's lips. Taking the hint, Mae opened her mouth and suckled Grace's fingers for a few moments, until Grace withdrew them, and put them to better use. Mae shrieked, in both surprise and trepidation as those damp fingers suddenly found their way between the cheeks of the Harlow blonde's firm buttocks, and pressed against the tiny entrance there. A moment later, one finger triumphed over the resistance of tight muscle and Mae found herself caught in the carnal delight of double penetration. Grace increased the pressure on Mae's clit, worked her fingers in counterpoint within the other girl's body, added a second finger to Mae's grasping pussy, then a third.

Mae had to cover her mouth with both hands as she rocketed into orgasmic delight. Grace was merciless, forcing the other girl to come hard and often, until Mae no longer had a choice about standing, and slid to the floor in a well-pleasured heap.

Lying on the floor, Mae watched, bemused, as Grace licked her fingers like a cat lapping cream.

"So, do you always fuck your girlfriend's girlfriends?" she asked.

"You're not her girlfriend," Grace said coolly. "At least, not yet. Now, tell me where it is." It took a moment for Grace to clarify exactly what "it" she was looking for. Mae chuckled when she understood.

"The top drawer of my nightstand, where else?" She watched as Grace retrieved the item. "Would you like some help with that?" she offered gamely. "Perhaps a bit of practice?"

"Don't be greedy, Mazie," Grace chastised her dryly. "It doesn't become you." But she helped the Harlow blonde to her feet and kissed her soundly before taking her leave, the torn dress draped over her arm, concealing something held beneath.

Eva had fallen asleep by the time Grace returned to their rooms, and slipped into the bedroom. Grace quietly undressed, and picked up Mae's little toy, before slipping into the bed beside Eva and drawing her lover into her arms. She woke Eva with a kiss, which, at first, Eva eagerly returned. Until she noticed something different about this kiss, which caused her to stiffen and push Grace away.

"My God," she said, horrified. "You smell like her, you *taste* like her!"

"I thought you liked that smell, that taste," Grace told her, pushing her back against the bed, grabbing hold of her wrists and pinning them to the pillow, forcing her knee between her lover's legs and spreading them wide. "I thought you wanted it." She settled between Eva's spread thighs, positioning Mae's toy at Eva's entrance. "And, my darling, I always give you what you want." She thrust the toy in hard, before Eva was ready, making the other girl whimper in something less than pleasure. At first. Grace pressed her lips to Eva's with bruising force, and soon the liquid warmth rose deep inside the other girl, so that she kissed Grace back, tongues battling for dominance, clutched her tightly, lifted her hips and raised her legs to wrap them around Grace's waist.

The tide had well and truly turned, drowning the moon in exquisite sensation. Eva was left sobbing her delight as Grace thrust into her in a hard, fast rhythm that built her lover's excitement to an unbearable degree. Faster she thrust, and faster, all the while telling Eva what a bad girl she'd been, how wicked, how naughty, and how diligently bad girls ought to be punished. When Grace outlined in exact and loving detail the precise means she intended to employ to punish Eva, Eva's world exploded in light and fire. Grace was forced to muffle the screams.

When Eva regained consciousness, Grace had discarded the toy and was delicately lapping at Eva's dripping sex. Eva stiffened as a gentle orgasm, more an aftershock to what had gone before than a completion of its own, swept over her. Her hands, she vaguely realized, had been bound to the top of the bed with a silk scarf. Eva wasn't entirely helpless, but the illusion that she might be was arousing, all on its own. She climaxed again. Grace seemed in no hurry to stop what she was doing, and Eva enjoyed three more ecstatic releases before pleasure came perilously close to pain, and she begged Grace to stop. Grace made her beg through another orgasm before she acquiesced, abandoning her feast, moving up on the bed to lie beside Eva, and take her in her arms.

"You've never been like this before," Eva said between slow, languid kisses.

"You've never given me cause," Grace told her. "Now you have. Actions have consequences, sweetheart."

"What kind of consequences?" Eva said warily.

"Well, for starters," Grace said thoughtfully, kneeling up and throwing a leg over Eva's head so that she straddled the other girl, and began to sink down until her own damp pussy hovered a scant inch above Eva's face. "You're going to fuck me with your tongue until I tell you to stop." Eva almost climaxed once again.

Grace did not tell her to stop until Eva's face was wet with Grace's juices, her tongue aching, her jaw tired. Eva made no complaints. She might have complained had Grace continued to demand her services, but given how early their call was for the next day, she decided that they should get some sleep so as to be at their best. Eva was released from her restraints, and allowed to cuddle next to Grace in slumber.

There was a subtle difference to the three girls the next day, so subtle, it went unremarked by most. The other young ladies at the boarding house noticed nothing unusual. Neither did the soda jerk at the drugstore where they had a quick breakfast, or the newsboy from whom they bought their morning paper. It went unnoticed by their fellow actors at the studio and by the crew. They were oblivious to the lingering touches, the heated smiles, the fond gazes. Eva and Grace had always been friends, and they had quickly become friends with the Harlow blonde. Seeing the three together surprised no one.

Arzner, it seemed, was not quite as oblivious as the rest of the world. She looked at them, smiled knowingly, and gave them directions for their next

scene. Costumes were found for them from stock, Grace offering suggestions on how to change the look of certain garments so that they could be
reused from other actresses in an earlier scene. Each of the three girls was
given a line of dialogue. Arzner was pleased with their performances.

"Women are made out to be so sappy in films these days," Arzner told
them as they wound up their work at the end of the day. "I can't abide it, and
I won't do that in my own films. And, if you want to last, try to avoid the
sappy roles." She fell silent, her dark-eyed gaze sweeping over them in
shrewd appraisal. "This is as much as I can do, for now. But I'm reading
some scripts, and I might want you for one of those in a few weeks. Provided
that you," she pointed an admonitory finger at Eva, "stop using that damned
peroxide. It'll turn your hair to straw, and I could use a brunette." Eva stammered her agreement.

The girls were ecstatic when they left the studio to enjoy a celebratory
dinner that was grander than the one they'd enjoyed the night before.
Afterward, when they returned to the boarding house, there was no pretense
of sending Mae off to her own room.

"It might be a tight squeeze," Grace said, linking hands with the other two
women and drawing them into the bedroom. "But I'm sure it'll be worth it."

"I'm sure it will," Mae said, amused, as Grace dropped their hands to
retrieve the toy from her lingerie drawer, where she'd placed it after having
cleaned it up that morning. Grace dangled the toy by its straps and looked
at the other two women thoughtfully.

"I'm still very angry," she told them. Eva flushed, her gaze dropping to
the floor. Mae merely looked at Grace in surprise.

"That was anger?" Mae said. "Hmm. I might want to make a habit of ril-
ing you up."

"No, darling. You truly don't want to get into that habit, at all," Grace
warned, stepping forward, the toy in her hand. "I forgive you because I
understand. You gave Eva something she didn't think she could get from me.
But that won't happen again, will it, Eva? You've learned, haven't you, that
there's nothing that you want that I can't give you?"

"Yes," Eva whispered tremulously. "I've learned."

Grace favored them with a beatific smile.

"Wonderful," she said happily. "Then it's time for the two of you to give
me what I want. It's only fair."

"And just what is it that you want?" Mae asked.

"Well, for starters, why don't you take off Eva's dress?"

Grace, it appeared, wanted an apology. A sincere, profound, lengthy apology. Groveling was required, so that the offenders knelt at Grace's feet, Eva before and Mae, unexpectedly, behind.

"Where in the hell did you learn to do that?" Grace moaned as Mae's tongue slid against her back passage. For a girl who'd been startled to have a finger thrust up her ass, the Harlow blonde seemed to be awfully familiar with the ways of back-door pleasure.

"Do you really care where I learned to do that?" Mae asked sweetly, before returning to her task. Grace, whose clit was being gently nibbled by Eva, decided that she really didn't. Her first orgasm came when Eva slipped a finger inside Grace and bit ever so lightly on her clit, while Mae continued to rim Grace. It was lovely, and certainly took the edge off, but she wasn't sure she was ready to let either girl up off her knees. Grace sat on the edge of the bed, and made Eva kneel between her thighs. Mae was ordered to kneel on the bed, behind Grace. As the Harlow blonde lazily ran her tongue along the shell of Grace's sensitive ear, her hands slowly massaging Grace's breasts, Eva continued to lap at Grace's drenched pussy, and finger her core. Two pairs of hands seeing to her pleasure were ever so much more delightful than one. Two tongues bathing her did more than double her pleasure. And having two sets of breasts to play with, while her own were lovingly fondled, was an experience not to be missed. Grace climaxed again, her hands tangled in the bed sheets, gripping for dear life, even as her thighs gripped Eva's bobbing head. Mae shifted, leaning over so that she could capture Grace's mouth in a long wet kiss, stifling her cries of pleasure.

Two long, hard orgasms, nice as they were, hadn't quite felt like enough of an apology for Grace. When Eva complained that her knees were getting sore from kneeling, Grace shocked the other girl by hauling her over her lap and spanking her bottom smartly, until the plump cheeks were a lovely bright red as Mae watched with flushed cheeks, parted lips, dazed eyes and very erect nipples.

"You should have thought of that before fucking another girl without permission," Grace said primly, before pushing Eva off her lap. But, she relented. After a fashion. Grace slid back on the bed, and told Mae to strap on the toy. Eva was ordered to bend over the bed, spread her legs, and stand absolutely still.

"I want to watch," Grace said huskily, spreading her legs wide, and letting her fingers drift down to her own aching pussy. "I want you to give Eva the fucking of her life, and I want to watch. And while I'm watching you, you can watch me." She emphasized her point by twisting her fingers on her clit, hips bouncing on the bed. Mae, still contrite, hastened to do what Grace wanted, and stood behind Eva, who moaned as the other girl gripped her sore ass, and shivered as the toy was driven into her own wet flesh. Grace licked her lips, watching as Eva's pert breasts jiggled and jounced with the force of Mae's thrusts into her cunt. "Talk to her," Grace ordered, fingers rubbing, twisting, sliding over slick and delicate flesh. "Tell her all the things you want to do to her, tell her what you want her to do." Mae obliged, whispering wicked carnal, lusty promises, enticements, desires. Eva moaned, thrusting her hips back, not caring as her tender bottom slapped against Mae's pelvis. Watching her lover helpless under the driving force of the Harlow blonde made Grace hotter and wetter than ever.

"Fuck us," Grace panted, using her left hand to thrust into her hungry pussy as her right rubbed her clit. "Fuck us with your hard cock," she demanded. Mae raised her face, eyes dilated with passion and fucked them with her hard cock until Eva muffled her screams in the quilt on the bed and Grace was writhing on the mattress and the Harlow blonde was shivering in climax, draped over Eva's pliant body.

It took another hour, and eight more orgasms, before Grace decided that they had apologized enough.

They slept in a tangle, like sleepy kittens. Mae's cock was buried in Grace's wet cunt, while Grace's fingers were buried in Eva's pussy, and her other hand was filled with Mae's soft, large breast.

They skipped the next day's casting call.

Arzner had work for them a few weeks later. Other offers began to come in. Eva let her hair grow out. Grace bought a toy to match Mae's. And the girls found the perfect bungalow.

In some ways, the times were generous. Or perhaps the place. However straight-laced the rest of the country might be, however Protestant and prudish, Hollywood was more forgiving. No one talked about Dorothy Arzner and Marion Morgan, though the two lived together quite openly. No one cared. And no one cared when Eva, Mae and Grace moved in together. The girls got work, separately and together, began to become household names… though those names, in the end, were not Eva or Mae or Grace, after all. Eventually, the Hayes code took hold, and the open secrets had to become a little more confined. There were marriages, carefully arranged by the studio. Scandalous, highly publicized love affairs with men whose boyfriends weren't inclined to be jealous. And, once in a while, very public quarrels, so that a gullible public would think the three starlets were rivals and enemies, instead of the most intimate of friends.

So much of their success, in the end, was owed to Mae. She'd taught them how to draw the right kind of attention from the right kind of people, how to show themselves to best advantage, how to make the most of every opportunity, and how to change with the times. All in all, Grace reflected one night as they lay together in their large Hollywood bed and Mae slid her fingers along Grace's clit while Eva suckled at Grace's breast, she could only be glad that Evelyn had lead and she had followed… into the arms of the Harlow blonde.

Diane DeKelb-Rittenhouse
MAKE DO 1940's

Beloved Martha,

I miss you. There are no words to say how much. There is only the simple ache of emptiness. It isn't so bad, days, when I'm ferrying planes, or studying navigation charts or working with the other girls. It's nights that are hard, when I lie alone in my bed in the barracks, surrounded by friends to whom I would trust my life, but dare not trust my secrets. It is then that I hold close my memories, and dream of our last night together I remember the feel of your long russet curls as they brushed against my skin, the firmness of your small breasts, the cool smoothness of your supple skin, the honey-sweet taste of the intoxicating dew that poured from you at the lightest touch of my eager tongue, your pink sex unfurling beneath my lips and fingers like a rose greeting the sun. I remember how you held to me, fingers tangled in my hair, the exact timbre of your voice through each anticipatory moan or pleasured cry. I remember your face, an angel suffused by rapture, at the exact moment that I brought you to pleasure. And I remember your laughter and your smile, as you changed from angel to temptress, your fingers finding me, cherishing me, pleasing me, bringing me to a rapture of my own.

My dearest, my love, how can I not miss you, not yearn to be with you once more? There are times when I bitterly reproach myself for the course I took, the one you have taken. But then I imagine you shaking your head at me, russet curls bouncing, your smile bold and sassy as you laugh at my folly. Because I know that our paths were set from the moment the bombs dropped on Pearl Harbor, and that, no matter the cost we knew we should pay, we would still have chosen to serve our country with the separate skills vouchsafed to us.

That knowledge does nothing to soothe my loneliness, but I will endure it, warmed by the memories of what we have shared, until that day when we are reunited, never to be parted more.

Always your
Elizabeth

* * *

There are three things in the world I love above all else. One is gone, so I'm making do with the other two: thundering through the sky in a *real* plane, not one of those tiny Cessnas that are all most women get to fly, and the taste of a warm, wet, fragrant cunt on my tongue. For the former, I can thank the fact that the military is short of male pilots, and has to make do with women to ferry planes from the factories where they've been built to the departure points to embark for Europe, and for a dozen other tasks that need doing. For the latter, I can thank my lucky stars.

The current lucky star sings with a band that's doing a USO tour of stateside bases to entertain the military. Not that we qualify. Despite our zoot suits and our silver wings, or the patches on our uniforms, we are reminded at every turn that the Women Air force Service Pilots are not military. Fortunately for me, Peg doesn't much care about the details. She'll be glad to see me tonight, when she's done her show.

Jimmy winks as I walk past the stage. He's tickling the skins, laying out a fast rhythm for the boys on the gobble-pipes to follow when we arrive. Couples are responding, jitterbugging wildly, guys tossing their partners hard and fast. No one seems to care overmuch about modesty right now. Look closely and you can tell who paid the monumental price of seventy-five cents for a rare pair of nylon stockings, and who is getting by with pancake make-up on her legs and brown eyeliner drawn down the back for a seam. I'm told that ladies don't sweat, they perspire, but it's so hot, I've got damp patches on my zoot suit. I can't believe the girls' make-up isn't melting, especially with the energy the dancers are expending in their daring gyrations and flashy moves. There's a sense of urgency, almost desperation, on the floor. It's as if it's the last night before the troops ship out and there's never going to be a chance to jitterbug again. With most of the boys in this crowd wearing uniforms, maybe that's not so far off.

"Man oh man, it's been a long time since I've seen a rag like this," Mabel says wistfully as we skirt the dance floor on our way to the back counter where the servicemen can get a free cup of coffee, and we'll buy ourselves whatever they've got that's cold and wet. The way she's eyeing the dancers, I know she's missing Tommy, who's stationed overseas. I give her arm a supportive squeeze, letting her know that I understand.

I hope she never has to return the favor.

"What's knittin', kittens?" the middle-aged man in charge of the counter asks, as we step up to order our tea. I don't recognize him, but I'd bet he's been around the WASP for a while, because he's not eyeing our clothing with disapproval, or accusing us of impersonating officers. The WASP are issued male military uniforms, and the sizes are so large that we have to wear them with the cuffs rolled up and belts around our waists to keep the trousers from falling down. I think the guy behind the counter likes a gal in uniform. He's certainly favoring Mabel with a warm look.

"No go, Joe," I laugh. "Mabel's a married lady, aren't cha, toots?" She stares at me with wide pansy-brown eyes, utterly oblivious.

"Well, gee whiz, Libby, what's that got to do with getting something cold to drink?" She's so damned green, that girl. It's a wonder they let her off the farm. Twenty-five thousand gals applied, and less than two thousand were accepted, with only half of those managing to get through training. There is no way in Hell sweet, green, dim little Mabel should have been one of them. But underneath the sweetness is the scrappy, and here she is, silver wings pinned to her too-large zoot suit, a genuine WASP.

That and the right ration coupon will get her a pound of coffee.

"So, what can I get for you ladies?" the gent at the counter asks, manfully hiding his disappointment at Mabel's unavailability. We tell him. He pours. We pay. Mabel drinks.

And I wait.

I've timed things well, and I don't have to wait long. Peg joins the band on stage to generous applause. Like Mabel, she's small but scrappy: even in her platform shoes, she's barely five-foot-two, but she has a voice large enough to reach into every corner of the club. Unlike Mabel, she's not a slender brunette, but a curvy, hazel-eyed blonde. She wears her sleek hair in an intricate coronet of braids atop her head, and an evening dress with the regulation 59-inch length and 144-inch sweep prescribed by the War Production Board. The dress isn't new fabric, but has been remade from something longer and older that probably belonged to her grandmother. Like the rest of us, Peg has to make do with the scraps and remnants already on hand, as just about all production is geared to the military.

But the dress is a pale violet color that makes her eyes look misty grey, and on her, make do looks good.

Peg flashes a klieg-light smile at her audience before launching into a ballad, "You Go To My Head." It's a great song for dancing cheek-to-cheek, and that's what people are doing, now, recovering from the frenetic activity of a few moments past. I raise my glass and sip my drink. Mabel sees our barracks mates at one of the tables in the back, waves and asks if I want to join them. From the table Doro, one of our new girls, sends me a pointed look, which I just as pointedly ignore. There's something about Doro that gets to me. I can't figure her out. Is her regard a sign of interest? If so our situation – six girls in a barracks, everyone knowing almost everything about everyone else – is too dangerous for that. Best to back off. But it's much more likely that she watches me because she's unfriendly and suspicious, and that's something I cannot afford. I ignore Doro's glances and tell Mabel to go ahead. With a smile, Mabel heads off, leaving me to my solitary enjoyment of the show.

And I do enjoy it. Peg has one of those honeyed voices that wraps around you like heated silk, so that you can almost feel the slide of her words against your skin. For the moment, I can pretend that every word is meant for me alone.

Peg's set lasts a full hour. Forty-five minutes into it, I leave the bar and make my way back stage. The other girls can find their way back to the barracks without me, and usually do.

The tour has been here for a week. I know where to find Peg's dressing room or, rather, the storage closet she's using as one. Most of the stagehands ignore me, and though one does give me a curious look, that seems more to do with my zoot suit than my having wandered from the audience to the chaos behind the scenes.

Soon enough Peg is finished, and free to join me.

"Hey sugar, you rationed?" I tease as she enters the little alcove they've set aside for her.

"Not for you, darlin'," she teases back, and then she's kissing me.

She smells like gardenias and tastes like heaven, soft and fragrant in my arms. Her little tongue wraps around mine, hungry and demanding. There's an urgency to her kisses, reminding me that her tour is due to move on tomorrow, and it's going to be months before we see each other again.

If ever. She could die on a tour overseas and I could crash ferrying a poorly repaired plane back to the factory for service. We know this and while we don't dwell on it, it does make the urgency more poignant, adds a little bitter to the sweet.

Pushing such thoughts from my mind, I give myself up to kissing Peg, running my tongue over her plump lips, gently biting down. She moans into my mouth, sways closer, totters on her platform shoes so that I'm holding her body up, pressed the length along mine.

"Want you," she gasps out, pressing kisses along my jaw.

"Want you, too," I growl back, holding her close. She giggles and pulls away.

"Give me a minute to change," she says breathlessly. "I'll meet you out back and give you a lift back to your barracks, all right?"

"Yes, ma'am," I tell her with a grin, looking forward to a lovely ride home.

And it *is* lovely, despite the dust and the heat, and the wobbling of tires patched together from the rubber soles of old shoes. There's no way we can risk Peg's hotel room, which she shares with a couple of the other girls on the tour, and my barracks is out of the question. But there is the back seat of the car Jimmy lets her drive. Once we're clear of town, we pull off to a side road. We're hidden from view by an outcropping of rock, which is as much privacy as we're going to get. I'd opt for the ground and making love beneath the stars, but Peg is antsy about snakes, and I can't really blame her. I had to pull a rattler from my cockpit, once. Not something I care to do again.

And so, we crowd together in the back of the old jalopy, and then I'm kissing her and running my hands under her skirts, skimming them along her nylon-clad legs, reaching under her garter belt for the edge of her panties. Even through the cloth, I can feel her wetness, lush and scented with something heavier than gardenias, her own female musk telling me of her desire. Peg moans into my mouth, lifts her legs to wrap around my hips. We rub together, now like eels, sleek and smooth, wriggling and playful. Then my fingers probe a little higher, delve a little deeper, and she arches off the backseat like a bow drawn tight, her fingers biting into my arms where she's holding on to me.

Just there, that wet and liquid place, velvet heat on my fingers. Slow and deep, teasing, driving her to frenzy so that she's whispering hot, dirty things into my ear and I feel my own wetness pour out to match hers. A little deeper. A little harder. In a minute, I'll add a second finger but not yet, not until she's begging.

Peg's not long on patience.

"Oh, Libby!" she's panting within moments. "More, baby, more!"

I smile against her mouth and slip a second finger inside, turning my hand so that I can reach her nubbin with my thumb. She whines and whimpers, rubbing against me, soaking my hand. I manage to get my other hand between us, though how, in my frenzied state, I maneuver the buttons out of their holes and the bra straps down her shoulder so I can pull the cups away from the rosy mounds beneath is a mystery, even to me. But I do, and her nipples are hard and swollen like ripe little grapes, and I can't possibly refrain from wrapping my mouth around one.

Keep your sugar. Peg's tits are all the sweetness I need.

She's so hot and so responsive. The moment I bite down on one little grape, she's off like a firecracker, hips pumping as she croons my name on a long wail and sticky sweetness pours out of her like lemonade from a pitcher at a summer picnic. There are times I wouldn't mind drowning in lemonade.

It takes her a while to recover, time during which we simply lie in each other's arms, cuddling, kissing, touching, tasting.

But not talking. There are no sweet nothings for me to tell her, and nothing she really wants to hear. We're having a grand time, and maybe we'll have a grand time on her next tour, but she's not leaving the stage, and I'm not leaving the cockpit. This is enough for us, this moment when we bring another kind of heat into the desert. At least, it is enough for now.

Soon, Peg is restless again, pushing me back against the seat, and going to work on my zoot suit. We don't have the luxury of stripping down completely, but Peg is inventive and flexible, and she manages to get enough of me bare that she can maneuver her head between my thighs, even as I lift her legs over my head and pull her panties out of my way.

And now I can indulge myself in one of my very favorite things, sucking on her cunt as she laps at mine, tongues exploring soft folds and humid recesses, secret darkness, private places. Her tongue is small but skilled, and she knows just how hard to lick, and where, exploring all over before setting up a hard, quick rhythm on my clit. A finger slips inside me, and I whimper, sucking harder on her own sweet nub. She's ruthless, reaching her other hand down to slip underneath my bra, twisting and pinching a nipple that aches for her touch. It's a race to climax, something of a contest, and I have an unfair advantage. She's already hot and primed from her last orgasm, so it isn't going to take me long to tip her over the edge into another.

But she's a competitive gal, is Peg. She forces her attention from her own pleasure until she brings me off, creaming on her fingers and melting on her tongue. I close my eyes, coming so hard I see flashes of light in the darkness and she ravishes me with her hot little fingers and her wicked little tongue. And, of course, I'm coming so hard, I suck and lick and bite with frenzy rather than finesse, which seems to be what the situation requires because she squeals and stiffens and comes apart, shuddering over me, drenching my face with her release. It isn't enough, is never enough, and we work each other to climax again, and once again, before we finally collapse, spent and exhausted, against the worn leather upholstery of Jimmy's old car.

* * *

Beloved Martha,

Not a day goes by but that I wish you were here. No matter what I am doing, who I am with, I am aware of your absence, as one would be aware of the loss of a limb, so vital are you to me, so much a part of my very essence, my very soul.

I know that you don't mind Peg. I think you'd quite like her if you'd ever met. So much so, I might have been jealous that she'd steal you from me. After all, she's a blonde, and you've always had a soft spot for them. I don't know why you ever settled for me, with my hopeless black thatch that won't be tamed into a smooth bob, or one of those sleek styles that look so luscious on Veronica Lake. I finally gave up, when I got here. Yes, my darling, the long black ringlets you loved are gone, and I'm getting along nicely with a short crop of bushy curls that stay the hell under my helmet when I'm flying, and keep the hell out of my way.

I can imagine you laughing at the very idea, or perhaps favoring me with a sultry look and telling me to come closer, so you could try out my new curls for yourself. What would it be like to have your hands in my hair when it's so much shorter now? I remember how you used to wrap my long curling tresses in your hand, pulling me to you, holding me to your pussy as I lapped at you, suckled you, fucked you with my tongue. You couldn't do that now, could you? Would my curls provide enough purchase for your long slender fingers or your graceful hands? Would they give you enough to grip? Or would you simply clutch onto me, grasping at my skull, holding me so tight and so close to your scented, delicious heat, the honeyed core of you?

Your absence breaks my heart, and not even Peg can mend it. I have moments of forgetfulness, especially when I am free and in the sky, soaring through the clouds. But you are all I ever desired in this life, my darling, and I won't be whole again until I am with you once more.

Always your
Elizabeth

* * *

It's an hour later when Peg pulls up to the entrance to the barracks. We exchange a long, slow, lingering kiss.

"You have my tour schedule, right?" she asks.

"Yes," I smile, patting the pocket into which I've slipped the little card. "If I have to ferry something close to where you are, I'll come and see you."

"Promise?" she asks, hazel eyes searching mine.

"Count on it," I tell her. We kiss again, and she promises to send me her next tour schedule, when this one is complete. She doesn't promise to write, and neither do I, and we don't promise to wait for each other, or to find each other after the war. Perhaps we will, but we are sweet friends rather than sweethearts. She is not the love of my life nor I the love of hers. We're good together, for now, and for now, that is enough. I kiss her good-bye, long and slow, then I get out of the jalopy, and stand, watching as she pulls back onto the road. She waves once, then drives off. I watch until she disappears around a bend, and then I head inside.

The barracks were designed for men, of course. Even now, they won't acknowledge that they need us, and the WASP are not officially a military group. Nights like these, we shower in our clothes for relief from the heat. I figure the others are long in bed, but I do that now, regretfully letting the cold water carry off the scent of gardenias that lingered on my skin. Soon enough, I'll change into my night things, stuff an old cotton sock into one of the urinals and wash out my under things, like all of us do, every night. For now, I am content to let the water pour over me, as I linger in the memory of my evening with Peg.

Unfortunately, I'm wrong about everyone else being in bed. The door opens, and I am not alone.

"You're back late," Doro observes, pulling the door shut behind her, and leaning against it. She hasn't been to bed yet, still in her own zoot suit rather than her nightgown.

"Yep," I say, affecting nonchalance. I'm wary of this new girl, who looks at me too intently, whose silver eyes see too much. Like Peg, she's a blonde, but that's all they've got in common. Peg's fun and easy and open, with a big heart and a quick smile. Doro is... something else. Reserved, and quiet and intense. I don't think she's smiled once in the weeks since she got here. She's on the tall side for a WASP, like me, and she's another farm girl like Mabel, only built along tight, solid lines, with wide hips and plentiful breasts. Even the overlarge zoot suits can't obscure her figure. Peg is beautiful, with a movie star's glamour and a pin-up's seductiveness. Doro might be pretty if she smiled, but there's something too raw, too edgy, too angry about her for real beauty.

"Don't know why you're always so late," she says now, moving closer, as if she's going to shower in the space right next to mine.

"Don't know why you care," I return, watching her warily.

She's beside me now, turning on the water over her own head, so that it pours over her body, wetting her silvery blonde hair, turning her into something cool and sleek, like one of the naiads of ancient myth.

Weren't they feckless, deadly little strumpets? I seem to recall them drowning unwary suitors. I'm neither, so I should be safe.

I'm wrong.

"I guess you're blind, then, as well as stupid," Doro says coldly.

Her words freeze me, shocking in their implication. She knows, I realize. She's fathomed the secret I won't tell. And like a few others who I think have guessed – but who will respect my privacy and never say a word, and to whom I won't ever say anything, just in case I'm wrong – she's clearly not a friend, not someone who is willing to protect me, but someone who wants me revealed for what I am.

Or, she thinks she knows. She can't have any proof. I haven't left any.

"What the hell is your problem?" I snap, turning off the water, stepping away. "What's it to you if I come back later than the rest of you, so long as I'm back before curfew? Mind your own beeswax, Doro."

"You'd like that, wouldn't you," she snaps back, giving up the pretense of showering and turning off the water, following after me. "That would leave you free to go off with that little slut from the USO and—"

That's as far as she gets before I slap her.

"You vicious little—" And that's as far as I get before she retaliates.

Doro grabs the hand that slapped her and gives a tug. I guess the work she did on her farm was more demanding than whatever Mabel did, because this girl is strong, and not just from the calisthenics they make us do every morning. I'm no match for her, and I find myself hauled up and tight and...

...I am being kissed, kissed in anger and in hunger and with a passion that leaves me weak-kneed from desire even more than shock, and the shock, believe me, couldn't be greater. I have been wrong, it seems. Not about what Doro watches, or what she's seen, but about why she was looking in the first place. And in those first unforgettable moments, I am helpless to do anything but kiss her back, my lips responding to the insistent pressure of hers, my mouth opening for her, my tongue caressing hers as she thrusts it into my mouth, hungry, devouring the taste of me. I think she's trying to suck away the gardenia taste of Peg, leave me with her own darker, deeper tang, something smoky, earthy, less glamorous and far more real. I'm too far gone to think about why I shouldn't let her, caught up in the maelstrom of that kiss, the feel of her body tight against mine. Doro thrusts her leg between mine, so that I'm riding her thigh, rubbing against places that are already sensitive and responsive, eager for more. And because I'm kissing her back, moaning as I rub against her thigh, she relaxes, just a little, stops clutching at me, holds me gently, instead, and the kiss becomes less desperate at the same time that it becomes more intense.

It is her mistake, backing off from that desperation. I remember who she is, what I am, where we are. And I break the kiss.

"No, sweetie," I say gently, with more reluctance than she will believe, forcing myself to pull back from her, pull away.

"What are you doing?" she asks, her voice soft, dazed. I look at her, and wonder how I ever thought of her as anything less than beautiful. Her hard edges have faded with her anger, leaving her softer, unbelievably vulnerable, unbelievably appealing in that vulnerability.

"You haven't thought this through," I tell her. "What it means to be... what we are... while we're trying to be one of the WASP."

"You think I've thought about anything else?" she tells me incredulously. "You think I didn't know, when I applied, what it would mean if I were found out? Hell, I was kicked out of home at fifteen because I couldn't keep my hands off my girlfriend. So, yes. I've thought it through."

"Not very clearly," I say, backing a few steps away, needing the distance for the sake of my own clarity of mind. "Because if you had, you'd know that this is too risky." Doro leans away from me, hands crossed beneath her breasts, angry all over again. But I've found her out, seen that she is beautiful, and I can't see her as anything less, now.

"It's not any more risky than you gallivanting all around town with every skirt who blows past with the USO," she huffs indignantly.

"Now hold on there, sister," I say crossly. "I do not —"

"Suzie. Babs. Peg," she bites out. Suzie and Babs were before her time, so how did she find out about them? Which is beside the point.

"Three gals. Over six months. That's not every skirt who blows past," I tell her coldly.

"It's every skirt who isn't going to stick around," she says just as coldly. "What the hell are you afraid of, Libby?"

"I thought that was obvious," I tell her. "I'm afraid of getting caught. I'm afraid of being stripped of my wings and sent back home. I'm afraid of losing what we have here, of being forced back to flying little two-seaters that get blown off course by a strong wind, and never having a Liberator or a Marauder under my hand again."

"And you think you don't risk it with those hussies in the USO?" Doro asks, silver eyes flashing like sunlight reflected off ice. "Do you think everyone on this base is as blind as you are?"

"I'm still here, aren't I? So, yes, I think that most of the gals here are as blind as the rest of the world, not seeing what they don't expect to see." I sigh, leaning against the wall, looking not at her, but at the white plaster of the ceiling above us and not seeing that, but the faces of the women I've worked with and bled with and cried with and triumphed with for the past eighteen months. "They think I'm just one of the girls," I explain. "And that I'm a bit of a loner. I always come back to base on my own, not just when I'm with someone. So, it's nothing out of the ordinary, nothing to raise suspicion, just Libby being Libby. And, no, I'm not so stupid to think that no one has a clue. I can see it from a few of them. They've caught on. But, they aren't judging me. They're my friends, my comrades. They won't come out and say what they suspect, and I won't come out and tell them I know that they know. We'll keep our secrets and we'll keep on. As long as our country needs us."

"And you, Libby?" Doro asks, coming closer again. "What about what you need?"

I look at her, really look, into those silver eyes I thought saw too much. And I realize I haven't seen enough. Those eyes aren't pure silver. They're flecked with palest blue, like hints of sky behind storm clouds. And they aren't cold, not like ice at all. More like mercury that's heated and liquid. There's a world of heat in Doro's eyes. A world of longing.

And a world of sorrow. I know what I'm going to say.

"I have what I need."

I just didn't realize, until I looked into her eyes, that it was a lie.

She looks back at me, and says nothing for a long moment.

"No, you don't," she says simply. "But I'm damned if I'm going to break my heart on the wall you've built around your own." She steps closer and kisses me for what we both expect will be the last time, a kiss that's as sweet and tender as the others were hungry and hard. And then she steps away, and leaves the shower.

I realize that I'm hot and sticky all over again, and go back to turn the water on once more.

* * *

Darling Martha,

Wish you were here. Wish you'd never gone. Wish I'd never let you go. I'm so confused, so indecisive. I think I've found something worth keeping, but I'm too afraid to try. For once, I don't even know what you would tell me. Would you laugh, and say I was worried over nothing, or would you shake your head, curls tumbling over your cheek, your mouth curved in a wry smile as you told me to buck up, that it was all for the best, and that some sacrifices have to be made? And would you tell me that the war won't go on forever, and that I had time?

I need you, my love, my darling, more than ever. And it hurts, more than ever, that I can't have what I need.

Always your
Elizabeth

* * *

It seems everyone is up late, tonight. Doro is pretending to sleep when I get back into the barracks, but her back is too stiff for the act to be convincing.

Mabel isn't even trying to pretend.

She's sitting up in her bunk, staring out the window at the moonlight, when I get in. I grab my nightgown – it used to be a tablecloth – and head for the washroom. Mabel slips out of bed and joins me.

"Rough night, sugar?" she says sympathetically as I head to one of the stalls to change. She's closed the door behind us, so we won't disturb the other girls.

"Why would you think that?" I sigh. I've had enough surprises for one night. It seems I'm due for one more.

"Libby, how long have we been friends?" she asks.

"How long has there been a WASP?" I reply as I emerge from the stall, heading for the urinal so that I can wash out my under things.

"That's right," Mabel agrees. "As long as there's been a WASP. We went through training together, training I think I'd have failed if you weren't there to study with me, encourage me, bully me when you thought I wasn't working hard enough, coddle me when you thought I was working too hard. So, let me ask you something. Do you trust me?"

I look up from my washing, holding my breath. And then I let it out.

"With my life, doll. You know that." But not my secrets. I can't trust her with those, can I? I turn back to finish my laundry, quickly rinsing my things, hanging them up the line stretched between some nails that we've fashioned. It's so hot, they'll be dry in just a few hours.

"My best friend, Kitty, was in love with my brother Pete as long as I can remember. Took him long enough to figure it out. He ran around with all the fast girls in town, dated the prettiest girl in school, and never looked twice at Kitty. Well, not for a long time. He caught on, though. But not until just a few weeks before he shipped out. War-time wedding, a month as newly-weds, then Pete is off. And a U-boat sinks his ship, six months later."

"Oh, Mabel…" I say, hurting for her. But she's not done.

"I think if I ever lost Tommy, I'd want to die," she says softly. "And I did-n't realize, when we found out your friend, the nurse, had died overseas, just what you'd lost. But that's what Martha was to you, wasn't she? A lot more than just your friend."

"Mabel—" I try again, but differently, warningly this time.

"So, you probably wanted to die, too," she goes on, ignoring the fact that there are tears gathering in my eyes, that she's pricked at a wound that will always be too raw to scar. "And that's why you haven't let anyone get close, since. You're making do with what you find, because you think that you'll never have the real thing again."

There's nothing I can say to this. Sweet, green, dim Mabel is not so dim or green, after all. She comes closer, takes my face between her hands, and looks at me, her pansy-brown eyes filled with more fire and determination than I've ever seen in them. "Well, you listen here, Elizabeth Marie. Love isn't like that. Love is something rare and precious, and you don't turn it away when it comes knocking, you open the door and let it in, grab on with both hands and don't let go." She smiles, letting her hands drop from my face. "Love is the one thing that you shouldn't have to settle for make do."

It occurs to me that Mabel may not be the smartest girl I've ever met, but she just might be one of the wisest women I've ever known.

* * *

My sweet Martha,

I will always miss you. I will always love you. And this will be the last letter, but you know that. I can see you laughing at me, even now, shooing me off, telling me I'm wasting time, and that I should make my move before it's too late. But this one last letter is one I have to write, before I lock it away in the little strong box beneath my bed with all the other letters I have written to you in the two years since the letter your brother sent, the letter I always dreaded would come, but was so unprepared to receive.

I think you'd like her, this brash girl who's willing to risk so much for a chance at happiness. And I think you'd love Mabel, and Jane and Mary and all the other gals I serve with. I wish you could have met them, and oh how I wish they could have met you.

In time, my love, in time. I believe that one day, we shall all meet again, in a better place and a sweeter rest, and that I shall have the whole of the sky to share with you and all of those whom we love.

But for now, I will say a final good-bye, and I will turn myself to building the life you would want for me.

Until we meet again, my love,

Always your
Libby

* * *

Doro doesn't immediately come around. She makes me work at things. But she's more discreet than I expected, and she doesn't make me work too hard.

It's a week later that we find ourselves some privacy. The other girls have gone off to another USO show, so we've got the barracks to ourselves. For the first time in a long time, I've got the luxury of a bed, if not the most comfortable bed, or the biggest.

"That's all right, baby," Doro giggles. "I've got enough padding to keep you comfortable."

She does, at that, being a girl with meat on her bones. Not a surplus, mind, just a deliciously curvy and abundant handful. It's sweet to have her here, sweet to be able to take my time. Sweet to be able to make love. Doro's breasts are full and heavy, beautiful with their faint tracery of blue veins beneath the pale skin. Her nipples are small and tight, pink little rosebuds, and responsive to my least touch. I trail my fingers over them, watching them tighten and pucker, watching her whole body quiver in reaction, in anticipation. Her eyes are wide and stormy, watching me, her plump lips glisten, swollen with my kisses, wet from the touch of my tongue.

Where will I touch her next? Where will I taste?

Where won't I?

My tongue learns her terrain, every salty inch of flesh, every bend of her joints, every fold and hidden chamber. I swirl it along the shell of her ear, nipping at the lobe, then trail it along her neck, and over her collarbone, down her shoulder, to her arm and wrist and fingers. Then it is time to travel back upward, and tease downward once more. But it is merely a tease because I cross over to the other shoulder... arm... fingers...

She's whimpering and bucking beneath me, and I know that she wants me to move on, but I'm not in any hurry. Eventually, though, I give in, and trail more light kisses down across her breasts, over her ribs and to her belly. She lifts her hips anxiously, invitingly, but I'm not about to give in so easily. She made me wait a week. She can wait a few more minutes.

And so I trace a path over her hips, to her thighs and down the long, lean curve of thigh and knee, trim ankles, long narrow feet, dainty toes. No make up here. No painted seams. Just soft and fragrant girl-flesh, naked to my touch, spread before me like a banquet. I finally have mercy on her, parting her thighs and lying between them. I breathe in her heady musk, staring at her dewy sex, flush and rosy, begging for my attention.

I give it to her. I give her my all. Tongue and teeth, lips and fingers. I swirl my tongue over the seam of flesh between her nether lips, lap at the tender folds, give her little bud of a clit my deepest, wettest kiss. My fingers are busy, exploring her, fondling her, seducing her and delighting her, abetting the hard work of my tongue. She writhes on them, delicious, whimpering moans coming from her mouth. I plunge in another finger, going deeper, going faster, suckling harder… And then I see it, the look of an angel suffused by divine rapture, as she comes apart in my arms.

We linger in the bed for a while longer, and she pleases me, in turn. But our time together must be fleeting. The other girls will return soon. When they do, we are blamelessly in our own bunks, me reading one of Mabel's old magazines, Doro sound asleep.

I don't know how much longer the war will last, or how much longer the WASP will serve. But I do know that I won't be drifting, as I feared I might. Doro will anchor me, as Martha once did, and I will have, after all, a life filled with the love and companionship I thought I'd never find again.

Mabel was right. Some things are too precious to let go of once we've found them, and love is something that should never just make do.

Acknowledgments

This book began, sadly, because my good friend of more than twenty-five years, Tee Corinne, was unable to do it because she was diagnosed with cancer. She requested that I take on the book, and I agreed to do so. I have tried to do the kind of book she would have done – historical, ribald, sexy, serious, important, literary, and groundbreaking. This era was Tee's favorite and we talked often of new artists or photographers she had discovered from these years. Thus, Tee deserves the first acknowledgment, for without her, I would not have done this book.

I could not have done this book without Judith M. Redding, who stepped in when I was mid-way through the project and going down (no pun intended) for the third time, foundering in international searches for erotic material from the period that wasn't owned or controlled by this or that estate and striving to uncover the missing link of lesbian erotica. Her editorial assistance and fortitude has been extraordinary.

Richard Kasak has been publishing groundbreaking erotic and political work by people of every sexual orientation for decades. Among his many queer authors have been Michael Bronski and Patrick Califia, whose work I have long enjoyed. Richard is the perfect editor in that he steps back and waits, without interference or pressure. He is also a great purveyor of bon mots.

Diane DeKelb-Rittenhouse has been a friend and colleague for two decades. Her retinue of information on the vast world of the erotic, as well as her keen knowledge of literary history, was immensely helpful with this project, as was her research and editorial assistance.

Early in the project Sarah Granlund, whose own erotic writing is terrific, provided research and editorial assistance.

Greg Herren, eroticist par excellence who as an editor has nurtured my erotic writing, was friend, confidante, and editorial sounding board.

Barbara Grier, co-founder of Naiad Press, brought the out-of-print work of lesbian writers back into print, which made my life as a college student

Acknowledgments

immeasurably richer. My only regret is that I have no work of hers from that period to interpolate here. Barbara provided permission to reprint some of that wonderful work, like the extraordinary writing of Gale Wilhelm.

The Lesbian Herstory Archives was a rich source of material and the women who run the Archives were, to a one, helpful, kind, interested, encouraging and generally delightful on our visits there. We are so fortunate to have this marvelous resource, which would not exist without co-founders Deb Edel and Joan Nestle.

Thanks to my good friend Deborah Peifer for her rapt and careful reading of material.

Thanks to Joan Poole for her friendship over the years and her consistent support of my work.

Thanks to Judith P. Stelboum, Reese Syzmanski and Greg Herren for their editorial critique and blurbs for the book and to Karla Jay for her archival work.

Thanks to Roberta Hacker, whose friendship over the past thirty-three years has sustained me on occasions too numerous to count. Thanks to my sister, Jennie Goldenberg, for the cheering section.

Thanks to my partner, Madelaine Gold, for her love and encouragement.

And finally, thanks to all those writers who strove to bring lesbian lives fully and realistically alive in their stories, in all their richness, during a time when it was often both illegal and "immoral" to do so. This book is most of all for them.

—*Victoria A. Brownworth*

Permissions

Permissions

Victoria A. Brownworth

Victoria A. Brownworth is the author of nine books, including the award-winning *Too Queer: Essays from a Radical Life* and editor of 14, including the award-winning *Night Bites: Vampire Tales of Blood and Lust*. A syndicated columnist, her work has appeared in numerous mainstream, queer and feminist publications, including the *Baltimore Sun*, the *Philadelphia Inquirer*, the *Village Voice*, the *Advocate*, *OUT* and *Curve*. Her erotic writing has appeared regularly in anthologies and magazines, and she is a former contributing writer to the lesbian sex magazines, *On Our Backs* and *Bad Attitude*. She has published several erotica collections, including most recently, *Bed: New Lesbian Erotica*. She also publishes gay male porn under a psuedonym. She teaches writing and film at the University of the Arts in Philadelphia where she added two new courses to the literary curriculum: *Writing Below the Belt* and *Smut*. She has also taught safe-sex education classes as well as classes on S/M and B/D for various lesbian and bisexual venues. She lives in Philadelphia.

THE COLLECTOR'S EDITION OF THE IRONWOOD TRILOGY

by Don Winslow

Fiction/Erotica • ISBN 0-9766510-2-5
Trade Paperback • 5 3/16 x 8 • 480 Pages • $17.95
($24.95Canada)

The three Ironwood classics revised exclusively for this Magic Carpet Edition
IRONWOOD, IRONWOOD REVISITED, IMAGES OF IRONWOOD

In IRONWOOD, James Carrington's bleak prospects are transformed overnight when the young man finds himself offered a choice position at Ironwood, a unique finishing school where young women are trained to become remiere Ladies of Pleasure. James faces many challenges in taming the spirited beauties in his charge, but no test will prove as great as that of mastering Mrs. Cora Blasingdale, the proud Mistress of Ironwood. In IRONWOOD REVISITED we follow James' rise to power in that garden of erotic delights, that singular institution, where young ladies were rigorously trained in the many arts of love. We come to understand how Ironwood, with its strict standards and iron discipline, has acquired its enviable reputation among the world's most discriminating connoisseurs. In IMAGES OF IRONWOOD, the third volume of the infamous Ironwood chronicles, the reader is once again invited to share in the Ironwood experience, and is presented with select scenes of unrelenting sensuality, of erotic longing, and of those bizarre proclivities which touch the outer fringe of human sexuality.

MASTERPIECES OF VICTORIAN EROTICA
Edited by Major LaCaritilie

Fiction/Erotica • ISBN 0-9774311-6-9 • Trade Paperback
5 3/16 x 8 • 320 Pages • $17.95 ($24.95 Canada)

There is no shortage of great works to compete for the title "masterpiece of Victorian erotica." Indeed, as readers familiar with Dickens or Trollope can attest, the Victorians were nothing if not prolific. Yet to be a masterpiece, a work has to distinguish itself in many ways. It can be without equal in its subgenre or the apotheosis of its tradition. It can offer a deeper insight, a more vivid image, or a more surprising turn. Or it can be unique, truly peerless in its style, plot or execution. Having distinguished themselves in these ways, the works in this volume represent the very best of the Victorian erotic imagination. There's poetry and prose, narrative and instructional guide; there's fetish, queer, s-m, and vanilla; and there's bawdy, tender and daring. For the newcomer to the Victorian erotic universe, these stories are the place to start. For the connoisseur, this collection offers undiscovered delicacies. For everyone, these stories cannot fail to arouse, stimulate and amaze with their delightful sexiness and bold originality.

HOWEVER YOU WANT ME
by Les Bexley

Fiction/Erotica • ISBN 0-9774311-5-0 • Trade Paperback
5 3/16 x 8 • 320 Pages • $17.95 ($24.95 Canada)

Pity poor Heritage College. It's hard to be a holier-than-thou Christian girls' school without a dirty little secret or two. And that was before April Cartier even set foot on campus. The banned activities listed in the college's morality code are April's to-do list; the college's dirty little secrets, her major. But it's not just the college that has secrets. Professors Jessica Rowley, Klaus Binder and Alex Gould have made secrets a way of life, and April isn't the type to leave anyone's skeletons in their closets. When this cast of characters finds itself in the perfect storm of desires and taboos, naked appetites and raw emotions, they become more exposed and more intertwined than any of them could have possibly imagined. Sexy and daring, unflinching and humane, *However You Want Me* tells the story of people whose deepest secrets are kept not from others but from themselves.

Back in Stock

MY SECRET FANTASIES
Fiction/Erotica • ISBN 0-9755331-2-6
Trade Paperback • 5 3/16 x 8 • 256 Pages • $11.95

Secret fantasies...we all have them, those hot, vivid daydreams that take us away from it all as we wonder, *what if...* In *My Secret Fantasies*, sixty different women share the secret of how they made their wildest erotic desires come true. Next time you feel like getting your heart rate up and your blood really flowing, curl up with a cup of tea and *My Secret Fantasies...* Beneath the covers of *My Secret Fantasies* you will find 60 tantalizing erotic love stories.

THE COLLECTOR'S EDITION OF VICTORIAN EROTICA
Edited by Major LaCaritilie

Fiction/Erotica • ISBN 0-9755331-0-X • Trade Paperback
5-3/16"x 8" • 608 Pages • $15.95 ($18.95 Canada)
No lone soul can possibly read the thousands of erotic books, pamphlets and broadsides the English reading public were offered in the 19th century. It can only be hoped that this Anthology may stimulate the reader into further adventures in erotica and its manifest reading pleasure. In this anthology, 'erotica' is a comprehensive term for bawdy, obscene, salacious, pornographic and ribald works including, indeed featuring, humour and satire that employ sexual

elements. Flagellation and sadomasochism are recurring themes. They are activities whose effect can be shocking, but whose occurrence pervades our selections, most often in the context of love and affection.

THE COLLECTOR'S EDITION OF VICTORIAN LESBIAN EROTICA
Edited By Major LaCaritilie

Fiction/Erotica • ISBN 0-9755331-9-3
Trade Paperback • 5 3/16 x 8 • 608 Pages • $17.95
($24.95Canada)

The Victorian era offers an untapped wellspring of lesbian erotica. Indeed, Victorian erotica writers treated lesbians and bisexual women with voracious curiosity and tender affection. As far as written treasuries of vice and perversion go, the Victorian era has no equal. These stories delve into the world of the aristocrat and the streetwalker, the seasoned seductress and the innocent naï f. Represented in this anthology are a variety of genres, from romantic fiction to faux journalism and travelogue, as well as styles and tones resembling everything from steamy page-turners to scholarly exposition. What all these works share, however, is the sense of fun, mischief and sexiness that characterized Victorian lesbian erotica. The lesbian erotica of the Victorian era defies stereotype and offers rich portraits of a sexuality driven underground by repressive mores. As Oscar Wilde claimed, the only way to get rid of temptation is to yield to it.

THE COLLECTOR'S EDITION OF THE LOST EROTIC NOVELS
Edited by Major LaCaritilie

Fiction/Erotica • ISBN 0-97553317-7 • Trade Paperback
5-3/16"x 8" • 608 Pages • $16.95 ($20.95 Canada)

MISFORTUNES OF MARY –Anonymous, 1860' s: An innocent young woman who still believes in the kindness of strangers unwittingly signs her life away to a gentleman who makes demands upon her she never would have dreamed possible.
WHITE STAINS – Anaï s Nin & Friends, 1940' s: Sensual stories penned by Anaï s

and some of her friends that were commissioned by a wealthy buyer for $1.00 a page. These classics of pornography are not included in her two famous collections, *Delta of Venus* and *Little Birds.*

INNOCENCE — Harriet Daimler, 1950' s: A lovely young bed-ridden woman would appear to be helpless and at the mercy of all around her, and indeed, they all take advantage of her in shocking ways, but who' s to say she isn' t the one secretly dominating them?

THE INSTRUMENTS OF THE PASSION — Anonymous, 1960' s: A beautiful young woman discovers that there is much more to life in a monastery than anyone imagines as she endures increasingly intense rituals of flagellation devotedly visited upon her by the sadistic brothers

THE COLLECTOR'S EDITION OF
VICTORIAN EROTIC DISCIPLINE
Edited by Brooke Stern

Fiction/Erotica • ISBN 0-9766510-9-2 • Trade Paperback
5 3/16 x 8 • 608 Pages • $17.95 ($24.95 Canada)

Lest there be any doubt, this collection is submitted as exhibit A in the case for the legitimacy of theVictorian era' s dominion over all discipline erotica. In this collection, all manner of discipline is represented. Men and women are both dominant and submissive. There are school punishments, judicial punishments, punishments between lovers, well-deserved punishments, punishments for a fee, and cross-cultural punishments. These stories are set around the world and at all levels of society. The authority figures in these stories include schoolmasters, gamekeepers, colonial administrators, captains of ships, third-world potentates, tutors, governesses, priests, nuns, judges and policemen.

Victorian erotica is replete with all manner of discipline. Indeed, it would be hard to find an erotic act as connected with a historical era as discipline is with the reign of Queen Victoria. The language of erotic discipline, with its sir' s and madam' s, its stilted syntax and its ritualized roles, sounds Victorian even when it' s used in contemporary pop culture. The essence of Victorian discipline is the shock of the naughty, the righteous indignation of the punisher and the shame of the punished. Today' s literature of erotic discipline can only play at Victorian dynamics, and all subsequent writings will only be pretenders to a crown of the era whose reign will never end.

Maria Isabel Pita

Maria Isabel Pita is the author of three BDSM Erotic Romances – **Thorsday Night, Eternal Bondage** and **To Her Master Born**, re-printed as an exclusive hard-cover edition by the Doubleday Venus Book Club. She is the author of three Paranormal Erotic Romances, **Dreams of Anubis, Rituals of Surrender, The Fire in Starlight** and of three Contemporary Erotic Romances **A Brush With Love, Recipe For Romance,** and **The Fabric of Love**. Three of her erotic romances (Dreams of Anubis, Rituals of Surrender, The Fabric of Love) were re-printed under one cover as **Cat's Collar – Three Erotic Romances**. Maria is also the author of the critically acclaimed **Guilty Pleasures** – a book of romantic erotic stories set all through history – and of two non-fiction memoirs – **The Story of M – A Memoir** and **Beauty & Submission**, both of which were featured selections of the Doubleday Venus Book Club. **The Fabric of Love** and **The Story of M – A Memoir** have been translated into German and published in Germany by Heyne/VG Random House GMBH. Maria won second place in the New England Association For Science Fiction & Fantasy for her story **Star Crossed**. She was also a finalist in The Science Fiction Writer's of the Earth Award and the L. Ron Hubbard Award for Science Fiction Fantasy. You can visit her at www.mariaisabelpita.com

BOUND TO LOVE: A COLLECTION OF ROMANTIC BDSM EROTIC STORIES

Edited by Maria Isabel Pita

Fiction/Erotica • ISBN 0-9766510-4-1 • Trade Paperback
5 3/16 x 8 • 304 Pages • $17.95 ($24.95 Canada)

In **Bound to Love**, Maria Isabel Pita has gathered together nine erotic love stories written by some of today's hottest writers of erotica. In each story the darker side of sexuality is explored through realistic, well-developed characters deeply in love with each other and otherwise leading normal lives together. The men and women in **Bound To Love** are involved in serious, long-term relationships in which their deeper feelings for each other are inseparable from their erotic interaction. The stories in **Bound to Love** are some of the best in their genre precisely because they transcend it.

CAT'S COLLAR – THREE EROTIC ROMANCES
by Maria Isabel Pita

Fiction/Erotica • ISBN 0-9766510-0-9 • Trade Paperback
5 3/16 x 8 • 608 Pages • $16.95 ($ 20.95 Canada)

DREAMS OF ANUBIS: A legal secretary from Boston visiting Egypt explores much more than just tombs and temples in the stimulating arms of Egyptologist Simon Taylor. But at the same time a powerfully erotic priest of Anubis enters her dreams, and then her life one night in the dark heart of Cairo's timeless bazaar. Sir Richard Ashley believes he has lived before and that for centuries he and Mary have longed to find each other again. Mary is torn between two men who both desire to discover the legendary tomb of Imhotep and win the treasure of her heart.

RITUALS OF SURRENDER: All her life Maia Wilson has lived near a group of standing stones in the English countryside, but it isn't until an old oak tree hit by lightning collapses across her car one night that she suddenly finds herself the heart of an erotic web spun by three sexy, enigmatic men - modern Druids intent on using Maia for a dark and ancient rite...

CAT'S COLLAR: Interior designer Mira Rosemond finds herself in one attractive successful man's bedroom after the other, but then one beautiful morning a stranger dressed in black leather takes a short cut through her garden and changes the course of her life forever. Mira has never met anyone quite like Phillip, and the more she learns about his mysterious profession - secretly linked to some of Washington's most powerful women - the more frightened and yet excited she becomes as she finds herself falling helplessly, submissively in love.

GUILTY PLEASURES
by Maria Isabel Pita

Fiction/Erotica • ISBN 0-9755331-5-0 • Trade Paperback
5 3/16 x 8 • 304 Pages • $16.95 ($20.95 Canada)

Guilty Pleasures explores the passionate willingness of women throughout the ages to offer themselves up to the forces of love. Historical facts are seamlessly woven into intensely graphic sexual encounters. Beneath the covers of **Guilty Pleasures** you will find eighteen erotic love stories with a profound feel for the times and places where they occur. An ancient Egyptian princess...a courtesan rising to fame in Athen's Golden Age...a widow in 15th century Florence initiated into a Secret Society..a Transylvanian Count's wicked bride... an innocent nun tempted to sin in 17th century Lisbon...a lovely young woman finding love in the Sultan's harem..and many more are all one eternal woman in *Guilty Pleasures*.

THE STORY OF M – A MEMOIR
by Maria Isabel Pita

Non-Fiction/Erotica • ISBN 0-9726339-5-2 • Trade Paperback
5 3/16 x 8 • 239 Pages • $14.95 ($18.95 Canada)

The true, vividly detailed and profoundly erotic account of a beautiful, intelligent woman's first year of training as a slave to the man of her dreams.

Maria Isabel Pita refuses to fall into any politically correct category. She is not a feminist, and yet she is fiercely independent. She is everything but a mindless sex object, yet she is willingly, and happily, a masterful man's love slave. *M* is erotically submissive and yet also profoundly secure in herself, and she wrote this account of her ascent into submission for all the women out there who might be confused and frightened by their own contradictory desires just as she was.

M is the true highly erotic account of the author's first profoundly instructive year with the man of her dreams. Her vividly detailed story makes it clear we should never feel guilty about daring to make our deepest, darkest longings come true, and serves as living proof that they do.

BEAUTY & SUBMISSION
by Maria Isabel Pita

Non-Fiction/Erotica · ISBN 0-9755331-1-8
Trade Paperback · 5-3/16" x 8" · 256 Pages ·
14.95 ($18.95 Canada)

In a desire to tell the truth and dispel negative stereotypes about the life of a sex slave, Maria Isabel Pita wrote *The Story of M... A Memoir.* Her intensely erotic life with the man of her dreams continues now in *Beauty &*

Submission, a vividly detailed sexual and philosophical account of her second year of training as a slave to her Master and soul mate.

THE TIES THAT BIND
by Vanessa Duriés

Non-Fiction/Erotica • ISBN 0-9766510-1-7 • Trade Paperback
5 3/16 x 8 • 160 Pages • $14.95 ($18.95 Canada)

RE-PRINT OF THE FRENCH BEST-SELLER

The incredible confessions of a thrillingly unconventional woman. From the first page, this chronicle of dominance and submission will keep you gasping with its vivid depicitons of sensual abandon. At the hand of Masters Georges, Patrick, Pierre and others, this submissive seductress experiences pleasures she never knew existed...

MAGIC CARPET BOOKS

Order Form

Name: _____

Address: _____

City: _____

State:_____ Zip:_____

Title	ISBN

Send check or money order to:

Magic Carpet Books, PO Box 473
New Milford, CT 06776
magiccarpetbooks@earthlink.net

Postage free in the United States add $2.50 for
packages outside the United States

Visit our website at: www.magic-carpet-books.com